ON THE THRESHOLD OF TIME

BY KATHERINE A. KITCHIN

Sequel to

A TINY STEP

McKnight & Bishop Ltd

About The Publisher

McKnight & Bishop are always on the look-out for new authors and ideas for new books. If you write or if you have an idea for a book, please e-mail info@mcknightbishop.com

Some things we love are undiscovered authors, open-source software, Creative Commons, crowd-funding, Amazon/Kindle, social networking, faith, laughter & new ideas.

Visit us at **www.mcknightbishop.com**

About The Author

Katherine Kitchin is a retired midwife and holistic therapist.
She is married, has four adult children and lives in North Yorkshire.

Cover Images:

Compilation of author's own photos and illustrations by Nina
ninakitchin@hotmail.com

'Pocket watch, by ArtTower via Pixabay (Image has been edited)

'Plant pot', by MunmxArt via Pixabay

'Red petaled flowers' via Pinterest
 merged with
'Anne Boleyn Climbing Rose' by LilipilySpirit
lilipilyspirit.deviantart.com (Image has been edited)

ISBN 978-1-905691-79-1
A CIP catalogue record for this book is available from the British Library

First published in 2024 by McKnight & Bishop Ltd., 35 Limetree Avenue, Kiveton Park, S26 5NY
http://www.mcknightbishop.com | info@mcknightbishop.com

This book has been typeset in Garamond-Normal and Chopin Script.

Printed and bound in Great Britain by Lightning Source Inc, Milton Keynes. The paper used in this book has been made from wood independently certified as having come from sustainable forests.

This book is dedicated to my grandmother's brother

2458 Private J. Robinson

of the

West Yorkshire Regiment

who died 29th September 1916

age nineteen, on the Somme

and is remembered through the character of Francis.

R.I.P

Acknowledgements

To Simon, Nina and Josie for their editing advice.
To Steve for help with police matters.
To Nina again for cover illustrations.
To Darcy for advice on the correct use of English language.

To my family for everything else.

PART ONE

Prologue

1878

What the young boy saw that day was indescribable, no two ways about it, and it absolutely freaked him out. He could neither understand it, nor even begin to explain it, but then, could anybody? No one would believe him anyway. Far easier for him to say nothing and keep it forever a secret.

He'd been walking along the dirt-track roadway by the edge of the meadow on his way to school when 'it' happened. A loose and bothersome bootlace had slowed his progress, and then the perpetual baaing from the nearby flock of grazing sheep stalled him some more. He watched and listened intently, unable to imagine what they may be saying to one another over and over again. The school bell sounded on the breeze telling the boy to hurry, but there were greater troubles in his life other than his own tardiness to worry about, and the sheep were a welcome distraction. Finally, after tripping on his loose bootlace for a third time, the tired, and now near-broken boy came to a total halt so he could retie it.

In all honesty, he was worn out. His woebegone little sister had kept him awake most of the night with her incessant coughing. It had been getting worse lately and he knew how it was going to end. His older brother Mark had been like that, and then he'd gone and died. He supposed the same would happen to Molly. Losing Mark had wrecked him, he couldn't bear for Molly to go too, his young heart was hurting enough. All the same, he hadn't want to show his sorrow in front of his mother and father, for they seemed to have forgotten all about Mark. Mother had cleaned and folded away any memory of him and had carried on with the day-to-day business of looking after the home. And Father, well, he didn't see a lot of him on account of him being in bed catching up on some shut eye before his night shifts at the factory. So that Father may stay napping, the young boy would keep Molly occupied and quiet, and away from under their mother's feet, especially when he could hear Mother sobbing; something, he noticed, she'd done a lot of lately.

On getting up from managing to tie a double knot to ensure the lace stay firm, he noticed Mikey at the other side of the road - a delivery boy nowadays, and an old pal of Mark's. He dallied on further, thinking he might as well be hung for a sheep as a lamb, and watched Mikey knock on the door of the corner house while pulling out a parcel from the large bag he had slung over his shoulder. At length the door opened. Alas, Mikey hadn't waited long enough, and had left fast paced, having stuffed the parcel back in his bag.

A maid appeared at the open doorway and ran after Mikey, who was rapidly disappearing round the corner. The boy watched attentively but then his curiosity was drawn back to the open door, there was something there on the ground wriggling in a towel. The boy walked a bit nearer to get a closer look. It was a baby. He liked babies, especially his little sister. Dear little Molly had appeared in a cot one morning after he'd lain awake listening to Mother crying out as if in pain. He'd been so fearful of the noise she was making that he woke Mark to ask him why Mother was doing this. But Mark had been nonchalant, saying it was probably because another baby was coming like the one that came last year that went straight to heaven, and to go back to sleep. But the boy hadn't been able to leave it there, and had sat up listening further. The sounds, although intermittent, were intensifying, and as much as it had frightened him to think what might be happening to his mother, it was also curiously fascinating. He could see Mark was still awake, his face was lit by the moonlight and his eyes were open. He had to know more, so asked if he knew where the baby might be coming from and why Mother had to shout so much. Mark had then become somewhat furtive, looking from side to side. He rose up slightly, supporting himself on his elbow, and let out a large sigh before imparting his knowledge of such matters.

"Mother told me she found you in the meadow and brought you home, but I know different now. Mikey says," he continued in clandestine whisper as if imparting secret information, "they come out of ladies' bottoms, and that's why she's crying out, because it's hurting."

Shocked, the boy wished he hadn't been so inquisitive and asked no more questions after hearing *that*, the very thought! And indeed, Mark was correct. A sister no less, and the boy had delighted in his new responsibility; to keep Molly entertained while Mother could get on with her chores.

A pitiful sound began to emit from the doorstep's writhing bundle which burst through the boy's reveries. He looked for the maid, but she was nowhere to be seen. He wanted to go nearer and pick up the baby to comfort it, but he didn't think he would be allowed to do that, so he decided to keep guard from his standpoint until the maid came back. He'd be well and truly late for school now, but looking after a baby was important, so he waited. What happened next however, would alter all that he knew to be true.

There was a strange sensation in the air, a sudden stillness, and it seemed to go right into him and out the other side. He looked skyward to see what the cause might be, but there were no rain clouds and the breeze he had felt snapping around his bare knees had ceased rather than whipped up again. There was none of the usual birdsong; even the interminable sheep talk had stopped. All was eerily quiet, broken only by the urgent yells from the baby which were so much louder now, more piercing, echoing, hollow sounding. Something was going on and already easily panicked, it was scaring him half to death! This wasn't normal, yet seemingly horribly familiar. A peculiar feeling came over him, as if he were about to faint, just like he had when catching the measles. He didn't want to feel like that again, especially not now, when he needed his wits about him. His breath came quick, and his heart thumped fast. He sat down on the path which made him feel a little better, his lonely vigil continuing from there.

Then out of nowhere, a heavy mist appeared and hovered in the road spooking him even further. He did not like fog, it always disturbed him for some unfathomable reason. The baby's cries reverberated in his ears more and more oddly as if they were coming from another place. He covered his ears with his hands to try and shut them out, only he didn't need to, for they stopped abruptly... and the baby was nowhere to be seen. But more than that, he had watched it disappear into thin air! One minute it was there, the next, it was gone. Poof, like magic!

The mist then lifted as quickly as it had appeared, the birdsong returned, the sheep resumed their bleating and once again he felt the cold wind wrapping around his knees. It was as if the world had stopped for a moment, and then started up again. Impossible, yet he'd seen it take place with his own bare eyes.

The maid reappeared from around the corner. Hastily, he jumped over a garden wall out of sight, wanting no part in this, for he was afraid. Young he may still be, but surely old enough to know that this was no magic act, for they were just clever tricks and sleight of hand. Babies aren't supposed to vanish into the mist, they're just not! After the maid had finished going in and out of the door and running around the street like a headless chicken, she finally went inside. The coast looked clearer, so he slunk off to school swinging his bag over his shoulder in an attempt to stop it crashing into his cold-chapped legs. With goosebumps all over, his very soul shuddered. There was *no way* he was going to tell anyone what he saw, *not ever.*

Chapter One

Saturday, January 1st, 2000, noon

Perhaps the best way of putting it, was that Steve 'came to' around midday. Groggily, he disengaged his legs from the nether realms of the couch, sliding his supple torso along the floor with his arms, soldier-like, and pulling himself up to a standing position, of sorts. He rubbed a hand through his blond locks and across his bleary eyes remembering where he was. Trevor's flat, not at home where he should have been, cuddled up to his lovely wife Jasmine. But then she would be at work by now, so that idea was a no go. He blinked hard for better focus and slumped towards the bathroom, picking his way through the detritus from last night's party littering the floor.

"All right mate?" Trevor asked tentatively, raising his thick eyebrows as far as he could manage above his huge chocolate-brown eyes. He was slouched at the dining table trying to force down some toast and black coffee. He was apprehensive because he had inadvertently, or so he had tried to persuade himself, embraced and kissed Jasmine, a few hours earlier, thinking there was no tomorrow. He had to admit to himself, considering that now he was experiencing an almighty hangover, he'd been a teeny bit toasted. It was only a New Year kiss and besides, he was sure he'd seen Steve all over his girlfriend Penny, so it had to be quits. They were best mates, allegedly, it could surely be smoothed over.

"Yeah fine," answered Steve as he disappeared into the bathroom. Trevor thus concluded that everything was fine and blew a small sigh of relief. He hadn't meant to kiss Jasmine, well not especially, it just sort of came about. But he had always liked her, even though they got off on the wrong foot when they first met. Similarly, Steve, who taught history in the local secondary school, had also had a rather awkward introduction to Penny, when she joined the school as a new teacher in the science department. He had mistaken her for someone else, an old girlfriend, and when he realised she wasn't who he thought she was, he was so relieved, he'd become a little too enthusiastic, manic even. Fortunately, she hadn't taken offence and they'd subsequently got on well as colleagues.

"Do you think it's happened?" asked Trevor as Steve returned.

"Do I think what's happened?"

"The millennium bug they've been promising for years, that's what. The thing that everyone's been worried about."

For a long while, the media had been stirring up a frenzy over concerns that the year two thousand would be read by computers as the year nineteen hundred, and would thus cause world-wide chaos. Now the day had arrived, and he was still here, and all appeared normal around him. Apart from having overshot his alcohol tolerance the previous night for which he would pay, Steve deduced that all the alarm and apprehension had been unfounded.

"Oh yeah that. Doubt it. Oh look," declared Steve, "I've just switched my phone on and it's still working. So much for that theory. Blimey!" He could see several missed calls from Jasmine's work number along with two voicemails. He listened to the messages and as he did so, Trevor saw the colour drain from his friend's face. Trevor was a dentist. He was used to noticing the faces of people change colour when undergoing treatment, or being told what sort of work they needed in their mouths. He knew it wasn't due to any bad technique on his part. He was, after all, quite a good dentist, or so he thought, and had plenty of appreciative messages from his patients. It was, of course, that they were fearful of the drill noise or injections, or potential pain, or any of the other horrible tortures they thought they might be forced to endure that were associated with dentistry. However, as far as he knew, Steve wasn't experiencing any dental problems at this point, so it must be something else.

"All right mate?" Trevor asked Steve for the second time that day.

"Jas hasn't gone into work, and they can't reach her at home or on her mobile," replied Steve, ringing Jasmine's mobile at the same time. The call went to voicemail. He tried their home number. No answer. Penny emerged from the bedroom where she had been keeping a low profile. The tones of anxiety coming from the lounge made it obvious there were more important issues to address other than her embarrassment. She'd been far too hasty last evening and had pounced on Steve while both under a bunch of mistletoe, and now rather regretted her faux pas. It was out of character. They were colleagues as well as friends, and it had only happened because she saw

Trevor in a drunken tryst with Jasmine moments earlier. It had been a tit for tat, that was all. She also suspected that Jasmine thought there was something between her and Steve, for Jasmine had remained rather cold towards her whenever they'd met before, and now she'd made things worse by making it look as if it were true. Steve was a good co-worker, and they got on well, but that was all. As for Trevor, she doubted whether he would remember much about last night. He'd been completely blotto when eventually falling into bed.

"I need to go and find out if she's okay."

"Trevor and I will follow as soon as we're dressed," said Penny. Steve glanced at her briefly and muttered an appreciative thank you as he left.

"Where on earth do you think she is?" asked Penny to Trevor when they were alone.

"How should I know?" was Trevor's reply. He wasn't one for hypothesis, things were as they were until proved otherwise, as far as he was concerned.

"Well, you know her better than I do. Maybe she slept in?"

"Jas, sleep in? No, I don't think so. Steve told me that she sets several alarms to make sure she's up for an early shift and it drives him mental. Fancy some coffee? I've made plenty."

"Thanks yes, I'll have a cup."

Trevor poured out another coffee from the cafetiere and topped up his own. He needed to come clean, he didn't like any secrets from anyone, least of all his girlfriend. They hadn't known each other for very long, but they both felt comfortable with each other, even from their first meeting. They had quite literally, bumped into each other. Both had been without their cars that day, both were walking towards the same corner, but from a different direction and both hurrying as they were running late. Together, they turned into the corner, Trevor glancing at his watch as he did so, Penny shifting her gait to off-balance while moving her heavy bag from one shoulder to the other, and wham! Penny's bag fell to the floor and sheets of A4 scattered over the pavement. Trevor grabbed hold of her arms to steady her, and their eyes simply met, and that was it!

"Oops!" said Penny, laughing. She knew immediately that the face she was looking at her was going to be significant in her life. Those eyes! She was amused at how fate could work. 'Out of the blue, when you least expect it,' her girlfriends had advised, following her laments that she never met anyone she might be remotely interested in. Trevor grinned back, more because he liked what he was looking at, fine-looking face, long crinkly hair, curves in nice places, rather than finding any humour about the situation. They both bent down to collect up the flapping papers, and ended up running even more late, but neither appeared to care about that anymore.

"Er, Penny, I think I might have disgraced myself last night, I hope no one got the wrong idea, I was just being friendly because it was such a special occasion."

"You mean your pathetic attempts at trying to get a kiss from the entire female population? No Trevor, I don't think anybody took it seriously, I'm sure your reputation is still stainless, just like your Colgate smile." She wasn't ready to admit, even to herself, that there had been a slight pang of jealousy when she saw him kiss Jasmine, that was why she'd retaliated with Steve. But when she saw Trevor attempting to get a kiss from every girl in sight, she regretted what she had done. He had been so drunk, not realising what he was doing, and she should have known better.

Unlike Penny, Steve hadn't given their kiss under the mistletoe another thought. His mind was on Jasmine, and where she could possibly be. It wasn't in Jasmine's nature to not go in for work or leave a message. Something was wrong, something had happened to her, Steve could feel it in his guts. He splashed a glass of water down his throat and set off for home, but a rising wave of foreboding was catching him in its swell.

There weren't many people out and about that he could see. Steve wondered if, like himself, they'd been up most of the night celebrating the first day of the new millennium and catching up on sleep. He felt strange, in a bubble, the world was not quite as it should be, and it wasn't just a lack of sleep or alcohol over-indulgence. He didn't know where Jasmine was and that was odd in itself. If there was a change of plan, she would have messaged him, and her work colleagues had expected her to arrive for a shift starting at seven-thirty. What could have happened since she had left the party and not turned up for work? The very point of her leaving for home when she did was to get enough sleep before an early shift! He tried desperately to stay calm and not let ugly thoughts into his mind without knowing any facts. Yet there was still a knot in his stomach. Something was definitely amiss.

Usually Steve would have enjoyed his walk home despite feeling cold and hungover. He and Jasmine often went for walks around the park. He could picture her now, her unbridled yellow hair bouncing around her face, or stuffed under her hand-knitted woolly hat when it was cold. When they had the time to spare they liked to spend it in nature, it was one of their favourite pastimes. Today however, was different. Steve swept past the park's main gates and followed Jasmine's probable route. If it had been in the middle of the day as it was now, she would have been walking through the park down the main walkway, passing the bandstand, rounding the play area and out again by the east entrance and the little group of standing stones. Two ancient circles of two-foot-high monoliths, one inside the other. But it had been night-time. No way would she have wanted to cross paths with any unsavoury characters skulking in the shadows. Anyway, the main gates get locked at twilight, she'd have gone around the park boundary on the streets. Snow had fallen a few days ago and was still around on higher ground but none here. There was a bit of fog though, he could see patches in the park as he hiked on. All had seemed clear the previous evening when they had watched the fantastic display lighting up the midnight skies. Fireworks had been let off from every corner of town, a magnificent night never to be forgotten. Standing hand in hand with Jasmine, they had felt, like everyone else, a connection with the entire world as the explosions in the sky heralded the new century. The windchill was cutting, he turned up his collar trying to keep warm and carried on. If only he'd retrieved the bedsheet off the floor that had been his Marley's ghost fancy dress costume, he could have wrapped it around him.

Near the east gate entrance, almost out of sight, wedged between the park wall and a lamppost, a tendril of overhanging shrubbery concealing all but the tip of it, there lay a phone. Steve almost missed it, his brain still being fuzzy. He picked it up and let out an expletive. It was Jasmine's. Totally stunned, he stared at it as if it had no right to be there. Minutes went by. What should he do now? He couldn't fathom it. Then very gingerly, he started pressing its buttons. There were calls from her workplace and an outgoing call she must have made to her mother at one-fifteen that morning and that was it.

Steve put the phone in the back pocket of his jeans and looked round for anything else, but saw nothing. Only there was something, he could sense it. He listened intently while the wind whipped around his ears. He heard a rustling, someone was nearby. The knot in his stomach got tighter and even though he was trying to stay calm, that increasing sense of fear and alarm simmered inside him.

"Jasmine? Jas, is that you?" he called, hoping his beloved was close. Steve kept as quiet as he could, trying to hear a response from her, hoping that she would call out to him. She may have fallen and sprained something and been unable to walk. He began to believe he was going to find her round some corner. The wind dropped momentarily, a bird screeched and rose up from the bushes and flew away, its wings flapping loudly disrupting the eerie stillness. "Jas?" he called out again tentatively. But only silence wrapped around him and he realised he wasn't going to find her there. With fast beating heart his fear increased, and many wild thoughts spun around in his head while he made his way home. The straying dead leaves still hanging on from autumn were caught by the returning wind, swirling around the ancient standing stone rings nearby as if by attraction.

He was glad he had decided to stay a while and know that the phone had been picked up and by who. He watched Steve notice it and double back to retrieve it. It was evidence, the proof of the route she had taken a few hours earlier and was now someone else's responsibility rather than his own. They would never be able to establish anything, never be able to find out the truth, only he knew that. He waited until Steve had gone, and crept away unnoticed, wondering what his next step should be.

"She's not here," Steve's trembling voice told Trevor over the phone, "and it doesn't look as though she came home. Her car is in the drive, and everything is as we left it, all neat and tidy. That's why we were so late last night, for some reason she felt an urgent need to clean the kitchen. And I've found her mobile phone by the park entrance. Something bad has happened, I just know it. If only we'd come to yours by car then Jas could have driven home and been safe."

"Oh mate, I don't know what to say I really don't, but she has to be somewhere." Trevor tried to calm him as best he could and then had a thought. He suggested Steve call Jasmine's parents to see if they knew anything and that he and Penny were on their way. Steve called Jasmine's work, desperately hoping she'd turned up. She hadn't, and the only thing Steve received from Jasmine's mother was her anxiety and concern in addition to his own.

"We need to go to the police and report that she's missing as soon as possible - like now," said Penny as soon as she and Trevor had caught up with Steve.

"Really, are you sure?" asked Steve. "But they don't do anything for forty-eight hours because they say most people turn up by then. She's going to be all right, isn't she? I mean, where could she have gone, do you think she found another party? Yes, that's probably it, she's at another party, she'll be home soon." He paced the same piece of floor, back and forth.

"Mate," said Trevor, "if she'd wanted to party, she would have stayed at mine with you, with us. I think Penny is right, we need to go to the police, they might have some information."

"What information? Like she's had an accident and is in hospital?" replied Steve desperately. "No, she would have called and told us."

"But she hasn't got her mobile, you found it, remember," Trevor answered, trying to be encouraging. "She might be lying there unconscious so they won't know who she is," he added.

"The sooner we go to the police station the better," said Penny trying to rally the two faltering men. "Come on, let's get going." They headed back past the park, past the way to Trevor's flat and into town.

The police officer needed much information and Steve could barely answer any of his questions. No, she had never been reported missing before. No, he hadn't thought to bring her credit or debit card or bank details. No, he hadn't brought any photographs and no, he hadn't got her toothbrush so they could collect a DNA sample either. He could, however, remember his in-law's address, having grown up in the same street. He had their number in his mobile phone and produced it immediately. "Glenda and Tony Simmons," he told the officer." My in-laws, Jasmine's parents." He could also remember what she had been wearing. As it was a fancy-dress party Jasmine had gone as a lady from the Edwardian period. It was a beautiful dress; cream in colour with lace at the front that Jasmine had sworn must be handmade. They'd found it underneath the floorboards of their home along with some hairbrushes. Neither of them had been able to understand why anyone would hide such an exquisite thing, wrapped in brown paper, beneath the floor. However the policeman said he didn't need that amount of information.

Jasmine had been waiting for the right opportunity to wear it, for it fitted her exactly, and she had looked amazing. He'd watched her twirl around in front of the mirror, enjoying the spectacle, his desire mounting, hoping his inclinations might be reciprocated when the opportunity came. Not then though, her thoughts had been elsewhere, tied up in hairstyles and housework. He'd had to wait until later, at the party, secretly, in the dark and in haste. Steve wasn't going to tell the policeman all that though.

The officer went on to ask about any distinguishing features that Jasmine may have. Steve said she had a birthmark on her left buttock.

"Like a star," Trevor interjected. Both Penny and Steve shot him a questioning look, their curiosity piqued. But then Steve, at least, remembered how Trevor must have known of it. It was while they still lived at their old flat and Trevor had been coming down the stairs and into the communal hallway. He'd just moved into the flat upstairs and Jasmine hadn't got used to it being occupied. To her mortification and to Trevor's delectation, she was there collecting the post while in a state of undress thinking she was alone. He and Steve had soon become firm friends however Jasmine preferred to keep her distance from Trevor, not knowing quite how to manage her embarrassment from that first encounter.

Trevor cleared his throat and swallowed hard in an attempt to get rid of his inopportune statement. He was only trying to help. Steve broke the tension by saying that no, he didn't have a photo of her birthmark, but might be able to draw it.

The officer, who carefully recorded every important detail with great diligence, and the duty sergeant, who had appeared briefly, were both ninety-nine percent sure the errant Jasmine would turn up. It was the first day of a new century after all, and everyone had been out partying. Still, it was part of his job to file comprehensive reports; dot the i's and cross the t's. And unfortunately after that, but fortunately for the world, there had been no millennium bug invasion, (well not in this nick anyway, he couldn't vouch for anywhere else) he would then have to copy it all onto a computer file. So much for an easy afternoon.

He kept all this to himself though, appearing on the surface to be very sympathetic and said how he understood that it must be a very traumatic time. "And just to recap, is this the correct number for your mobile phone I have written down here, and this one is your home number?"

"Yes, that's right," replied Steve.

"And your address, it's the same as the person you are reporting missing?"

"Jasmine House. It has a name, Jasmine House," Steve answered, pointing at the address that the police officer had written down on the form.

"Oh, after the mis - er, your wife, who is missing."

"No," replied Steve, "it was already called Jasmine House. That's one reason why we bought it, its name, like it was meant to be ours when we saw it."

"Ah yes, I see," replied the police officer, wishing he never asked and keen to dismiss them so he could get his report finished and filed. He encouraged the trio to return home in case Jasmine had surfaced, and to find all the other information the police needed for further investigation if she didn't turn up. He also emphasised Steve should make his own enquiries. His closing statement was they, the police, would help support him and give him any information they received promptly. Steve interpreted this as proof of his original theory that they weren't all that interested, she couldn't be classed as missing, and they weren't going to produce his beloved Jasmine for him any time soon.

"At least they're going to put her onto the computer, so it's bound to go national," Trevor said, trying to be helpful. "Choose a decent picture of her, not her passport one, everyone's passport photo is rubbish, a really nice one will make people more sympathetic and look for her." But Trevor's good intentions weren't having any effect. Steve had never had to deal with any actual crisis in his life, and usually left it up to Jasmine to get wound up about things. Largely, he just let life happen. But this was different. All those cases about kidnappings and murder and rape reported in the news, plus the three combined, were now happening to him and worse, to Jasmine. If only he'd walked her home, if only she'd not needed to go home early to get some sleep before her early shift at work, if only she'd not been on duty on New Year's Day! He felt utterly helpless.

He had a long list of 'if onlies' by the time he was back home and had got off the phone to Jasmine's mother, Glenda. Glenda said she and Tony would come over straight away. Steve persuaded them to stay where they were, he couldn't cope with his in-laws quite at this moment. Well, his mother-in-law anyway. "Just in case she'd thought to come and wish you a Happy New Year in person" he had said to her. It worked. Glenda said she would try to keep herself occupied by ringing everybody and see if they had any ideas about where Jasmine might be. However she was already fearing the worst. Long-held emotional trauma was brimming to the surface. She couldn't possibly lose another child, she just couldn't.

Steve then rooted out some photos of Jasmine for the police.

"This one, no, this one is better."

"Why don't I take both, I'm sure the police will be fine with two," said Trevor. Steve handed over both, along with bank details.

As soon as Trevor left for the police station, Penny tried to get Steve to eat something. She put bread into the toaster. "Do you think she saw us," she asked sheepishly after putting a round of toast in front of Steve, "and went off in a huff?"

Steve picked at the toast half-heartedly. He'd forgotten about their kiss under the mistletoe, until now. He might have remembered sooner, but Jasmine's disappearance had over-ridden it. Penny was one of those dangerously alluring females who attracted wandering eyes, and Steve had to admit if only to himself, that he had always 'admired' Penny. But his excuse to that was because somehow she reminded him of Jasmine. Tired and confused, he fiddled with the toast in his fingers, tapping its edge onto the plate distractedly while his mind continued to fill up with discombobulated thoughts that refused to go away. Penny was a work colleague, a friend, and worse, was Trevor's girlfriend! It had been quite unexpected, that kiss, and quite delicious. How could he have done it? His perception of how he felt towards Penny was all over the place, a blurry mixed-up mess and he was ashamed. Yes, she was really lovely, but he in no way fancied her, not 'like that.' It should have been a quick peck, not a long smooch! In the heat of the moment, he had forgotten himself.

While his mind wrestled, Steve's eyes rested on what his knotted fingers had destroyed. Unable to face any food, he let the innocent piece of toast drop back onto his plate.

"Oh God, do you think so. It was only a... Penny I'm so sorry, I shouldn't have, I wasn't thinking, and now she's left me because of it. What shall I do?" Head in hands, he curled his head down onto his knees, he couldn't take much more.

Penny responded by shrugging the whole thing off, saying that she thought they should forget it happened as they were both a little drunk, and that it was more her fault than his. "I sort of made you," she added. Steve peeped an eye through his fingers, he wasn't entirely sure how he could ever have been forced into anything so nice. Penny continued, "I'd seen Trevor trying to get a kiss from Jasmine and I was, I think, getting my own back. I'm the one who should be saying sorry. Anyway, the point I'm trying to make is, she has probably gone to a friend's house to brood about it and so that means she's okay."

Steve raised his head to speak. "Do you really think so? I'm not so sure. She would never miss work, especially without calling them, and it doesn't explain why she dropped her phone. She was kissing Trevor?" He sat up straight, Penny's words had just sunk in.

"I think it was more Trevor trying to kiss her, I don't think she had any actual part to play in it. Please don't be upset with him, he was so drunk I don't think he had any idea what he was doing last night, he was going around everyone later, it wasn't just Jasmine."

With Penny's explanation of events, Steve felt he'd been given a pardon. He was exonerated! No guilty thoughts necessary. Phew! And if Jas had kissed Trevor... he'd have to think about that one. But not now, not when, not when; he swallowed hard. "No, of course. I'm glad we're sorted about it, and anyway there are more important things to think about. You're right, we should forget about it. It's happened and that's the end of it. I'm far more concerned about where Jas could be now. Something isn't right about all this. It's not like her. I know her, she would never not go in for a work shift, she's dedicated to that place, that job. Jas loves her work. No, it's far more than seeing us kissing. Something bad has happened to her Penny, I just know it."

The constant knotting pain that had been churning inside Steve's guts all day was getting worse by the moment. Jasmine really *was* missing. The realisation had sunk further and further down into him, but he couldn't, or didn't want to take it in, it was too indigestible, but it had to go somewhere. Then it did. Gripping his abdomen tightly he made a sudden move towards the door. Not since his stag night had this happened. Rushing an apology to Penny that he couldn't eat the toast, Steve reached the bathroom just in time to empty the entire contents of his stomach into the toilet, but still the pain remained. He returned to the kitchen, wrung out.

"Any better?" asked Penny. He made a half-hearted shrug and walked to the window and stared out, hoping that Jasmine would be there, walking down the path. She wasn't.

It looked drab and dismal outside. Steve checked his watch, it was only half past three, too soon for dusk. He squinted, trying to sharpen his vision towards a sudden movement in the road. Had he seen something disappearing hastily out of his line of sight? Hard rain began to fall from the heavy skies, preventing him from seeing anything clearly. He did see Trevor though, dashing up the garden path returning from the police station. Steve rushed to open the front door to let him in, poking his head into the rain as he did so, looking for something.

"Did you see anything outside, Trev?" Trevor was preoccupied checking out how leaky his supposed waterproof jacket was.

"Like what?"

"Like anything suspicious?"

"Er, no, I don't think so. No, nothing suspicious. Why?"

"Just thought I saw something. It's nothing, forget it."

He wasn't entirely sure why he felt compelled to watch the husband, but he had kept vigil, nevertheless. There was nothing he could do, not yet anyway, and now he was cold and wet. When he saw him at the window, he thought he was looking straight at him. He had to go; he didn't want to be seen. He stooped down below the hedge and scurried away out of sight.

Chapter Two

Saturday, pm.

The kettle venting its contents in clouds of steam was not enough. It took the shrill shriek of its whistle to tear through the fogginess of Steve's mind and force him to pull himself up and take it off the boil. He made coffee. He needed something to keep him going to fight off the exhaustion that was creeping over him. His hangover may have all but gone, but he wasn't feeling anywhere near normal.

The ever-present knot in his stomach was gnawing at him with intent, his heart was heavy with pain and his head ached. He lumbered into the sitting room and drew the curtains, shutting out the gloom and slunk down into a chair and anxiousness. He hardly touched his coffee. Darkness had fallen long ago, and the rainstorm reduced to a mere drizzle, but he barely noticed. All he could think about was Jasmine. The doorbell rang. His heart gave an extra thud, and he sprang into action in case it was her having lost her keys. It wasn't.

"Mum, Dad, what are you doing here?" He was astonished to see his parents standing on the doorstep. He'd only just managed to dispatch Trevor and Penny. They'd gone to clear up their flat after the party but promised to return soon. Steve thought that might take some time, but they insisted on coming back thinking it wasn't a good idea to leave him all alone for too long. In fact, he was glad to shut the door after them, he needed some space so he could think. That was not to be however, not now he had to open the door to his parents.

"Stephen, of course we have come, what else could we do? As soon as Glenda let us know, we packed our bags. Happy New Year by the way. Well, under the circumstances, perhaps not so happy." Anne, his mother, tall and striking, walked into the old Georgian hallway with an authoritative air and glanced lamentably at the Christmas tree as if it had no right to be there. She took off her coat and handed it to her son hoping he'd do something with it while she removed her heeled court shoes claiming they were killing her. Steve draped her coat over the banister rail and Anne, clearly agitated, padded about in her stocking feet. His father, Paul, followed her inside and shut the front door against the evening's shadows. He took her coat along with his into the cloakroom.

"You've told the police of course?" asked Paul, emerging from the cloakroom. He was taller than his son and despite having more years behind him than he cared to have, he retained an engaging presence. Steve had always looked up to his father with the greatest respect and although he very much appreciated his support, along with his mother's, he hadn't thought he would be opening the door to them just now. It made it all too real.

"Dad of course I have, they took all the details, only at the moment, they are still expecting her to show up. But they don't know her like I do, she wouldn't leave or anything like that."

"Stephen are you sure you haven't had a squabble?" asked Anne, cupping his face in her hands at the same time. Steve took hold of them with his own hands and put them down to her sides, holding them for a moment before taking a step back. "No Mum, I wouldn't normally ring my mother-in-law every time we disagreed about something, would I? This is different, it's not right. Something's happened to her, and I don't know what, and I'm thinking all sorts till I don't know what to think. Mum, this is awful." And then it came. The emotion that he had tried to suppress all day. Steve started to weep. He couldn't help himself, and it came from his gut, and he howled as if in great pain. Anne wrapped him in motherly arms, like she always had when he was hurting, and he yielded to them, like he always had.

Paul paced about the hall floor, his shoes clattering on the inert cold tiles, echoing his failure to rectify the matter. How on earth could he comfort the poor boy? He was a mathematician; everything could be solved by mathematical measurement, in theory at least. All he required were the correct equations. Solving problems, sorting things out, finding truths were all part of the normal routine for him. However, with neither facts nor figures, there was nothing for him to work with and was no use to his son whatsoever.

Anne led Steve into the kitchen where he hung about finding solace by watching his mother organise some food. He hadn't eaten all day - hadn't wanted to, and he didn't know if he would ever want food again. Anne found a lasagne in the freezer and was heating it through and preparing a salad. Paul joined them and helped himself to a beer from the fridge. Drinking something would give him a better option than pacing the floor. He gestured to Steve if he wanted one. "Er, no thanks Dad, I really don't fancy a beer, but please, you go ahead." The thought of any more alcohol was making his liver shout out for mercy.

Over the meal, which Steve managed to pick at, Paul encouraged Steve to recount everything that he knew to have taken place. Wearily, Steve tried to piece the day's events together, but it wasn't enough for Paul, he needed absolute clarity. He determined he would go out later and retrace the route Jasmine would have taken. "Just so I can get a better understanding, son. It will help me, I think. Let everything sink in, so to speak." Anything was better than sitting twiddling thumbs.

The doorbell rang again. Steve's heart raced. It would either be good news or bad news at the other side of the door. He couldn't look at his parents, he knew they were thinking the same. He drew out the walk to the front door for as long as he could, eventually opening it gingerly... to Trevor and Penny returning from cleaning the flat. He let out a large sigh and ushered them into the kitchen, introducing his parents to Penny (they already knew Trevor) and instructing them not to take off their coats and settle down as he was about to show his father Jasmine's way home. His mother had other ideas though. Seeing as his friends had come, they could be his father's guides. She ordered Steve to stay put in case there was news, and she would keep him company. He simply obeyed and sat down limply.

The spitting rain had stopped for now, and Trevor, Penny and Paul started out on the route back to Trevor's flat. Trevor had by this time traversed it several times and he wasn't sure if doing it again would make any difference, but understood Paul might need to look around. Paul and Penny, already in deep conversation, quickly determined they both shared a leaning towards the sciences, she in physics and chemistry, he in mathematics. Penny was enthralled that Paul had spent time in the U.S. observing the research being done by theoretical physicists into wormholes and black holes.

Trevor switched off. He remembered Steve explaining about black holes when they were at the local pub one time. He and Penny had just met, and Trevor was trying to learn more about the things she was interested in. Steve had endeavoured to help and had made a stab at enlightening him. He had done quite a good job, as his practised father had put it to him in such a way that Steve had been able to retain some sense of it all.

However, the conversation between his girlfriend and Paul was sounding far more technical, and Trevor had begun to lag further and further behind as they walked the perimeter of the park to the main entrance, and back again. They had rounded the corner and were coming up to the east gate. Trevor pulled the torch Steve had provided for him out of his pocket in readiness for the streetlights going out; they were notorious for never working properly around there. Surprisingly, they appeared to be functioning normally. Trevor switched on the torch anyway and shone it at the ground searching for what, he couldn't say. On reaching the entrance he then directed the beam into the park's lightless walkway. It was generally poorly lit at night to discourage people from entering. Near the main entrance, as it was Christmas, a few fairy lights were stung up between the trees for a bit of cheer, but that was it. Nothing round here.

"Not much going on in there." The unknown voice made Trevor jump. "Sorry, I never meant to startle you, I saw you shining your torch." The old man, to whom the voice belonged, gestured into the park. He had a dog with him, a West Highland terrier which Trevor bent down to stroke.

"What's his name?" Trevor asked. He liked dogs, as long as they belonged to someone else.

"He's a she, and her name is Bessie." The old man replied.

Trevor had a brainwave. Dogs got walked regularly, and more than likely, dog owners kept to the same routes most of the time.

"You didn't happen to be walking your dog, I mean Bessie, here abouts, last night?" he asked hopefully. "After midnight," he added, trying to pinpoint the right time frame. The old man looked at him for a moment before asking Trevor why he wanted to know. Bessie wagged her tail enjoying the attention she was receiving. Trevor began telling him about Jasmine going missing on her way home and that her phone had been found nearby. He continued to stroke Bessie as he did so, who was reaching her paws up in excitement.

"After midnight you say?" The old man sounded thoughtful but then answered a little scornfully. "I really don't think I would have been out walking a dog at that time of night, and in amongst all those fireworks. Far too much noise for them. They don't like fireworks you know." He tugged at the lead to bring Bessie down from Trevor. "No, I kept her inside where it was safe. Took her out earlier though, this sort of time, but no, nothing unusual to see. Er, have you been to the police?" Before Trevor could say any more, Penny and Paul came over. They had walked further along, immersed in their conversation, but now, remembering Trevor had been with them, returned to retrieve him. The old man nodded to Trevor, straightened his cap and went on his way.

"I was asking him if he'd seen anything last night, I thought he might have been out walking his dog," Trevor explained, feeling the need to give an account of what he had been doing as it was far more important surely, than conversations on relativity, astrophysics, quantum fields, or whatever the heck they'd been discussing.

"Good thinking!" said Paul. Penny put her arm through Trevor's. She wanted something. He had very quickly come to know his girlfriend's ways.

"I thought," she began, "that we could show Paul the stone circle while we're here. It won't take a minute."

They passed through the park entrance and over to the ancient standing stones, Trevor conceding meekly to the plan. He knew how much Penny was attracted to them and wasn't surprised she'd suggested showing them to Paul. She would often carry a pair of divining rods and show him how they twitched and swung about, saying it proved the stones caused changes to the electro-magnetic fields. In truth, Trevor didn't share her curiosity in any of the ancient menhirs that peppered the land and the myths and legends surrounding them, although he never admitted it. He required more solid evidence than quivering rods before he would hold any belief in such things even after, for his girlfriend's sake, he'd read up a little about it. His feet felt far more comfortable planted on the solid ground of the here and now. Paul, however, appeared keen.

Regrettably, it was too dark to make much out, even with three torches. Though definitely not Stonehenge, Paul was enamoured. "We need to come back in daylight and take some measurements, there is much to consider here, a magnitude of computation." With that, they agreed to regroup first thing. Trevor was a little bemused, he thought they were out looking for clues to help find Jasmine, not getting excited over a few ancient lumps of rock. Penny said she would explain later.

Again, his instincts had led him back to this place just at the right time. How interesting that they were intrigued by the stones, but he had heard all he needed to. It was time to leave.

"Anything?" asked Steve when they returned.

"Not really," replied his father. Whatever was on Paul's mind, he favoured keeping to himself. "You?"

Steve reported that the police had rung to give an update and to see if Steve had any more information for them. There had been no admissions to hospital of anyone of Jasmine's description and that her parents had been in touch for any news. Also, for reasons he perhaps didn't want to fully understand, the police had asked again for her toothbrush, so they could collect a DNA sample for their record. Trevor said he would take it in. He would walk back to the flat with Penny, drop her off and then go on to the police station. The route was becoming ingrained, he could almost do it in his sleep. Steve brought him Jasmine's toothbrush. Trevor asked Anne if she could find a plastic bag and he put the toothbrush into it, careful not to touch it himself so he wouldn't contaminate the 'evidence', like Morse on the telly. He liked to be efficient. They said their goodbyes and went back off into the night, leaving their disconsolate friend slumped at the front door, watching them go.

Anne missed nothing. Her poor son was empty; too tired to reason, and there was nothing she could do. She sighed. "We can't do anything but wait for news, so I suggest we all have an early night and catch up on some sleep." Steve reluctantly made his way upstairs in zombie-like fashion just managing to turn out the lights on the Christmas tree as he went past. They'd been shining practically unnoticed since the day before, when Jasmine had switched them on at dusk. But now, it didn't feel right that their star-like twinkling should evoke any suggestion of festivity, for that had all gone. Neither was affording the self-indulgence of slumber. Jas was nowhere to be found, and there was no place Steve could hide from that. Resignedly, he got into bed and reached his arm across to the other side of the mattress and into emptiness. Jasmine's warm and inviting body should be there, nestling into him. Instead lay desolation itself. Steve felt for her nightie she always kept under her pillow and pulled it out, pressing it to his face and breathing in her scent. It was sacred nectar for him; he hugged it close, across his chest. It took him a while, but thankfully, he slept hard and fast.

Chapter Three

Sunday, January 2nd, am.

It had been a surprisingly quiet New Year, as New Years go for the town's police force. It looked as though it was going to be an easy run-of-the-mill morning, no surprises and just what DI Jim Manning was hoping for. The last of the rowdily intoxicated who'd been rounded up for their own safety over the festive period had finally been cleared from the cells, bringing a little bit of peace and calm; acoustics weren't the best attribute of the building. All that was left outstanding from the day before were two reports of car thefts, one break-in and one missing person. Along with the relief that morning Jim Manning had worked throughout Christmas, but the rota system had given them four days off over the New Year and this was the first early turn back. He had made the most of the time off, catching up with his side of the family and making merry like everyone else. However, like most of his ilk, he needed to be in the saddle and on the job and most likely the missing woman situation was all that would require his attention.

It was now half-past eight and he picked up the misper report, drank some of his now tepid milky coffee that he hadn't had time to drink earlier and beckoned two of the relief's officers to join him to look over the file.

It looked straightforward enough; husband reports missing wife who had left a New Year party alone and on foot but had never reached her intended destination of home a mile away. Chances were, she'd gone off in a huff after an argument and was holed up with some girlfriend somewhere. Nevertheless, they would still have to investigate, but Jim Manning imagined she would turn up in a day or two. They usually did. He checked the information they had already received to see if all was in order and then, as soon as nine o'clock arrived, picked up the phone and dialled the husband's number. Being a thorough policeman, he wanted to conduct the interview himself and derive whether this was the aftermath of a simple domestic problem, or there was anything more at play. After all the years he had spent on the job he could get a sense of what might be really going on, his intuition having become quite well-developed. He liked to think he would soon glean if some foul play was involved and if so, would instigate a fuller police inquiry. The quicker the better for he had seen it too many times, officers reluctant to do this, and those vital initial hours were thus lost.

The husband answered the phone; no, the Inspector did not need to come out, he would come into the station straight away. An interesting sign, in Jim Manning's book, that the probable suspect number one, the husband, was willing to help with enquiries. Over eagerness to help often pointed to being 'Chummy'; the name police gave to the one they ultimately arrested for a crime that had been committed. And he might have something to hide by not wanting the police in his home, but that would be part of their routine investigation anyway. He assigned the two officers to ring round the taxi firms and check the hospital admissions again and went to refresh his coffee with some hot water and more coffee; he wanted to stay alert.

A room had been set up by the Holmes Unit in readiness for any major incidents over the millennium that may or may not transpire. It could, Jim Manning thought, be put to good use if the woman - he looked down at the report to instil her name in his memory - Jasmine Bartram's body turned up and it all became nasty. But then murder squad would be taking over if that happened. Meanwhile, it would stay on his desk.

At the same moment that Jim Manning was examining the misper file, a Ford Mondeo pulled up outside Steve and Jasmine's house. Paul, returning from an early morning foray in and around the park, recognised it as Glenda and Tony's, Jasmine's parents. He knew them well. As well as being Steve's in-laws, they were also Paul and Anne's neighbours. It was how Steve and Jasmine had first met; they had grown up together.

Glenda's personality oozed from her as soon as her large mouth, needlessly embellished by an intensely loud red lipstick, opened. "We couldn't keep away any longer," she yelled to Paul while heaving her generous torso out of the car and veering towards him. Paul gave her a hug and nodded to the bespectacled and balding Tony, the complete opposite of his somewhat histrionic wife. He was quietly and unobtrusively taking their luggage out of the car boot and carrying it inside into the hall. Steve had seen them arrive and hiding his reluctance about that, was ready at the door.

"Darling," exclaimed his mother-in-law as she fluttered her arms around him. "I just had to come, I know you understand, she is my daughter after all."

"Our daughter?" corrected Tony under his breath, but she hadn't heard him. The telephone rang and Steve rushed to pick it up.

"Hello, Steve Bartram." Everyone's eyes were upon him, no one daring to breathe. "I see, okay. No need, I'll be there shortly." He put the phone down. "No news, they just want me back at the police station to go over a few things."

"No news is good news perhaps," said his mother encouragingly.

"Is it though?" Steve replied bleakly.

Steve grabbed his coat from the cloakroom, pulled his hat out from the pocket, put it on his head and stalked off. He was in no mood to play host. He'd woken that morning from a very deep sleep and was immediately confronted with the stark reality that Jasmine remained missing, while he had luxuriated in bed. The guilt was intense. Hands stuffed deep into his pockets, he listened to the dull sound his feet made on the pavement, like a heavy clump; weighed down and dense. It wasn't his customary way of walking, that was almost like a skip. But things weren't normal because he didn't know where Jas was so nothing made any sense... and now it appeared, the police wanted to know of his movements and were investigating *him* instead of looking for *her.*

On reaching the park, Steve lifted his focus from the ground to look around him in the vague hope of finding Jasmine. He couldn't see her anywhere. She had to be somewhere, but she just wasn't there. He clutched at his head and screwed up his eyes. This couldn't be happening, it really had to be a dream - a nightmare even. It couldn't be real. It was surely someone else experiencing all this, someone who was like him but wasn't actually him, and he was merely watching; observing without the throttling emotion that wouldn't leave. Alas, not. He dropped his hands and plodded on past the quiet of the unmoving stone circle, past the silent bandstand. On and on, clump clump.

Suddenly, he came to an abrupt halt in both breath and step. Someone was following him, he could feel it in his bones. He turned around and surveyed the central path which he'd just joined and rubbed at his dog-tired eyeballs to have a better look. Peering as best he could, he scrutinised the grand walkway and the steps that led to where the shaft of the war memorial stood in the centre of the promenade terraces, and all of the spectacular Tuscan colonnade behind. However, it's magnificence was lost on him today, all he wanted was to see who was there hounding him. Alas, he couldn't see anyone. In fact, he'd barely noticed a single other person in the park while he'd been walking. He hadn't exactly been aware of much though, apart from Jasmine being missing and a depth of despair he never knew existed. He turned back round to see a woman coming towards him pushing a buggy filled with a small sleeping child. He recalled there had been a couple of youths hanging about the swings, and then he noticed a person walking on the path that ran parallel to this one, the rhododendron bushes separating the two. Steve gave a long sigh and trudged on through the park and into town towards the police station. He tried hard to shrug off how he was feeling, but with the continual drizzle of rain and the wearing wind, all he managed was to further wrap himself up in a cloak of doom and desperation, wondering what he was going to be accused of and worrying where Jasmine could possibly be.

Arriving at the police station, Steve took a long deep breath before he dared himself to enter the small stark reception area. He rang the bell on the counter where a frosted glass hatch was protected behind a criss-cross iron grid. The shrill sound of the bell announced his arrival. The hatch obligingly slid open to reveal the duty police officer, just like it had the day before. It was almost déjà vu, except that it was a different officer to the one he had seen previously. Steve explained who he was and that he had been asked to come in for questioning about his missing wife. The officer appeared unimpressed that his wife was missing and he was merely asked to take a seat on a bench opposite the desk. The hatch closed leaving nothing for Steve to do but watch the peeling paint on the wall to his left and look at a notice pinned up on the wall to his right about not drinking and driving, which looked as though it was about to fall off. He almost felt inclined to stick it back up but then thought better of it - he didn't want to be accused of interfering in police business as well as not taking proper care of his wife.

A door at the side opened. He hadn't noticed it before but deduced it must have been there all the time. Another police officer emerged and introduced himself. Well into his fifties, with a somewhat ruddy complexion and a waistline that was begging for a larger size in trousers, he cut an imposing figure. He seemed friendly enough - just a tactic to give him a false sense of security before being arrested for getting rid of his wife most likely. Meekly, Steve followed him through the door, down a corridor and into another bare interior to await his fate. A desk, some chairs and a window were the only adornments. The media were correct, the police force really didn't get enough funding, bare necessities only. The policeman, who had introduced himself as Detective Inspector Manning pulled out a chair for Steve, while seating himself at the other side of the desk. Then, instead of being given the third degree, DI Manning appeared warm, sympathetic and caring. He explained that he wanted to go over what Steve had reported already, and was he able to remember anything else, "... as every little thing helps, even though it might not seem relevant, it might be a clue."

Steve relaxed a little and when gently probed, related everything he could about the night before. 'No, they had not had an argument. Far from it. They had spent a lovely evening at Trevor's party, a friend of theirs, and had been together most of the evening until it was time for her to go home. She had left early because she was on duty the following morning. He'd offered to walk her home, but she'd said she would be fine on her own, and not thought anything about it until waking up to messages from the hospital, her place of work.' Jim Manning jotted things down in a matter-of-fact sort of way, but when Steve said about finding Jasmine's phone at the edge of the park, he leaned forward in his chair so abruptly, Steve felt a shockwave go right through him and sat upright and uptight.

"You found her phone in the park?"

"Yes, when I went to look for her, when I followed the path she would have taken, I saw it just near the entrance."

This was definitely disturbing, DI Manning deduced. A young woman would be unlikely to get rid of her phone even if she had decided to lie low for a while, which was one line of possibility. However, in this case it didn't sound as though she was ready to disappear. Leaving a party early so she could get some sleep prior to working an early shift, that was the sort of thing he would have done himself. "Midwife, you say?" asked the Inspector, his voice as a rule well-versed to hide the alarm that had now begun to clamour inside him. The situation had just become more serious. The officer taking the initial statement should have obtained this important intel. They were most likely dealing with an abduction. No woman would just drop her phone without reason.

"Yes, she works on the delivery suite at The Royal. Both she and I have messages from the staff there asking where she is," replied Steve warily. There had been a subtle change in the reassuring intonations of the Inspector's voice and now Steve was on the edge of his chair as well as poker straight. "I checked what was on her mobile phone," he gulped, not wanting to miss anything out.

"We need that mobile, and you need to show us exactly where you found it. We will want to look at it to know who the last caller was and who was the last person she called," he said perhaps more abruptly than he should have. Maybe if they'd had this knowledge earlier, it would have helped build up a picture of events more quickly and to know which lines of enquiry to follow first. He tried to remain calm in front of Steve, who he knew from experience must be going through hell, but he was annoyed that this important piece of information had been missed, and his irritation had just got the better of him.

He changed tack and spoke in a more methodical manner and kept to an established framework that was known to help worried relatives to feel that the police, whom he was representing at this moment, were doing all that they could. He started by telling Steve exactly what they, the police, had done so far and where they would go from here. "This would be to obtain a list of names and addresses of the people at the party if you could procure that for us. Meanwhile, we are in the process of contacting all the local taxi firms and will look carefully along the route your wife most likely took; especially where you found her phone." DI Manning rested his hand on the desk ready to heave his heavy frame up but before doing so asked one more question, if Jasmine was suffering from depression?

"Good God, no!" came the reply. Satisfied with the answer and the interview over, Jim Manning ushered Steve out of the room and ordered him to remain in the waiting area. There was something not right, he could smell it and he sought to get his relief up to speed and organise searching the area as soon as possible while there might still be clues to be found.

Back in reception Steve was once again looking at the flaking paint and droopy posters. He decided it was best not to mention that Jasmine had kissed Trevor and he, Trevor's girlfriend. It had nothing whatsoever to do with anything as far as he was concerned and he was certain that no one at the party would have followed her home. The side door opened and he was handed a cup of tea. He managed a 'thank you,' but the police officer disappeared as quickly as he had come. Steve drank the tea from what must have been the smallest cup on the planet and put it down, empty, beside him. Slumped low in the chair with only his thoughts as company, he cut a melancholic and solitary figure.

DI Manning knew what he was doing, he had lots of lines of enquiry to begin and he was already putting plans in place to find Jasmine and Steve had been hopeful. Now though, this renewed optimism had fallen away and replaced by unanswerable questions. Where was she, how could they possibly find her and even more than that, find her safe and well? She clearly wasn't safe and well, but in some unknown place alone and afraid. Steve stood up and paced about, feeling powerless. He couldn't even do that effectively; two steps and he was at the bare wall with the peeling paint and then two steps the other way and the 'don't drink and drive' poster loomed at him. He decided to stick it up properly. There was some hardened Blu-Tack on the back. He pressed firmly, his thumb turning white with the prolonged pressure. It did the trick; it was back up - for now anyway.

The door opened once again and the police officer who'd delivered the tea reappeared. Steve was to show him where he had found his wife's phone and the probable route she would have taken. Finally he could do something positive! He followed DC Downey - the name he had used to introduce himself - into a police car. They drove to Trevor's flat, then to the point where Steve found Jasmine's phone at the park entrance and then home. He grabbed the phone quickly while DC Downey waited outside and handed it over with great reverence, as if it were the vital clue to finding Jasmine and bringing her home. DC Downey explained that they would be able to get the phone company to look at any calls Jasmine had made on it, triangulate her location and get an approximate fix on her whereabouts in case it was different from the picture they had built up.

Steve returned indoors thinking how quiet the police officer had been during the car journey. He concluded he'd been concentrating on the drive, and it probably wasn't the protocol to chat with passengers, who were for the most part probably miscreants and undesirables. His meandering thoughts vanished instantly though when the two anguished mothers wanted to know what had happened. Tony hovered in the background, making space for them, but listening intently all the same. Paul stuck his head out of the dining room door where he was ensconced but grasping quickly there was no news, said he was in the middle of something and closed the door. Over coffee, as Steve related the morning's events, the conversation became one of positivity as they persuaded themselves that all would be well now the police were doing something about finding her. "After all," explained Glenda, "she has to be somewhere, it's just a question of finding where that somewhere is."

Anne felt she and Glenda needed something practical to keep themselves occupied. "Would you like us to take down the Christmas tree dear?" she asked.

The Christmas tree. He and Jas had chosen it together along with new baubles and lights and it had looked amazing in its spot in the hall, in the alcove under the stairs. It was the first Christmas they had bought a real tree. When they lived in the flat there hadn't been much room, so they'd improvised with a twig sprayed with silver paint and some fairy lights, and hung their Christmas cards from it. This time though they'd made an occasion of it and opened a bottle of fizz, dressed the tree, turned up the music volume on their lovely old jukebox and danced and sang until the wine was all gone.

"Take a picture of it Steve; isn't it pretty," Jasmine had said, and he took several, mostly of her, with the tree in the background. How forlorn it now looked, now the celebrations were over, but he wasn't ready to do anything with it. He should wait for Jasmine to return first.

"No Mum," he replied. "Not yet, not until twelfth night anyway."

"Oh of course," replied Anne. "I just thought it was something we could be getting on with to help. Maybe we could go and get some provisions. Tony, would you drive us please?"

Tony dutifully obliged and they left Steve relatively alone; his father still being occupied with his own matters in the dining room. "I'll be fine," Steve told them. He had things to do and began making a list of all the people he could remember who were at the party. Trevor would give him the names and addresses of those he didn't know, there weren't that many, but he doubted that any of them would be able to offer any clues.

While Tom Downey was escorting Steve, Jim Manning had wasted no time. He called a meeting with all the officers still in situ and brought them up to speed, asking them to make a priority of this now escalating investigation. He insisted everyone should have a full picture of what had happened. Uniform was to be brought in to investigate the area of the park entrance and each member of his team delegated a line of routine enquiry. He would be going to the park himself to meet Tom Downey, who was waiting for him there after he had retrieved the phone from the husband. When he was satisfied that the investigations at the park were underway, Jim Manning would then be making a surprise visit, along with one of the female officers, to the missing woman's residence. He would see if he could pick up any clues about what her state of mind prior to her disappearance had been. It was turning out to be no ordinary day after all.

Considering it had her name written on it, Jasmine had told Steve from the first moment they laid eyes on it, that Jasmine House was the house for them. Now the only reason Jim Manning had cause to knock at its front door was because Jasmine wasn't there. Steve was taken aback when he opened it to find DI Manning standing there with a young female officer by his side, so soon after leaving the station. It could only mean one thing, he thought, that they'd found her... dead. He began shaking uncontrollably, he didn't want to let them in, he didn't want to hear news like that.

"Mr Bartram," began Jim Manning, "do you think we might come in? We would like to have a look around as it will help us with our enquiries."

"Oh, yes of course." Steve opened the door fully and let them in. His relief was insurmountable. They hadn't found her and that had to mean she was out there somewhere, didn't it? And now they were looking for clues to see if she had intended to disappear. He understood that from their point of view. But there was no way she had thought of leaving, just no way. Part of him wanted to tell them they would be wasting their time. He knew though they had to do their job, and if that meant going through Jas's things, then so be it. She would be mortified though if she ever got to know about it. Everything that could be found out about her, would be found out. The police would look over every tiny little detail, including what her knickers looked like. He then remembered that before they went to the party, Jasmine had insisted on making sure the whole place was neat and tidy. 'Please no Jas, please don't tell me you intended this.' For the first time since her disappearance, Steve wondered if he'd got it all wrong and she had deliberately disappeared. But why?

Steve sat down at the foot of the stairs after showing the female officer his and Jasmine's bedroom upstairs, in the knowledge that she was turning over every last item of Jasmine's personal belongings. Meanwhile, DI Manning busied himself in the dining room, looking over the household's receipts, bills, bank statements and the rest. Steve had shown him where they kept them all, but not before having to extricate his disgruntled father, who unhurriedly took up all his morning's workings off the table so the Inspector could sit at it. Paul paced obstreperously around the hall, not only annoyed that he had been disturbed, but alarmed that the police seemed to have thoughts that his son was in some way involved in his daughter-in-law's disappearance. 'Well,' he thought, 'they are wasting their time, there's nothing to be found here.'

Glenda, Anne and Tony returned, Paul letting them in. They burst through the front door in alarm having seen the police car parked outside. They had immediately jumped to the same conclusion as Steve, that Jasmine had been found dead, and the police, had come in person, to break the news.

"They're looking for clues as to her disappearance," said Paul quickly in reassurance. Their glacial expressions thawed back to an ashen hue, which had now become the new normal. Tony went back out to the car to get their purchases before his wife had time to tell him to do so, and Anne went to sit beside her son on the stairs. It seemed the right place to be for her.

"There are two cars in the drive," said DI Manning as he came back into the hall.

"Yes," replied Steve. "The Citroen is mine and the Fiesta's Jasmine's."

"May I take a look at the Fiesta?"

"Certainly, but I don't think it's been anywhere since Jasmine last used it," replied Steve. He picked the car keys up from a tray on the hall table and handed them over to the Inspector who then went outside to give

Jasmine's car the once over." He returned several minutes later and handed the keys back.

"One last thing," said Inspector Manning on his way back out after they had finished their search, "did Jasmine have a handbag at the party, only we can't find one here?"

"Yes, she has only one. It's quite old and she's quite attached to it, doesn't want to replace it," replied Steve.

"So that is also missing. Did she keep her phone in it as a rule?"

"Yes, unless she put it in her pocket, but she doesn't have a pocket in that old cloak she was wearing, so it must have been in her handbag."

"She rang me during that night," said Glenda, "only I didn't pick up the message till we got in, which was around two-ish and by then I thought it was too late to call back."

"And you are?" asked the Inspector.

"Jasmine's mother!" Their eyes locked together for a moment, each thinking there was something about the other.

Jim Manning gave a small cough, breaking the spell. "Thank you," he began cautiously. "Forgive me if I sounded abrupt, but the quicker we can establish a picture of events, the quicker we can get the investigation heading in the right direction. We'll take a look at that call and any others, and the times."

The police left, and the house was theirs again. Paul was trying to answer his wife's query of where on earth he had been earlier that morning and saying he'd been out for an early morning walk to the park to try to clear his head. Tony interjected with some other information. He and Glenda used to live very near here when they were first married, right by the park. Glenda then spoke of giving birth at home very unexpectedly and all by herself, to Jasmine and her twin brother, who was tragically stillborn.

"Just behind the front door of all places," she explained.

"On the doorstep, so to speak," remarked Anne. "That must have been very traumatic for you."

"Yes, it was, and I can't think for the life of me why I should bring it up now. It must be seeing the police here. They had to be involved; you know, in case I had..." Glenda tailed off, not wanting to give voice to what the police might have suspected her of doing before continuing in another direction. "...Anyway, so you see, I have already lost one child, I am not prepared to lose another." Her words had hung in the air only briefly before the depth of their meaning hit home. She started to cry. Tony reached for his handkerchief that he always kept in reserve for just such occasions, from his trouser pocket and proffered it. She took it appreciatively and dabbed her face and managed to compose herself, hoping that this couldn't really be happening. "It was seeing that policeman, he seems; well, I don't know what he seems, he just made it all come back to me."

"On the doorstep?" asked Paul, picking up the conversation when he thought Glenda calm enough to continue.

"Well, when I was compos mentis again, Jasmine was on the doorstep, yes."

"Inside the door?"

"Yes!" Glenda replied, a little bemused. She hadn't realised that tiny details of what happened were requiring so much scrutiny; she almost wished she hadn't mentioned anything.

"Er," began Paul, "which street was it and what house number?"

"Really Paul, does it actually matter? I was just making conversation. I didn't know I was going to get the third degree!"

"Sorry, I was just curious. I've been in the vicinity of the stone circle this morning and wondered if it was round there, or around another side of the park, that's all."

Very gently, Anne steered Glenda away and into the kitchen with the excuse that time was getting on and they needed to prepare a bite to eat. The tension was near snapping point, and they had enough to contend with. They could all do without needlessly causing each other more distress and suffering.

"Flat one, number twenty-three, it's just at the intersection of Park Road and Meadowsring Road," whispered Tony when their wives were out of earshot.

"Ah, thank you," replied Paul, trying to remember the number of the house where he'd found himself earlier that morning, but couldn't. However, his interest was sparked, and even more so when Tony then began revealing more information. Passed down the years by those who liked gossip and tittle-tattle and tell tales of woe, there was a story from a century before which was never resolved. Tony got to hear of it when the tragedy of his own son got out. A new-born baby had disappeared many years previously from that very doorstep. Taken, most likely, by some vagabond or other. When Tony heard the story, he wondered if there was some sort of curse upon the house which had caused his only son to be stillborn. "Well, you clutch at any sort of explanation, just so you have some sort of answer, don't you?" Tony offered as a perfunctory excuse to his outlandish reasoning.

"Indeed, you do," Paul agreed. He then excused himself and retreated into the dining room to sort out the bits of paper he'd been working on before being interrupted by the intrusive police.

It wasn't too much later before he wandered into the kitchen, sneaking a cherry tomato, and popping it into his mouth. "Go do something useful and find Tony and Stephen," snapped Anne. Paul shrugged his shoulders wondering what he had possibly done to offend his wife and went back to the hall to look for them. He found them walking around the sitting room, wearing out the floorboards. He couldn't imagine what they must both be feeling. One was missing a daughter, the other a wife. Being one step removed, as he was only missing a daughter-in-law, he didn't feel he was qualified to understand their respective pain

"Come on you two, I believe we are about to be served lunch." He guided them tenderly towards the kitchen

It proved difficult for Tony to eat, his appetite had failed him and he'd struggled through a morsel of bread and cheese. Concerned and anxious, he needed to be out and doing something instead of sitting idly waiting for news. Fresh air, that was what he required and after lunch offered to show Paul where he used to live. Steve tagged along; he needed something to do too, even if it was just walking. The hapless trio were soon standing outside flat one, number twenty-three, which was precisely the doorstep Paul was hoping it would be. It was most definitely a standing stone he decided, as he studied it for the second time that day.

Uniformed police were at large, looking as though they were combing the area. Paul, Tony and Steve walked a few yards from the door and its step to watch them. "They'll be looking for evidence. DC Downey said they'd be coming," said Steve hopefully. "I'll go and see if they've found anything. They can find all sorts from the tiniest of clues, and that might lead them to Jas."

"They won't let you anywhere near any crime scene," said Tony. He had to hold Steve's arm; he was about to cross the road over to the park.

"Crime scene, what are you saying? She's just missing that's all. They *are* going to find her, there will definitely be clues." Steve shrugged off his father-in-law's hand, but failed to cross, sinking his hands into his pockets instead. He pulled out his hat and wrenched it as far down on his head as it would go in attempt to shut out the world. He was feeling very low and had snapped at everyone over lunch. He'd been so rude to Jasmine's mother, but it had come after years of holding his tongue and right now he had no strength of mind to contain himself. While immersed in his own distress he'd completely overlooked that she, like him, was suffering.

A black VW Golf pulled up. It was Trevor's. He was just passing. "On call," he explained, and on his way to a local care home. One of the residents had been having trouble with a tooth but was too incapacitated to come to the surgery.

"Greenhead Care Home?" asked Steve.

"Yes, as a matter of fact that is exactly the one," replied Trevor. "You know it?"

"I was just there on New Year's Eve visiting the old lady who used to live in our house before us. It's not her is it, with the tooth ache?"

"No, I've been given a man's name," answered Trevor.

"Oh, I'm glad of that. She was a nice old lady; I would like to see her again some time."

"Well, there's no time like the present, hop in."

"Perhaps another time," replied Steve. "I'm not in the mood for talking to strangers right now, and I don't think she was, you know, all there."

"Okay, I'll see you later. Maybe I should say hello to her on your behalf. What's her name?"

Steve thought for a moment trying to remember. "Rose, Miss Rose Brown. Oh, and I nearly forgot, the police want names and addresses of all the people at the party. I've written some down but didn't know everyone there, so if you could do your dentist friends and have Penny do hers." Trevor nodded in reply and roared off, waving his hand as he saw their shapes retreating into the distance in his rear-view mirror.

"That's interesting," said Tony softly. Years of experience married to Glenda had taught him to speak quietly when in her company, and he was rarely out of her company. "Glenda," he continued, "spoke of someone called Rose when we lived here. Maybe it's the same lady. She was there when..." He paused as thoughts of losing his new-born son came to mind for the second time. Although he had accepted matters and moved on, it still pained him to talk about it; he felt it to be a personal matter rather than one for public discussion, and there had been enough of that already during the morning. A young innocent who had never had the luxury of taking a breath, not even one. However, it was about Jasmine that he wanted to speak, so he carried on. "Glenda said that when she was getting into the ambulance with Jasmine to be taken to the maternity hospital, just here," he gestured at the road in front of them, "an old lady appeared and started talking to her. Funny story actually. I think it was the old lady who said to call our baby Jasmine, because that was what her grandmother had wanted her mother to be called. Don't understand it myself, but the story has always stuck in my mind for some reason."

"But what has that got to do with the name Rose, other than both being the name of a flower," asked Paul, somewhat befuddled by Tony's tale.

"Ah well, I'm coming to that. Glenda met her again later, just before we moved away. We'd had Lucy by then, she must have been about a year old. Jasmine was around three when we bought our current home, so that must be about right. Glenda said she had sat next to the same lady on a bench in the park, and that the lady had said repeatedly that her name was Rose. Apparently, she took hold of Jasmine's hands and was saying 'Rose' over and over again as if it were important that she had to remember it."

"She did," said Steve slowly. "Jas did remember her name. It was on the day we first went to view our house. Jas saw the rose climbing up the side wall and it triggered a memory in her. She started saying Rose, Rose, the lady at the park's name was Rose. Or something like that, I can't remember exactly."

"Well, there you are then," said Tony. However, before he could say anymore, there was an interruption. A female voice was shouting so loudly and with such urgency that their conversation paled into insignificance.

"Quick officer, that's him, the one in the middle. That's the one who was snooping around claiming he was from the council. Quick, arrest him before he gets away."

Paul recognised the woman. She'd slammed the door in his face earlier that morning, on the doorstep of flat one, number twenty-three and was now standing with hands on hips looking daggers at him. He wondered how he was going to explain to the police why he had been 'investigating' her doorstep. "Er yes, hello officer, I'm very sorry if I have caused alarm, however I don't recall saying I was from the council, I think that may have been an assumption on the good lady here's part. However, it wasn't snooping exactly, I'd been looking at the standing stones in the park and noticed this doorstep - her doorstep," he explained and gesturing towards the doorstep and then the woman who was now tapping one of her feet impatiently. "You see it looked so like them that I came over to have a closer look. I was curious to know if they were connected to each other in some way. I have an interest in the stone circle and was in the process of measuring the distance from it to the doorstep when the lady happened to open the door."

"We are investigating a possible abduction in this vicinity," began the police officer, satisfied by Paul's explanation for the moment. "Did you notice anything unusual, or happen to pick anything up?" Paul thought it best to come clean.

"Actually officer, that's exactly what I was looking for, something unusual or out of place. You see, the girl who has gone missing is my daughter-in-law." The police officer looked at Paul, looked in the direction of the standing stones and then back at Paul.

"And did you find something that you think would help with our inquiries?" he said again a little more forcefully, wondering what they were trying to achieve by measuring how far a front doorstep was from the stone monument. However, he understood that the natural stress of a family member going missing may have been a cause for his bizarre behaviour.

"Er, no Officer, nothing at all."

"All the same, we will need your name and contact details if you would care to give them to my colleague here, that would be most helpful."

"Is that it?" the woman asked. "Are you going to let him go, just like that? I can't believe it. So much for the police, no wonder the place is like it is, girls going missing, lights never working, people allowed to snoop about as they please." She threw her hands in the air in utter frustration and stalked off back into her house muttering to herself and anyone else within earshot. The police took Paul's details and asked Steve and Tony who they were. On finding out, suggested that perhaps they should wait at home in case the search proved fruitful.

"If they find her body, he means," said Tony under his breath. Normally mild-mannered, he was livid. It was his daughter who was missing, and the police thought he'd best be out of the way! "Don't they understand?" It took the biscuit as far as he was concerned.

"They may well be a little tactless, but they are doing their best," whispered Paul, overcoming his annoyance with the police intrusion earlier. His frustrations and distresses were nothing in comparison to Tony's who must be going through hell itself. Tony looked searchingly at Paul and was about to say he knew that in reality but Steve, who had managed to remain quiet in front of the police officer, could contain himself no longer and prevented him.

"Dad, that's all we need, you nearly getting arrested. What do you think you were doing anyway? I can't believe you'd be doing cockeyed science stuff at a time like this!"

"Sorry, I was trying to keep myself busy, that's all," replied his father, deliberately not mentioning who'd been with him. "Anyway, we're done here. Let's go find a pint and think of something else to do without being interrupted. Steve, where's your local?"

Steve was becoming increasingly bewildered by his father. He walked around a bit with head bowed and hands on hips, pondering. Finally, he spoke. "You think beer is going to help keep you occupied? Honestly Dad, I cannot fathom you sometimes."

"Son, we're all trying to keep it together, I thought it might help us stay occupied that's all."

"Well it doesn't occupy me," Steve retorted. "But if beer is all you can think of right now I suppose you're best going to The Junction from here, it's nearer. Straight up there and out through the top gates and you'll see it over the road." He gestured towards the park walkway that flanked the bowling greens and tennis courts.

"I know it," said Tony. "At least we'll need to come back this way, they can't make us go home."

"No, they can't," replied Steve. Beer was the last thing he could think of though. How could he?" He walked off in a huff in the other direction and left them to it.

"Best leave him," said Tony to Paul, who was ready to go after his son. "Wherever he is emotionally right now, we can't reach him. Let him walk some of it off, he knows deep down that you care."

"Yes, you're right I suppose. I must say how well you are holding it together," replied Paul.

"What else can I do Paul, what else is there to do?" Tony asked pleadingly.

"I understand, I get you. Come on, let's drown our sorrows." They set off in the opposite direction to Steve and towards the pub.

Perhaps it was a good thing that Steve had absented himself Paul thought, for it gave him an opportunity to sound Tony out on the ideas he was exploring. Three pints each later, they were in deep conversation about theories of relativity, the mysteries of stone circles, and the enigmatic Rose. They were so engrossed they hadn't noticed there was someone nearby and listening to their every word.

He ought to make contact. He had planned what to do - to make himself known and to divulge information about where to look for her. Easier said than done though. Having spent the morning walking and thinking, he still wasn't sure what his next move should be. He didn't want to expose himself just yet, he wasn't ready. If he stayed quiet, no one would suspect him of any involvement. He needed to see her again first, see what she had to say, and maybe then... but it needed to be sooner rather than later... before they got to her first. This was a very tricky situation, he was uncertain how to handle it, but at best, information concerning Jasmine's whereabouts needed to come out little by little. He thought it would be better for all that way.

Chapter Four

Sunday afternoon

The emergency appointment at the care home turned out to be an easy tooth extraction, Trevor's favourite part of dentistry. Today though, his thoughts were focused on Steve and Jasmine. He wanted to do something to help find her but like everyone else, felt useless. Then just as he was finishing up with his patient, an idea struck him. Like he'd told Steve, he would seek out his Miss Brown and say hello on his behalf only at the same time he might be able to solve another mystery. It might not have anything to do with what had happened to Jasmine, but it was a riddle, nevertheless.

When Steve and Jasmine had bought their house, it was still full of the old lady's goods and chattels. To Steve's astonishment, they included an old jukebox. "...And not any old jukebox, but a genuine 1015 Bubbler," he remarked to Trevor one day when they were propping up the bar at their local. Why an old woman would have such an iconic thing like that in her house had become the big conundrum, an unsolved enigma. It couldn't have been one of her children's, as she was a spinster; but even so, any children she may have had, would surely not have left it behind. At least it meant he was doing something, and it might help to cheer Steve up a bit if he managed to find an answer.

Trevor leaned his head around the office door and found a couple of nurses sitting inside, one staring at a computer, the other appearing to be writing something. They looked up at him vacantly. He reminded them who he was; that he had finished with Mr Woods; what they should look out for, and was Miss Brown available? They were concerned whether she had a booked appointment, especially as it was Sunday, but he stated it was merely a social call. Trevor had no idea if she was a patient at his group practice or not but deduced that the staff probably wouldn't know either. Both nurses looked at one another before one of them realised it was her turn to move.

"Come with me," said the elder one of the two. Trevor dutifully followed the now hurried caregiver into a very large sitting room. It was peppered with elderly citizens, who were either dozing away their twilight years, or staring blankly at a deafeningly loud television that was placed next to a very grand but sadly unlit fireplace. They came to a windowed alcove, in which Trevor spotted a very old-looking faded chair. Contained by its winged contours huddled a lady so ancient and lifeless she appeared almost transparent. He approached cautiously, making sure the nurse was in front of him. "Rose, the dentist has come to see you," said the nurse. There was no response. Tenderly, the nurse took hold of one of the old lady's fragile-looking hands and held it in hers before repeating the announcement. "Rose, the dentist has come to see you." Trevor was becoming increasingly uncomfortable; he was being a sneak; he should not be disturbing her; he ought to make his excuses and leave. He shifted his feet nervously while the nurse tried again. "Wake up Rose, the dentist is here."

There was a slight stir. An ancient eyebrow arched as the old lady flickered into wakefulness, and then lowered into a frown as if she were puzzled. Slowly, her body came to life. "Dentist did you say?" It was a whisper of a voice, as if she hadn't the strength to project it outwards. Her elbows went back, she was trying to straighten herself up and sit forward in her chair to give more force to her voice. "What do I need from a dentist? I have dentures," she bared them in a grimace to make the point.

Trevor stepped forward tentatively. "Good afternoon, Miss Brown, this is just a social call, I don't need to look at your dentures, unless they are giving you any trouble. Are they giving you any trouble?"

Rose thought about his question for a moment before saying, "not especially," and then settled back into her chair. The nurse excused herself and bustled off. Trevor, now a nervous wreck and with knees knocking, asked permission to sit down. Rose responded with a feeble open arm gesture towards a nearby seat but then with eyes half closed, appeared to be drifting off again. He was indeed encroaching on her time. Maybe, he thought, this had been another one of his idiotic ideas, like agreeing to Penny moving in. Penny by herself was fine, but what he had failed to foresee was what came with her; mountains of clothes, boxes of books, bits of furniture, not to mention all the lotions and potions that now covered the top of his chest of drawers. His flat was already full, now it was overflowing - even the bathroom cabinet had been invaded! But then he'd been warned about having a serious relationship; that freedom becomes merely a word rather than a state of being. However, there were fringe benefits which he rather enjoyed, and he was kind of in love with her, so he felt he shouldn't really complain. Wondering how on earth he was going to begin a conversation that would lead to information about the jukebox, he pulled up the chair and sat down anyway before he collapsed in a heap of jelly. He'd never felt so nervous, even drilling into his first ever tooth wasn't this bad. This had to be a first!

"I came to see how you were, er," he began hesitantly, "how you are settling in here." He saw the old lady's eyes flicker and look a little vexed, but it showed she was awake and listening. He attempted to rephrase his query. "Are you liking your accommodation here, I mean after moving from your home." He wondered if he had said the right thing, she seemed disturbed. He continued with his monologue, for that was what the conversation was rapidly turning into. "It must have been difficult to leave after living there for so long." With that, her eyelids opened to a vacant stare. Oops, too direct, any further and he might upset her. He tried another tack, a last attempt before admitting defeat. "Miss Brown, as well as being a dentist, I am also a good friend of the fellow who came to see you the other day, Steve, er Stephen Bartram." He got an immediate and reassuring response. Her cloudy eyes transformed quite noticeably, becoming bright and shining. Result! He thought she would have been quite stunning in her youth, there was still a deep brown colour to them even though her pupils had the distinct haze of cataracts. The glow was short lived though, her face soon changing to sadness once more. Damn! He didn't know what he could say next; everything he'd tried so far clearly wasn't working.

Thank goodness, a timely distraction. A nurse had appeared with two cups of tea. Trevor was surprised she didn't spill any the way she was bounding merrily about. She put them down gracefully on the small coffee table next to Rose. "Quite the popular girl, eh, Rose? Two young gentleman callers in nearly as many days. What's your secret? I could do with a man in my life just now." She placed her hand on her hip coquettishly before turning her attention to Trevor. "She's perked up no end since her first visitor a couple of days ago. Bring it on, that's what I say. I hear you are the visiting dentist," she continued. "Great idea to socialise with your clients, putting them at ease, long may it continue." She waltzed off. Trevor followed her with bedazzled eyes, almost entranced.

"She's the best one, that nurse, Maria. Always happy, always dancing and full of cheer," began Rose, her quiet voice drifting across towards Trevor.

He turned back around to face her. She was going to say something else, her expression kept changing as if she was wondering how to put it. Eventually she spoke. "What day is it today?"

"It's Sunday, the second of January," he answered politely.

"Has it happened then?"

Trevor hadn't a clue what she meant, but then remembered the millennium bug. "No, it didn't happen, the computers are still running, all is well." He thought she looked confused, a little crestfallen maybe. He tried to steer things towards finding out about the jukebox, for that was the whole point of speaking to her, even though he was being rather indirect. "I hope you don't mind me asking, but I am a little curious. I know Steve and his wife Jasmine well, and have been to their house, your house, several times. It's a lovely place, and full of its own history. They've kept many of the pieces of furniture." Rose was looking pleased with the information he was imparting, so he carried on. "There is one piece that captivates me though and that's the er, the jukebox." He stopped there and waited with expectation. It would be great to tell Steve a bit of positive information and try to take his mind off things. But then again, maybe not. It was complete trivia compared to Jasmine's disappearance. Why had he thought it was a good idea? Now he felt completely stupid. Here he was, sitting in front of a particularly old and quite vulnerable lady, trying to extract information from her when he had no right to be there. He really should have made his excuses and left.

"Ah that..." She looked wistful, sad almost, yet continued speaking slowly and deliberately, as if most of her strength was going into the projection of her voice. Trevor was forced to pay precise attention; her breathy words weren't easy to catch, but he was determined nonetheless; it was why he was there. "It was given to me by my colleagues on my retirement from nursing at The Royal. My mother said I should get one, but she didn't tell me why and I have no idea how my colleagues found out, but somehow, they did. She even told me which records to put in and in what order. Anyway, it doesn't matter, I'm pleased you like it. Do they like it too, my er, the new owners?"

"Yes, very much. You say your mother said to get it. I find that intriguing, did she like all that sort of music then?"

"I haven't the slightest idea," Rose said dismissively. She looked tired, Trevor thought he should let her get back to her slumber, but then she took him by surprise by asking, "Are you sure it didn't happen?"

"I'm sorry, are you talking about the millennium bug?" She shook her head to the question. "I'm afraid I don't know what you mean then. I had better leave as I've other things to do. I need to get back to my friend Steve, the new owner of your house." Trevor hesitated, he didn't know why he would suddenly blurt this out, but he carried on anyhow. "Jasmine, his wife, has gone missing." He saw Rose's withered hands go up to her mouth as she took in a sharp breath, and then down to her chest where they wobbled noticeably. She sank back in her chair and began to cry. That did it, he thought, he could be a complete bastard at times. Now he really *had* upset her. "I'm very sorry," he muttered, "I didn't mean to make you cry, I don't know why I mentioned it." Trevor looked round for a nurse but couldn't see one. "I'll go and find help."

"No, it's all right, I don't require a nurse. I'm a little emotional, and very tired. Perhaps you could leave now?"

"Yes, of course. Er, nice to meet you," said Trevor, attempting a rather insipid smile. Grateful to have been dismissed, he got up to leave. Rose smiled back and making a grab for his arm, managed to take hold of a bit of his jacket sleeve.

"The letters. Ask him about the letters."

"Er yes, all right, I will," replied Trevor. Letters? he didn't know what she meant. Letters as in written correspondence, ABC letters, like a child's learning tool, or Scrabble even? He hardly thought Steve would hang onto something like that. They had most likely been thrown out, or sold on eBay, if they'd been of any worth. He was pleased to be out of the building and in the fresh air.

Trevor jumped into his car and checked his mobile. There was a missed call from a number he didn't recognise with a voicemail attached. It was the police. He'd given them his name and number at the police station when handing over Jasmine's photograph and now they were asking for the names and addresses of everyone who'd attended the party like Steve had said. He didn't see how the information was relevant, but appreciated they could leave no stone unturned and would be looking into the possibility of someone at the party following her. Was one of his friends some sort of reprobate? He grew cold at the thought, but then dismissed it as nonsense, and headed home, narrowly missing a pedestrian who appeared suddenly in his rear-view mirror as he reversed out of his parking position. Trevor thought the figure was somehow familiar, but by the time he'd finished manoeuvring his car and swivelled round to have a better look, they were no longer in view and Trevor was none the wiser.

Chapter Five

Sunday afternoon.

Posters and placards heralding the seasonal sales adorned every high-street store, enticing the masses. Eager shoppers filled the streets, sporting their bargain buys in logo-enriched bags of every texture and bulky size. The chaos and the frenzy, the inescapable shoves and jostles, mirrored Steve's state of being exactly, but was also a soothing balm. A tortured man in a state of limbo, had sought the company of strangers and sunk further into solitude. He wandered aimlessly around the town for a couple of hours, moving wherever he was propelled by the herding throng.

Steve barely knew who he was any more, or who he was supposed to be. A happily married man, a man whose wife had left him, a widower through murder, a man whose wife was being held against her will, a man who was having a very bad dream? And Jas? What was happening to her? Rape, torture, death? Oh God, it was too painful to think about. Being amongst a crowd of anonymous people brought a weird sense of comfort as an alternative. Here, he didn't have to be worried, sad, scared, happy; he could just be...nothing.

He was in the middle of C&As, mindlessly rummaging through a rack of jeans, when he felt his phone vibrating in his trouser pocket. He yanked it out quickly, hungry for good news, any news. It was a text from Penny asking if he was okay. He texted back asking if she was at the flat as he was heading that way. She was. He put his phone away, departed the bedlam of the town centre into the peace of the residential quarter and onwards towards someone who cared.

The front door of the flats opened as soon as Steve had rung the bell. He still had a spare key from when he and Jasmine lived in the ground floor flat, having never handed it in when they moved. He must leave it out on the kitchen table to prompt him to give it to Trevor, he thought. Steve crossed the hall and climbed the stairs to the first floor. He saw Penny waiting on the landing. Such an open, friendly face and her long wavy hair left loose today, framing it. He needed a hug so much. Each stair he climbed brought Steve closer to Penny's outstretched arms and he almost leapt up the last few towards them. She took him into the temporary sanctuary of her loving embrace, and as she did so, her friend and colleague, turned into a blubbering wreck.

Several moments passed before any words were exchanged - they weren't necessary. Steve needed to let go of the emotion; Penny and her obliging shoulder were fully present while he did. When he was spent, they moved, arms round each other, inside the flat. He sat down on the sofa and watched Penny fill the kettle and put teabags into mugs. "I think maybe you should ring the National Missing Persons Helpline," she told him, thinking it would be good for Steve to stay positive and focused. She brought over the hot, welcoming tea and sat down next to Steve, who took a sip before answering.

"The what? Isn't that for kids who've run away?"

"It's much more than that," Penny replied. "It's a free helpline for families and those who have any information about missing people. People use it to make contact for all sorts of reasons. For instance, someone might want to tell their family that they are safe and well, but they don't wish to be contacted. Or someone may know something about someone who is missing, but doesn't know the family, or they don't want to go to the police about it for whatever reason." Penny paused to have a drink of tea but then thought to add, "Of course I'm not suggesting for one minute that Jasmine is in hiding and doesn't want you to know where she is, I just think it a good idea to spread the net wide, that's all." She took another sip of tea to swallow down her words that were spoken earnestly, but not with absolute truth. After her and Paul's conversation in the park, whatever she thought or imagined was mere conjecture and best left unsaid. Better that Steve was kept occupied with things to do, like the suggestion she had just voiced.

"Mmm, perhaps it's a good idea. I'll look when I'm home, that is, if they're open on a bank holiday weekend. Thanks for that," he said, perking up. He sipped his tea. "This tea is lovely, I needed something hot and sweet, just the thing to warm me up, thanks again."

The front door swung open and Trevor walked in, shedding his coat and workbag. "Ah Steve, any news?"

"No, not yet, but I'm going to ring the National Missing Persons Help Line when I get home. It was Penny's suggestion."

"Ah good idea," replied Trevor but secretly thinking Steve was clutching at straws. "The police rang me this afternoon, they want names and addresses of everyone at the party like you said."

"Waste of time from my point of view," replied Steve, "but I've written down a few that I know." He pulled out a piece of paper from his back pocket and passed it to Trevor who was re-boiling the kettle.

"Oh good, thanks. I don't know everyone's addresses, I'll have to go round those I do know and hope they will know," said Trevor resignedly.

"I'll do it," said Penny.

"Oh great, thanks," said Trevor and passed Steve's list over to her, glad to have it all off his hands.

Steve finished the last of his tea and left in sombre mood but with spirits a little raised. At least the police were looking for her, and he was able to do something positive too by asking for help from a big and caring organisation. She had to be somewhere, maybe they would be able to help.

As soon as Steve left, Trevor confessed to Penny what had happened during his afternoon. Remorse was creeping over him and he wanted to offload it somehow. "Er, I met Ms Rose Brown today, while I was at Greenhead. I er, thought to enquire about that jukebox they've got. I know Steve's always wondered about it. I um, thought it too good an opportunity to miss"

"You sound almost guilty of something Trevor," said Penny. "And... what did you find out?"

Trevor added some milk to his second cup of tea and took a large swallow before answering. "Well," he continued, "she gave a really strange answer. She said it had been her retirement gift from a nursing career at The Royal because her mother had told her to get it."

"Her mother?" retorted Penny. "Why would she be choosing her retirement gift, surely that would have been up to her employers?"

"I know, that's what I mean, peculiar. Apparently, her mother had chosen all the music and in which order to arrange the records."

"Bit odd don't you think? A couple of old biddies jiving around to Jailhouse Rock, the mind boggles!" They cracked out laughing and Trevor felt better.

"I'm pretty sure Jailhouse Rock isn't there though," he said. "Ask Jas, she knows all the tracks on it. Oh..." His voice tailed off as he remembered.

Meanwhile, Steve walked home through the now twilight-lit park absorbing the serenity of evening and the power it brought. It didn't matter what was happening in the world to any individual, whether good or bad, the sun would set despite it all, and the day would come to its inevitable conclusion. He passed by the tranquil lake and the noiseless bandstand, the idling swings in the playground, the shuttered café. The early January night was rapidly descending, preparing to cocoon all in its wintry blanket. Despite the cold wind that had begun to stir up again, Steve felt moved to sit for a while and take in more of the ambience. It felt almost timeless; day followed night relentlessly. If night and day were conscious, they would still know no other cycle. So, he pondered, 'day' was a continual phenomenon, as was 'night.' If Jasmine had been here so recently, she was a part of that day, or that night, which was a part of all the nights and all the days, including this one. With that thought, Steve stood up, shook himself and headed for home feeling he was beginning to sound a bit like his father. All the same, he really had felt her presence all around him, she'd seemed so close, as if she'd never left. He took comfort from that at least.

Neither Glenda nor Anne was particularly impressed that their husbands had ended up at the pub, given the present circumstances. It wouldn't have entered the head of either woman to go out for a social drink at a time like this. However, keeping their thoughts to themselves, they asked for news. They were informed of the police presence in the park, but, due to sheer embarrassment, the two men declined to relate any details about the altercation concerning the present resident in Tony and Glenda's old flat. "Well, no news is good news I suppose," proffered Glenda dubiously, and carried on chopping copious amounts of onions. In her wisdom gained from previous tragedies, sticking to some form of routine helped to stay sane; preparing food was hers. Everyone had to eat, and she liked to provide hearty meals, and food could be very comforting when going through emotional pain. She was making spaghetti bolognese - everyone liked that. Tony helped by preparing some salad.

"Well, you clearly have dinner sorted between you, and if we were to speak in proverbs, too many cooks spoil the broth; we'll leave you to it," said Paul, and ushered Anne out of the kitchen.

"Glenda," began Tony hesitantly; she was dabbing her onion-filled eyes with kitchen towel, "do you remember when we lived here, and you spoke of the old lady you met?" He paused, waiting for her to recall. "I think you said her name was Rose."

Glenda continued with her onion dissections. "Oh yes, I remember. Why bring that up?"

"I have just had a thought that maybe she used to live in this house," said Tony. Glenda stopped her chopping, which had begun to become somewhat manic.

"Really, what on earth possessed you to draw that conclusion?" Tony proceeded to tell her what Steve had said, that the previous owner of the house was called Rose, and Jasmine had recalled meeting her and she had kept saying 'Rose'. Glenda's eyes lifted upwards to her forehead thinking back to all those years ago.

"Yes, she did, it was Jasmine's birthday. She seemed most insistent that Jasmine should know her name. Most odd," she said thoughtfully, and then sniffed, her nose now full of onion vapour. "Anyway, just because her name was Rose doesn't mean that she was the Rose that used to live here, and what does it have to do with anything?" Glenda resumed her frenzied attack on the components of the bolognese, this time being the turn of the peppers and mushrooms.

Her husband could be so absurd sometimes, she thought, just missing her finger with the knife. Slowing the slicing down a little, she continued to reflect. What if it had been the same woman? How strange, and what a coincidence. Or was it a coincidence? When Glenda had first met Rose, when she was in the ambulance, just after giving birth, she'd thought Rose was some sort of mystic. She'd told her something, Glenda tried to remember what it was; something about Rose's mother being called Jasmine, or wasn't called Jasmine like her grandmother had wanted, or something like that. It was too complicated for her to understand then and with the passage of time, no easier now. Nevertheless, it had prompted her to call her new baby Jasmine. She never thought to reason why, maybe she just liked the name. She took in a deep breath and breathed out forcefully, unconsciously attempting to blow her thoughts away and poured some oil into a pan. Turning the gas on to full, Glenda then put in the onions and swished them round absentmindedly. Something niggled; something she wasn't understanding. Why did that old woman's words still bother her? While she was pondering, smoke began to billow, and the over-sautéed onions were turning almost black. Glenda carried on cooking, but on a lower setting. Tony said nothing, it was better that way, continuing to concoct the salad.

A rather paranoid Steve arrived back home, believing he was being followed. He'd imagined it a few times since Jasmine disappeared and felt it again just now as he came out of the park. However, when he stopped and tried to listen and look, there was nobody around. Maybe, because nothing made any sense, it was making him hear things that weren't there. To calm himself down, he stood and took a moment of sanctuary in the welcoming hallway with its galleried landing. When he and Jasmine had entered it for the first time they felt they'd stepped into a time-warp, the place having been untouched for years. They'd seen beyond the peeling paint and aged clutter though, running and dancing from room to room in wonderment. Like Steve told the officer when reporting Jasmine's disappearance, they knew immediately the house was meant for them, it had all but spoken to them even before they entered through the front door.

Steve sighed at the memory, breathed in the pine aroma emanating from the Christmas tree, checked out the jukebox which had remained unusually silent and walked over to pick up a sheet of paper that was lying on the floor tiles outside the dining room. He looked at it quizzically but then recognised immediately to whom it belonged. On it were his father's interminable mathematical equations, but there was something else, something familiar. Heavily filled in with over-lapping pencilled lines that formed countless triangular, diamond and other nameless shapes, was the distinct outline of a star. Why had his father, who had no knowledge as far as he knew, of Jasmine's birthmark, drawn something very similar, and why had he applied so many maths equations to it? Yet another thing to muddle him up and he'd had plenty of that already.

Steve had come home to company whether he had need of it or not. The parents and in-laws were busying themselves, as far as he was concerned, in monopolising much of his house and all the while Jasmine was most likely in great danger and there he was, being completely ineffectual in doing anything to find her. Frazzled emotionally and mentally, it was no use him even trying to do any reporting to the National Missing Persons Help Line. He needed space to think, not more confusion and went into the sitting room hoping for peace and quiet. Instead, he found his father standing at the window. Steve thrust the piece of paper towards him so forcefully, Paul was forced to take a step back.

"Is this yours?" he asked. Paul looked at his son, and then down at the piece of paper. He took it into his hands and examined it.

"Yes, it is, why do you ask?"

"It was on the floor in the hall. I picked it up and realised it was one of your calculations, but could you please tell me about this drawing?"

"Yes of course," replied Paul relaxing; he thought he was about to be accused of something. He wasn't the best at neatness, partly why he and Anne were in the habit of continually decluttering their home. "It's essentially a diagram of the standing stones in the park, but when I drew lines so I could begin to see all the relationships, or angles between each stone, it became heavily filled in. Why do you ask?

"It's only that it reminds me of something, that's all."

"What does it remind you of," replied Paul interested in what his son had to say. "The denseness of all the lines in the middle makes a rather distinguished shape don't you think? Like a star, I'd say."

"Exactly," said Steve. "But more than that Dad, you can't have known this, but Jasmine has a birthmark which is almost exactly the same shape!"

Paul could hardly contain himself. "Well, there's a coincidence for you," he replied as calmly as he was able. "I'd been looking at all the different angles one could generate with a plan of the stones, and this is the result. How fascinating that Jasmine has a mark just like it!" He had to really try to remain nonchalant, but the information was dumbfounding. When discussing matters with Penny at the circles, vague abstract ideas had formed in Paul's mind which he'd attempted to discuss with Tony in the pub but hadn't gone as far as he thought he might. Realising it would be too much for him to absorb, Paul stopped himself short. Now though, his work, all those calculations, had just entered yet another dimension and he didn't know how long he could keep his theories to himself. But keep them to himself he must, for they were mere speculations, nothing more. Until he had proof then that's how they'd have to stay; he would just have to control himself and say nothing.

"Let me have a look then." Glenda had walked in; she had needed a rest from vegetable preparations and left Tony to watch over the bolognese. "Oh yes, I see what you mean, it does look like it. Though of course, I haven't seen it for years, being where it is, on her bottom."

"Did you really have to say that?" said Steve rather angrily. Yet again Jasmine's mother had annoyed him. Normally, he was able to keep his fury under control. There'd been so many times when she second-bested Jasmine after her sister Lucy, and she was such a drama queen; he was always exhausted after being in her company. And now she was embarrassing Jas. Well, he knew she would have been embarrassed, had she been here.

"Well, that is where it is!" Glenda replied indignantly.

"Would anyone like something to drink?" asked Anne. She'd been taking time out in her guest bedroom upstairs and keeping out of the way of things but couldn't help but hear Steve and Glenda's rising agitation. Their reverberating voices had made their way into the hall and up the stairs towards her. She rushed down quickly to try and defuse a potentially awkward situation before it got out of hand. "Glenda, what would you like? Should we make some gins and tonic with that bottle of Gordon's we got at the supermarket?" Anne looked at the blank faces but continued regardless. "Five G&T's coming up then. Steve where are those nice tumblers we got you for Christmas? Better still, come and show me."

The five gin and tonics turned into seven when Trevor and Penny arrived unexpectedly, and straight away invited to stay and eat. Trevor had forgotten to mention earlier, when Steve had been round at theirs, what the old lady, Rose, had asked about some letters. When he remembered, he thought it important enough to come over and ask him about it. However, by the time he and Penny got there, it had escaped his mind yet again. This time, due to what had happened on their way over which Trevor revealed, but not before taking a long draught out of the glass he'd been offered first.

He and Penny had been walking past the bandstand in the park, when he noticed the old man who he'd seen the other day, walking his dog again. The man had come from the direction of the lake, and their paths met by the temperance drinking fountain. Trevor thought the old man seemed surprised to see him, even a little shocked. Nevertheless he'd bid Trevor and Penny a good evening and begun to continue his walk, but then hesitated and asked if there'd been any further developments "...er, on your missing friend." Trevor replied with a no, but was conscious of the old man's hesitation, as if he wanted to speak further. Meanwhile, the ever-enthusiastic Bessie was jumping up Trevor's leg wanting to say hello, so he bent down to pet her, thinking it might give the old man time to say what he wanted. The man started to speak. "I, er, think we may have a mutual acquaintance. It was you, wasn't it, visiting Miss Brown today? She said she had been visited by a young gentleman, and I believe I saw you leaving as I was approaching Greenhead."

"Yes, I was there," replied Trevor curiously, realising it had been him he'd seen in his rear-view mirror earlier.

"Yes, I thought so. And do you know her well?"

"Not especially well, no," replied Trevor, wondering if he could get out of this without having to explain himself in too much detail.

"You see, I have known her for quite some time, and she has never mentioned you."

Oh dear, the old man was probing a little too far, he would have to say something by way of an explanation. "Ah well, she perhaps wouldn't have. I am a dentist you see, part of the practice down Fitzwilliam Street. I happened to be seeing another patient, I just thought I would say hello and see how she was keeping." He hoped that would suffice. It did. The old man changed tack and began divulging precisely what he and Penny had rushed over to tell them all. Apparently, he was on his way to the police to tell them what he knew.

"What he knows about Jasmine do you mean?" asked Steve. He got up from his seat and was striding around, unable to keep still.

"Yes, I think so," replied Trevor, "but he wouldn't elaborate. Said it was best told to them, but he didn't think it would help."

Steve took in a large gulp of air, as if he was about to hear what had happened to Jasmine and headed for the door. "Right, I'm going there now, to see what he knows."

"No you don't," said his father restraining him from reaching the door. "If he has anything useful the police will tell us. Sit down and have a drink. Here." Paul pushed an unclaimed glass of gin and tonic into his son's hand. It was no use diving down to the police station every time there was a possible lead, and he knew his son knew that too.

"What on earth does he know?" wondered Steve, taking a sip of the colourless fizz. "Do you think he saw something?" He set his glass down, he wasn't in the mood for alcohol.

"Well, he said he wasn't there when I asked him about it last night," began Trevor. "Wait a minute, he said he wasn't there walking his dog, but I suppose he could have been there on his own." Trevor accepted the drink offered by Paul and carried on talking. "I remember him saying he'd walked her earlier, and it was too noisy with the fireworks to take her out at that time of night, but he could easily have gone out without her. He must have seen something, don't you think?"

"I'm sure the police will let us know of any developments," said Paul. "Meanwhile, there is nothing we can do, so let's keep calm and let them do their jobs. If she's out there, then they will find her."

"What do you mean 'if'?" Steve retorted. "Of course she's out there, she's just got to be, hasn't she? She can't just vanish, can she?" The question went unanswered as Tony declared the food was just about ready and could Paul move his papers off the dining table so they might all sit down?

Although the table was laden with a deliciously aromatic spaghetti bolognese and colourful salad, it was only picked at. None of them had much of an appetite, apart from Trevor who tucked in with enthusiasm.

Meanwhile, at the police station, Jim Manning had called in his troops for an update. An incident room had been set up with code name 'Operation Birdwing' as the evidence, or rather lack of it, was pointing to a possible abduction.

"Please, anyone, tell me something we can go on. Has anybody got anything concrete?"

"None of the taxis had a call from that area, and there weren't any buses operating at that time."

"No one matching her description was admitted to hospital."

"Okay, have we got the phone triangulated?"

"Not yet sir."

"Get onto them first thing tomorrow, anything on CCTV?"

"Haven't got them all in yet Guv, but there's one from the off-licence on Fitzwilliam Street showing her walking in the direction of Greenhead Park, timed at five past one in the morning."

"Excellent. So that would correlate with the time she left the party on New North Road. Can someone get a map on the board so we can record her route please? Do we know where the surveillance cameras are in the area?"

"Working on it, Sir."

"Well work faster. And look for private houses that have CCTV, there are loads of pricey places in that vicinity, some of them are sure to have cameras. We must be able to come up with something useful. Anything else?"

"A description of what she was wearing, and her photograph has been circulated to our local units, and I'm expecting a list of names and addresses of the party goers in the morning Guv."

"Good, keep me posted if they come up with anything. This is a young woman, a hard-working midwife, who, from what we have ascertained so far, respects her job so much, she doesn't have an alcoholic drink on the biggest night of the century and leaves a party to get enough sleep so she can be ready for duty in the morning. In my book, this doesn't fit someone who intended to disappear. Far more likely she has been taken by a person or persons as yet unknown. We need to find out what has happened to her as quickly as we can, the longer we take, the colder the trail will get. Ben, have another look at the CCTV footage we have already and see who else was around at that time. Anything from the house to house?"

"Not really, Guv."

"What do you mean not really, either there is or there isn't."

"Then no, Sir."

Jim Manning dismissed them with a wave of his hand. They, or rather he, had been too slow off the mark, but if he jumped to attention, all guns blazing every time people got lost, he would have no resources for anything else, plus the fact that it would be inappropriate. He could only do his best, so he stopped himself there and went to top up his coffee. The kettle hadn't yet come to the boil when Tom Downey interrupted him. Apparently, there was an elderly gentleman at the front desk saying he knew something about the missing girl.

"Genuine or crackpot?" asked the Inspector.

"Don't know Guv, he'll only speak to the 'officer in charge,' and I'm quoting."

"All right Tom, I'll see him." He put the heaped spoon of coffee back in the Nescafé jar and screwed on the lid sighing heavily, wishing his sergeant wasn't on sick leave. There were always the inevitable fruitcakes who felt the need to confess at any given opportunity and DS Bradbury could have dealt with it had he been here. However, the fact that Jasmine Bartram was missing wasn't on general release until the morning, so maybe he really did have some information. 'Well, you'll never know unless you ask, Jimbo,' he muttered to himself, 'a hot coffee will have to wait.' He adjusted his posture and went off towards the front desk while putting on his meeting the public face.

Chapter Six

Monday, January 3rd, am

There was a loud knock on the front door. Nobody spoke, no one dared move. Who would be knocking at this time of the morning, unless...? They looked at one another over the breakfast table, none of them wanting to answer it. It was Tony who, in the end, felt brave enough. He took a deep breath, opened the hefty main door and faced up to two uniformed policemen. He gulped hard in anticipation of what they might be going to say.

"We would like to speak to Mr Paul Bartram please."

"Is it to do with my daughter's disappearance?"

"We are just conducting routine enquiries Sir. May we come in?"

With a great sense of relief, he led them into the sitting room and gestured for them to sit down. Paul was by then in the hall, he'd followed Tony out of the kitchen in case he needed backup support. "It's the police, they want to see you."

"See me, what on earth for?"

"Routine enquiries they said. Better go and see. The longer we keep them waiting, the longer they'll take to find my daughter." Tony couldn't bear to say her name, it would be like an acknowledgement of her disappearance. Calling her his daughter kept her close to him, and therefore safe. He watched Paul shrug his shoulders, walk into the sitting room and close the door behind him.

Twenty minutes later the police left and Paul returned to the kitchen. All eyes were upon him.

"Okay okay, they wanted to know why I was hanging around the entrance of the park yesterday. The police that we spoke to there yesterday had put it all in their report, they were just following things up."

"Paul," enquired Anne, "what were you really doing when you went out yesterday for your, so called, early morning walk?" Hardly pausing for breath, she carried on. "You went to look at those standing stones, didn't you? I knew you wouldn't be able to keep away. That's what these calculations and diagrams that you've been doing are all about. Really, at a time like this, I can't believe it! Well, actually, I can. You cannot stop trying to prove it all can you? Give it up Paul, please give it up; I can't take anymore." With that, she got up from the little breakfast booth, and walked out. All eyes were fixed on the kitchen door she had slammed shut behind her. They then, as one, swivelled round in their stunned sockets, turning towards Paul.

"Paul, what on earth *were* you doing so early in the morning?" The request this time came from Glenda, seemingly picking up an imaginary baton in support of Anne. She stood up with arms crossed; she wouldn't move until she had an answer.

"I'm so sorry, I didn't realise it would have caused so much trouble," Paul replied reluctantly. Then hesitantly, attempted to excuse his alleged faux pas with; "I simply couldn't sleep and thought to do some measurements on the standing stones. It was to do with my work, I couldn't resist the opportunity."

"Well, like your wife said, maybe you should give it up. Is it really the time and place for doing your calculations?" continued Glenda.

"Glenda please," Tony said, trying to keep the peace, "Paul's doing what he can to keep sane, like we all are."

"Can you all please shut up?" Steve shouted. "I can't stand this any longer. I'm off to the police station to see what the old man had to say." Steve got up from his chair and stormed off, and for a second time, all eyes pivoted onto the kitchen door.

"Now look what you've done, don't you think the boy has enough on his plate without us all getting at each other? He needs peace and calm, not mayhem." Tony was always one for keeping the peace, he didn't think any good came of arguing, but things were getting a little too much. Normally, he would let his wife have her way, life was simpler when he did, but she had been plainly rude to Paul, and he felt he had to say something. "We are all feeling the strain. Please, let's not fall out. We need to do something constructive rather than destroying each other."

"Yes, you're right," said Glenda, surprisingly meek. "I'm sorry Paul."

"No need to apologise, Tony is right, we are all feeling it."

Glenda's phone rang and made them all jump. It was Lucy. She'd been on holiday abroad but had at last managed to get a flight home and was now at the airport getting a taxi. She would be with them in an hour or so and had ideas for making and distributing some missing person leaflets.

"There you are, she's been reading my thoughts," said Tony, pleased his wife would have at least one daughter by her side to help her cope. Glenda had hoped that Jasmine might have turned up by the time she and Tony arrived at Jasmine House, but that not being the case, had thought she'd better let her younger daughter know of their concerns. The news hit Lucy right in the middle of her stomach, as if she'd been punched. It was a pain like no other, she couldn't rest, and she couldn't eat. There was no point continuing her holiday in this state and no question of not coming home. She'd twisted and turned with the news and taken the first available flight back. She needed to be with family, not stuck thousands of miles away and feeling totally useless. Her idyllic Mexican dream holiday had evaporated with the words 'your sister is missing'; the beautiful beach resort had lost its appeal. Her mother had tried to dissuade her, for she'd been so looking forward to it.

A bit of a workaholic, she rarely had any time off. Lucy was a costume designer and had worked on some of the BBC's major period dramas, as her mother delighted in telling people. After spending Christmas day with her parents and Jasmine and Steve, she'd set off by herself on the twenty-seventh to Mexico, for sun, sea and some peace.

Unlike Jasmine, Lucy looked like a younger version of her mother with a comparable fiery temperament. She'd obtained her efficiency and capable nature from her father though. However, much to the incredulity of Glenda, she seemed totally unable to find a boyfriend.

"I can't imagine why you would be in the position of having to holiday by yourself." Glenda had chided recently. "Surely you come across single men in your line of work. What about your friends, they simply must know someone? Such a shame you stopped seeing that lovely boy Thomas, he was utterly charming."

"That was years ago Mum, and he'd been two-timing me, and then he dumped me, so I was well out of it. Anyway, I'm not interested in a relationship at the moment."

"Not interested? I've never heard the like. Oh, you're not, you're not, you know," Glenda continued in a whisper, "one of those," she cleared her throat, "lesbians?"

"No Mum I'm not, but it might be easier if I were, you might get off my case." And so the conversations between mother and daughter had continued.

On this occasion, however, Glenda's thoughts were far from any relationship Lucy may or may not be having, and she embraced her daughter before she'd barely stepped over the threshold. At least she had one child safe and sound.

What else could he have done? No one would understand why, and now he'd no idea what he was supposed to do next. Maybe provide clues as to her whereabouts? Would that help speed things up for them to find out where she was, or should he let sleeping dogs lie and leave her location for them to discover? But he didn't think that would happen; never in a million years. Anyway, it wasn't his fault that she was there, in that place, in that exact position. He hadn't been able to help himself, he had to experience it, he had to know... and now he had to make himself scarce, for he'd seen her husband marching along the main path quite near; he didn't wish to be noticed.

Steve was oblivious of Lucy's arrival; he'd already left in fury. After storming out of the kitchen, he'd pulled his coat off the hook in the hallway and stomped outside, slamming the front door behind him. It was some time before his rage subsided and he'd hiked almost the entire length of the park before something caught his eye and he slowed his pace. A figure. He'd seen it before, he thought. He looked again but it was gone. He shuddered a little, this was getting spooky. Someone was spying on him, he was sure. Did the police suspect him, and were they following his every move for clues? It was ludicrous, and he would tell them so.

Absurdly, the police station felt like a place of refuge for Steve. He could sense the same ambiance as the first time they'd gone to report Jasmine's disappearance and when he'd visited subsequently. It wasn't a good atmosphere, it was stark, cold, uninviting even, but it was continual; the constancy of it somehow reassuring. The same poster was stuck on the wall, still up (but Steve pressed at its corners just in case) the same criss-cross iron grid over the frosted glass hatch. There were no spots for strange surprises to hide; everything was measured, even the tedious form filling, he decided, had been a comfort. He rang the bell and the endless rhythm, the daily beat of the station carried on as it always did. The duty receptionist slid open the hatch.

"Hello, I'm Steven Bartram," Steve began, "the husband of the missing woman," he continued as he didn't recognise the uniformed officer on the other side of the grid. The police officer checked the open page of the desk diary.

"Right, I see. Were we expecting you?" he replied quizzically but without altering his poker face.

"No, I have come because I wanted to know what the old man had to say."

The police officer's face had a brief look of surprise before returning to dead pan mode. "Please take a seat a moment," he instructed and slid the hatch shut leaving Steve wrapped back in the atmosphere of the place and considering what good it would achieve by being there.

The door to the street opened. Steve looked up automatically. It was Trevor of all people. "Hello there, I didn't expect to see you here. Any news?"

"No," replied Steve. "I'm trying to find out what the old man you saw last night had to say. Can't have been much maybe, otherwise they would have got in contact, wouldn't they?"

"I don't know mate, I don't know."

"What brings you here anyway?" asked Steve more cheerfully. It was good to see a friendly face; he'd felt the support Trevor had been giving him and he was glad of it.

"Oh, I'm just dropping off the list of names of the people who came to the party they asked for. Penny sorted it for me and typed it up last night. Thought I'd drop it off before I went to work." Trevor looked at his friend sitting alone in the soulless room and sat beside him. He really felt for him.

"You know," he continued, "everyone was really shocked when Penny and I rang them for their addresses, they couldn't believe it."

"I know," replied Steve, "I've had loads of text messages, I realised that the word was spreading. I couldn't be bothered to reply back; I couldn't face it you know?"

"I understand, and I'm sure they do too," replied Trevor with real compassion towards Steve. He didn't feel the need to say more, and they both sat down in a slump to wait. There was something about the moment that seemed to mean so much somehow. They were being sucked into a palpable vacuum of space. A void was silently wrapping its blanket of emptiness around them, insulating them from the rest of the world. Two good friends sharing something intangible, but nevertheless, real.

"I think there's someone following me," declared Steve and startling Trevor.

"Really, why would somebody be doing that?" He sat up straight to be more attentive.

"No idea, but I've felt it right from the start when I found Jas's mobile in the park."

"You sure?"

"Well, as sure as I can be. It's hard to explain, I just feel it, you know?"

Trevor looked at his good friend empathetically. "Do you think that it might be that you are a little bit stressed out at the moment, you know, with what has happened?" He really did wonder how Steve was coping so well, the strain had to come out somewhere.

Steve carried on as if he hadn't heard what Trevor had said. "It's happened a few times, usually as I'm walking through the park, but not always. And then when I was looking out of the window at home, when you came back from here after bringing them Jas's photos and stuff, I'm sure I saw something."

"Like what?"

"I don't know, a movement, a shadow or something."

"I remember you saying, but I had just walked down the street, I saw nothing in particular; a few people about, that's all."

"Okay, well maybe I'm paranoid or some such, but it keeps happening. Look, I'll take that list in, you'll be needing to get to work."

"Great, thanks. I do I suppose, see you later." Trevor got up just as the side door to the inner sanctum of the police station opened. Trevor raised his hand by way of saying goodbye and Steve turned to the opened door. DC Downey came through, nodded a 'good morning,' and ushered him in.

Although outwardly dismissive, Trevor had been rattled by what Steve had said about someone following him. It was exactly what he'd imagined about Jasmine when the police had asked for the list of names and addresses of the partygoers. Had someone been following her, and now they were after Steve? But why? It didn't make any sense at all. He decided that maybe he might try and keep an eye on Steve; follow him so to speak and see if he could see anyone suspicious. With a plan formulating in his mind, he fired up the Golf and headed for the surgery.

"Trevor the super sleuth," joked Penny when he spoke to her of his idea. She wasn't in school until Wednesday, when the new term started and so he'd returned home to spend his lunch break with her, for the simple reason he missed her. He didn't know why, he'd only seen her that morning, still luxuriating in bed after a brief but very gratifying embrace. He wanted to see her face as he had left it, after kissing her goodbye, with an expression of complete bliss. However, she'd been on another plane, studying her course notes and lesson plans in readiness for school spring term, and so he poured himself a glass of cold water instead.

"I'm not doing it for fun, and I've got to do something. I must help him if I can. Goodness knows what's going on inside his head. He was at the police station this morning when I dropped that list in, he looked a total wreck."

"The poor thing," agreed Penny. "Should we go round again do you think?"

"I'll call in on my way home from work and catch up."

"Okay, that's good. I don't suppose for one minute he's contacted the head about the new term, I'll do it for him. He won't be in any state to return, even if Jasmine is found tomorrow."

Penny's afternoon continued the same as her morning, deep in schoolwork, Trevor was deep in the mouths of his dental patients and back at Jasmine House, 'operation poster' was deeply under way. As far as the two sets of parents were concerned, Lucy had arrived with a whirlwind behind her. She'd barely taken off her coat before handing out instructions.

"Mum, Dad, can you find a street map, make a list of the areas and share them out into five please. Anne and Paul, where is Paul? Oh, never mind. Anne, will you help me with the poster design and printing? Where's their computer?"

Lucy, already knowing the password from using it on a previous occasion, commandeered Steve's computer and printer and began expertly planning out some A5 sized flyers with the heading, "HAVE YOU SEEN JASMINE?" She put a few details of last known whereabouts and the police phone number to ring with any information. Steve had looked out some photos of Jasmine earlier and left them on the dresser. Anne and Glenda leafed through them to sort out the ones that were most representative, the best likeness. Lucy chose two from their shortlist. One of her face, and the other of her in uniform. She thought it might help the public be more obliging with any information if they knew what her occupation was. NHS workers were always well-respected; it had to gain the sympathy vote.

Tony wondered if the idea of a poster campaign should only be sanctioned by the police. They were the experts after all and surely ought to have been consulted. What if it was the wrong course of action and frustrated the investigation massively? However, these thoughts he kept to himself; at least it gave them something to occupy themselves with and a feeling that they were doing all they could.

Steve arrived back, gave Lucy an enormous hug and apologised for ruining her holiday, to which she replied that it would have been so much worse not to have cut it short. She then asked inquisitively, what information the old man had about Jasmine. Only then did Steve tentatively let go of Lucy; he was so pleased to see her, and it felt so good to hold her close, he was missing Jasmine so much. Unfortunately, he didn't have much he could relate. Apparently, the police had been dismissive with whatever the old man had to say, claiming it was the rantings of someone who was either not in control of the better half of his faculties, or he was after some notoriety. They had taken down his statement but didn't think it was of any help to their enquiries.

"So, what did he say?" asked Paul. He had reappeared when Steve returned, hoping for news.

"Now he makes his entrance, we could have done with your help getting the printer to work, and Mum and Dad could have utilised your skills, I'm sure," said Lucy. She wasn't used to people not jumping to attention when she was coordinating proceedings.

"I deduced it was yet another case of 'too many cooks' as the saying goes, so I kept out of the way," he retorted. Lucy, he thought, even though she was semi-jesting, was too much like her mother, and perhaps more manageable in small doses.

Steve answered his father's query dismissively. "Oh, some story about thinking he may have known her long ago and perhaps killed her by giving her the flu."

"That doesn't even make sense," concluded Glenda.

"Exactly, that was what the police thought."

"Killed her with flu, what on earth is he talking about?" Glenda continued, unable to let it go.

"If the police aren't interested, then I don't think we need to be dear," interjected Tony. He knew where this was going, his wife would continue down a path of whys and wherefores and he wanted to nip it in the bud.

Like his father-in-law, Steve also had reservations about distributing leaflets without asking the police first. He rang the station and asked to speak to DI Manning; he would know if it was okay or not. The reply was that the Detective Inspector was in a meeting, but almost as soon as Steve put the phone down, it started ringing. He picked it up to hear DI Manning on the other end who, when Steve asked, replied that they were in the process of putting Jasmine's missing status on general release so he couldn't see a problem with it.

Relieved to hear this, Tony could now throw himself whole-heartedly into the project and steer his wife away from going down a rabbit hole. "Let's get on with finishing and sorting where we're going to distribute these things. The quicker we get them out there, the better it will be in finding our daughter, don't you think dear?" he declared.

Later, armed with a wad of leaflets each to hand out, or stick up wherever they could, the family spread across town covering as many areas as possible. Steve chose to stay local and walked around the park, asking everyone he came across if they had seen Jasmine, and giving out leaflets to anyone who would take one. He'd been out about forty-five minutes, when a feeling that was becoming a little too familiar came over him. He was being followed again, and it was giving him the creeps. This time, he was determined to find out. Carrying on with what he was doing, but remaining alert, he tried to pinpoint where the person or persons were, and how they were managing to stay undetected. So far so good, but he still couldn't be sure who it might be. Had that lady in the blue coat passed him before, and those youths that had been hanging round at the swings; were they watching him? He was sure a couple of them were now on his tail, but then why would a bunch of lads be interested in him? And he'd noticed someone earlier who was around fifty metres behind him and seemingly keeping the same pace, for he was still there when he glanced back for the third time. However, the task of discovering who it was, was proving to be tough. There were too many people and they were merging into a blur, Steve couldn't remember clearly who was where and if they were acting oddly. He needed a crafty plan of action. He thought that if he turned at the next corner away from the main path and pretend to go round the lake but instead hide in the bushes, he would catch them unawares. That way, whoever it was wouldn't know which direction to take and be forced to stop. It would then enable him to get a good look from his hiding place, who it might be.

Steve took the path leading to the lake and dived into the thicket of rhododendrons and into a little oasis of calm, nature's gift of presence. He could almost feel the life force in the branches as their leafy fingers reached out and brushed his cheeks. He recalled hearing the language of the winged insects as they buzzed about when he was last there in the summer with Jasmine. All was quiet now though, in the sleep of winter, only nature's spirit still lived. A robin looked inquisitively at him before it hopped off, and an earthworm wriggled through the undergrowth close to his feet - he'd probably just saved its life. But either the atmosphere was changing, or it was Steve himself, for it was like being amongst phantoms; a world without substance; a world that wasn't real to him anymore; lost among the shadows.

The waxy leaves of the rhododendrons obscured the rays of filtered light from the setting sun, projecting their form beyond themselves; their quivering dance creating an ethereal blanket covering all, including Steve. He waited there, panting slightly in anticipation. Of what he wasn't sure, but it was making his heart quicken, nevertheless.

Footsteps pounded down hard and hasty on the path and Steve's unworldly sojourn was broken. Someone was running very fast, their thudding feet getting nearer and louder... and then stop, leaving only silence behind. Sweat appeared on Steve's brow, he could barely breathe. They were very close, just where he'd come off the path to hide. Somebody, dark and inscrutable was but an arm's length away. He tried to keep as quiet as he could, but needed to move, ever so slightly, to get a better view through the bushes. Then it came, a sharp cracking noise, his foot had stepped on a twig. What a complete idiot! Next thing, the looming figure's head turned towards him and peered into the shrubbery, right where he was; too late to do anything; he was sunk.

"Steve, thank goodness, I thought they'd got you!"

"Trevor, what on earth are you doing?"

"Trying to see who might be following you. I thought the best way was to follow you myself and catch them at it. What are you doing in there?" Steve pulled himself free from his woody hideaway and brushed himself down. "When you suddenly disappeared like that, I thought they must be bloody good, I've never run so fast in my life trying to see where they were taking you."

"Who was taking me, did you see someone following me?"

"Actually no," replied Trevor sheepishly. "But that's why I thought they were clever." Steve gave him a sardonic smile.

"Well, if you didn't see anyone, seems as though the only person stalking me was you. If you've nothing better to do, you can help me dish out these leaflets."

"Sorry mate, just trying to help," said Trevor meekly, knowing he'd given Steve a shock.

"It's okay, I suppose I would have done the same thing myself."

"No worries," replied Trevor, relieved he'd been forgiven. "So, what were you doing in the bushes, call of nature was it?"

"Trying to find out who was following me, never thought it would turn out to be my best mate!"

"But as I said, it wasn't me! Well, it was this time, but not other times. Look, there's that old man walking his dog again, the one who went to the police." Trevor was glad he was able to steer the conversation onto something else.

"Looks pretty normal to me," replied Steve. "Hold on, I think he's coming this way. Good evening, Sir, could I give you this leaflet?" said Steve as the old man approached. "It's about my missing wife," he added after seeing the old man eyeing it with suspicion.

The old man paused, asked Bessie the dog to sit, and observed Steve with slow and careful deliberation as if he was under some sort of assessment and then came out with the remark "Ah yes, I can see it in the eyes," and took the leaflet Steve was proffering. He then began to scrutinise the photographs of Jasmine. "Lovely girl. You don't remember me, do you?"

"Er, no," mumbled Steve, "I don't think I do."

"Nor would I have expected you to, the encounter was very brief. You were coming to view your house; your wife was appearing very enthusiastic about it. She'd read the name on the gate and said it was the same as hers."

Steve thought back. "That's my name on the gate, 'Jasmine', it must be a sign for us to buy it," he recalled her say to a passer-by at the time who had struck up a conversation with them.

"That's right, I *do* remember! You explained how the house had been empty for some time and needed someone to love it."

"Ah, is that what I said? Anyway, pleased to meet you again. I'm very sorry about you know, the fact that she's missing. If I can be of any help, just let me know." He doffed his cap, pulled Bessie by her collar and walked on.

"He's definitely a bit weird," decided Steve.

"Definitely," agreed Trevor. "What was that about meeting him before?"

"Just as he said. Jas and I were viewing the house for the first time, and he happened to be walking past and a few words were exchanged, that's all."

Later, when he'd no leaflets left to give out, Steve was ruminating in attempt to get everything straight in his head. "Trev, how do you think he knows we actually bought the house?"

"I assume you are talking about the old bloke with the dog. Probably seen you going in and out of it; he's obviously local, and old folks like to nose a bit at who's doing what and where they're doing it. And he also knows the old lady, Rose, so you can take that into account too."

"I suppose you're right. Even so, there's something odd about him, seeing as he went to the police with that far out story of his."

"And the way he was looking at you, at your eyes, or whatever it was he said. Anyway, I'd best be getting home. See you later."

"Same here, I've been out long enough, 'bye for now."

Trevor decided to keep eyes on the old man; he knew something, he was sure of it. In the meantime, he carried on back to his flat and to Penny, whose image he had not quite been able to get out of his head since the morning.

Steve had not long been back home when the doorbell rang. Wearily, he went to see who was there and was surprised to see the old man with Jasmine's handbag! "Found it in the park a few days ago; been meaning to take it to a lost property somewhere, but then thought to check with you after, you know, to see if it's hers."

"Where did you find it?" asked Steve. He had a quick glance inside it to see if anything was missing. He couldn't tell. Purse and keys were there but he'd no idea about anything else Jasmine kept inside it.

"Oh, it was outside the park, by the gates up yonder. Shouldn't have sat on it for so long I suppose." He waited for a reply, but got nothing; Steve was lost for words and stared avidly at Jasmine's bag. It was like a bit of her coming home, and maybe the rest of her was close behind. "Well, is it hers then?"

"Yes, yes, it is," replied Steve clutching hold of it when the old man had proffered it. "Thanks for finding it, I'll have to take it to the police probably. Oh, and they'll most likely want to ask you exactly where you found it. I'd better have your name and address so I can give it to them. Please come in while I get a pen and some paper."

The old man took off his cap and stepped into the hall. He looked upwards and around, taking in his surroundings, his eyes coming to rest on the Christmas tree, while Steve went to find some paper from the kitchen drawer. "Nice tree," he remarked when Steve returned armed with a pen and a writing pad.

"Thank you," replied Steve appreciatively. The adorned and fragrant boughs were indeed lovely, though lately had lost their charm upon him. Even so, he was still reluctant to take it down. He looked at the old man expectantly, his pen at the ready.

"Arthur Pickford, 24, Regent's Grove, but they have it already I believe. Also, my phone number is 427035."

"Steve Bartram," replied Steve, offering his hand, which Arthur took and shook gently. "That's just a couple of streets away from here, isn't it?"

"Yes, that's about right," the old man replied. Steve then thought to find out more about him, not wanting to miss an opportunity, and anyway, he knew instinctively that this man knew more than he was letting on.

"Did you know the old, erm, the lady that used to live here before us?"

"Yes, and I still do. Known her a long time I have, since she was quite young."

"You must have grown up together," said Steve, wondering how some people remained relatively young and sprightly for their age, and others became frail and infirm.

"Well, not exactly," replied Arthur.

"But you are of a similar age, or are you younger?"

Arthur was thoughtful. "Hmm yes, I suppose we are of an age. But then looking one's age is a funny thing don't you think? I always looked old when I was a younger man, and then never really aged after that. That's what Rose said anyway."

Steve changed the subject; the man was talking in riddles, and he needed an answer to the question burning on his lips. "I was curious why you went to the police yesterday and said you had something to do with my wife's disappearance."

"Oh, you heard about that. I'm sorry, it wasn't what it seemed, it was a mistake, I should never have gone."

"But you *do* know something?" Steve wasn't going to let him get away with any excuses. He was unconvinced and the old man knew it, and he was becoming more forceful by the minute. "Anyway, how have you come into possession of Jasmine's handbag?"

"I told you, I found it," he said defensively. "Look, I don't think I can tell you anything that will help you, and I think we should leave it at that." He turned to go, then paused, looking as though he was remembering something. "On a different subject," he began hesitantly, "when I saw Rose last, she was wondering what you had done with the letters. Not that I would know, and I told her so but, seeing as I'm here, I'm telling you what she said."

Steve was becoming more and more agitated. "Rose? Letters? What *is* all this, and what has it got to do with my missing wife?" He paced about the harsh unforgiving floor, the sound of his frustration coming through his feet and echoing around them both. "And" he continued, "why in heaven's name would she get you, a complete stranger, to come and ask me about something that neither of us know what she's talking about? It's completely irrelevant to anything that's happening right now. Does she know my wife is missing?"

The older man could see the younger man's frustration, and he really felt for him, but there was nothing he could do. "Sorry son, I'm just the messenger. Maybe it was the wrong time for me to bring it up."

Steve softened; there was no way this old man could have abducted Jas, she had twice his strength, easily, and the old woman in the care home wouldn't have a clue about the present situation likely as not. "Look, thanks for bringing me the bag, I'll take it to the police station in the morning, they can contact you for the details." With that, the old man, satisfied he'd done his duty and keen to get away, moved towards the front door, popped his cap back on his head and bid goodbye, leaving Steve to himself.

The others arrived back soon afterwards and when they had all gathered, Steve told them about Arthur Pickford turning up with Jasmine's handbag. They were all keen to look at it, but Steve said the fewer fingerprints on it, the better. "So they can pick out the monster who snatched it from her," declared Glenda.

"Yes, exactly," replied Steve, but not really agreeing with his mother-in-law; he'd rather not think of any monster attacking Jasmine.

"Is everything still in it?" Glenda asked. She was moving back and forth, sitting down, standing up, stepping to and fro.

"I don't know, but it's not empty," replied Steve.

"Sit down dear, you're on edge; calm down," Tony entreated.

"Don't tell me what to do when my daughter is missing."

"Our daughter," Tony interjected. But it got lost in the diatribe that followed.

"How could you not have walked her home, Stephen. I can't think why you wouldn't do such a thing. Jasmine's your wife, my daughter, and you let her walk home on her own. What were you thinking? Don't you have any sense of responsibility?"

"And you think I haven't wished the same? I can't stop thinking 'if only this, if only that.' I'm tied up in knots," replied Steve, trying his best not to show more annoyance towards his mother-in-law. But Glenda hadn't finished.

"Of course, you never think things through do you, like the time when you bought this house. Just look at all the hours of work Jasmine has had to do to make it habitable, and she's always so busy at the hospital. You should have stayed renting so it would be easier to move back home like Jasmine wanted."

"What on earth are you talking about? Jasmine loved this house as much as I did, and she has never shown any inclination to move back to where we grew up, never." Steve's tolerance of Glenda was solely because she was Jasmine's mother, but it was wearing thin. Tony, the eternal peacekeeper, intercepted before things got out of hand.

"I think we are straying off the point a little. We would surely all have twenty-twenty vision with hindsight, but sadly not one of us possesses that quality until it is too late. No one is to blame here; the situation is what it is and we should all support each other. Glenda, Steve has got enough on his plate without you haranguing him, and Steve, please realise your mother-in-law is overwrought, let's give each other some slack here."

"The thing is," said Lucy, who was just as distraught, but trying to keep it together, "we need to focus on how best to find her. For a start, this chap Arthur Pickford has already gone to the police, and they dismissed him. Are they going to be quite so quick now that he's produced Jasmine's bag? There must be a link."

"Maybe, maybe not," said Paul. "We'll have to see what the police say. Perhaps we should take the bag now rather than wait till morning. Would you like me to take it in Steve?"

Steve declined his father's offer, deciding to do it himself.

Chapter Seven

Tuesday, January 4th, am

There were no seats left in the incident room. DI Manning had called an urgent meeting to keep everyone in the picture, a regimen he observed when deeming it useful. There had been a significant development in the misper case they were handling. He stirred two heaped teaspoons of sugar into his mug of coffee and sipped at it. It was still hot, and everyone was still milling around, so he thought to enjoy his little moment of coffee bliss.

Eventually, he pointed at the new photo on the evidence board when everyone had quietened down after the usual banter and crack. "A handbag, believed to belong to the missing woman, has been recovered," he began. "More than that, it appears that Mr Pickford, the old man, who only two days ago came forward saying he was responsible for her disappearance, has had it in his possession all this time. It's gone straight to forensics. I'll keep you all updated if they find anything on it. So, from becoming someone who we were perhaps a little too keen to dismiss as an eccentric, Arthur Pickford Esquire, has just been promoted to a person of supreme interest and is currently here after being invited to come in for questioning. He clearly knows something. I'll tell you what that something is after I've spoken to him."

"What made him come forward with it, Sir?"

"He didn't, exactly. He took the handbag round to the missing woman's husband claiming he happened to find it and wondered if it was hers. The husband handed it in last night, telling us how he'd acquired it."

"Is the husband telling the truth, Guv?"

"It seems so; the old man has corroborated this. Says he picked it up while out walking and intended to hand it in at some point, but when learning of the woman's disappearance, thought he should take it to her husband to see if he recognised it."

"How did he know where he lived?"

"Wouldn't be too difficult to find out, and he may have known them already - he lives fairly close by. He could have picked up one of those leaflets the family has been distributing around the town. But we'll find all this out when we have questioned him in more detail. Meanwhile, how far are we getting with private security cameras picking anything up?"

"On with it, Guv."

"Good, I want to see all significant footage by this afternoon. I can also tell you a press release has been approved. Anyone else got anything to offer?"

DI Manning intimated that the briefing was over when no one spoke up, took a mouthful of coffee before it got too cold to be worth the caffeine injection, then called after DC Downey to come with him to converse with their improbable, but so far, only suspect.

Alas for any further progression in the case, Arthur Pickford was seemingly able to convince the two police officers that he was telling the truth about finding the handbag lying on the ground. However, when the interview was about to be terminated, he appeared to want to say more. The officers didn't stop him. He looked from one cop to the other almost furtively, as if he were giving away something hush-hush. Clearing his throat, he blurted out, "It's those stones - that's why she's gone. They can do that you know."

The two officers shared an almost imperceptible glance at one another. "The stones?" replied the Inspector.

"Aye, the stone circles in the park there. First saw it happen when I was a lad. A baby it was, disappeared into thin air."

"You mean abducted?"

"Well, that's what everybody thought, but I knew different. Took me years to find out where she ended up."

"And where was that?" asked Jim Manning, letting the old man have some space, at the same time trying to work out what he was talking about. He knew that when people talked, through all the rubbish, little bits of information appeared that may seem irrelevant at first but might turn out to be a useful piece of intelligence.

"Like I said, from a doorstep opposite those stones. Right where she was in the first place. She hadn't moved anywhere at all. It got me thinking, that did."

Jim Manning, sitting forward on his seat now, quizzed him further. "You mean there was a baby who had gone missing but was then returned?"

"Yes, but not till a long time after."

"Did you know the baby?" asked the Inspector.

"No, not then, anyway."

"Then how did you know it was a 'she'?"

"Well first off, the newspapers said so, but I met her when she was grown."

"Right then, we'll leave it there for now, shall we? Thank you for helping us, but we may want to speak to you again."

DI Manning got up from his chair and moved towards the door saying to Mr Pickford that the detective constable would show him out. Tom Downey threw a quick glance of raised eyebrows at his superior and left with his charge. When the door had closed behind them, Jim Manning sat back and brooded for a while on the jigsaw puzzle ramblings of the old man. He pulled open his desk draw and rooted around for an old notebook from years ago, there was a coroner's case he'd been involved in. For some indefinable reason, the old man's revelations of doorsteps and missing babies had reminded him of it.

He needed to speak with Tom Downey and found him in the corridor. "Tom, I want you to look into historic reports of babies going missing in this area. Go back as far as the records take you, or as far as what records we have."

"How far do our records go back Guv?"

"I've no idea. If you don't get anywhere, then look at old newspapers. Let me know if you find anything."

"Yes, Guv, I will."

"Oh, and just one thing."

"Yes, Guv?"

"Keep this between ourselves, won't you?"

"Yes Guv, understood."

Tom Downey went on his way unperturbed at what his senior had instructed him to do. He always did as he was told, and sometimes he was told to do the strangest of things. Even if he thought the things he had to do were silly, ridiculous, a waste of time, he did them anyway and to the best of his abilities. It kept him busy and the day turning. One day, he hoped, things would be different - more exciting perhaps than searching the archives for details of an alleged missing baby. His low spirits weren't because he didn't enjoy police work because he did. It was more that he'd lost something very precious, and now everything else palled into insignificance. If only he hadn't been so stupid way back when - but then he'd been so very young and not thought about any consequences. His boss, meanwhile, enroute to a meeting about police recruitment, took time to visit the ambulance station in search of an ambulance crew that, around thirty years ago, was involved in a case of his. He was hopeful they were still on the job. He still was, after all.

He found a lad peering under an ambulance's bonnet and started there. 'How long had he worked there, had he come across crews who'd been there back in the seventies, did he know anyone who did?' Jim Manning was in luck and was given the name of someone who the lad thought had been working there forever but hadn't seen him around lately. Jim Manning thanked him and was looking round for someone else to ask, when an ambulance pulled in. He hung around till it was parked and the crew had jumped out, and then made his approach. 'Did they know when Tim Reynolds would be back on shift?'

"Too late mate," said the well-built one who Jim Manning concluded was too cocky by half.

"He's retired and gone to live the high life in Spain," added his partner, the smaller of the two who seemed more amenable. "Is there some trouble?" the second one inquired.

Jim Manning assured him not. "No, just looking into an old case of mine and wanting to ask if he could recollect anything."

"Then hold on a minute and I'll get you his email address," said the second ambulance man.

It was getting on for four o'clock by the time Jim Manning got back to the police station. He'd procured Tim Reynold's email address but hadn't had any time to follow it up. What turned out to be a very arduous meeting about cutting costs rather than recruiting more bobbies, had drained him completely. He needed coffee, but DC Downey was coming in at the same time and he put his desire for caffeine aside. "Ah, Tom. Did you get anywhere with the task I set you?"

"Yes, I did, but it was way back in eighteen seventy-eight. The old man's old, but not that old, he couldn't possibly have been there." They moved back outside so they couldn't be overheard, and Jim Manning encouraged Tom Downey to continue. "I looked at reports of missing kids and kidnappings, and believe it or not, it was still on file, but reported as a kidnapping. It was a baby, less than a day old, and had been taken from a doorstep."

Jim Manning took in a sharp intake of breath. "You sure it was a doorstep?"

"Yes, it's quite clear, the address as well."

"Which is?" hissed the Inspector in anticipation; he wasn't sure whether he wanted to hear the answer or not. If it was the address he thought it was going to be, then the tenuous link he'd begun to make with the past case of his, was about to become stronger... and decidedly weirder.

"Flat one, number twenty-three, Meadowsring Road. Well, that's what it is today, back then it had no number, and hadn't been divided into flats. It was called Bolton House. I've just got back from taking a look. It's just over the road from the park, by the gate where the standing stones are and where we've been investigating for anything on the misper."

"The east gate; I see." Jim Manning recovered quickly and swallowed hard. Just because he was concluding that he'd a lot more to fathom about the world's inconsistencies, didn't mean he was going mad. There had to be a logical explanation, he just didn't know yet what it was. All he could do was what he always did, police work, joining the dots and putting it all together. "Did I hear correctly that the missing girl's father-in-law had some sort of altercation there the other morning with the house owner?"

"I believe so. I think he'd been trying to find some answers for himself and wandered too closely to her doorstep. Taking some measurements from it as I understand, and the house owner took offence."

"Hmm, you see, it's that doorstep, there it is again. I've come across it before in a coroner's case I was involved in many years ago. There's a link somewhere, I can feel it, but I've no idea what."

"Doorstep, Guv?"

Inspector Manning took the DC's reply as a cue that he ought to elaborate. "A woman had given birth at home on her own to twins after some sort of haemorrhage which caused her to lose consciousness. When she came round, she discovered one twin to be dead and behind the stairs, and the other, according to the notes I took at the time, was to be found by the front door, alive and well."

"On the doorstep?"

"Yes, precisely. More than that, the lady's name was Glenda Simmons, our misper's mother."

"Simmons?" replied Tom Downey. "That's the missing girl's mother?"

"Yes, keep up lad. I thought she looked familiar when I saw her the other day. Now then, there's more. That baby found alive and on the doorstep, grew up to become our misper. And then the old man is saying he saw a baby disappear and turn up in the same place years later? But the baby he's talking about went missing in eighteen seventy-eight!" Jim Manning looked Tom Downey in the eye and then down on the ground shaking his head. He breathed in deeply and let it go with a long sigh. "I don't know, I really don't know where we're going with this, but we've got a lot to think about here. This case is becoming a little complicated in more ways than one." He looked back at Tom Downey. "I think it best for the both of us to keep this new information to ourselves, at least for the moment, don't you think?"

"Yes, of course, Guv. I understand." DC Downey was a straightforward type of a guy, and this case was moving into uncharted territories as far as he was concerned. He understood the need for discretion; things didn't fit, and yet they did, but not in any logical way, which meant he was quite happy to keep quiet. Being a laughingstock was not part of his plans.

Keeping this part of the investigation separate from the main one, which was finding the missing woman, was fine by him. Anyway, he'd got plenty of his own stuff to think about, especially now after what the guvnor just said. "There's one more thing, Guv. It was reported that the missing baby had a distinguishing feature. It was a birthmark, in the shape of a star, on her buttock."

The two men looked at each other. Both knew they were getting into something that neither of them comprehended, but which was too curious to ignore. "There's an answer to everything, and the answer to this is out there somewhere. Police work, we'll keep plodding on until we find it," stated the Inspector.

Hot coffee was on Jim Manning's desk, but the information spilling from his computer was of far more interest. He'd emailed Tim Reynolds, the old ambulance worker, and got a reply almost immediately. Retirement in Spain can't be much different to being in the office if one was sitting in front of one's computer all day, he mused.

"Greetings from sunny Spain" the email began. *"Curious regarding your email. Funnily enough I remember you from the coroner's inquest as the investigating officer. It's such a shame in these cases that the police must be dragged in, as if the parents aren't suffering enough, but that's for another discussion. So yes, I remember the case. Quite well in fact, as I was one of those at the scene. Bill Crowley was the other; dead now, poor blighter. It was one of those instances that you never quite forget; poignant if you like. But I don't know if I can help you with anything, other than she'd had a BBA (born before arrival to a medical facility if you aren't familiar with the term). Unusually, she'd tied off the cords to both twins. She said at the time she could barely remember but had a vague image of her sewing box and holding scissors and a length of twine. As you will recall, and why you were involved, the boy infant was showing no signs of life, the post-mortem later concurring that he was stillborn. Such a tragedy."*

Jim finished reading still baffled, nothing stood out. There must be something somewhere that no one had thought about. He looked around for inspiration and spied his yet untouched cup of coffee. He picked it up and took a sip, and then another, and another, then put it back down abruptly, for he had it!

"Did you collect the afterbirth? Were there two afterbirths?" he wrote.

He didn't know much about these matters but understood enough to realise each baby would need a placenta of its own. He'd watched kittens being born way back; he must have been around nine or ten at the time. The family cat, Pepper, had produced a litter of four; Eeny, Meeny, Miny and Mo, and they all had their own and individual afterbirth, eaten so ravenously by the new mother, that Jim thought she was going to eat the kittens as well. Fortunately, she'd stopped after devouring the umbilical cord, millimetres short of their belly buttons.

"That's a story in itself," came the reply quickly.

He really didn't have much to do in Spain, concluded Jim.

"There was a pet dog; massive thing it was too! While we were seeing to the woman and babies, it had sniffed the placentas out and seen its way through much of them before we'd noticed. We bagged up what was left and took it with us to the hospital."

Jim Manning wrote back a reply of thanks, knowing his next task was to contact the maternity department of the hospital, but even he knew it was a long shot. Records of thirty years ago would most certainly have been destroyed by now, and anyway, he wouldn't be allowed to gain access to them. But there might be a midwife still there, and the missing woman was a midwife, she may have known who amongst her colleagues had worked there back in the seventies. Time to talk to the husband again, he surmised. He surely would be able to find through her colleagues somebody who was working back then and maybe they might remember something. But he then immediately rejected the idea. To involve the husband of a missing person whose whereabouts he was in the middle of investigating was not correct procedure. He lifted his coffee cup to his lips and drank from it, but quickly put it back down. It had gone cold. He hated cold coffee. He considered refreshing it, but then thought better of it. He checked the phone book and dialled a number. "Maternity please," he answered when the operator asked him which department he required. "No, hold on, have you the number for the maternity manager?"

"I can put you through to their secretary."

"Yes, that will do thank you." He waited while music played, quickly being interrupted by a ringing tone.

"Hello, Patricia Roberts' secretary speaking."

"Good afternoon, my name is Jim Manning. I am a Detective Inspector from the local police department and I'm hoping you will be able to help me with one of our investigations."

"Oh, you mean about Jasmine Bartram?" replied the secretary.

"Er no, not exactly. It's concerning an incident that happened many years ago that I've been looking into. The thing is, I'm looking for midwives who worked at the old maternity hospital in the early seventies, around thirty years ago. Do you have any midwives who were working there at that time who still work now?"

"Just a minute," said Patricia Robert's secretary, and put him on hold. Jim listened to more music that was supposed to be calming. 'What if you didn't like what was playing?' he thought. It would make jangled nerves even more so, or it might instil a false sense of security, or send you to sleep... The phone clicked. Jim jumped.

"Hello, Patricia Roberts, matron speaking. I understand you would like to speak to a midwife of a certain age; I'm intrigued. I have been here since nineteen sixty-nine, will I do?"

DI Manning arranged to see Patricia Roberts straight away. "As long as it won't take too long, I'm winding up for the day, you're lucky to have caught me at a lull," she told him firmly.

Within twenty minutes he was knocking on her door at the hospital and introducing himself. Patricia Roberts, matron, was in a formidable navy-blue uniform, with maroon epaulettes on the shoulders, denoting her status. However, she didn't match the uniform, coming across as warm and generous, inviting him to take the seat across from her desk and offered him a chocolate from an open box of Thornton's Continental. Jim Manning declined, he didn't want to be hampered by gooey caramel sticking to his teeth, not at this juncture anyway.

"It's about an old case I worked on where a dog chewed on the placenta. It was a B.B.A.," Jim Manning began, using the medical terminology. "Boy and girl twins had been born at home, the boy unfortunately, stillborn. Nineteen-seventy, it was."

Patricia Roberts sighed before replying. "Goodness me, that was a long, long time ago. I remember it well. I was the midwife who received her. It was so sad, that little lifeless soul, my first one, you never forget. The poor mother, her sorrow was everywhere, we all felt it. Back then, women were discouraged from holding or even seeing their little departed ones. It was all wrong, but being a very junior midwife, I had no say in the matter. That's what it was like then though; so cruel." She then hesitated, realising she had said too much. "Forgive me, the recollection is bringing all the emotion I felt at the time."

"No problem, I know how you feel. We have to stomach things we don't want to in our job too, it's not straightforward dealing with the general public sometimes. I had no wish to upset you, I came looking for someone who was involved and I found you. Can you remember anything else?"

Patricia Roberts thought for a minute. "She was very apprehensive in handling the surviving twin and she needed lots of support, but that can be completely normal with any new mother. However, I won't be able to give you any specific information."

"I understand. It's the afterbirths I'm interested in. I believe the pet dog had tried to eat them. Was it still possible to see if there were two, one for each child?"

"Oh, now you're asking something, let me think a minute." She pondered for a moment. "Do you know, I can't remember the placentas. I wonder if one of my colleagues looked at them for me while I was busy with the woman. They will have been looked at, and the findings recorded, it's part of what we do. We check that the placenta is complete and what condition it's in - if it is healthy or not, amongst other things. Sometimes with twin deliveries, especially with some types of twins, the two placentas can be very much fused together. Without further analysis by the laboratory, it can be difficult to know if the twins are identical. However, a boy and a girl twin would have had separate placentas." She paused again, this time for just a few seconds. "Something is ringing a bell; I'm pretty sure it wasn't me who looked at them. Look, can I get back to you? I would like to ask one of my colleagues if they remember anything. May I ask why you are wanting to know?"

DI Manning replied with his usual response in such circumstances, which seemed to fit the occasion. "Just pursuing lines of enquiries about an old case of mine that I had a particular interest in. Dotting the I's and crossing the T's so to speak." He then added, "Like you, it got to me." He got up to leave but not before thanking Patricia Roberts for her time and making sure she had his mobile number; he didn't want any messages left back at the nick which he might have to explain.

Chapter Eight

Wednesday, January 5th, am

The following morning Patricia Roberts was as good as her word. She called Jim Manning just as he was levering himself out of his car. It was a tight fit in the police station's car park, the only space left. Seemingly everyone had been called in this morning. More meetings, he supposed. His mobile always rang at inconvenient moments, like when poised to do something radical with a pile of disorderly paperwork and having to answer it instead, only to let the papers fall all over the desk. Or in the toilet when both hands were required, or getting out of the car as he was doing today. Nevertheless, he liked to answer it if he could as the caller might have something crucial to say and the sooner he knew it the better. He prised it from his pocket squeezing himself between his four-year-old Volvo S90, and some swanky BMW that he hadn't noted before.

"DI Manning here," he bellowed, seeing as he was outside. Patricia Roberts had an answer for him. Her colleague, after a prompt, had also remembered the case and had taken charge of the afterbirths. Memorable because they had been half-eaten by a dog, and she could only be sure of one placenta being there that was not quite complete, due to the dog having helped himself. She'd always presumed, as did her colleagues, for she had them check too, that the dog had eaten the other one in its entirety. She also said, although she couldn't remember actually doing so, that it would have been sent for reporting to the histology department, so they would have tested for any signs of the second placenta.

Jim Manning thanked Patricia Roberts very much for her information, put the phone back in his pocket and walked inside his workplace to begin his day. No doubt the histology department's findings would be in the coroner's report, but he already suspected what it would say. Like the midwife said, there were no signs of a second placenta. So maybe there had never been one, which was what Jim had begun to wonder the day before. And so maybe, the baby on the doorstep wasn't Glenda Simmons' baby at all and that she never had twins. She had given birth to just one baby, a stillborn boy.

Interestingly, he'd written in his notes at the time, that the doctor who had attended her antenatally hadn't suspected twins. Scans weren't performed as routinely back then as they are now, so it could never be proven that she was carrying twins, which made the old man's story of a baby disappearing and then reappearing later, years and years later apparently, seem rational in an odd sort of way. That is, if the girl baby on Glenda Simmons' doorstep really wasn't hers but rather the baby that Arthur Pickford was talking about. Also, that would make Arthur Pickford well over a hundred years old and that had to be an impossible fact. 'No no no Jimbo,' he chastised in his head, 'that can't be right, definitely not. Where do you think you are going with this? Stop it right now!' But he couldn't and he headed towards the incident room with thoughts that would not go away.

There were seemingly unexplainable and muddling phenomena that went beyond the bounds of standard police detection and procedure. Indeed, his fellow colleagues had resorted to calling in mediums to help solve cases before now while he'd always preferred to keep both of his feet firmly on the ground. There had to be a rational explanation to all this he argued with himself and being both a determined man and a conscientious police officer he would continue to sniff about until he found it. Meanwhile, he had to get all this weird stuff straightened out. The link to all of it was that doorstep; he needed to go and have a look for himself.

Meanwhile something else had come up. There was some footage on an infra-red security camera that was fairly close to the east gate of the park, where the phone and handbag had been recovered. The owner had thought to take a look at the recordings after noting the police activity and being handed one of the leaflets Jasmine's family had been giving out. His camera had been directed to view the front gates to his property which included a view across the road and onwards to the park. Around one-twenty am, according to the clock on the footage, a female figure was to be seen walking on the pavement along the park's boundary. There was an interval of time between every frame, so the film didn't flow in real time, but nonetheless, her progress appeared to be staggered, and at one point she could be seen holding onto her head as if in pain. The footage then blanked out for a few moments, and when it returned there was no girl on camera.

"What's wrong with her?" asked Tom Downey. "She looks as though she can't see where she's going, and what's the matter with her head?"

"That's what we need to find out," replied Jim Manning. "We can see she still has her handbag at this point, and this is very near to where it was found, and she's holding something in her hand, her mobile phone perhaps? So, the question is, has an attack on her already happened, and has she managed to escape thus far, only to be apprehended a few moments later? Is she attempting to phone for help? We've nothing on record apart from a call which we have since discovered was to her mother, which was recorded at one-fifteen, a few minutes prior to this recording. Pity it fogged up just when we needed to see her next step. Can we look at either side of this to see who else was about?"

"Will do, Sir."

"Anyone else with a camera in the vicinity?"

"Yes, Guv, there's one just around the corner on Heaton Road, the route she would have taken to get home. However, she doesn't appear to be on it."

"Nothing at all?"

"No, Guv, nothing apart from a lone figure walking away from the park area, timed at a quarter to two. Definitely not her though."

"So, it's looking like she's been taken just after the last sighting on the camera from number nineteen, Meadowsring Road, the one we've just viewed. Can we identify the person on this other footage?"

"Can only see the back of them unfortunately, and the footage isn't that clear."

"Okay, thanks. Has the house to house been completed?"

"More or less, Sir, no one saw or heard a thing."

"I'm going to have another word with the husband, but can we scour the neighbourhood for any more hidden cameras, especially by the park gates?"

"On it, Guv."

"Okay, get to it, time is becoming less and less on our side."

He didn't know what had moved him to observe the footage from the camera on Heaton Road, but Jim Manning was glad he had. One might not have a clear view of the face of the person on the film, but the way the figure walked gave it away. That gait was unmistakable; the slightly bowed legs; a lean to the left; the bearing. "And there you are. Bingo!" Jim Manning declared aloud and wondered how much involvement that innocuous old gentleman actually had in all this. It would certainly deserve more investigation. Carefully though, and by Jimbo himself - it was too delicate a situation for dragging in any other well-meaning copper for questioning. DC Downey, the only person who knew what was on his mind, was too junior, and it wouldn't be fair to make him party to not declare that he knew who it was. He thought for the moment, it would be better all-round not to let on that he'd identified who was in shot.

On his way to visit Steve Bartram, Jim Manning parked up outside the east gate of the park, near where the film footage of the missing woman clutching her head was recorded. He wanted to get a feel of the place for himself now he had more information on the case, and while he was on his own.

Just as well, he hadn't realised just how close the two points were to each other. Number nineteen was literally only a few metres away from the park entrance. Frustratingly though, the entrance was just out of view of the security camera. Jim Manning looked into the park towards the standing stones, which weren't far from the perimeter across the grass, but were further along if one followed the formal pathway from the entrance. He thought about what Arthur Pickford had said about them and their so-called power. Initially he'd all but dismissed it as the ramblings of an old man; Jim Manning had never really bothered about the mysteries of the two stone rings, or even their history. If he'd ever taken a walk in the park, something he may have done to entertain the myriad members of his wife's family on their dutiful visits; the circles had just been part of the scenery; he didn't necessarily take much notice of that either.

But Arthur Pickford had, and so had Mr Bartram senior. There must be some reason for their existence. He regarded them now, a few innocuous slabs of granite. He supposed they formed some sort of ancient calendar that marked the position of the sun as it rose and set; 'pretty clever for a caveman,' he admitted to himself, and perhaps not that much different to today. How would we function without knowing whether it was a Friday or a Monday? He sighed, blowing away his thoughts on the inconsequential. He heaved himself out of the Volvo and lumbered across the road towards the house with the doorstep he was interested in. Incredibly, it was next-door-but-one to the house with the camera; the house numbers were not sequential.

Memories of the interview with the parents of the deceased baby all those years ago crept into Jim Manning's mind. A task which every officer hated but had to implement. It was part of procedure as foul play was always a possibility. It hadn't been easy, he knew the mother thought that they were accusing her, the last thing she needed. Her despair had been palpable.

Jim Manning arrived at the door of number twenty-three and looked down at the doorstep. It was a little uneven, thicker at one end and, as he remembered, the door was positioned over the middle of it, so one half was on the outside, the other half on the interior. He looked at it intently and, when the door opened, he saw it in its entirety.

"Don't tell me you're from the council about the streetlights, because I won't buy it."

Jim Manning looked up to see a stony-faced woman eyeballing him so mercilessly that even he was slightly taken aback. "Good morning, Madam; police. DI Manning, carrying out investigations." He flashed his warrant card while she looked down at the doorstep, and then, very slowly, looked back up at him, not at all impressed by the policeman, or his rank.

"Then it can only be about my doorstep," she snarled back. "You were looking at it weren't you, just like the others. What in heaven's name does everyone want to look at my doorstep for? So what if it is one of those standing stones, it wasn't me who nicked it, you're wasting your time and mine. Goodbye." She shut the door, and left Jim Manning staring at the rather nice brass letterbox positioned halfway up it. He stood for some time.

Something had happened that he couldn't define, and he needed to stay still and take it in. It was when the woman had said the doorstep was a standing stone. He felt this was a really crucial bit of information but had no idea why. Paul Bartram had been seen looking at it, so he must think it of importance too. Why it seemed so critical, Jim Manning had no idea, but he was surely going to find out. Somehow a baby from eighteen seventy-eight was bearing remarkable similarities to the one from nineteen seventy, which just so happened to be their misper. "Come on Jimbo," he urged himself, "piece it all together." It was an itch, and he was desperate to scratch at it, but he just couldn't quite reach it; unless... but that's not possible, it could never happen. Or could it? He shook his head in disbelief, but at the same time something changed within him. Maybe, just maybe, there was more to this world than meets the eye, and perhaps Jim Manning the unshakable, was ready to concede that there were some things in life that couldn't be explained within normal parameters.

"It's the police at the door again," remarked Tony. Staring out of the kitchen window, he'd seen a car pull up and recognised the man who got out as the Inspector who'd called the other day.

"DI Manning, police. I would like to speak to the two Mr Bartrams please. Are they in?"

"Yes, I remember you, please come in. Have you got some news?" asked Anne who had opened the door to him. She showed the Inspector into the sitting room.

"Just continuing with the investigation, er Mrs?"

"Bartram, I'm Paul's wife, Stephen's mother. Please take a seat."

"Thank you. I would like to speak to Stephen first please." Anne went to fetch him, and Jim Manning made himself comfortable in an armchair. Steve entered presently and sat opposite, the detective subtly altering his position to vertical as he did so and cleared his throat. "Good morning. I'm here because we have received some footage of Jasmine on CCTV which was taken near the east entrance to the park."

"Oh," said Steve in answer. He had run out of words to say and had no energy to think of any.

The Inspector continued. "It shows her holding her head. What I would like to establish is whether it is an injury, or does she suffer from severe headaches that would make her clutch at her head?"

"Oh my God," replied Steve. His hand went to his mouth and his eyes were wide. "No, she doesn't get headaches, but..." he tailed off, he was thinking hard.

"But?" said Jim Manning expectantly.

"Oh, this is going to be embarrassing," said Steve.

"Go on," encouraged Jim Manning. "Every little detail is important."

"Well, I can't think how it can help, but, at the party…"

"Yes?"

"Well, we, we were in a cupboard, the er, broom cupboard, for, you know, a bit of privacy, and there wasn't much room, and then a ladder came off the wall and fell onto her head. But she seemed okay after."

"So, let me get this clear, she sustained an injury to the head from a ladder that fell off the wall while you were both in a cupboard at the party?"

"Yes, that about sums it up."

"And whatever you were doing in the cupboard is the embarrassing bit?"

"Yeah, you've got it," replied Steve sheepishly.

"Thank you, I believe I get the picture. I have the information I need. May I speak to your father now?" Jim Manning got up knowing where Mr Bartram senior would be found and deciding he may as well talk to him there.

"Is that it?" asked Steve, surprised at the swift conclusion of the interview.

"Yes, you have been very helpful, thank you." Steve stood up as well, glad the Inspector hadn't made him say outright what he and Jasmine had been up to in the cupboard but appalled with himself that he hadn't even thought about her having a head injury, and that it could easily have led to swelling and pressure on the brain causing headaches, concussion, or even haemorrhage. He'd not been married to someone who worked in the NHS and not learnt anything. A bleed on the brain and he'd sent her out into the night on her own. He was a monster, there was no other word. But then that wouldn't have made her disappear he argued with himself, she couldn't have been that bad, she'd have realised if she was, and got help. No, it wasn't that; something else had happened and now; nothing, zilch, nada. There was no trace of anything. He followed the Inspector out into the hall where the others seemed to have gathered expectantly, including Paul. Jim Manning looked towards him.

"Mr Bartram, may I have a word?"

"What about?" asked Paul curtly. "I've already been interviewed by your colleagues."

"Yes, you have, but this is about another matter. I understand you are a mathematician and have been taking some measurements at the stone circle in the park and its position relative to a doorstep. I would like to ask you a few things about certain theories you have been looking at."

Paul looked at the Detective Inspector dubiously. Did he have any idea of what he'd been sounding out? He doubted it, not a down to earth plodding policeman. But then he thought that's precisely what he did himself, gather information, make measurements, do all the donkey work. He would never further his scientific knowledge if he didn't. Perhaps they weren't that different.

"Paul, there's something you've been keeping to yourself isn't there?" Anne was annoyed, she knew he wasn't letting on about something. "Just what were you doing the other morning? You're doing more than just having a passive interest in that stone circle, you've been investigating something, I just know it. Come on, admit it, even the police are on to you."

Paul looked at his wife in defeat. "Okay okay, I've been looking into some theories of my own, but let's not keep the Inspector. What do you want to know?"

"Could we go somewhere a little more private?" the Inspector asked.

"Come in here." Paul led the way to the dining room and when they were both seated at the dining table, the Inspector spoke first, his amber eyes looking from left to right beforehand. "Look Mr Bartram, Paul, may I call you that?" Paul nodded in the affirmative. "I'm speaking candidly now, you understand?" Paul nodded his head again. "Something strange happened here and I believe you understand what I'm talking about." Paul nodded for the third time. "I'll come straight to the point. I don't know of what relevance this has with your daughter-in-law going missing, but I know you have been looking at a certain doorstep which is in the vicinity of her last known whereabouts." Paul nodded again, wondering where the detective was going with this. But Jim Manning had deduced that Paul Bartram would either know exactly what he was talking about, or that he had been investigating something entirely different. He doubted the latter; his mind would have been engaged wholly in the hunt for his daughter-in-law.

The question, on Jim Manning's lips, was blunt. If anyone might want to help him with an explanation as to how a baby that disappeared in eighteen seventy-eight might then turn up in nineteen seventy, then it would be Paul Bartram.

"What do you know about time travel?

January 2nd, previously, six-thirty am

They had arranged to meet early as soon as it was light enough to see to work. Paul slipped out of the still sleeping household and collected some measuring equipment from the boot of his car. It felt damp and cold, the morning mist still hovered above the wintry ground, the skies looking set to stay grey and bleak. He'd forgotten to bring his scarf in the rush to support his son, so he turned up the collar of his coat and walked swiftly, in an effort to keep out the cold. Penny and Trevor arrived in Penny's car at the same time as he reached the east gate.

Trevor hadn't been keen on coming, but Penny persuaded him that he would be of help with recording the measurements. She said that Paul wanted to obtain a detailed plan of the stone circles; precise angles, lengths, distances apart, as much detail as they possibly could. Trevor thought that maybe there were more pressing matters than measuring a few chunks of rock, like searching for Jasmine, but perhaps Penny had forgotten about that already. After all, she barely knew Jasmine and getting together with a fellow scientist was possibly far more gripping. He was quite annoyed with her, but didn't want to show it, so he kept his mouth shut and listened to what she had to say instead.

Penny explained that Paul, on learning about the stone circle, had immediately wanted to go and examine it and consider the possibility of it being an elaborate mechanism for manipulating the earth's energy field. That took the biscuit, Trevor couldn't stop himself from laughing. From what he understood from Steve, Paul was a bit of a genius when it came to maths, but then maybe the flip side of a genius was indeed a madman. Steve seemingly, had completely forgotten to mention that his dad was completely potty. He already knew that Penny was, for she had divining rods that were brought out at any given opportunity and especially when around the standing stones. He could, to a certain extent, forgive her for being this way as she was in constant contact with dodgy chemicals in the school's chemistry lab. Besides, she was gorgeous and that overrode everything. He hoped that she wore gloves like he did when dealing with anaesthetics, but sometimes he wasn't so sure.

Penny had been insistent though, about the authenticity of Paul's hypothesis and said it was based on Einstein's theories of general relativity. She tried to explain to Trevor that basically space-time, or gravity, given the right conditions, could bend back on itself and so create a closed time-like curvature, or, in other words, a loop back in time. A spinning black hole could create just this situation; a wormhole or bridge would have been made to go from one point in time to another and an object, or even a person, could travel through it faster than the speed of light, but without breaking the rules because it was taking a short-cut!

Trevor heard all the words, but he couldn't make sense of what Penny was trying to explain and compared the likelihood of it to Alice falling down the rabbit hole. Then he thought about it. "So if you did somehow manage to go back in time, wouldn't that distort things? What if, for instance, you met your parents before you had been born - might that one encounter perhaps prevent your own conception? Then you would have never been there in the first place to go back in time!" Trevor's brain was reeling after thinking that one through, but he thought it clever to have thought it; having to repeat it might be another matter. Penny left him a little deflated though when she said that scenario had already been thought of.

"Ah, that's described as the grandparent paradox. But at least," she claimed, "it's flummoxed many acclaimed physicists and their kind."

Thus, the reason for arriving in the car for no one, Trevor thought, had discovered how to press a button and get him from 'a' to 'b' in a nanosecond, which would have been rather helpful yesterday, and Trevor had no intention of doing all that tooing and froing again.

Between them, Penny and Paul had mustered the tools they needed, and set about measuring distances, heights, angles and the relationships of the stones to each other, shouting the results to Trevor who recorded them on a notepad. Paul photographed the site from as many angles as he could. Penny then drew his attention to one of the houses over the road, or rather the doorstep of the house. "I've always been intrigued by it, I'm sure it's one of the stones on its side. I've dowsed from the stone circle and towards it, and there is a definite line of energy linking it to them." Paul took out a pair of binoculars from his coat pocket and focused on the step."

"I think you may be right," said Paul after seeing it magnified, "I wonder if it would help or hinder matters. I think we need to get some measurements from it and the other stones, it shouldn't be too difficult to get. Trevor, take this end of the tape measure and hold it still just here." Paul pointed to the base of the standing stone nearest to the step. They laid the tape down several times along the line before Paul realised they weren't going to get a sufficiently accurate measurement. "We need to come back with a piece of string we can pull tight, we are making a complete hash of it this way, the line is too higgledy-piggledy."

"I've got a ball of string in the car; it was for an experiment with the year eights at school. I'll get it now," said Penny and walked back towards her old, but trusty little red Mini that she'd bought as soon as she'd left university and had a regular salary. It was definitely showing its age, but she didn't want to part with it. It was while she was fishing around in its boot that something made her stop what she was doing and listen. There had been footsteps, and then there hadn't been any footsteps. She straightened up from her bent position to seek an explanation and thought she saw someone disappearing from the flowerbed and into the bushes. "Kids, even at this hour," she muttered, shrugging it off. She found the string and took it back to the others.

The string was easily long enough for their requirements, the only snag being Trevor getting caught by the house owner when he was holding his end of the string on the edge of the doorstep.

"Er, hello," was all he managed to verbalise as he gave an abashed cheesy grin to her when she opened the door to find him crouched down. She looked upon him quizzically, head to one side.

"Have you come about the leak? It's not here, it's at the back door. It comes right through when it's been raining hard. I'm surprised they've sent you out today, it being Sunday. I thought you lot would be on holiday."

"Oh right, the back door, I see," replied Trevor, trying to bluff his way out. Then he thought better of it. "Actually no, I haven't come about the leak, I'm examining your doorstep."

"So, you haven't come about the leak, but you still want to look at my doorstep?"

"Well, it's a very interesting step, as doorsteps go. It's very old we think."

"Well, it would be, this is an old street of houses. Just a minute, who's 'we'?"

"I'm dreadfully sorry to have been so impertinent, Madam," said Paul. He'd seen the door open and had come over to take a closer look. "We have been doing some problem solving at the stone circle and I'm afraid curiosity got the better of us. We think that your doorstep maybe a standing stone."

The woman, still in her dressing gown, looked Paul up and down and concluded that Paul was an idiot, like most men she encountered. "Well, it's not standing anymore," she replied indignantly and was just about to shut the door on them but decided to ask them a question instead. "Are you from the council, because I would like to ask when are you going to fix the streetlights? They're always turning on and off, like Belisha beacons. You come along, take a look, and still it goes on and nothing ever gets done."

Paul's ears pricked, his enquiring mind immediately wanting to delve further. This piece of information could be evidence of magnetic interference and help with their investigations. "Really," he replied, "that is very interesting. I wonder, could you have noticed, is there a particular time when this happens, for instance, before a storm, or when there is a full moon?"

Deciding he was indeed a complete moron, the woman retorted that she had no idea and wouldn't be bothering to find out.

"Just one more thing, would you mind if we photographed your step?" That was the last straw, she'd had enough of these ridiculous fools raving on about her doorstep.

"Yes, I would mind, and you can get lost!" She slammed the door shut.

"It definitely is one, did you see the width of it, there's just as much of it inside the house as there is outside, and look at its length, it goes far beyond the door frame. I think it is the biggest of all the stones, maybe used as a conductor. However, it will likely as not been moved from its original position to become a doorstep, so the original intent of it may have become distorted." Trevor had no idea what Paul was talking about but still nodded excitedly. "Anyway, we have, I believe, assembled enough information for me to get started. What we will need later, most likely, is a decent magnetometer. Dowsing is all well and good, but it doesn't give us any hard facts and figures." Trevor had a light-bulb moment.

"A compass? I have a compass."

"Well good, a compass would be a start, but I was thinking of something a little more sophisticated. However, there is plenty for me to do before we get to that stage. At the moment I simply want to get a plan of the site onto paper and make maths of it by turning it into distances and angles. I can then compare my findings with what we know about black holes and see if they bear any resemblance to each other."

Trevor and Paul collected Penny at the stones where she had been keeping a low profile. Three strangers on a doorstep might have been a little too intimidating, she thought. All three then returned to the Mini and drove the few hundred yards to the top of Steve and Jasmine's road so their car wouldn't be seen and dropped Paul off. They thought it best to keep quiet about what they'd been doing, deciding it was in Steve's best interests. Trevor agreed wholeheartedly, needing to distance himself as much as possible from this lunacy.

Perhaps Paul was using his suppositions as a diversionary tactic to get away from the reality of the situation. Nonetheless his daughter-in-law was somewhere, and he was merely exploring a possible occurrence. As to where that somewhere was precisely, Paul had no idea. He may be clutching at straws but getting stuck into his calculations was all he could do to keep himself in control and served him better than doing nothing at all. The not just possible, but probable, vibrational aspect of the standing stones had really sparked his curiosity, and he found Penny's experiments with dowsing the electromagnetic fields fascinating. If the seemingly unfeasible had in fact happened, that Jasmine had fallen through a black hole, then there was the whole of time and space to consider, if it were at all possible for someone to survive that sort of journey. In any case, Paul was only at the very beginning of what most critics would consider to be a virtually unprovable and very flimsy hypothesis. Maybe it was easier to keep things simple; she had been taken by person or persons unknown. That was terrible in itself.

When Steve had left for the police station and Glenda and Tony were settled in, Paul opened the door to the panelled dining room at the back of the house and went inside. It was, he understood, to have once been a library, back in the days of opulence, the shelves forming part of the panelling. Today though, preoccupied with recent events, Paul ignored his resplendent surroundings. He seated himself at the dining table, opened his notebook, and began drawing diagrams. Apart from when Steve returned from the police station with one of the officers, he was left undisturbed.

The time ticked by unnoticed by Paul. Eventually he put down his pencil and studied the sheets of notes in front of him. He'd been making a plan of the stone circles and then drawn lines, with a ruler, between all the stones so each stone was connected, by line, to every other stone in both the inner and outer circles. He hadn't yet got as far as measuring the angles that were appearing. He would need his computer and trigonometry programme for that, although he knew already what would be created. The crudely pencilled pattern was in essence, a mandala.

Paul was absolutely in his element, forgetting temporarily of present circumstances. He loved discoveries, and he believed he was finding something here. He was aware the word mandala meant circle, and that mandalas were what could be called cosmic diagrams; each mandala having its own vibration, its own tone. He had researched, for instance, that when a human voice intones the most sacred of Hindu symbols, the syllable om, or aum to be exact, the vibration induced would create what was known as the Sri Yantra mandala. It could be observed when powder sprinkled on a diaphragm, moves into the shape when a device called a tonoscope is used. In other words, in Buddhist teachings, a beautiful representation of the universe. He also understood that some mandalas reveal the individual's path in life, that the shape and patterns formed, represent the vibrational qualities of one's own being.

Paul hadn't expected a question about time travel from anyone apart from possibly Penny, and least of all from a senior police officer. It caught him off guard and he wasn't sure how to react. Even though it was exactly on the same lines as his own thinking, he wasn't ready to divulge that, and definitely not to a policeman. Any plausible explanation to demonstrate time travel would need scientific proof from facts and figures. To be able to do that would take a lifetime, or two; it was beyond him. He could possibly discuss it with like-minded colleagues, but who had the time or financial resources to prove it? A conundrum certainly, but he would have to say something in reply.

"Why on earth are you asking me that Inspector, surely you can't be serious?"

"As your wife said, you've been investigating the stone circle, and as you have just admitted, you have some theories, so I say again, do you think there is a possibility that someone can travel through time?"

For a few seconds they eyeballed each other, both searching for answers from the other; Paul quickly yielding to the eagle-eyed Jim Manning. He removed his glasses and covered his face with his hands and rubbed his brow, his elbows firmly on the table. After a moment he looked back at the patient policeman sitting opposite who, he realised, must have suspicions of his own. Eventually some words formed in his reticent mouth. "It's just a theory," he conceded, "and the science to back it up is very flaky to say the least. I don't know how it could ever be actually proven. Why do you ask?"

"This isn't about Jasmine's whereabouts as far as I know, and this, if you don't mind, is between you and me for the moment."

"I understand," replied Paul. He knew the Inspector wouldn't want it broadcast that he had asked about time travel, but there must be something he knew, and Paul wanted to hear it.

The Inspector cleared his throat. "Many years ago," he began, "I participated in the investigation in a coroner's case about a stillborn baby who was born in the house, or rather the flat, which has the doorstep you were investigating."

"Glenda's child, Jasmine's twin brother," declared Paul; his curiosity piqued.

"Yes, the very same. Now Glenda's statement said that her memory of Jasmine was that she saw her on the doorstep, not that she gave birth to her. I understand that the whole experience was extremely traumatic, and she barely remembers giving birth to the boy. But suppose she hadn't given birth to Jasmine?"

"What?" cried Paul. "I'm not following this."

"I haven't finished yet, I will elaborate. Many years ago, there was a report about a baby going missing from the same doorstep."

"Yes, I know that story, Tony related it the other day."

"So, what if this baby, that everyone assumed had been abducted, genuinely disappeared, and then reappeared, still on the doorstep, just as Glenda was delivering a stillborn child? I know this is very tenuous, but there's more. The baby that went missing had a birthmark like Jasmine's." He paused so Paul could compute, and Paul did just that.

He'd been correct in his thinking that her birthmark was of significance. It was an imprint of her vibrational essence, her mandala. Could this particular set of standing stones then, have resonated so completely with Jasmine, that in a particular moment she'd somehow merged with its energy field? In other words, she hadn't really gone, but had moved through time instead. Jasmine was still in this vicinity, but in another year! This is exactly what he'd felt almost by instinct when Penny had shown him the stone circles, and now he had the confirmation. But this wasn't the beginning, and neither was it the end and now the detective was adding yet another dimension; that Jasmine had come from some other time period as a baby. Had she gone back to where she belonged? He looked across at the policeman almost plaintively. "So where do we go from here? It's not like your usual sort of investigation, is it?"

"No, it isn't, you're spot on there," Jim Manning agreed, albeit a little reticently. He stroked at his mouth, deliberating before speaking again. "The way I see it is this. The police will continue carrying out routine investigations. Meanwhile, for my own peace of mind, I'd like to dig deeper into this other, erm, possible cause of Jasmine's disappearance."

"If we are to continue along these lines," Paul began in measured tone, "are we presuming then, that Jasmine is now somewhere else in time? Am I correct?"

"Well, against my better judgement, I'm beginning to take on this idea, yes. The question is, are you with me on this?"

Paul nodded in the affirmative yet again, and the two men spent some time revealing to each other what they had discovered so far. It wasn't long before Jim Manning got onto Arthur Pickford.

"The old man who had her bag?" Paul interrupted.

"Yes, that's him. I think he knows a lot more about all this, and I think we need to talk to him but I'm not sure that bringing him into the station is the best way. When he has tried to hint at things, he's not been taken seriously, and I include myself in not looking further into what he was trying to tell us. I suppose he didn't know where to start. But what he has said, if one puts it into the context of time travel, starts to sound like factual evidence. Want to come with me to speak with him?"

"You bet I do."

"Er," began Jim Manning awkwardly, "this line of enquiry is in my own time; not part of the official investigation, if you get my meaning."

"I understand completely," replied Paul.

They left the house together; Paul giving the briefest of explanations to the others that he was helping police with enquiries and thus yet again avoiding his wife's perceptive questioning concerning his movements early on Sunday morning.

On the short drive to Arthur Pickford's house, Paul asked the Inspector if he'd heard of the Philadelphia experiment. He hadn't, so Paul proceeded to explain what it might be like for someone to disappear and reappear somewhere else, although the Philadelphia experiment had not been about time travel.

"In nineteen forty-three, a complete ship, the USS Eldridge, was said to have disappeared from the Philadelphia Naval Shipyard, only to materialise in New York at exactly the same time, using large electromagnetic field generators. Eyewitnesses (those who had survived, for many of the sailors on board had not) reported a severe vibrational noise, a green-coloured fog, and nausea following the alleged events."

"I've never heard of such a thing," replied the policeman, open-mouthed but eyes remaining firmly on the windscreen; there were roadworks ahead; the traffic was backed-up.

"No, the 'powers that be' attempted to keep it secret, and when the truth of it began to filter out, suppressed it again by claiming the story was perpetrated by a hoaxer. It became known as World War Two's Philadelphia Experiment, which had been exploring Einstein's unified field theory, which is, in simplified language, uniting electromagnetic radiation and gravity into a single field."

"I'll take your word for that," said Jim Manning.

"They wanted to bend light around an object by refraction to render it invisible, but they had discovered much more, so much so, that the secrecy of the experiment was paramount. It was claimed that in order to maintain the silence, people were subject to brainwashing, others simply disappeared, shall we say? When I heard of this, I could hardly contain myself. I had to know more. If they were getting rid of people, it had to be something big."

"Sounds big all right."

"It took some time," continued Paul, as the car came to a stop at some temporary traffic lights for alleged roadwork operations, "but I managed to land myself a two-year sabbatical in the U.S. I was accepted into the Institute of Technology in California to observe, or even help with the mathematics in the department of theoretical physics. It was a once in a lifetime opportunity that had come my way, and it involved working alongside renowned professors who had interests in the astrophysical implications of Einstein's general theory of relativity. From a small boy you see, I have been curious about time travel, and whether it was possible. And then to work with these renowned scientists to try and prove it; well, it was a dream come true."

"So, what you're telling me, is that they were trying to prove that time travel is possible?"

"Amongst other things, but it was certainly *my* objective."

"Well, you've got me there, I had no idea about this stuff. I just like sniffing around and finding the facts from out of the hogwash and drivel so to speak."

"Then we're not so different," concluded Paul.

"No indeed, perhaps not," agreed Jim Manning.

After an overly long wait the lights turned to green and the car crept forward, deftly avoiding the rogue traffic cones that had become misplaced from the rest of the neat row along the road. Put there for seemingly invisible workmen to have a safe environment to carry out their business. There was no evidence of that either. It may have been quicker to walk the short distance and thus avoid the frustrations of having to experience the idiosyncratic workings of road diggers, or in this case, the lack of them, thought Jim Manning.

"Steve was sixteen when we moved to the States," continued Paul. "He told me he was nervous about it at first, you know, leaving everything and going into the unknown. But I suspected he really meant leaving Jasmine. They grew up together, Glenda and Tony are our neighbours. I don't know if you knew that already. I told him it wouldn't be forever, and in the meantime, he would have a whole new world open up for him. And indeed, he did. He went as a boy, and returned as a young man. I didn't think he'd look at Jasmine twice when we got back, how wrong I was. I don't mean that I didn't think much of her," Paul added. "On the contrary, she's a lovely girl. I simply imagined that after two years of separation they would most likely have grown apart."

"Here we are," Jim Manning declared, pulling the car to a halt and reversing into a parking space with much finesse. He took a pride in his driving, including parking with precision. They were in front of number twenty-four, Regent Grove, Arthur Pickford's address, at precisely the time he was coming down the street towards them walking a dog. "Ah, the man himself," he added. They waited in the car until he was alongside before getting out.

"We need to talk," said Jim Manning.

"Yes," replied Arthur Pickford, "maybe we do. Would you like to hear my story?"

"We think so," Jim Manning replied, glancing over at Paul. "This is Paul Bartram, the missing girl's father-in-law," he said by way of introduction.

Arthur Pickford nodded his head at Paul. "Then I think it would be most beneficial for you to meet someone else who can support what I have to say, and maybe give you some more information that will be of interest to you."

"Then lead on," replied Jim Manning, gesturing at Arthur Pickford to sit in the back of the car along with Bessie, who sat quietly on his lap.

"I would like to speak now; I need to get it all off my chest," declared Arthur Pickford.

Before the engine was turned on, the old man held a very captive audience as he told the story of his life with all its remarkable experiences. He then directed the Inspector to drive to the location of where his friend lived, the latest person of interest.

Much later, Paul was dropped off at Steve and Jasmine's by Jim Manning, but he didn't know what to do with himself. He'd heard a story, two stories even, both told in truth and sincerity and, in essence, proof that his hypotheses were indeed correct. He should be happy, but instead, he was deeply melancholic, for the news was bitter-sweet; Jasmine was gone, and much, much more. How could he possibly tell his son what he knew?

Meanwhile Jim Manning was back in the incident room updating everyone. "We now have a possible explanation as to why Jasmine was clutching her head on the film from the security camera located in a private residence near the east gates of the park. I have ascertained from Stephen Bartram, the husband, that both he and Jasmine had gone into a broom cupboard for some privacy while at the party. During the, er, privacy, a ladder was disturbed, and fell onto Jasmine's head. An injury sustained in this manner, although appearing minor at the time, has a potential capacity of developing into something far worse, and by the time she was caught on camera, may have been experiencing a bad headache, or even concussion. Although we can't rule out an attack, this misper case may be the result of accidental trauma rather than an abduction. Can we check hospital admissions again and get a team out to search the locality; ditches, neglected gardens; everywhere in fact. Also, can we look again at any other stuff we've got of her on cameras and see if she's bothered with her head? Also, the husband's father, Paul Bartram, has told me that she and her husband were childhood sweethearts, information that may prove useful or may not, we don't know at this point."

"Bonking in the broom cupboard. Well, that's novel!" someone commented.

"No snide remarks please, we are dealing with a serious matter."

"You're thinking she may be bleeding inside her head, Guv?"

"We need to consider everything," replied Jim Manning. "Anyone else got anything?" He closed the meeting as no one was forthcoming with information and spied DC Downey standing by the door. "Tom, have you got a minute?" They left the room together and went into Jim Manning's office.

That evening, after he arrived home late, Jim Manning's wife Mary, felt obliged to ask him about the case he was on. She didn't normally ask, but she knew her husband well enough to know he wasn't happy about something. He'd eaten the chicken supreme that she'd prepared for their meal without enthusiasm, and he was abnormally quiet. She usually ignored the fact that he couldn't leave his job behind, but this was different; there was an air about him, like he was wrestling with something that wasn't fitting into the normal way of things.

"There's something that I haven't come across before, nor, I don't suppose, has anyone else, nor likely to either," he admitted to her after her query. "Something, I'm not sure... do you remember me telling you about that case old Bob had, the one where he got that woman in who called herself a medium or some such? Well, I was thinking I might like to speak with her. She managed to find the location of the victim by looking at a map."

"Have you a murder case on the go then?" Mary asked.

"It's rather a missing person at the moment, but it's complicated."

"Ah," Mary nodded, "but isn't it always?"

"Yes, I suppose so, but, but this is different."

"Is it that different though? I'm surprised you are giving up like that. It's not like you."

"I'm not giving up. What makes you think that?"

"Because of what you just said. In all the years I've known you Jim, I have never for one minute thought you would resort to a medium. Surely you don't believe in all that rubbish, do you?"

"I don't, not really, but that shouldn't stop me from looking at every possibility in order to solve a case, and if that's what it takes, then who am I to stand in the way? Old Bob spent weeks on that business and got nowhere, and as soon as that woman said where her body was, it was solved by the DNA found on her. Mind you, he was never able to say officially that he'd spoken with a medium, it wouldn't do that the police were collaborating with the occult. The official version is that they got lucky with the search area."

"Well, there you are, they just got lucky."

"I feel I have to do something more though, something different. We've no leads apart from CCTV confirming the route she took, but that's it. Apart from..." Jim trailed off; he was obviously perturbed.

"Apart from?" Mary encouraged. "Come on Jim, think it through, what's being calculated in that brain of yours."

"Hmm, we thought we had a suspect, but it turns out he isn't. It's more about something he has said to us, and it ties in with an old incident I remember, that's all," he replied, not wanting to reveal any real information to her. "Anyway, didn't you know Bob's wife? Might you still have her phone number?"

"Yes, somewhere, I'll look it out for you, but Jim, be very careful. The police turning to mediums? Don't become a laughingstock."

"Don't worry about that, if I do anything at all, it'll be for my own peace of mind. I shan't involve the nick, not if I can help it, I'd never live it down."

"I can believe that. But you had a suspect, for what?"

"It's that woman who went missing on New Year's Eve. We brought an old chap into custody for questioning, but we had to let him go, he found her handbag, that's all."

"Oh that, it must be such a worry for the family. I do hope she turns up safe and sound."

"Don't we all," her husband replied, "don't we all." They sat in silence for a while. But Jim needed to get it off his chest, she would know he wasn't at ease; she knew everything about him, every gesture, every facial expression, he couldn't keep this to himself, she would know it was big. "The old man, he's been coming out with crazy stuff that doesn't add up. He says he knows the missing lady, but from a long time ago, and I mean a long time ago, like in the early nineteen-hundreds."

"What?"

"Precisely! Claims she didn't go missing exactly but went through time."

"So, he's off his trolley then."

"Well, that's what I thought at first, but then he started telling us a story, and it sounds so plausible that I feel I ought to follow it up. Just out of interest, you understand."

"Jim, I know you better than that. You have seen everything, done everything, nothing is new to you, there must be a proper explanation. Why are you giving him the time of day?"

"Because he told me to talk to someone who would corroborate what he was saying. I did and it was the missing woman's daughter. Now this'll get you, like it did me." Jim moved forward on his chair before he delivered the next bit of information. "The misper's husband says they have no children. Even if they did, they'd be youngsters. Guess what, her daughter, their daughter, is ninety-nine years old! Don't laugh, I knew you'd laugh, that's why I didn't want to say anything."

Mary could hardly speak for laughing. It was so out of character for her husband to lap up the ridiculous and it had unnerved her. Her defence mechanism had been hysteria, so much so, that she was incapable of responding for some time. However, she finally composed herself. "Jim, maybe it's time you retired. We've talked about it over and over, but I think now is the time."

"You think I'm losing it don't you? Maybe I am, but you know what I'm like, I will follow every lead regardless of how absurd it seems, and I'm not nearly old enough to be retired; what on earth would I do? Anyway, I went to see this alleged daughter, and the reason I'd thought about asking a medium if she could help is because if what both she and the old man says is true, there won't be any body to find alive or dead other than in their grave, seeing the age of the daughter."

Mary Manning was lost for words. She didn't really have any reasoned response to her husband's wild statements. It was all too absurd, and Jim really needed a holiday. Clearly, the few days over the New Year hadn't been enough. She gave a little cough and got up to start the washing up. They mostly did it together, but today Jim Manning stayed at the table brooding and then turned on the television when it was time to watch the news.

Chapter Nine

Wednesday, January 5th, pm

As soon as his father had gone into the dining room with the Detective Inspector, Steve went out. He craved something - fresh air, freedom, escape? Anything other than what he had at present. However, dragging his feet to the park didn't bring him much comfort. He walked past the swings where a few kids, ever willing to brave the cold, were hanging about; past the bandstand, its very presence echoing the brass bands playing underneath its silent roof; past the idling paddling pool awaiting budding skaters to glide across its top as soon as its icy skin is formed and through the main gates. The crushing agony that followed him everywhere these days was the only thing he noticed. He walked on, round into New North Road and abstractedly towards Trevor's flat. "Come on up," he heard a muffled voice speaking through the speaker after ringing the doorbell.

"I would be surprised if the bang on her head was anything more than a bad bump. Surely she would've had more symptoms if she was having a bleed inside her brain." Trevor knew that brain haemorrhages didn't necessarily manifest immediately, but he was trying to reassure his friend. Steve had relayed the latest from the police as soon as he'd entered the flat and also confessed as to why Jasmine may have already been suffering from concussion. "Did she complain of any pain?" asked Trevor, wondering how on earth they had had time to make a 'visit' to his junk room and also racking his brain in an effort to remember if Jasmine was showing any sign of a head injury while he was trying to kiss her.

"No, I don't think so," replied Steve.

"Well, there you are then, couldn't have been anything much."

"So why was she looking as though her head was hurting in the police video?"

"Maybe someone had attacked her, but she had managed to get away?" replied Trevor awkwardly. He didn't want to alarm his friend, but that's what it was looking like.

"You think?"

"Well can you think of anything else?"

"I don't know what to think any more," said Steve. He sat down with his head in his hands.

"I know it's not much, but I'm here for you mate," said Trevor, full of compassion for his desolate friend.

Steve looked up, "Thanks, I know you are."

They hugged each other, and from the stillness of that moment, Steve drew strength.

Trevor coughed as they pulled apart and the moment was gone. "Oh, I keep forgetting to say. That old lady: Rose, she asked if you had looked at the letters."

"What?"

"I didn't understand what she meant either, unless it was some Scrabble pieces she'd lost."

"Scrabble pieces? We didn't find any of those I don't think. When did she ask you that?"

"You know, when I went to see one of our dental patients there, she spoke to me, and she asked me to ask you if you had looked at the letters. What's up?" Trevor could see a look of realisation on his Steve's face. "Do you know what she meant?"

"Yes, I think I do," replied Steve. "Sometime before Christmas, Jas and I found several letters which looked as though they'd been written to some lost boyfriend. They were behind a drawer in a dressing table. Jas wasn't bothered by them so much, but I found them fascinating. They were all about what was happening in the writer's life, how she was missing some bloke who she couldn't go back to." He shrugged his shoulders dismissively. "The old woman, Rose, she knew I'd found them. They must be important for her."

"Yes, I suppose you're right. Maybe you should give them to her."

"Yes," Steve agreed, "maybe I should. She'd asked the old man if I'd found them too."

Trevor thought for a minute. Concentrating on other things might help prevent Steve from pulling himself further down a vortex of misery and despair. "Perhaps you could go and get them now and take them to her."

"Yes, I'll do it," replied Steve. "At least someone will have some pleasure out of today."

"I'll come with you. Penny's out visiting, not sure when she'll be back. Let's go in my car, I'm not as keen on walking all over the place like you."

Trevor drove the short journey and Steve picked up the letters. They had been placed very neatly behind one of the top drawers of a dressing table in a bedroom that had a connecting door to the main bedroom at the front of the house. He and Jasmine found them there one day along with an old photo of a young soldier while they were clearing out the room ready for redecoration. After reading a few of them, Steve had replaced the letters back behind the drawer as carefully as he could manage but given the photo to Rose when he'd been to see her on New Year's Eve to glean information about their house.

They'd planned to get on with refurbishing the room in the New Year. 'Fat chance of that now though,' he thought. He pulled out the roll of letters which were tied with ribbon as gently as he was able, called out to his mother to say he was with Trevor on an errand, jumped back into the passenger seat of Trevor's car and headed towards the care home, Trevor spinning the wheels slightly as he set off. Unbeknown to them, the detective Inspector and Steve's father had just left there.

PART TWO

Chapter Ten

Monday, January 1st, 1900

It was now well after midnight, but he still remained. He was near the stone circle in the park, close, but not too close, to where he had seen the baby disappear years before, when he'd been but a young lad of eight. The park hadn't been constructed back then, but the standing stones had, laying unobserved for countless years, covered by meadowland belonging to the great Greenhead Hall which, following the death of its last owner, now stood derelict. They had only come to light during the park's creation. Being hidden from view hadn't diminished the power they held though. That power, had caused a baby to disappear.

several years earlier ...

Market stalls aplenty swiftly encompassed the ancient stones following their discovery, satisfying the needs and desires of the sightseers who came to see them in their droves, but with the greater intention of filling the rapidly deepening pockets of the stallholders. Like everyone else, he, a youth back then, had been drawn by the archaeological dig and the lure of the street traders. He had purchased a pendulum from a stand that was full of the strangest of widgets and artefacts. Only having a few pennies, it was the cheapest thing he could find. Nonetheless, he later chastised himself for getting it, realising he could have made one for nothing out of a bit of turned wood, like a bobbin, and some yarn. To feel better about it, he persuaded himself into thinking it was special because he had bought it, therefore it was a 'real' pendulum because it hadn't been merely homemade. Whatever its origins, it grew to be an invaluable tool as he gradually discovered and trained himself in the ancient art of dowsing. He was soon able to tell if there was water beneath the ground. "An old well lies under here," he would tell his pals. "Careful the ground doesn't open up and you fall in, you never know when strange things might happen, and then you'll be stuck down there for ever."

Either his associates began to stay clear of him, or his strange hobby kept him away for hours, for he began to spend most of his spare time alone. He learned the wondrous secrets that the mysterious earth revealed to him through the use of his pendulum, but deprived himself of human company in the process. No one else shared his enthusiasm for dangling something resembling a plumb line above almost anything, but for some reason that he could never account for, he felt compelled to continue to do.

The stone circle and the area around it, he found, was very different from anywhere else, even more than finding hidden wells. His pendulum would start to swing and twirl as he moved in and out and around each stone. He observed that, at certain times, the pendulum was livelier than at other times. It changed with the seasons, it changed with the months. Even night and day were different. There seemed to be a connection to the moon and stars as well. His harmless hobby had changed into a passion. He spent hours in the library studying books on divination, stone circles, astronomy and anything he could find to enhance his learning on similar subjects. And that's how he came to the conclusion that those stones had had something to do with that baby's disappearance.

That was the reason why the man lay in wait. For quite what he did not know, but he had calculated that if anything was to happen it would have to be this night. The moon although waxed, remained almost full and the constellations of the heavens were lined up. And most of all, a century was turning. That had to mean something. At least he hoped it did and then he would have the proof he sought.

He'd been in town earlier that evening observing the crowds gathering in St. George's Square in front of the railway station. There had been an atmosphere of expectancy. A new beginning was coming, a century was turning and everyone sought to see it happen. Even the young children had been allowed to stay up. But he hadn't hung around, he wanted to be positioned in the park well before midnight for he was prepared to skip a night of revelry for this, whatever it was. Anyway, he wasn't one for painting the town red being too reserved for that sort of thing. He enjoyed the odd half in The Regent and listening to the crack from the locals, but he was mainly a solitary fellow. He still lived with his elderly and widowed mother, and he worked as a librarian in the town.

The church bells rang out announcing the new century (in case anyone was unaware) and the air was soon thick with the smoke of fireworks that had been lit in celebration. There were explosions of light from every point in the skies and he couldn't help but raise his eyes to watch. He could even hear the cheers coming from the crowds in town after midnight had struck. As speedily as it had sprung, the spectacle died down and the vapours from the spent gunpowder floated away. He saw a few people drifting home, but then all became quiet. It was getting late; surely something should have happened by now.

The man was beginning to doubt himself. He fumbled for the pendulum in his pocket; he wanted to check if he could pick up on the energy. His pendulum was strangely still. He moved to another vantage point where he could see the stones and still have a good view of the road. Well, he would have had if the streetlights had been lit. Again, nothing from the pendulum. He heard footsteps; someone was approaching; a tall man, not old, yet stooped. It was Dr Brown, the local doctor who must be coming home from a busy night at the hospital. The man knew where the doctor lived; he would soon be turning left. Suddenly his attention was drawn away and onto a carriage coming at great speed from behind the doctor. It only just missed him as it careered past before turning sharply into Heaton Road, the road that he assumed the doctor would be taking. It was fortunate to have managed the manoeuvre at that speed, the driver must have been either very lucky, very drunk or more likely both. There was something at the side of the road. It was difficult to see properly in the dark and hazy atmosphere of the night. He screwed his eyes tight trying to see more clearly. A body maybe. Perhaps it had come from the carriage and fallen off as it rounded the corner but it didn't seem likely, the orientation was all wrong. It hadn't been there before though, so it must have come from somewhere.

He stayed in his hiding place, looking attentively. He saw Dr Brown approach. It *was* a body; a person; a woman. Dr Brown was talking to her but the man couldn't quite catch his words. She was talking too, seemingly dazed and trying to stand up, but very unsteadily. She was losing her balance and couldn't stay upright and heading for a fall. He thought he should go and help, but he didn't need to. At the moment he was about to break cover, Dr Brown had scooped up the young lady into his patently strong arms and carried on walking home, his footsteps sounding a little more laboured than before.

The man, in solitude again, pondered. Had she fallen from the carriage, or what would be much more exciting, appeared out of thin air? He tried his pendulum again; there was movement; the energy had returned; seemingly there had been some form of hiatus when everything was at a standstill. Or maybe it hadn't all stopped; maybe there had been increased action at the midpoint. He gathered himself, watching the swing of his pendulum as he walked towards the stones and into the centre. It was indeed doing some curious things. He followed the activities of his trusty weighted twine back out from the standing stones and across the road... to the doorstep from where he had seen the baby disappear. He could hardly believe it; the energy was reaching directly to it! After all his observations and study over the long years, now he had real credible evidence. Better than that, the woman in the road had appeared directly on the line he had just dowsed. This was what he had been waiting for, he just knew it.

He hurried along the road just in time to see the good doctor going to his front door with the woman cradled in his arms. He wouldn't be taking her anywhere else, not at this time of night. The man had got what he wanted, this was the reason why he'd spent years taking careful measurement and had lain in wait for so long. He would now have to keep very close observation on Dr Brown's comings and goings in order to get as much information as he could about the woman. But right now, it was late. Time for bed and sleep. Only sleep was long in coming as he grappled with his thoughts. Where on earth had this lady come from? He resolved to keep a watchful eye as she might provide a key to what had happened to that baby. He'd kept abreast of any news coming in about a stray or abandoned newborn that Lord and Lady Peters, the distraught parents had claimed was their daughter. There'd been nothing whatsoever.

Chapter Eleven

1955

She was on her way through the park towards the hospital as usual, but today it was as if she were pulling an unknown monster along and trying to dodge its invisible mouth. The jaws snapped at her heels trying to eat its way into her very being. Everything felt so heavy. She walked as briskly as she could against it. It wasn't the weather; the new day, already warmed by the autumn sun, was yet unspoiled by the morning's comings and goings. She knew why this was so of course; it had taken months. of paperwork and planning but finally the day had arrived. The very last day of her working life, the final time she would wear that dress and walk away from a very large and significant part of her life.

It was the year nineteen fifty-five and times were changing faster than ever. Four years had passed since males had been allowed to join the nurse register, and now two were rostered to start work on her ward. 'Male nurses indeed! Whatever next?' It was a step too far, in her mind. Over her time, she had witnessed many changes for the good and the not so good, the birth of the NHS, new and powerful antibiotics, and only this year, a cure for polio. But this, this just took the biscuit! Time to let the new breed of nurse take over, for it certainly wasn't her way of going about things. Having reached her fifty-fifth birthday, a very respectful age of retirement, it was time to go.

Pausing only briefly in her office to remove her outdoor clothing, and with barely a glance at the mirror to confirm its correct position, she pinned her frilled cap with white Kirby grips onto her French-pleated brown and slightly greying hair. With many years of repeating the exact same procedure; there was no real need to check. Already dressed in her navy long-sleeved uniform, she donned her starched white apron and was ready for duty. Clearing her throat of any unwanted emotion that had the gall to be stuck there, Sister Rose Brown opened the double doors to ward five and entered for her very last shift of duty.

There were two young nurses sitting at a small desk a few yards in front of her and a third of the way down the centre of the long Nightingale ward.

They stood up hastily and almost to attention as soon as they saw Sister Brown at the ward entrance. "Good morning, Nurse Smith, Nurse Thompson."

"Good morning, Sister Brown," they replied in unison, while fearfully hoping they had completed all their tasks to Sister Brown's satisfaction.

"Please turn off the desk lamp there is no need to waste electricity. There is light enough from the windows and I assume you have finished your reports as you appear to have found time for gossiping."

Nurse Thompson reached for the switch. "Sorry Sister."

"Efficiency is the key, Nurse Thompson. Now please tell me of any relevant occurrences overnight before the day shift arrives, you may give a full report then."

"Only one admission, Sister, in bed eight." Nurse Smith inclined her head indicating the bed as she spoke. "He was admitted for assessment after being found wandering the streets in a state of confusion; keeps asking if the year is nineteen-eighteen!"

"Indeed!" 'Nineteen-eighteen; if only it was,' Sister Rose Brown thought to herself. That was then when her mother... She cleared her throat once more and glanced over at bed eight. The occupant turned over and back again and then sat up.

"He has slept only fitfully," said Nurse Smith. Sister Brown walked to the foot of bed eight and picked up the chart holder clipped there. Seeing nothing of note to worry her about the patient's health; perhaps the pulse was a little raised, and blood pressure slightly erratic in the early hours, but now settled; she replaced it and looked up at the occupant. His face looked drawn, frightened even, but of what, she had no clue. There was something about him, something familiar that she couldn't fathom. Ordinarily Sister Rose Brown took all in her stride, nothing really rattled her, but now, she felt an odd sensation in her gut. Something wasn't right, something was out of place. She turned away with a mind to return after report.

A slight draught was discernible as the young student nurses who were on the roster for the morning shift opened the double ward doors and entered. Rose put her thoughts aside and took her spot at the head of the long multi-use table in the middle of the ward. The two night nurses flanked her, and the others took up places down either side. "Good morning nurses," she said by way of greeting.

"Good morning, Sister," they replied in one voice, only sitting down after Rose had taken her seat. Nurse Smith gave a report of her night shift and then she and Nurse Thompson waited to be dismissed.

"Off you go to bed, and sleep well."

"Yes Sister. Thank you Sister," they replied and scooted off, their beds beckoning. Rose led morning prayers then opened the workbook, trusting that her charge nurse had completed it the previous evening. She would have normally checked it over as a priority, but today she had been distracted by the new occupant of bed eight. Rose delegated the work; all of them to give breakfast to those who were unable to feed themselves, then two for the bed baths, two to make the beds of those who were mobile, and two to do the temperature, pulse and blood pressure rounds. In between, they would all do the two-hourly turns and pressure area care for those who were unable to move themselves; the 'up' baths could be done in the afternoon, along with the dressings. She would assess the new patient in bed eight and do the medicine round as usual. There was only one consultant round on a Thursday, so she would be able to prepare for that easily in between.

"But there's only one working sphyg, Sister, the others are down for repair."

"Well, it only takes one of you to perform a blood pressure reading. Decide between you who needs most practice in taking temperatures, pulses and respirations as opposed to accuracy in determining the systolic and diastolic of a blood pressure with the one operative sphygmomanometer."

Rose left them to sort it out and commenced her own ward round. "Good morning, Mr Pickford, is it?" she asked, having arrived at bed eight after starting at bed one. The occupants of beds one to seven had been on the ward for some time and Rose knew them well; she had checked their charts and distributed their medicines with exactitude; it hadn't taken her long; she was keen to learn more about the mysterious man in bed number eight. She checked his wristband to make sure it was in fact Mr Pickford and looked at him intently for a moment before hastily averting her eyes and read his files clipped at the bottom end of the bed instead. An imperceptible shiver coursed through her - there was indeed something familiar about him and it was making her distinctly uncomfortable.

"Yes, that's my name, and I live at twenty-three Dudley Road. But it's not there see, it's gone I tell you, disappeared, and everything looks different, it's like I'm not in the right place."

Rose searched for something in her mind, a memory. Then she had it. "But number twenty-three was annihilated during the Second World War, I live quite near there, I remember it well. My neighbour thought they'd heard the sound of a doodlebug but it turned out it was someone's exhaust falling off their car; a doodlebug could never have got this far north. No, it got hit by a stray incendiary from when they'd been flying over Bradford in forty-one. Still, a bomb nonetheless, but fortunately the house had been empty for years..."

She tailed off, realising who Mr Pickford was, although she hadn't known him by that name. Neither had she seen him for many a year, not since she was a girl, not since the end of the Great War, not since - nineteen-eighteen! And after all those years, he didn't look a day older. In fact, he seemed younger; she had remembered him as an old man, not someone who looked to be in his forties, like he looked now. But then, she supposed, to a child, anyone around forty years of age would appear old. She had known him as Mr Walkpast, a name that her mother had coined, as he always seemed to be 'walking past.' If one looked out of the window, he would be walking by, or if one were in town, or in the park, there he was, passing by and doffing his cap.

Sister Rose Brown did the unthinkable; something she chastised her nurses for, as it was against her way of going about things; she sat down on Mr Pickford's hospital bed. She was in such a state of shock; she couldn't help it, for she had had a realisation. Years ago her mother had told her that before she gave birth to Rose, something had happened that would be difficult for anyone to believe so she had kept quiet about it. Although trusting her mother absolutely, Rose had never been completely sure about it as it was too extraordinary to fully grasp. Until now that is, for the exact same must have happened to Mr Walkpast.

She didn't know whether to hug him for inadvertently giving her proof of her mother's outlandish story, or to say, very gently, of what had just befallen him. No wonder he was in a confused state. She remembered her mother had said she had not dared go anywhere for weeks following the event, and she was never far away from attacks of anxiety and panic for the rest of her life. But her mother had told no one, as who would have believed her? The only reason she told her daughter was because she had found secret letters, hidden from view, revealing another life, another man, her real father. At least Mr Walkpast, or rather Mr Pickford, would have her to tell his story to; perhaps the only one who would believe his bizarre tale, for she knew now with certainty, her mother had been telling her the truth.

Rose recovered herself. "Mr Wa... Pickford, this hospital ward is full of patients who need my attention. I will return when I have finished and have your consultant, Dr Fullerton, take a look at you on his round today and see where we go from here." She stepped round from his bedside and moved onto the patient in bed nine. "Good morning, Mr Williams, how are we today?" Rose barely heard his answer but nodded as though she had. She examined his charts at the foot of his bed, checked his pulse, and ticked off on his medication chart that she'd given his morning dose of digoxin and moved on to the next bed. She continued in this way until she'd seen every patient in every bed, greeting them with her usual air of confidence and authority. However, with thoughts of Mr Walkpast gyrating round in her head the whole time, her outward composure only remained solid through years of practice. Inwardly, she was finding it very difficult to concentrate and had switched to automatic pilot.

Before long, the ward doors opened fully, and Rose felt the familiar draught as they did. She turned to see the arrival of Dr Fullerton who was encircled by his team of doctors and a train of medical students. It was earlier than usual for the ward round; his junior doctors had had barely any time to prepare, but he wanted to get cracking after being informed of a rather interesting case on female medical. He was keen to spend as much time there as he could before his clinic started in the out-patients department. Why he insisted on doing it all on the same day nobody understood; there was always an urgency for the rounds to be finished so clinic wouldn't run late. But he was the consultant, and that was what he commanded. Only four of the total patients on the ward were his, so the round would be short. Arthur Pickford had been admitted under him as he'd been the on-call consultant during the night. Dr Fullerton's firm specialised in medical conditions of the heart, so if he didn't have a problem with his heart, it would be unlikely that the doctor would have much of an interest in him.

Eight beds on the ward were allocated to Dr Fullerton's firm by bed board but as per usual, they were mostly occupied by patients that weren't his. However, patients that required admission had to be put somewhere and his beds had been grabbed as soon as they were vacant. When Dr Fullerton finished chastising Sister Brown over the persistent inefficiencies of bed management – a problem which was no fault of hers, the ward round began. She took his haranguing with long-suffering patience, she was well-used to it, he always liked to complain about something. They arrived presently at bed eight, Sister Brown explained who the occupant was, and that he had been admitted after wandering the streets in a confused state. The assemblage then waited for the houseman to say what medical treatment had commenced. The houseman however, had been kept up most of the night with the particularly interesting case on female medical. He'd seen him only briefly in the accident and emergency department, and made the decision to admit him because he hadn't really known what else to do. He realised Mr Pickford was clearly not in a normal state of mind when he insisted that it was the year nineteen-eighteen and wouldn't have it any other way. For his own safety, after liaising with his registrar, it was agreed Mr Pickford should have a comfortable bed for the night and a more thorough investigation made by his senior when he could get to him. Dr Fullerton raised an eyebrow and looked at his registrar for a fuller explanation.

"I'm afraid I was unable to examine him myself as I was, erm, held up elsewhere and unable to get away." Dr Fullerton's registrar paused to clear his throat and then continued. "So, I sent instructions for the man to be admitted for observation and for the nursing staff to note any changes in his condition that they observe, and he would be clerked in as soon as someone was available."

"Sister?" Dr Fullerton waited for what Rose had to say.

"If you would care to look at the chart, it will show that pulse and blood pressure stabilised and are now normal." She thrust the chart under the consultant's nose continuing, "and the night nurses described him as having slept fitfully." The consultant cardiologist glanced at the chart briefly, looked at the offending patient in bed eight, looked at his registrar, and then towards the houseman who was ready to pen indecipherable scrawl in the medical notes from whatever words of wisdom his learned superior was about to dictate.

"Shell shock, refer to psyches," decreed Dr Fullerton, continuing with, "I will write to Dr Alistair, he deals with that sort of condition. Medical students, I would like you all to examine this man at some point and be ever thankful you weren't old enough to go to war." He finally spoke to the man in bed eight, who, completely overwhelmed, thought it best to keep quiet. "Don't you worry, old chap, you're in the right place. We'll get you sorted. Who's next, Sister?"

"Shell shock? I haven't got shell shock; I never went to war. They wouldn't have me, something to do with having a heart murmur, and the fact that I was already over the age limit," Mr Pickford appealed to Rose when she returned to his bedside a little later, Dr Fullerton's ward round having been successfully concluded without the usual difficulties. He'd clearly been eager to get away as soon as possible.

"Perhaps not, but you will need help as you were reported to have been rather disoriented."

"And what is a doodlebug and what do you mean by the Second World War, and what has happened to my mother, and if it isn't the year nineteen-eighteen, could I please be informed of what everyone thinks the year is?"

"Mr Pickford," Rose began gently. She could see how agitated he was, but knew she must tread carefully. "One thing at a time, I think. First, I can help you understand what has happened to you, because I will venture to say that I believe the very same thing happened to my mother." Mr Pickford looked at Sister Brown quizzically.

"Your mother?"

"Yes, my mother. Mr Pickford, do you think that the year is nineteen-eighteen?"

"Well, it certainly was when I got up yesterday morning; read the morning paper and then went out for a walk - first time out since catching influenza. Just a mild dose the doctor said but knocked me for six I can tell you. Couldn't get out of bed for three weeks." He looked Rose up and down. "How have you fared, Sister, has it caught up with you or have you managed to get away with it?" She took a deep breath. Not one for mincing her words, she decided to give it to him straight.

"Mr Pickford, I'm very sad to say my mother died from catching influenza, but that was many years ago." Rose did a quick calculation, she was good at figures, "Thirty-seven to be precise, and the year was nineteen-eighteen, shortly after peace was declared. Mr Pickford, to..." But before she could embark on any further information, she felt the gush of air from the double doors of her ward as they opened yet again, and watched in horror as an assemblage of nurses, doctors, consultants and ancillary staff spilled through. Rose was about to admonish them all for potentially destroying the peace and quiet of her ward, when she realised Matron, who was carrying a huge bunch of flowers, was at their helm. Rose looked back despairingly at her patient saying she would get back to him as soon as she could. She moved towards the centre table and taking hold of the nearest chair back, she gripped onto it tightly. Another interruption, but then wasn't it always so? This time however, it was by Matron, and no one took Matron to task not even the most senior of consultants, and certainly not Sister Rose Brown however she might be feeling inwardly.

It turned out Matron hadn't planned it in quite this way; she had intended to escort Sister Brown to one of the meeting rooms where a small function had been organised in honour of her years of dedication to the hospital. But, like the line in the poem says, 'the best-laid schemes o' mice an' men', things don't always go to plan. Matron Pilkington's statuesque frame had been observed walking along the long corridors of the grand old hospital building. The exquisite floral bouquet she was carrying had sparked the curiosity of others who were also going about their business and making their way along the corridor, and they had asked who the flowers were for. On being told they were for Sister Brown who was retiring today, out of respect the others had delayed their business and followed on behind Matron towards ward five, male medical, Sister Brown's ward. By the time Matron arrived in the vicinity, the group behind her had steadily grown into quite an entourage. Rose swallowed hard before speaking. "Matron, good morning. You appear to have rather a large party with you today."

"Good morning, Sister. Yes, none of my doing I can assure you but then I should have expected something like this, being the occasion that it is.

They want to give you their regards and warm wishes for a happy retirement. Word spread, I'm afraid, when they saw these flowers."

Spontaneous applause erupted from the assemblage. The ward patients, who had got wind of the sister's retirement from the nurses whispering to each other while they had been going about their business during the morning, clapped too. And then someone began to sing 'for she's a jolly good fellow' and of course everyone joined in immediately, and then there was another round of applause.

Rose didn't know quite where to put herself; it was the last thing she would have sought. She'd hoped to leave quietly and without any disturbance or fuss. She liked to do her job well with proficiency and efficiency, and that alone gave her a feeling of satisfaction, outweighing any praise that may be due. However, even she couldn't help but embrace the overwhelming sense of love and gratitude that was coming from everyone and felt quite overcome. She had all but forgotten they were in amongst the sick and the dying, especially as they were also joining in the singing and the applause as best they could. She felt a tear running down her cheek and letting go of her grip on the chair back, reached into the pocket of her uniform for her handkerchief just as Matron presented her with the flowers. Her ward nurses gathered around, one of whom tried to hand her an envelope, but as Rose was now heavily encumbered, placed it on the table in front of her. "We've all written something, Sister. Mine is to thank you for all that you have taught me while I've been on your ward, and how sorry I am that you are leaving, because it won't be the same without you."

"Indeed, it won't Nurse Simpson. But then all good things come to an end. We all, at some stage in our lives, move on towards pastures new. And I am sure that Sister Dawkins, to whom I will be handing over the reins this afternoon, will be more than adequate to carry you forward." Rose smiled affectionately at the young nurse, who, in her estimation, would do well. 'Very conscientious and hard-working,' she had written on her report at the end of her first year of training. Now in her final year, was shaping up splendidly. Rose looked round all her nurses, she was fond of each of them if she had to admit it to herself. "Thank you all for your cards and messages, I will look forward to reading them later. And thank you all for coming," she continued, addressing the crowd hovering at the door, "but I think the ward needs to return to the peace and quiet we all endeavour to adhere to."

"I agree entirely," said Matron and turned towards them to shoo them out with a flick of her wrist and a look that could not be misinterpreted. They dispersed quickly and without fuss, and Rose gave an almost imperceptible sigh of relief. "But my reason for coming to your ward, apart from bringing you these flowers," continued Matron, "was to escort you to the old meeting room for a rather more formal presentation. Nurse Simpson, please would you put them in some water, I'm sure you can spare Sister for half an hour. You may call on Sister Winterburn on ward seven if you need anything urgently. I have already informed her of the situation." Nurse Simpson nodded a 'yes, Matron' and took the blooms into the flower room to put them in some water.

Rose resigned herself to the fact that it was inevitable the occasion of her leaving day would be marked in some way. She had spent her entire career in the same hospital having begun her nurse training there shortly after the end of the Great War and was probably the longest serving nurse in the whole place. When the Matron's post had come up for the taking ten years previously, it was assumed that she would apply, and most likely be successful. However, she had preferred to stay nearer to her patients rather than be involved in what would have amounted to paperwork and meetings ad infinitum. Rose had always been a hands-on nurse and had wanted to stay that way until latterly, with the nursing profession seemingly changing all around her, she understood that she had had her day. It was time to let someone else, someone much younger, take the helm.

Reluctantly, Sister Rose Brown felt obliged to drop what she had been doing - helping Mr Pickford to reorientate - and murmured to him an apologetic; "I'm sorry, I *will* get back to you." She then instructed another of the student nurses to place the written messages she had received on the desk in the sister's office and turned to follow Matron who was already on her way out.

She managed to catch up with her outside the outer ward doors and they hastened along the windowed corridor, which presented uninterrupted views of the central courtyard garden. Rose would usually cast her eyes in that direction when passing. However, Matron's pace was swift, with no time for any dalliance. Sweeping past the chapel and reaching the main corridor, they descended the stunning cast-iron and stone split staircase which led to the main entrance hall. Here the Gothic arches and pillars and Victorian tiled floor never failed to impress. A little way along yet another corridor, they reached a large mahogany door which Matron opened. Inside was a large wood-panelled room and a further crowd of people standing talking to one another.

Rose looked about her, not at the people chattering noisily, but along the walls, where there hung many imposing pictures of the doctors of old. She had viewed them on many occasions but was always gripped by the way those faces looked down upon whoever entered their supposed domain. This was the Great Hall, where many a decision of note had been made. Professor Wilson's portrait always stood out for her, his eyes penetrating her very soul. He had been the bane of her father's life when he had worked there in his formative years as a doctor. Ever keen to bring new ideas to the staid old group of elders, her father would keep abreast of new research and inquiry with the intent to make a difference. However, his suggestions and theories only brought forth ridicule and scorn. Furthermore, he had recognised the need for an isolation ward when the Spanish flu epidemic was descending on the unprepared populace at the end of the Great War. But the 'great' Professor had refused, and precious lives had been lost. Rose shuddered at the memory and pictured in her mind the wonderful portrait of her father, his kindly brown eyes almost leaping out of the picture. It hung not here, but in the entrance of the maternity home that her wonderful mother had founded many years ago. It was there that her father was able, finally, to come into his own.

Matron picked up a handy paperweight and banged it down hard onto the top of the long refectory table, the centrepiece of the room, and brought everyone's attention to call. She then began to deliver a concise summary of Sister Rose Brown's career, the hushed assembly listening intently. Rose was surprised how much Matron knew, she'd forgotten a lot of it herself, and quite enjoyed the trip down memory lane. She was reminded of the time when she, as a young staff nurse, had taken a calculated risk and tackled a fire she'd discovered in the main linen room in the basement, which would have been of far graver consequence had she not done so. By some Divine providence, there'd been several fire buckets close to hand. It was discovered later that the porter had left them on a trolley nearby, while the call of nature had taken him unexpectedly via the back stairs to the nearest convenience. Luckily Rose had been passing; coming in at the little-used basement entrance and leaving her bicycle inside the door out of the way. She had seen the flames licking round a stack of towels heaped on one of the shelves. Fortunately, there'd been enough buckets of sand to extinguish the flames, which would have taken a hold in a matter of minutes. The police suspected an arson attack, but the culprit was never found.

Matron also spoke of the time during the war years, when Sister Brown had given up her ward for a time so it could be used for the casualties of war. She and her medical patients had been rehoused into extremely small quarters; rooms normally assigned to the teaching of student nurses. Beds, bed lockers, bed tables, filing cabinets and treatment area were easy to install, an automatic sluice for the cleaning and disinfecting of bedpans, not so simple. The service lift was nearby, the nurses having to load a trolley full of the used metal receptacles and take them via the lift up to ward two to use their sluice-room facilities. Sister Brown had managed to secure sterilising equipment for the instruments needed for wound care, "otherwise," she had argued, "how on earth do you expect me to keep this God-forsaken make-shift excuse for a ward, to a standard you'd expect?" Rose grinned to herself at the reminder, she'd been livid at the time and had wanted to split her beloved ward in half; fifteen beds for her medical patients, and fifteen for the wounded, but the hospital managers had made their decision and weren't interested in what she had to say. 'A mere woman,' she thought, 'how could she possibly have any plausible input to offer?'

Bringing her speech to a close, Matron began enthusing about the retirement gift they were going to give to "the well-deserving Sister Brown." Rose expected the gift to be a watch, or something to that effect, but couldn't believe her eyes when Matron removed a dust cover from what she had thought to be an item of furniture that had been put aside as surplus to requirement. She gasped in amazement, and so did everyone else, especially when Matron pushed coins into a slot and made her selection. Neon tubes of coloured flowing bubbles that arched over the machine's curving top gave a colourful visual accompaniment to Jimmy Durante's song 'Young at Heart'.

"A jukebox! However did you know?" gulped Rose when the rendition had finished, and everyone had stopped cheering and clapping. Her day was certainly turning out to be very eventful in more ways than one.

"Ah, I have my methods," was all Matron would say.

One might refer to Sister Rose Brown as being the type of woman that may prefer to keep her distance; keep herself to herself, which was fair enough in Matron's book. But Matron was astute and knew everyone had a soft spot, it just needed to be found, and she'd found Sister Rose Brown's purely by chance, but immediately knew it when she saw it. Almost a year ago, she'd been sitting in a café with Sister Brownette from ward two, female medical, drinking coffee and listening to the sounds blaring out of the jukebox in the corner at the back. They'd done their nurse training together, more years ago than either of them would care to remember, where a solid bond had been formed between them. At present, they were on a mission to find the best coffee shop in town. This café, they had agreed, was nowhere near the top of the list. Nevertheless, they'd got chatting to Old Burt, the proprietor, after asking him if he would mind turning down the music so they could hear each other speak. Afterall, they were the only ones in the place at that moment. Rather taken with the two attractive women who were much nearer to his own age than his usual clientele, especially the one wearing red lipstick, he obliged them at once and, learning that they were both in the nursing profession, asked them if they knew a certain Sister Brown, who worked at The Royal.

"Why yes of course," exclaimed the one with the red lipstick. Matron, who while not on duty, would discard the persona as quickly as she did her uniform when stuffing it into the wash bag for the hospital laundry to take care of. She was known when in mufti as Paula Pilkington. "Why do you ask?" Any snippets of information were gladly taken. Paula Pilkington liked a bit of gossip, though she always kept it to herself. She raised her Player's cigarette to her 'Coral by Max Factor' lips, and took a long drag, as if sucking in the information she was about to hear. She then lay back in her chair, making herself comfortable, and exhaled.

Old Burt continued, "She came in here once saying she was attracted by the jukebox. When I told her what make it was, her eyes lit up and she wanted to know all about it; how to get one, how much it cost, and the like. She said she'd been instructed by her mother, in no uncertain terms apparently, to procure one, but so far, her quest had been thwarted. Regrettably, I believe it was again, when I told her the price of the thing, that is."

"Whatever would her mother want with one?" asked Paula.

"That's exactly what I asked her myself, but she answered that she had no idea, but her mother had been explicit that she acquire such a thing for her father as some sort of sign."

Paula sat forward, crossing her legs as she did so. "A sign? How intriguing," she replied, her interest well and truly sparked.

Observing the flash of leg from his extremely alluring customer as discreetly as he was able, the proprietor was in his stride; he enjoyed a little tittle-tattle when he could afford the time. "And not only that, but her mother had also given her a list of forty-fives which were to be placed inside, and the exact order they had to go in."

"How extraordinary, she must be a thoroughly modern old lady wanting to keep up with the youngsters and their rock and roll, I have to say, it's all a bit brash for my taste."

"Not a bit of it; her mother is dead!"

"Well, doesn't the plot get thicker!" surmised Paula. "An old woman instructs her daughter, who is well past her jiving days, if indeed she ever had any, to get a jukebox and to load it with musical compositions placed in a certain order as some sort of, what, some form of gesture, or..."

"And," interrupted Old Burt, "the type of jukebox was specific too. The same as this one, the Wurlitzer 1015, otherwise known as the Bubbler. As I was saying, Sister Brown said she had noticed it through the window as she was walking by and thought to ask the make. But like I said, when she heard how much they are to buy, she looked decidedly deflated I can tell you, and went on to say it was a little too much for her pocket at the moment and that the purchase would have to wait. Anyway, excuse me." Old Burt bowed his head to the two women and moved back behind his counter ready to take the order from a group of youths who were trooping in.

'So,' thought Paula, stubbing out her cigarette as it was time they moved on, 'our reserved and unassuming Sister Brown is rather keen to own a jukebox known as the Bubbler.'

And that thought grew into an idea, when Paula Pilkington learned of Sister Rose Brown's decision to retire after her next birthday. She was confident there must be one somewhere going cheap, and continually bore this in mind when thinking about a retirement present; she liked anything unusual; the usual watch or similar was, to her mind, extremely boring and staid.

Then one day, Paula Pilkington got lucky. She unearthed one quite by chance when taking a wrong turning and finding herself down a back street behind a row of shops. Rather than turn around, she chose to walk down its length and pick up the main street at the other end. The place was desolate and decidedly unattractive; overfull dustbins spilling their detritus into the road, tall graffitied brick walls concealing the back yards of the buildings and dog dirt everywhere. Paula picked her way carefully through it thinking she had made the wrong decision when, through an open gate she was just in time to see a man throw a cover over, what she thought, what she hoped to be... a jukebox. She immediately hailed the man and enquired as to its make. It was the correct model, a Bubbler! Paula was delighted but played it cool. She asked nonchalantly if it was broken and was he throwing it out and might he be interested in her taking it away for him. The man sniffed in hard, and with a look of exasperation explained that no, it worked fine. However, because it only took American money, he was fed up with swapping English money for American, so his clientele could play it. More to the point, they continually lost the American coins, and he would run out of them, and so the "blessed machine" couldn't play anything which was losing him business. He had ordered a more modern version and it was being installed as they spoke, and "yes," she was "welcome to the bugger," for a modest sum of course.

So, Paula Pilkington, Matron of The Royal, had acquired the best possible retirement present that Sister Rose Brown would ever imagine she'd receive, and she had been keen to reveal it, hoping against hope that she'd made the right decision. Seeing Sister Brown almost in tears when she removed the cloth, she knew she had.

"Thank you, Matron, thank you everybody. You don't know how much this means to me. It's the best retirement gift I could have wished for, and I can't thank you all enough. How did you know?" Rose asked again, shaking her head in utter disbelief.

"However *did* you guess?" she repeated to Matron when the formalities were over, and everyone had drunk a toast. "No one knew; it's impossible; I am absolutely stunned."

"Well, that's for me to know," replied Matron, and tapped her nose with her forefinger. "All I can say is I hope you enjoy playing it. You will need to have some American nickels and dimes as that's all it takes, but apart from that, it just needs filling up with little black discs."

"Well, how you knew shall remain a mystery then, until I find out of course! Meanwhile I shall enjoy seeking out and listening to the little black discs as you call them, and I was forewarned about the nickels and dimes, so everything is as it should be. Again, I cannot thank you enough."

Saying goodbye and thanking everyone for coming seemed to take forever, but eventually the party dwindled as everyone needed to get back to work. At last! Rose could make her way back to her ward, for she had been away far too long. Matron had already left, but not before informing Rose that arrangements had been made for her to have the jukebox installed in her home the very next day if she wished. They agreed on a suitable time, and then Matron had excused herself.

Rose arrived at the double doors of her ward at the same time as Sister Dawkins. "Ah, Sister, is it that time already? I don't feel as though I've anything prepared for you. My time has been taken up unexpectedly, I give you my apologies."

"Sister Brown, no need for apologies, I've come early; first day, new post and all that. I know the ward well enough though."

Sister Dawkins had overseen it and the other wards in this wing of the hospital for the last three years as night Sister. She had also worked as Rose's senior charge nurse before that. "Please, you first." Sister Dawkins opened the door and waited for her senior to go in. On entering, Rose quickly cast her eyes around. She would know at once if there was anything amiss, she could almost smell it, coming from years of experience. All seemed well, and they both, rather than sitting in the office, took places at the small desk in the middle of the ward, the retiring sister giving the new sister a quick summary of any new developments in the patients' treatment plans.

Rose had been delighted that her former charge nurse was to take the reins of her beloved ward. She was kind, efficient, and very good at handling the senior doctors' humours and idiosyncratic behaviours - something she herself had taken years to accomplish. As Sister Dawkins knew the ward so well, Rose had no new directives to give her, meaning she could introduce her to the patients as the new sister and let her take over immediately. Thus, Rose was left essentially to do as she pleased, which she realised was a strange concept having never been in that situation before. She started by resuming her conversation with the patient in bed eight; asking Sister Dawkins' permission to do so first.

Chapter Twelve

It was the last thing Rose Brown had expected to do on the first day of her retirement, but it had to be done. Before she finished her final shift the day before, Rose had gleaned that Mr Pickford had a sister living but half a mile away from him. Mrs Clifton, Molly, was her name. Rose, duty-bound, set off the very next morning to an address he'd given her, hoping for the best outcome; that she was still alive, and still living there. She was cautious about it though. Telling someone their long-lost brother was alive and well after thirty-seven years was all well and good. Saying he didn't look a day older than the last time they had seen him would be the tricky bit. She thought it would be best not to mention it initially. That is, if Rose found who she was looking for. Afterall, she could easily be dead and gone after all this time. And if Mr Pickford's sister wasn't where he said she was, where could he go? He would never cope with today's world by himself and, having nowhere to live, would most likely end up on the streets. Rose couldn't have that on her conscience. She was determined to sort something out if it came to it.

The street was much the same as any other in that area; Victorian terraces with tiny gardens to the front, and a yard at the back that included an outside privy. It wasn't that far from where Rose lived, but in the opposite direction to where Mr Pickford had resided with his mother. Number twenty-four was as unremarkable as the others. The time-worn faded green paint was the only difference amidst the predominance of black front doors. Rose breathed in deeply, being perfectly practiced in concealing any personal perplexity. Then slowly and with great deliberation, she stepped through its small gate and up the short path and to the door. Her arm reached out and her hand took a firm grip of the doorknocker. With an interval of one second in between each, she struck it three times onto its plate, stood back and waited. Very soon she heard someone approach and fiddle with the lock. The door opened. A small and sprightly woman of mature age was revealed behind it and an inquiring look upon her lined face.

"Good morning," said Rose. "Forgive me for disturbing you but may I ask if your name is Mrs Clifton?"

"Er, yes?" The reply was inquisitive in nature, but at the same time apprehensive.

"Sorry, I should have introduced myself. I am a nursing sister, or rather," Rose corrected herself, "I *was* a nursing sister at the Royal until yesterday; I have just retired. My name is Miss Brown, Rose Brown, and I have something to tell you that I feel you would rather hear whilst you are seated."

"Oh well, in that case, you'd better come in then," the lady replied and opened the door more fully in order to let Rose into her home. Normally, she would never let someone she didn't know inside her house but sensed that this particular stranger standing at her front door in such a beseeching manner, was genuine, and was going to give her very important information. Besides, her husband was inside, so she wasn't alone. Rose was led into a narrow hall, as wide as the steep set of stairs at the end of it, and into the first of two doors, the front room. There was a tiled fireplace, but the hearth was empty. She hadn't been expecting visitors, the woman explained, by way of apology. Rose had replied that she rarely lit a fire in her front room during the day either, and anyway, it wasn't too cold today. She took the chair she was offered, and Mrs Clifton sat on the settee opposite, while her husband, Harold, who had been summoned to join them, sat next to her.

Mrs Molly Clifton, along with Harold, listened attentively to the news that she had given up hope of hearing years ago, that her brother was not only alive, but safe and well. He was currently resting in hospital but waiting to be claimed so that he could be discharged securely, as he had nowhere to go. The poor woman was in a daze, the information, although wonderful to hear after so many long and empty years, had come completely out of the blue. She took a gasp of air, and pressed both of her hands tightly to her chest as Rose gave her the good tidings. At length, when she had overcome the initial shock, she managed to say something. "Where on earth has he been in all this time? Why didn't he contact us?

"I'm afraid he wasn't able to, you see..." Rose continued falteringly, she was recollecting the conversation she had had with Mrs Clifton's long-lost brother. "… something rather strange happened to him." She wasn't sure how to proceed.

"Mr Pickford," Rose began, after handing the ward over to Sister Dawkins, "please take your time to digest what I'm about to say, it will probably be very difficult for you to take in at the moment, but I will try and help you as much as I can." Arthur Pickford said nothing but nodded in response. "I'm afraid there is neither rule nor formula to explain what I am about to tell you, so I shall just come to the point and say it how it is. I believe you've somehow slipped through a distortion of time into what would be the future for you but has now become your present. In other words, you have moved forward in time by thirty-seven years, and as a result, ended up in a confused state, as your body has not adjusted to what it has undergone. If you can think rationally and retrace your steps, I think I will be able to help you work out where and how it happened."

Mr Pickford stared wide-eyed at Rose, as if looking past her at something else. He held his slight and wiry frame in a rigid sitting position, clinging on to the bed sheets with clenched and whitened knuckles. Then, very quickly, his grip lessened, his taut shoulders relaxed, and his expression changed. He was smiling, laughing almost. Rose imagined he must be losing his mind and thought to get the houseman to prescribe a sedative. She got ready to move, but then wavered after his ensuing response, for on hearing what he had to say, finding a doctor would not be an appropriate plan of action.

"I've done it, I've done it, at last I've done it!" Mr Arthur Pickford laid back on the bed, exhilarated. He began to look intently at her, really look, peering with eyes now half closed. He was recognising her, she could tell. Maybe his state of confusion wasn't as bad as she'd first thought but she was still rather curious why he seemed so happy on hearing her explanation.

"Might you be the daughter of Doctor Brown living at the big house in Greenhead Road?" he asked.

He *had* recognised her, even after all these years, she surely must have changed from a young, naive seventeen-year-old girl to a rapidly ageing spinster. However, what he said next made her aware that it was what she'd said earlier, rather than how she looked, that had caused Mr Pickford to recognise who she was. "Yes, I know what happened to your mother, I knew her, dare I say it, rather more than she knew me. I followed her often, although I tried to be discreet. I needed to find the way, you see, and she was the key."

Rose was barely able to stand up. His revelations were not only quite shocking but were opening old wounds that she'd locked away a long, long time ago. As she had already disclosed, she'd lost her mother very suddenly and unexpectedly just as peace had been declared at the end of the Great War. Her mother had gone from being healthy and well, to dying in a matter of hours. She'd been a victim of the Spanish flu that had been wreaking havoc. For the second time in her then young life, Rose Brown had been grief-stricken, for she'd already lost her sweetheart. She had handled it by throwing herself into a life of nursing, hoping she might save the lives of others; even though she hadn't been able to save her mother's or that of her beloved Francis, who had never returned from the Somme.

Mr Walkpast had been following her mother. No wonder she was always noticing him, he'd been stalking her! Shivers went down her body; she was feeling repulsed, and she had to get away. "Please, don't go." Arthur Pickford was trying to stop her and grabbed her arm, "I have so much to tell you. I didn't mean to scare you, please stay."

Rose sat back on the chair, she must remain rational, this was not the time for personal feelings to get in the way and maybe there was a reason why he would do such a thing. Perhaps she'd been too hasty and hadn't understood fully. Her judgement of him was prejudicial and undeserved; she had to give him the courtesy of a fuller explanation, and after all, he wasn't quite himself and seemed like a nice man. She put her feelings aside and let her compassion take over to try and help her patient for despite everything, that was what he was. He would need to ask so many questions about the years he had, to all intents and purposes, lost.

"Thank you," said Mr Pickford as she sat back down. "Forgive me for sounding as though I was some sort of bogey man, but it wasn't like that at all. What I should have said is that I believe I witnessed the way your mother arrived here and spent years trying to study how and why this could have occurred. I learned that it had something to do with the vibrational field around the stone circles in the park, but more of that later. Please, tell me about the time now, I feel so at sea about what is going on. I feel rather dizzy."

"As of course you would be, having bypassed all of those years," agreed Rose sympathetically. "During that time the world has changed completely, we've seen another war, and it will take time for you to adjust. My mother found it hard to cope, indeed, I'm sure anyone would."

"Yes, as I've already asked you... there's been another war? For goodness' sake, did we not learn anything?"

"I'm afraid not."

"With Germany?"

"Yes, I'm afraid so."

"Please tell me we won," he said tentatively.

"Of course we won, what would you have expected? But it wasn't pretty, no war is, however I'm sure you can learn all about it later. But right now, we need to think of practicalities. Oh, and it might be wise not to mention what happened to you. I don't think people would understand and it may lead them into thinking you are a little unhinged."

He tittered with hilarity. "There's no chance of me saying anything that others may deem unearthly, I've spent a lifetime keeping things to myself about all that, but I hope I will be able to discuss it with you."

"Yes, I hope so too, especially about what you know about my mother. Meanwhile, you need time to get your bearings, and when discharged, somewhere to stay. Do you have relatives?"

"Unless my mother is still alive who I live with, I mean lived with, then it would just be my sister."

Rose thought hard; she tried to remember what she could about number twenty-three Dudley Road, for it wasn't far from where she lived... yes, an old lady had lived there. It was reputed that she'd gone out of her mind, waiting for her son to return home. It was assumed by everyone, that her son must have been killed in the Great War, but she couldn't accept it, and for years, just sat and waited for him to reappear. Only now, Rose was realising the truth of it; her son had simply vanished. No wonder she had never come to terms with it; she would always hope that he would come home someday. What Rose couldn't remember, or perhaps never knew, was what had happened to the old lady. "I'm afraid I don't know about your mother. What year was she born?"

"She would never tell me; I had no idea how old she was. My birth was in eighteen seventy I believe, although Mother would always gloss over that too! She didn't like birthdays seemingly."

"So, say she was in her twenties, it's nineteen fifty-five now, so if she's still with us, she's going to be over one hundred years old."

"Mmm, yes of course, she would be. Never thought of that sort of consequence, she must have been lost without me. Oh dear, I appear to have been a rather errant son." Arthur Pickford appeared somewhat crestfallen with the news and sat quietly among his own thoughts.

When Rose believed it to be the right time, she interrupted his reverie. "You say consequence as if what has happened to you was with intent; surely this has come about by accident? Certainly, my mother never intended it, although she came to accept her fate and all that came with it. She stepped into her new life and gave it purpose."

"I never knew where your mother had come from and that she'd come through time, just that she'd appeared in front of me. By all accounts, she claimed she'd lost her memory, and yes, she certainly did give her life a purpose. She orchestrated the birth of a maternity hospital; a truly great innovation; and a woman at that! My mother thought she'd done the local women proud, but I say she'd done far more than that." Arthur paused a moment. "But you see, there's the conundrum. For me, it was more by design than accident! I have wanted this, or rather wished to know what would happen and where I would go. To prove it possible I suppose. I'd always felt it was a case of being in the right position at the right time, and that took me years to work out, and even then, I was never certain."

Rose couldn't make any sense out of what her Mr Walkpast, or rather Mr Pickford (she must try and remember to think of his rightful name), was saying about wishing this upon himself and put it down to his confusion. Meanwhile, she wanted to deal with more pressing matters. He needed a place to live when he was discharged, for there would be no reason to keep him after he had been reviewed by Dr Alistair, she was sure of that. "You said you had a sister?" she asked.

"Yes; Molly."

"And where does Molly live?"

"Don't tell me he actually succeeded," exclaimed Molly. She leapt off the settee with her hands still pressed flat on her chest as if she were attempting to hold something in.

Rose regarded Mrs Molly Clifton closely. She was lithe and lean despite her years, just like her brother, and her stance was similar; head leading as she moved forward. Mr Arthur Pickford, alias Mr Walkpast, had made himself noticed to Rose and her family all those years ago, because of the way he walked! Head bowed, almost running; his sister was doing the same! But that was that as far as likeness was concerned. Even though his age had been held in suspension for the last thirty-seven years and he'd not yet gone through the ravages of time like his sister, their faces were still so very different.

It was an interest of Rose to see the similitude in families and she was disappointed not to detect much of a familial resemblance between sister and brother. She supposed the fascination had come from the fact that she'd never met her real father. She had had one stepbrother, George: tall, fine-looking but extremely hot-headed. He'd taken after his father in both looks and temperament and was completely different to herself. Rose, although very much like her mother, especially her rather prominent chin, had always wondered if she'd taken any qualities from *him*; that elusive man whom, so her mother had said, she would recognise when she saw him.

Mrs Clifton looked at Rose straight in her eye, almost accusingly. "Well, did he?" she asked, but then sat back down in a state of collapse and started to cry. "I'm so sorry, I didn't mean to. It's not your fault, it's just, after all these years of not knowing - it's been very hard."

Rose pulled a handkerchief out of her handbag and passed it across and waited while Mrs Clifton composed herself before asking what she meant by 'succeeding.'

"Oh, I knew what he was up to, always around those stones," Molly continued falteringly. "You know, the ones in the park, mapping out the magnetic fields or whatever it is that he can feel. Ever since he was a boy, he's been like it, it's all I've ever known about him. It's because of what he says he saw. He told me about it once, in confidence; he didn't want anyone else to know, but I'd kept pestering him to tell me. I think I threatened him by saying I would tell our mother he was swinging that pendulum of his around the stone circles all the time and not minding me like he was supposed to be doing. So, he told me. He said he once saw a baby vanish from a doorway just over the road from them there stones and right before his eyes. He said that he believed they had some sort of power over the atmosphere and had made that poor baby disappear. I always thought it was a load of rubbish until he showed me a newspaper report at the library with the story of her sudden disappearance. It was put down to a kidnapping, but Arthur said he knew better. I began to believe there might be something in it when he showed me how you could feel a kind of propulsion or pulling from something as simple as holding a bobbin on the end of a bit of string. I could see its swings changing when he moved from one area to another. He claimed that when the conditions were right, the circles would send out a pulse into the air in their near vicinity and cause strange atmospheric alterations and sometimes push something through into somewhere else. Like the baby." She paused for breath and wiped her eyes with Rose's handkerchief. She'd never spoken of this to anyone, except her husband, but he'd dismissed it as absolute nonsense

Rose sat quietly, drinking in this information, hardly believing it to be true. Yet she knew it was a corroboration of what her mother had told her, and she hung onto everything Mrs Clifton was saying, hungry for more. "Did your brother tell of any other things that he saw?"

"Oh yes!" she continued animatedly. It was a relief that someone was interested in what she had to say. "He'd worked out that when the century was going to turn - goodness! it's all so long ago now - the conditions would be right for another shift. So instead of going out revelling on such an occasion like the rest of us - mind you, he wasn't ever one for that - he was skulking around in the park, waiting. What for, he didn't know, but he said something did."

"And what was that?" Rose asked. She could hardly contain herself, knowing already what Mrs Molly Clifton was going to say.

"He said a woman appeared out of nowhere. I know it sounds incredible, but it happened all the same. He said one minute she wasn't there, and then after a coach and horses had gone by, she *was* there. He said there was a lot of mist and he couldn't see clearly but she was coming and going so to speak. And after the mist went away, she stayed. Anyway after that he knew there was some sort of entryway from another place. So, as well as keeping an eye on the woman to see if he could glean any information about it all, he became determined to do it for himself. To disappear I mean."

She stood up and brushed her hands down her pinafore continuing, "I'm sure I don't know why I'm telling you all this, you must think me fit for the nut house. It must be the shock of your information. Is my brother all right? I should have asked straight away, but part of me is so cross with him for going away and with no explanation as to why. What has he been doing with himself after all this time? Oh!" She stopped talking. It dawned on her then, after she said the word 'time'. The answer to her next question would be the proof of it all and she didn't know if she was ready to know. "He did succeed didn't he? I was half joking before. Oh golly gosh I daren't ask. W-what sort of age is he?" she asked, her voice faltering and unsteady.

"He looks no older than he did in nineteen eighteen, I can assure you," replied Rose. She got up out of the chair, went over to Mrs Clifton who had been stepping backwards and forwards across the room, with the purpose to calm her. However, the information had made poor Molly Clifton crumble, and for the second time, she sat back down in a heap of disarray. Rose thought it best to stay quiet and give her the space to take it all in. She sat herself down once again.

At length, Molly Clifton spoke, panting as she did so. "I thought maybe what he said, you know, if it was all really true, he'd maybe been shifted to another part of the world and couldn't get back. But then I couldn't stop wondering that if I could believe that, then anything might be possible; and it hit me. Maybe he couldn't come home because he'd gone to another time rather than another place. I was right. It's correct isn't it? It's all real, all of it! He was right too. I should never have doubted him. Goodness me. Oh dear, oh golly gosh."

"Well in your defence, it all sounds very outlandish," proffered Rose.

Molly stood up again and resumed pacing about the room, unable to stay still. Her mind was in turmoil and her movements reflected that. Rose understood and once again, let her be. A few moments elapsed before she was able to give voice to her disquiet. "I went along, you know, with all his ideas for his sake; he was very convincing. But the idea of jumping through the ethers into somewhere else, well really! And then when he went missing, and he had told me what his intentions were, I wondered if he'd been right after all. Only I'm a rational person and decided on a more logical explanation. Even now, when you said he'd turned up, I assumed he would be old like me and had done something daft like running away. I've been so cross with him all this time." She sat back down and glanced across at Rose unsure about her next words but said them anyway, albeit hesitantly. "You know between you and me, even though he was too old, he was ashamed that he didn't go and fight. He felt guilty at not doing his duty. But then when the war was over and he saw the state of our fighters, I think he felt relief that he hadn't. All those poor men, boys really, came home steeped in emptiness and sorrow. Well, you know how it was. And then there was another one to ruin the next generation. When will we ever learn?" After the rhetorical question, which echoed her brother's response after learning of the Second World War, she was contemplative, but then broke into giggles. "Hehe, as if jumping through time isn't daft enough. Oh dear, listen to me; I'm a gibbering wreck."

Harold Clifton had so far remained quiet but chose this time to speak up. "Molly, whatever has happened to your Arthur; you must go and see him. You need to hear the facts from him, but as far as I'm concerned he has an awful lot of explaining to do."

"Yes, I agree," Rose returned. "However, your brother will need a lot of tender loving care even though you may be angry with him, which I can understand. You must have had years of torment after he disappeared. But think of him for a minute. He has lost all those years that we have lived through, and for him it was only yesterday. He's going to have to educate himself about them so he can orient into the here and now. Also, the precipitous way by which he arrived in this present time may have injured his body or mind, so he will need time to recuperate in more ways than one."

"Yes," sighed Molly, "I expect he will. In the meantime he has a lot to answer for. Just wait till I see him; I'll give him what for, I can tell you."

"I expect you shall, but please go easy on him if you can," beseeched Rose. "Meanwhile, I'll telephone the ward and let them know his relatives will take care of everything when the doctors feel he is ready to be discharged, and get back to you." She got up to leave. Mrs. Clifton had had an enormous shock, albeit a pleasant one and she would need time alone with her husband so they might take it all in and prepare for Arthur Pickford's re-emergence accordingly.

Rose returned home to await the appearance of the jukebox. It duly arrived at the agreed time and was placed in the hall. She patted it with delight. It was what her mother had wanted, and Rose thought again how lucky she was to have been given it. Meanwhile, there were other things afoot. She still needed to speak to Sister Dawkins and so resignedly drew away from the jukebox and headed for the telephone. Her jukebox would have to wait - the first day of her retirement was certainly full!

Sister Dawkins had wasted no time in getting help for Mr Pickford. She knew only too well that if she waited for the medical team to get organised another bed would remain blocked without reason. She had seen Dr Fullerton's secretary in person to make sure he had dictated the letter of referral and signed it. She had then hand delivered it to Dr Alistair's secretary with the instruction that she must "stuff it under Dr Alistair's nose" as soon as he was back in his office. Sister Dawkins then rang switchboard to put her straight through to Dr Alistair. She asked him to come and see the referred patient as soon as possible, saying he would need to be transferred across to the psychiatric ward immediately as the medical ward that he was currently on would be highly inappropriate. She knew Dr Alistair wouldn't want another valuable bed on his ward filled with someone who quite clearly didn't need to be there. He would more than likely, she hoped, take one look at Arthur Pickford and hand him back to Dr Fullerton, who would then discharge him. Despite a benign heart murmur (which one of the medical students heard when Arthur had told him to listen for it) they would find nothing to detain Mr Pickford any longer. Dr

Alistair, as expected, had pronounced him fit and well, not suffering from shell shock, and, under his breath, making vague intimations of Dr Fullerton having wasted his time.

By late afternoon, all had been arranged. Arthur Pickford had been assessed by Dr Fullerton's registrar as fit enough after suffering some form of anxiety attack and to see his own doctor if it recurred. Naturally, Rose hadn't given Sister Dawkins the full story; just that the family had lost contact after the war. Neither did she mention which war! There were no formal visiting hours till Friday but Sister Dawkins had waived the rules. It appeared obvious to her that Mr Pickford must be reunited with his estranged family as soon as possible to help speed his recovery and discharge from hospital. She would argue it out with Matron later; that is, if she ever found out.

Rose was to be found retracing her steps and knocking on the door of number twenty-four Regent Grove for the second time that day and waiting for it to open. This time it was to tell its occupants that not only could they go and see Arthur, he was also to be discharged from hospital very soon. Molly and Harold got their coats immediately and, along with Rose, caught the bus into town - Molly didn't think she was up to walking all that way. At the hospital Rose guided her charges to the ward and Arthur's bedside but then left them to it. At first, the reunion was an emotional and tearful one for Molly and she held her brother close to her bosom. Arthur was bemused. He had only seen Molly, as far as he was concerned, a few days previously when he had escorted their mother over for tea. However, he was visibly shocked to see how his beloved little sister had aged since then. Molly's tears nonetheless were soon mixed with her wrath. 'How dare he do such a thing, what was he thinking? We spent years waiting for news; our poor mother went to her grave not knowing what had become of him.'

Something deep within had driven him to pursue his dream of achieving the inconceivable - slipping into somewhere other. He knew it was possible. He'd witnessed the baby disappearing and then the woman's arrival. He had to experience it for himself though. That would be the ultimate proof, travelling through time had been an unexpected bonus. Yet Arthur had never stopped to consider what effects he might inflict on those he would leave behind and now he'd lost all those years in between. He was learning that for every action there is an equal and opposite reaction. It had been such a shock for him to hear his mother was dead. She'd died many years ago, but for Arthur it was only yesterday when he'd last seen her. Arthur's remorse was unexpectedly sudden and distressingly painful and on top of that, he needed to mourn.

Molly's anger abated; she could see her brother's distress. He wept quietly, discovering how his mother had behaved after he'd gone. She'd never given up hope of his return always telling people he would walk back through the door one day. But people had only looked at her with pity in their eyes. Over time, Molly managed to persuade their mother to come live with her; she was becoming more and more forgetful and unable to manage. Mercifully she had done so, for only a few weeks later the house had been blown to smithereens. Her waiting for Arthur's return continued; imagining he would be home now the Second World War was over. When he still didn't arrive, as a frail woman well into her nineties, all her hope seemed to vanish and she simply faded away.

Rose had arranged with Sister Dawkins to pick up a few belongings that she had to leave in the office the day before; the flowers had taken most of her carrying capacity. A note saying 'please leave for Sister Brown' that she'd written lay on the top of the pile. Today though, she was simply Miss Brown. The note was an ominous reminder that her life was to change. But she would have to get used to that, she supposed. She sat down at the desk and fingered through the cards and messages the nurses had given her with a mind to open them, but she was distracted. It was the end of an era. No more would she see these walls and all that had occurred within. However, she had made her decision to retire, so that was that. Rose cleared her throat and stood up. She placed the messages carefully inside a bag (she would read them later), and went into the main ward to look for Sister Dawkins. She was at bed eight with Mr Pickford and his family.

"Ah, Sister Brown, I was about to come and find you," said the new ward sister. Mr and Mrs Clifton are about to leave and they wanted to tell you of the arrangements. I'll leave you all to it!"

"Thank you Sister, but I rather imagine my title to be Miss now," replied Rose.

"Oh dear, I don't think I could ever call you anything other than Sister," she replied, trying to stifle her giggles that had come from embarrassment. She had always looked up to her senior and mentor, and the thought of calling her Miss seemed somehow like a slight. Rose gave a short nod of the head and turned her attention towards the Cliftons.

"Sister says Arthur can come home," declared a rather vexed Harold Clifton. "But we've asked if he could stay another night. We haven't... we weren't..." he looked over at his wife, "expecting all this. Were we, love? We need time to get a room ready for him."

"And don't look like that Arthur," said Molly. "Of course you're coming home with us. Where else would you go? At least until we can get everything sorted. Isn't that right Harold?" She looked for approval from her husband.

"Yes, of course love. Of course," he agreed. A bit of male company would be welcome from his point of view, for a while anyway.

"That's settled then." The couple stood up as one, and made to leave, saying they would return in the morning at ten o'clock to take Arthur home. Rose bid them farewell but said, if they agreed, she would also be there for his discharge to ensure it all went smoothly. Both Molly and Harold said that would be very helpful and how grateful they were for her assistance. When they had disappeared through the ward doors, Rose turned to Arthur Pickford and asked if she might visit him in a few days once he was settled into his new home. They both agreed that there was a lot to talk about. Their paths had crossed, and they both knew why.

Chapter Thirteen

Meanwhile Rose had been busy. There was much to sort out from her nursing years. Correspondence, certificates, letters of thanks from grateful patients and their families, and miscellaneous papery items made quite a pile. Seeing no need for all the paraphernalia, Rose thought to throw most of it away - or rather save it to fuel the coal fires when she had a mind to light one or two of them. The only things she wished to keep was a certificate to say she was a registered nurse, her nursing badges awarded by the hospital and the General Nursing Council when she first qualified, and the written messages that the nurses had given to her on the day of her retirement. She packed them away in a small box along with her silver belt buckle, a gift from her father on qualifying, and placed them on a shelf in the library. A lid had closed on a large part of her life and she had nostalgia enough for the past without holding on to more. Rose knew well enough that the old had to be cleared for any new beginnings to appear, and Rose anticipated there would be plenty of those.

Today was one. She was to step into new territories by meeting with Mr Pickford and hopefully learn more about what had happened to her mother after she arrived in nineteen hundred. There was a chill to the morning, it was the first time in the season that Rose had put on her heavier navy-coloured coat along with her pale green headscarf. She looked up at the sky. The usual September warmth of late summer wasn't in evidence, the clouds were gathering, and the wind was getting up. Well-prepared for the fresher air, she stepped forward purposefully, a result of years of marching up and down the hospital's Nightingale wards, and arrived speedily at the Clifton household a few streets away. Mr Pickford, or Arthur, as he insisted Rose call him, was waiting for her. She was ushered into the front room just as it was starting to rain. She saw immediately that he was looking less distracted and more at ease and remarked on it. "A good sign that you are getting used to everything."

"I've been out and into town with Molly and I'm relieved to see the buildings are the same, though the shops therein have changed. But the traffic; it's so busy. So many cars and with no sign of a cart or horse. And those stop and go light thingamajigs and black and white stripes on the roads, what's that all about? Molly tried to explain to me, but there's so much to take in. Still, the park is still the park, thank goodness, and the standing stones; well, they've always been there..." He tailed off, but Rose wanted to keep him talking.

"Tell me about yourself Mr Pickford, Arthur, I would love to hear about the old days, and it is still so recent for you. What can you tell me about my mother?"

Arthur Pickford began to tell of when he first saw Rose's mother. She had appeared suddenly in a cloud of mist, and Rose's father had picked her up and taken her to his home and looked after her. Then later, he'd seen her out in the park with Miss Victoria, Dr Brown's sister (or should he say Mrs Jason Bartram, who she became subsequently) on a few occasions. He'd also seen the announcement in the paper of her marriage to Rose's father. Arthur Pickford, maybe a little injudiciously, then remarked how surprised he'd been as so little time had passed, but then read the announcement of a baby daughter and wondered if that had been the reason for the hasty nuptials. He'd wanted to talk to Rose's mother about what he knew, but could never drum up the courage. "After all, one couldn't just walk up to a relative stranger and ask how they'd appeared out of nowhere." So, he began to follow her in the hope that there would be an appropriate circumstance where he could broach the subject. "But of course, there never was," he stated dejectedly. "I still don't know where she'd come from."

"Ah! but I do," Rose said gently. "She told me. I'd discovered some letters you see, behind a draw in her dressing table that she'd written but never sent, to a man who was unknown to me. I realised that the man she was writing to was my father, my real father."

Rose's world had fallen apart on that day. Who she thought was her father apparently was not, and her mother was clearly in love with someone else, and the young innocent fourteen-year-old Rose didn't know who she was any more. She shouldn't have read them, but she had been curious as to why they were concealed and was now in desperate need to be consoled. Speaking to her mother was out of the question under the circumstances – the letters had been hidden! Obviously, Rose couldn't tell her father. It was perfectly clear from the letters he didn't know he wasn't Rose's real father and therefore was the last person to speak to. But she had to talk to someone about what she'd found, so her grandmother had become her confidante

Very soon after, Rose's mother had been summoned to Tiplin Hall, the family home of Lord and Lady Peters, Rose's grandparents. Rose assumed it was because of what she'd written in her letter. She assumed correctly, for when her mother returned from Tiplin, she proceeded to tell Rose everything. And what a story! Through the years the tale, be it truth or fabrication, had gone round and around inside Rose's head, she didn't know what to think as it was too incomprehensible to imagine. Rose's mother had told her she hadn't sent the letters as it was impossible to do so under the circumstances. She explained to Rose as best she could, that she had come from the future, and that the future was where he, Rose's father was!"

Still, so much of what her mother had said to her about future events had been correct. She'd told Rose of many world events including the outcome of the Great War before it had ended, and that there would be another war only twenty odd years later. Even more than that, she said she thought she'd already met Mr Walkpast when she was living in the future, and although elderly, he didn't look as old as he ought. Her mother had wondered if perhaps it was his son, but then remembered how he'd reacted when he'd bumped into her and knew it must have been him. Years had gone by before Estelle, Rose's mother (her name being given to her by her husband, Dr Brown) had deduced that he'd surely gone through time too, so she wasn't the only one.

As a girl, Rose had found her mother's stories intriguing, and if they were true, then the adult world was surely a magical place. It had helped to reduce the impact of the shock she received when she first found out about having another father. It was only as an adult however, that Rose began to understand what her mother must have gone through. If she really *had* moved backwards from the year two thousand to nineteen hundred, she would have been in a terrible state. Indeed, Estelle had told her how confused and scared she was. Rose had never forgotten the conversation, and she recalled it now...

"I need to tell you about something that happened to me a long time ago, but it involves you and it is time for you to know. Oh Rose, I hardly know how to begin, but I imagine I will have to start somewhere." Estelle, Jasmine, cleared her throat and breathed in and out deeply in preparation, for she was about to let go of something she had kept concealed for so long. "Before I met your father, I was, well I, I was already married to someone else. In fact, I suppose, I still am in a way."

Rose, who had been staring out of her bedroom window, felt her legs turn to jelly and her stomach lurch, the same way she had felt when she read her mother's hidden letters. She needed to sit down on her bed and clutch at her stomach before responding. "How can you be married to two people at the same time?" she asked rather truculently; but truthfully, she was near to tears.

"It's not quite what you think, and what I'm about to say will be so hard for you to take in. Rose, you know the story of when I was a baby and I disappeared from a front doorstep, supposedly kidnapped? Well," she continued after Rose had nodded, "I didn't actually move from where I was, well not in the normal sense anyway, I moved forward in time. For some reason I left the year eighteen-seventy-eight and arrived in nineteen-seventy, but I was still on the doorstep."

Estelle then described how she had grown up assuming that Glenda and Tony were her natural parents, as did they; there'd been no clue to assume otherwise. "I grew up thinking I had been a twin, but my brother was stillborn. My mother, Glenda, went on to have another baby; my sister Lucy."

Rose thought for a minute, her young mind accepting for now, what her mother was telling her. "But she wasn't your real sister, was she? Oh!"

"What is it?"

"It's like me and George, I thought he was my half-brother, but he isn't even that, only it still feels like he is."

"Yes exactly, she felt like my real sister, and like you, I didn't know that she wasn't. Anyway, so I grew up and when I was eighteen, I left home and trained as a nurse and then became a midwife."

"Mum, you were a nurse, a real nurse?" Rose's brain began calculating. "But that means you are still a nurse and still a midwife."

"Yes, that's right, I am. But how could I tell anyone here, now? How would anyone believe in nineteen hundred that I'd come from the year two thousand? They would think I was out of my mind and have me locked up! It seemed the only option was to say I'd lost my memory, and if I had lost my memory, I couldn't say I was a nurse!

Your real father and I had known each other from being quite small, and we both knew we would eventually marry, and then we bought a house; this house! It was such a shock to wake up in it and see it as it was in nineteen hundred, and that strangers were living in it. It was my house! I was so confused.

Let me explain. It was the last day of nineteen ninety-nine and we, your real father and I were at a party to see in the new century. I had to leave and go home shortly after midnight because I had to get up early the next morning to go to work; but I never made it home... that's when it happened. I fell backwards through time into the early hours of nineteen hundred, exactly one hundred years before. It was a shock... and then came another shock, or rather something beautiful. You; but a shock nevertheless; and I needed to get married, and quickly. You see," Rose's mother explained, "I couldn't be expecting a child and not be married, so I married John because I knew he would look after me, and everyone assumed he was your father; for why shouldn't they?"

"What's my real father called?"

"Stephen, Steve for short, you will meet him I know, because for me, it has already happened."

"How will I know him when I meet him?"

"You will, but I'm afraid he won't know who you are when you do, because he didn't know you were expected."

"Oh dear, then I shall have to tell him," replied Rose.

With a long sigh, Rose left her reminiscing, and began an abridged version of what her mother had explained to her while Arthur Pickford listened attentively.

"... Fortunately, as you already know, she was rescued by my father, who carried her to his home. He didn't know what else to do in the circumstances. He thought she'd been hit by a coach travelling at speed as it turned around a corner. Incredibly, his house was also hers, but in the future. To think she and her husband, Steve, my real father, will be living in my family home and I will get to meet him! That alone, brings me immense comfort. However, after arriving from the future, my mother soon realised she was expecting a child; me, so she had to think fast, as having a husband a hundred years away was of no help whatsoever. She knew my other father, John, was falling in love with her, and she needed to be married, so she took matters into her own hands, and sped things along. They wed before she was, you know, showing; the marriage had already been consummated when John had proposed."

At this point Arthur Pickford felt he needed to interrupt. "This is what I don't understand. Lord and Lady Peters claimed that she was their long-lost daughter."

"Yes, they did," replied Rose.

"But I saw her appear out of thin air, so I know she couldn't be."

"Well, there's more. My mother *was* their daughter! She went missing soon after she was born. The story was that she'd been kidnapped. A maid attending her had put her down at the front door to chase after some delivery boy who'd pulled the doorbell. However, too impatient to wait for an answer, he'd run off, not even leaving whatever he had been delivering. When the maid returned, the baby; my mother, was gone."

"Oh, my goodness, I know that story well. It's why I became so interested in the stone circles as I realised they must have had something to do with it. I saw it happen; I was on my way to school. The baby was your mother?"

"Yes, she was. You saw her?"

"Yes. And I knew the delivery boy, Mikey. I saw him there. But you're right, he didn't stay long, and was on his way before the maid opened the door. I watched her going after him down the street and around the corner. That's when it started... I began to feel strange, and my ears were ringing. And then there was a sort of fog, and then... the baby wasn't there; she'd disappeared into thin air!" Arthur's breathing began to change as he remembered. Sweat appeared at his brow and he was getting more and more anxious. "Oh no, talking of this is bringing on one of those funny turns. I need some air."

"Of course," said Rose and opened the doors for him as he rushed outside clutching his chest. He stopped by the gate and held onto its post for support, gasping for air as if there were none. "It will pass, just as before. Concentrate on taking good and even breaths. Count slowly as you breathe in, hold, now breath out, hold again," she explained. Rose had witnessed anxiety attacks many times; this was the second time with Arthur Pickford. The first time was after he'd been discharged, and they were leaving the hospital. Fresh air had triggered it; a sharp cold draft slapped across his face when he'd stepped outside and caught him unawares, making him gasp. The little party of Rose, Arthur, Molly and Harold, had successfully made it through the ward doors, along the corridor and down the grand steps of the entrance hall, and through the front door, but then had to quickly revert back inside and sit on a bench opposite the front desk. It had scared Molly half to death seeing her brother in that state; she was so glad that Sister Brown had chosen to stay with them and escort them out. It was almost one hour before Arthur felt anywhere near normal, but Rose had been holding space for him all the while, telling him what to do to help himself; her soothing words, her calmness, her very presence; eventually his affliction, as he later came to describe it; was stilled.

"You are doing really well, keep looking straight at me. Breathe slow and steady, that's good." After ten minutes or so, this present attack had subsided. Reassured that it hadn't lasted as long as before, and he would be all right and not about to die - it was his nerves remembering the stress of travelling through time, Arthur was back inside. They soon picked up from where they had left off, Arthur looking thoughtful. He joined his hands together as if in prayer and put the tips of his fingers to his lips.

"So, she reappeared, where?"

"She reappeared at precisely the same place in the year nineteen seventy. She had a towel wrapped around her."

"That's right, I remember the towel," Arthur interjected. "So that means, at this moment, the one that we are in now, she is outside of our world, but she is somewhere, because she is travelling from eighteen seventy-eight when she disappeared, and forward in time to nineteen seventy. My word! That is huge to get my head around."

"But you've just done the same thing! Surely you understand."

"Yes I suppose so, but when I arrived, it became my present, but nineteen seventy is the future for us all."

"Well nineteen seventy will become her present when she arrives," replied Rose. "It's the same. The thing is though, she comes while the woman who lives in the house is giving birth. My mother assumed of course that she was the daughter of that woman. She explained to me that the birth wasn't going as it should and that the woman, who was on her own, had managed to call an ambulance on the telephone in the hall, but had then passed out because she'd lost a lot of blood while giving birth to a son who was sadly stillborn. In the meantime, my mother appears by the front door, exactly where the maid had left her back in eighteen seventy-eight, and everyone thinks the woman has had twins. It wasn't until Mum was taken back to the nineteen-hundreds that she found out she was the long-lost daughter of Lord and Lady Peters. She had a hard time believing this herself initially, but then slowly but surely, managed to work it all out."

"But how did Lord and Lady Peters know it was their daughter? I always wondered how they could prove it."

"She had a very distinctive birthmark, that's how they knew."

"Yes, so she did, a picture of it was in the newspaper. So, your mother, she had the birthmark?"

"Yes, she did."

"So that has confirmed things for me, I didn't know your mother had the birthmark."

"Well why would you, it wasn't discussed publicly," Rose retorted.

Arthur was contemplative and put his hands back in the prayer position. "It's almost as if there was a mistake when she disappeared as a baby, like a glitch. In order to rectify it, she was brought back to where she should have been."

"Well almost," replied Rose, "but she would have had to be in the right place at the right time, and what are the odds on that? Also, she would have been twenty-two in nineteen hundred if she hadn't disappeared as a baby, but when she reappeared in nineteen hundred, she was thirty."

"Well, that may be so," agreed Arthur, "but all the same, as you say, the conditions would have to have been right. Hmm, that's got me thinking why I was also able to move through time. Perhaps we'll never know for sure, but I at least know it can be done. Ha, one up on H. G. Wells!"

There was a small knock at the door and Molly came in carrying a tray of tea and biscuits. "I thought you could do with a cuppa. You've been having such a long chat your mouths will be dry." She sat alongside her brother and poured the tea out of a brightly coloured teapot and into her best bone china teacups. "Sugar Sister?" she asked Rose while handing round her home-made shortbread biscuits.

"No thank you," replied Rose. "But please call me Rose, I'm not at work, and anyway I am now retired. Ah, there's nothing like a good cup of tea," she said after placing the cup back in its saucer.

Soon after, the conversation came to a natural halt. Both needed to digest everything, so Rose took her leave. She thanked Molly for the tea and biscuits, arranging to return shortly.

"I see he had another turn then," said Molly worriedly as soon as the sitting room door was closed, and they were alone in the corridor.

"Yes, I'm afraid so, although not as bad as the first time," replied Rose. She was conscious that Arthur needed to take things easy and come to terms with what had happened to him.

"He had one when I took him for a walk into town. Thank goodness I went with him, so he didn't have to cope on his own. Not that I would have let him go alone - too many changes for him to manage. That's probably what made it happen I expect. Just did what I saw you do and spoke to him calmly. I was in such a panic myself though; gave my poor old heart a right set to, I don't mind telling you."

"Oh dear, he never said. I expect he'll have a few more. My mother was just the same. Hopefully, each time they'll be less intense as he gets used to it. Well done you, though!"

"Just sat him down on the park bench and told him to breathe in and out; that's what I did. By them there standing stones it was, we were so nearly home. Done too much too soon I expect, but he always did like to be out walking. He never could keep still, always had the fidgets to be somewhere else other than where he was."

It was an incredible coincidence, Rose thought later, that Mr Pickford, Arthur, had been there at the two instances when her mother had slipped through time. She was thankful nonetheless, as it gave her mother's story credibility. How unfortunate though, that Arthur Pickford was experiencing the same sort of nerve trouble. Although Rose believed what her mother had told her, she had still questioned how it could all be true, and many a time wondered how and why it happened. Perhaps it was never meant to happen, and when the time was right, the 'powers that be' simply pushed her back again. "But if it hadn't happened, I would never have been born," she said aloud, thankful she was alone and there was no one there to hear her talking to herself.

There were other things to consider too. There were those blasted records for a start, and as there was 'no time like the present,' seemingly rapidly becoming her new motto, she may as well start filling up the empty jukebox with what records were already available. Rose could almost hear her mother's voice in her head. *"Put the records on,"* she had stipulated, *"in the following order. They must be precisely as they are on this list."*

Rose climbed the attic stairs, for she had kept the list that her mother had written down in one of the attic rooms along with the family photographs and other bits of stuff and memorabilia. She couldn't bring herself to part with any of it, but it brought back too many memories if she kept any of it out and on display. So there it all stayed and in perfect contrast to the way she was able to dispose of her nursing career so easily and without any fuss.

"Some you will be able to get hold of in the nineteen fifties, others you will have to wait till well into the nineteen seventies, so it will take you

years, but you will complete the task, because I have seen the result, so don't worry."

Her mother's words echoed down the years as she pulled out the list of song titles and who had sung them. A few of them she recognised, *Night Train*, by Jimmy Forest and *Blue Velvet*, by The Clovers; another proof that her mother had visited the future Rose supposed, for she would have no other way of knowing.

The following morning was heavy with grey wet mizzle. But it didn't perturb the birds devouring the few morsels that had been put out on the bird table. Nor did it upset Rose who stepped forth with her usual gusto and suitably attired. She was on a mission to investigate which records on the list were already in existence. She marched quickly, with her head down, through the park, coming out onto Trinity Street. She avoided the direction to The Royal, choosing the alternative way down to town, arriving at her destination which was Woods, the music shop on New Street. She wasn't disappointed. As well as procuring *Night Train* by Jimmy Forest and *Blue Velvet* by Tony Bennett, to go into slots four and six as per her mother's instructions, she also found *Crying in the Chapel* by The Orioles and *Kaw-Liga* by Hank Williams for slots eight and nine. "That's four, only twenty-one to go," she had told the assistant who, after discovering they were for a newly acquired jukebox, explained to Rose that she would have to remove the middle of the discs so they would fit properly onto the mechanism. Rose was thankful for the information and made her way out, but before returning home, thought she would pop into Woolworths along the street and have a look round. It had been a long while since she had done so, and so pleasant to have the time to browse.

Rose tried to remember; it was not since she used to come in with her father for his bag of sweets after accompanying him to the library to change his books. He would push his walking stick with determination at the glass doors, his other arm linked into hers. She smiled to herself; he had liked his sweets. He'd taken to buying them after his diminishing health forced him to cut his alcohol intake. The premature and precipitous death of her mother changed him. Once a strong and forthright man; perhaps a little overly opinionated, but with a heart that would help anyone who needed his ministry, Dr John Brown became someone who appeared to have lost something, and was never able to find it, or even know or understand what it was. He had been a highly regarded obstetrician in his day, but then all his fire simply fizzled away, and he had sought solace in a whisky bottle. That, and his age, nudged him into retirement. Rose had looked after him with utter devotion until he finally passed away as the Second World War was looming closer, which was just as well, she thought, as her brother had been killed in London during the Blitz. She knew her father would never have coped with the knowledge of that.

However, before Rose had managed to walk a few steps along the path, she was hailed. "Matron," she replied when she saw who it was, "what a surprise!"

"Please, we're not at work now, my name is Paula, as well you know. Fancy a coffee?"

Apparently Matron, or rather Paula, after visiting the café where she had purchased the jukebox to sample the coffee, had ascertained that it was an old model that only took the old seventy-eights. All the records these days were forty-five revolutions per minute and Rose would need a conversion kit in order to play them and she was on her way to sort it out. So, they both returned to Woods and ordered one before Paula trundled Rose towards Woolworths' café.

Paula was curious. She rather thought Rose had something clandestine going on. A special male friend perhaps since, apart from Kaw-Liga, which made one want to get up and dance, the records Rose had bought were mostly the kind one would need someone to dance with "right up-close like," which was how Paula had put it. Also, how had her mother known about the songs before they had ever been written? Paula sat forward in her chair puffing on her cigarette expecting answers. Rose replied huffily to her newly acquired friend that no, she did not have a special male friend who she might dance with (perish the thought) and it would probably be a long time before she would be able to get every single record on the list. While in no rush to listen to them anyway, there would be many years ahead of her to hear them and ponder on their relevance for her mother and how she knew of them.

Worn down by the inquisition, the whys and wherefores Rose managed to keep to herself, leaving the mystery of it all to Matron Pilkington's imagination. Later though, when welcoming her bed, she accepted the chance encounter had been all to the good and that Matron, although somewhat domineering at times, had her heart in the right place. She fell asleep that night content in the knowledge that she was doing what her mother had asked of her. Rose would have done anything for her mum, anything at all, if it had only meant not losing her in such sudden and traumatic circumstances.

Caring for her mother in the few hours before her death had made Rose determined to become a nurse, despite her father's feelings about his daughter working for a living. However, he'd observed such tenderness in the love and care Rose gave to his beloved wife as she lay dying, he changed his mind and gave her his blessing, thus allowing her to begin her training when a little older. Meanwhile Rose gathered some experience in nursing care at Tiplin Hall, the family estate of Rose's grandparents, Lord and Lady Peters. It had become a convalescent home for wounded officers during the First World War. After her beloved Francis had been lost, Rose helped out at Tiplin, caring for the wounded officers. It helped to take her mind off her grief, fill the emptiness in her heart and made her think of wanting to become a nurse.

Chapter Fourteen

1960

It was raining. Arthur was forced to admit the gardens needed it - the June sunshine had been extraordinary. He waited for as long as possible for the downpour to abate, but the drab grey sky showed no signs of brightening, and it came to a point where he couldn't delay any longer. With a degree of trepidation he donned his raincoat and galoshes, locked the front door, opened his umbrella against the relentless deluge and set off down to town towards, what was for him, a rather challenging enterprise. Arthur's fellow colleagues had found out about his propensity for dowsing and thought it a good idea that he might give a little talk on the subject at the 'Thursday Evening Group' meeting at the library. It was the first time he had ever spoken publicly about it, and he wanted to get there in good time so he could set up and have time to settle his nerves. Introvert by nature, Arthur Pickford was decidedly out of his comfort zone.

He'd continued to have occasional episodes of nervousness and anxiety. They would come upon him suddenly, out of nowhere and for no particular reason, ever since he'd arrived in the year nineteen fifty-five. This was coming up to five years ago, and Arthur had staggered along after his leap forward in time, in fits and starts. Sometimes he was gleeful about his covert escapade, other times full of remorse, but what was always in the background waiting to jump out when he least expected, was this jittery anxiety that he didn't seem able to shake off. He'd had a sense of unease since childhood, but that had grown into something so much worse. Rose, thankfully, had been there in the background with help and support seeming to know how he was feeling whether he had said anything or not. She could recognise the symptoms, she had told him, because her mother had been the same.

Alas, as well as the time travelling, Arthur had faced a sudden and tragic bereavement which had taken place only a few months afterwards, and this had set him back still further. Molly died. Complaining of pains in her chest one day she had taken to her bed. Harold had gone up to check how she was feeling and found her sitting up in bed, but with no sign of life whatsoever. The doctor said her passing would have been very quick, which was of some solace, but it was still an enormous shock. Six weeks later, it had been Harold's turn. The doctor said he'd simply died of a broken heart. "He couldn't live without her," is what Arthur had relayed to Rose.

Through all this, a bond had gradually formed between Arthur and Rose. He'd leaned heavily on her for support during the time of losing first his beloved little sister Molly, and then Harold so soon after he'd arrived in, what was for Arthur, such alien surroundings. The world had altered so much and so shockingly fast that he'd no idea of what code of conduct people followed. Their behaviour was so changed, but then what of his own conduct? How his mother must have suffered, and now she was dead and gone. She'd spent years and years waiting for his return, with poor Molly having to take all the strain. Arthur had left his family in precisely the same boat as the one he now found himself in, and without even thinking twice. If only the inexplicable wheels of time had sent him to an earlier date, before his mother's death, but she would still have had to grieve for her missing son wherever he'd turned up. Whatever scenario Arthur imagined; he would still carry guilt on his conscience. Rose, thankfully, was always there, pulling him through his ups and downs and slowly but surely, Arthur managed to pick out a path in this strange new world.

It hadn't all been doom and gloom for Arthur, for out of tragedy had come a welcome surprise. As well as his sister's house being left to him, for she and Harold had updated their wills to make it so, shortly after Arthur was back in their lives, there was also a sum of money that had been Arthur's in the first place. It had been passed to his mother when Arthur was presumed to be deceased, who left the money to Molly in her will with instructions to give it to Arthur when he returned, being ever hopeful that he would. Molly had kept it in a savings account, and it amounted to quite a tidy sum. He was financially secure at least, which certainly made his life run more smoothly than it might have done.

Arthur walked through the lending library and into the back room, having first left his dripping outer garments in the small staff cloakroom just off the entrance hall. "Good evening, Mr Pickford," said Miss Jennings, one of Arthur's colleagues. "We're all looking forward to tonight."

Arthur had been working part-time at the library for some years. When first adjusting to life in the nineteen-fifties, Arthur became a frequent visitor to this new and handsome edifice. Built in nineteen thirty-seven it was a complete change from Church Street where the library had previously been located. Arthur could remember 'the new library' had been under discussion in planning meeting after planning meeting for year upon year in the days before he'd moved forward in time. And now, here it was, a long-awaited feast to behold, despite the fact he hadn't had to wait as long as everyone else! Arthur had worked as a librarian thirty-five years previously at the old place, so for him it was like a home from home, even though the staff from those old days were long gone. Books were still books however, and he felt as though he belonged there. Library procedures had changed little over his lost years, and he still enjoyed pulling a reference book from a shelf and sit gleaning information from it.

On one of his regular library excursions one day, Arthur happened to see some information about a job opportunity as a library assistant pinned on the notice board in the reference library. When he expressed some curiosity about it, the staff, who knew him solely as one of their regular customers who had a passion for books, urged him to apply. With their encouragement, Arthur took his chance and applied for the job; successfully! His new colleagues welcomed him with open arms, especially after he said he'd had previous experience as a librarian in former times. He even managed to secure his old national insurance number; no one from any government department had queried it. He was back as a salaried employee, that at least had given him some continuity.

"Good evening to you too Miss Jennings. How many do you think will be coming tonight. Not too many I hope."

"Oh, go on with you, you will be fine," replied Miss Jennings, sensing his nervousness.

"I hope so, I do hope so," said an unsure Arthur. "I've never known anybody that was remotely interested in what I do."

"Just tell them how to look for gold, that'll get their interest." Arthur chuckled, he'd never found any gold, a few old coins which seemed like treasure because of the thrill of finding them, but nothing of any real value. But finding the odd coin had never been his main interest. Any spare time he could muster, he would dowse for, and then map the lines of energy he found, and try to work out what they all meant. The energy lines around the standing stones in the park had always been his particular fascination. He would record the lines and note the subtle changes in them from season to season, and moon phase to moon phase. However, he was well aware that it wasn't everyone's choice of entertainment, and formulated the talk into a light-hearted discussion, hoping most of the time would be taken up with people's questions.

It looked as though the talk might be hard going at first; there was a deal of scepticism around.

"Who, ahem, 'discovered' all these lines then? Do you think they tripped over one in the street one day that nobody had noticed before?"

The question brimmed with scorn and the mischief-maker, looking round for support, gained a few titters of approval. However, Arthur was by then voicing his passion and his nerves had melted away.

"It was William Black, whose expertise during the nineteenth century was with Roman roads. He studied his theory of grand geometric lines for fifty years before releasing what he had found, which was that the roads linked major landmarks in a very precise manner and could be seen to define the county's boundary markers."

"Really?" someone else retorted, "sounds to me there were some good architects about, that's all." More laughs resounded and Arthur joined in, unnerving the doubters somewhat.

"Yes, you are right, there were, even in ancient times. Their architecture was based upon knowledge of, shall we say, the currents of the earth. A chap called F. J. Bennett published what he'd found in nineteen hundred and four, which was that prehistoric sites and old churches have a link, in that they usually have north-south alignments and regular divisions of about a mile between them. Also, the appearance of ley-lines which have been linked to underground streams and the magnetic currents of the earth. But it is where these lines cross that is the most interesting, because many of these are where sacred sites are found."

Arthur's answer shut the hecklers up. From then on he held the group in the palm of his hand. "We have our own historical site as I'm sure you all know, the stone rings in the park." He looked round the group; they were all ears. "Megalithic and monolithic structures in the British Isles have been traced back to at least three thousand years B.C. and seem to have been based on a very refined philosophy of sacred science. These places appear to magnify the energy of the magnetic field. I think it's time now to show you by what means I find how strong the currents are in any particular place." He then pulled a simple pendulum from out of his pocket and make clear that expensive equipment wasn't needed. The string was of hemp, the pendulum, a small turned bit of hazel wood. He explained that all that was required was to remain relaxed and have a precise question in mind, keep the mind empty of unnecessary thought so as to let the answer come, and the pendulum would swing accordingly. He was soon finding bunches of keys in people's pockets, a sixpenny piece under the rug, and a gold necklace down the back of a leather-upholstered seat that Miss Jennings stated had been reported as lost by someone in the library the day before, for which Arthur received a round of applause.

He finished by explaining other forms of usage, such as how to dowse over a map to get a feel for the general area before proceeding on foot for a more detailed search, and even what would be the best vegetable to have for one's supper, which brought the house down. Miss Jennings thanked him for giving such an interesting and informative talk which provoked a warm-hearted further round of appreciative hand clapping. That night, having had to battle against the unrepentant rain on his way home for a second time, a tired Arthur sank into his bed surprised yet satisfied that he'd been able to hold such an engrossed audience. It would be over to Mr Hebden next time, talking about his exploits in genealogy. Arthur would then be able to relax and listen intently, along with everyone else.

There was no change in the skies the following morning and the drizzle looked set to stay for yet another day. "Flaming June!" exclaimed Arthur, by way of greeting his next-door neighbour as they simultaneously locked their respective front doors but then setting forth in opposite directions, and both trying to avoid the large puddle that had formed over the path and most of the road.

"Aye, 'appen t'ducks'll like it," came the reply. Arthur chuckled in response and walked towards the park and into town. He'd almost reached the library but then happened to catch a glimpse of Rose going into Woods music shop. He felt a slight pang of guilt. He'd been avoiding her somewhat ever since she had turned him down, very politely he had to admit, to his suggestion that perhaps there could be a romantic liaison developing between them. He'd been embarrassed by her rebuff. Apart from when age eleven, when he was bowled over by a classmate with ringleted hair and beautiful smile who he quietly worshipped from afar, Arthur had never been drawn to anyone, until Rose. He was rather shy and unsure of things of that nature, so it had taken much courage for him to ask, and he'd borne the rejection ever since; their relationship as friends suffering as a result. He'd grown very fond of Rose over the last few years; he found her to be warm, generous with her time, and incredibly supportive of him, especially in the beginning, when it took a while for him to adjust. He sidled into the door frame of the bank and waited till she disappeared through the shop door and into its musical depths before carrying on towards his destination.

Maybe, he thought later, after replacing the morning's returned books to their appropriate places on the shelves, it was because of what they both kept close to their chests, what they both concealed from everyone else; that secret they held that bonded them together. Mistakenly, he'd believed there was more to their relationship than merely friendship, for Rose had told Arthur plainly. Her heart was given to another, to Francis. Although long dead, having perished like so many other young boys in the Great War, he was nonetheless still dear to her and it wasn't conceivable for her that he would ever be replaced.

Yes, as a result of his inexperience in this sort of thing, Arthur understood he'd misinterpreted her affection as a friend, as something else. Nevertheless, he was missing her company and accepted he had to take her rejection of him on the chin. He would telephone her, not from the call box at the end of the road like he normally did, but from the telephone he'd just had installed in his home. The library staff had persuaded Arthur to get one, but so far, apart from ringing the library one day to say he would be a little late for work, he hadn't had cause to use it. Nobody had rung him, as nobody had his number, apart from the library, and he hadn't had the thing long enough for him to appear in the directory. Ringing Rose to tell her of his new telephone number was the excuse he needed, and it would break the ice.

He needn't have worried, Rose was not only pleased to hear from Arthur, but delighted she would now be able to ring him instead of waiting for him to ring her from the call box. There had been no mention of the awkward conversation that they'd had a few weeks previously. In fact, she was keen to meet up and tell him about her latest acquisitions for the jukebox. Previously she had bought *That'll be the Day* by The Crickets, *Ain't it a Shame* by Fats Domino, *The Great Pretender* by The Platters and *Tutti-Frutti* by Little Richard, and had placed them in slots five, seven, twelve and sixteen accordingly. And just yesterday, when Arthur had seen Rose go into Woods, she'd bought *Oh Carol* by Neil Sedaka and *I Only Have Eyes for You* by The Flamingos, which were now in slots seventeen and ten, respectively.

Red-faced, Arthur sipped at his cup of tea with eyes cast down while hearing what Rose had to say. He was being forced to listen to a love song. *I Only Have Eyes For You* had been playing over the radio at the café, just as they had sat down. "That's one of them playing now, what do you think?" Not noticing she hadn't received an answer, she continued chatting, much to Arthur's relief, seeing as he felt like slithering off his chair and hiding under the table. "So that's ten down, fifteen more to go," she announced. "More tea?"

"Er, yes please, that would be nice." Rose poured for them both and Arthur tipped in the milk. "Tell me," he continued, after taking a large bite from a custard cream biscuit, "how do you know when it's time to get them?"

"I don't," she answered "Every month or so I pop into Woods and ask what's popular. I also listen to the radio from time to time to see what is current and check if it's on the list. It would have been so much easier if Mum had put dates on as well, but I don't think she knew. In fact, she said how hard it had been to remember the artists. She found it much easier to recall the song titles from the order they were in."

"Oh well, I suppose it keeps you on your toes, and the records will keep, even if you miss the odd one or two, you don't have to get them as soon as they come out."

"No, I suppose not, but I don't want them to be out of print as it were, like a book might be."

"Yes, there is always that, but if your mother gave you the list in the first place, then it must mean you get them all, including the correct artists, so there can't be any need to worry."

"I'm not in the least bit worried, I've had to cope with far worse than collecting a few records. Anyway, enough of all that, would you care for another?" Rose picked up the plate of biscuits in front of them and offered it to Arthur as he'd quickly polished off his first. He took another custard cream, as did Rose, she was rather partial to those. As a girl, she would nibble at the top layer until it was destroyed and the cream in the middle exposed. She would then lick at the cream until it had virtually gone, and then munch the bottom layer. Of course, Rose would never be seen to do that now, but the thought was always there in her mind. Smiling to herself, she took a small bite of the top layer but then stopped her fancy and immediately took a bite of the corresponding middle and bottom layer. Arthur, meanwhile, dunked his in his cup of tea, and leaving it a little too long, lost half of it in the bottom of the cup.

"Blast it," he said quietly and fished it out with a teaspoon and into his mouth wishing he'd been more careful while in front of Rose. Her manners and poise, he thought, were perfection itself; what must she think of his uncouth behaviour?

"It's so annoying when that happens isn't it," declared Rose sympathetically. "Please, have another."

"No thank you, it'll spoil my tea, as my mother used to say. Anyway, I'll be getting on my way soon, I need to do a few bits and pieces before it gets too late. I'll be happy to have more on another occasion though. I'm quite partial to custard creams, ever since they came out."

"I was about eight I think," said Rose. "When they were first produced," she added as she saw Arthur looking quizzical.

"Oh right," replied Arthur after he'd caught up with Rose's thought processes.

When they were both ready to leave, Arthur picked his cap off the coat stand and even though the June weather was for the moment behaving itself, for the sun was shining gloriously, he settled it upon his head. They walked back together until they reached Rose's home.

"Oh, I nearly forgot, I picked some roses from the climber up the back of the house, too many by half, I got carried away. Please take some, they're beautiful at the moment." Rose disappeared inside and returned readily with a bunch having wrapped the stems in newspaper. "They're a bit drippy, they've just come out of water, be careful."

"They are very beautiful, thank you, I shall enjoy having them. Molly doesn't, or rather never had roses growing in the garden, and I'm not much of a gardener to think of planting any. Can't think why, their scent is lovely."

"I was named after that rose."

"Sorry, what did you just say?" asked Arthur, not quite understanding what Rose meant.

"I said, my mother named me Rose because of the rose bush these roses came from. I will elaborate, I can see you are confused. Sometime in the future, my real father will say that he would like for the both of them to start a family and they will be underneath this very rose bush as the petals come fluttering down like confetti. My mother told me she thought later it had been a sort of omen, as when she was thinking of a name for me, she realised that she and her sisters from her nineteen-hundred family, the Peters, had all been named after flowers. It was then she remembered the rose petals, and that when she had been a very young girl, she'd met me in the park, and I'd told her my name was Rose.

Mum said it had made her cry when she, years later, realised who I was. That it was me, her daughter, she'd been talking to, because it was another link to the future and where she'd come from. Of course back then, she couldn't tell anyone her real name of Jasmine, because she'd had to pretend to have lost her memory. My father suggested her name might be Stella. However, she preferred Estelle; so that was who she became. And even after the Peters reclaimed her, it didn't get changed back to Jasmine because she said she was used to Estelle. She told me once that the real reason she wanted to remain as Estelle was because it helped her to keep secret where she'd come from and keep up the pretence of having lost her memory.

"Look," countered Arthur, sensing Rose's need of some support. "I know it's still several years away, but she'll be here as a baby before you know it, and you'll be able to see her in the park for yourself and live out your mother's memory."

"Yes, I've thought of that, it's one of the so very precious things I still have to look forward to; that, and when she arrives as a baby, although I'm troubled by it if truth be known; how to manage it, you know."

"Well, you've plenty of time to think about that one, just think of what she told you, because that is what you will do, so you can't go wrong."

"I suppose so," replied Rose, dubiously.

"Oh, I've just realised; Stella, as in star, as in her birthmark," observed Arthur.

"Yes, precisely," Rose agreed. At least she was convinced of that.

Chapter Fifteen

1965

"How's the jukebox project coming along?" asked Paula Pilkington. She had taken to popping round to see Rose once or twice a week, ever since she'd retired the year before. Her old friend and colleague Sister Brownette had, in Paula's own words, "... gone and got herself spliced and has upped sticks to Leeds, not so handy for the odd chinwag anymore." It appeared Rose had taken her place.

"Mmm, around ten so far."

"And how many more are there to go?" demanded Paula. She was determined to glean more information.

"Fifteen I think," answered Rose, indifferently.

"When was the last time you bought any?"

"Oh, let me think, I would say around five or six years ago."

Paula needed to take action; it was obvious her friend was losing heart. After all, it was she who'd found the jukebox in the first place and therefore surely had some authority in the matter. "There must be some more by now. Hand over your list then, I'll see if I recognise any."

A while back, Rose had not been able to fend off Paula's high-handed inquisitions any longer about how her mother could have known the songs that were on her list before they ever existed. She'd finally given in, telling her not the whole truth, but certainly no lie, claiming her mother had been able to foretell the future and that was how she knew of the songs that would be released in years to come. The revelation had shut Paula up, even if only momentarily. However, today Paula was back on the case, so Rose produced the list, albeit reluctantly.

"Oh, number one on your list, The Beatles *I Want to Hold Your Hand*, I recognise that one, and *White Christmas* by Bing Crosby, number two. Surely you must know that one Rose. And look, number fifteen, another by The Beatles, *Eight Days a Week*, that's a new release. They're rather good don't you think? Saw them on Top of the Pops on the telly. Have you seen it?"

"Not really; I caught a glimpse when the programme first started last year. It's for the youngsters I feel, not for the likes of me; not at all. But I have heard of The Beatles. Liverpool boys, aren't they?"

"Mmm yes, they are oh and look, number twenty-one, The Rolling Stones *Satisfaction*, I've heard that on the radio. So that's another four to get. Fabulous, that's what I say."

'You would,' thought Rose.

Before she could have any say in the matter, Paula had organised for them to pop into town to see if Woods had any of the records, and to buy them. "And then we'll try out the new coffee shop on the corner near the station," decided Paula in a fait accompli.

They travelled in Paula's white Triumph Spitfire convertible. She'd acquired it as soon as she'd retired from nursing, and it was her pride and joy. She liked to drive with its roof open as often as the British climate would allow, enjoying the admiring glances that the car brought her way. Today was no exception and Rose made sure she was well-wrapped up in her thickest coat before climbing in. Paula checked her lips she'd just retouched with bright pink lipstick in the rear-view mirror and started the engine. As soon as it had fired, she engaged first gear and set off with a jerk; the screech of the tyres objecting to the sudden pace. Never having considered covering her now whitened and bitten lips with anything other than a bit of Vaseline during winter, a grim-faced Rose composed herself in the passenger seat, clutching on for dear life.

"And how much are they?" asked Paula to the man behind the counter in Woods.

"Six and eightpence each, so that will be one pound six and eight altogether," he replied.

"Look Rose, I can see *Jambalaya* by Fats Domino, that's on your list too, isn't it? We'll have that as well please," declared Paula in her usual assertive manner.

"So that now comes to one pound thirteen and four," said the shopkeeper, his eyes looking upwards towards his brain while he did the arithmetic.

"I'll have to write a cheque I'm afraid, I wasn't anticipating spending so much today," explained Rose.

"No problem, a cheque will be fine," said the shopkeeper, "as long as I can have your address written on the back." He dropped the slim black discs, all in their individual papery sleeves, into a brown paper bag emblazed with the shop's logo, while Rose pulled her cheque book out of her handbag. "Planning a party then?" he asked Paula.

"And who wants to know?" she replied, while her eyelids fluttered.

"It's usually the young ones who come in to buy all the latest releases, I wondered what you planned to do with them, although, may I say, I didn't mean you were old, on the contrary."

"Stop right there before you put your foot further in it," goaded Paula. The man grinned, accepted Rose's cheque, bowed courteously and bid them a polite goodbye as they made to leave.

"I don't know how you do it," said Rose when they had settled down in the coffee shop; a milky coffee for Paula, and a cup of tea for Rose and a scone each.

"Do what?" asked Paula.

"Manage to get every man on the planet to make eyes at you. You even succeeded in making the young lad serving our drinks blush, poor thing."

"I just like to play, that's all, there's no harm in that is there?"

"I suppose not," agreed Rose.

"It's all right for you, you have a man," continued Paula, reaching in her handbag for her cigarettes having finished eating her scone. "Want one?"

"No thank you Paula, I don't smoke as you know. And what man are you talking about? My man, although hardly a man; just nineteen he was, died in The Great War, or rather The First World War, as they insist on calling it nowadays. No man has ever taken his place; nor could I ever imagine that to happen."

Francis. The thrill of their fleeting romance emerging as she thought of him. His muscular arms around her and full lips seeking hers; stirrings inside her; heat rising, desires she could never have believed, yielding, giving, taking and then succumbing. And then the numbing pain after she heard of his death and years and years of longing for him to just come home. But only her ghostly reveries of him ever came, and her grief fell through the transparent image of his soul.

"I mean Arthur, he holds a candle for you, surely you know that?"

"Oh Arthur." Did Paula think she and he? Never in a million years. "He and I; we're just friends, we could never be more than that. There's been too much history between us, we couldn't. No, it's not possible." Rose shuddered at the thought of it. Besides, she always saw Arthur as a generation above her own, although the workings of time had changed all that, she now being marginally older.

"Yes, but he's there for you, isn't he?" Paula lit her Player's cigarette and took a long pull on it before continuing. "You see, there's never been anyone for me, I rather think I frighten them all off, but you would have thought there would be someone on this wretched planet of ours that would match up don't you think?"

Rose thought about what her friend just said. All Paula's bravado was a cover for her loneliness. What she craved was someone who needed her; someone to love. She felt sorry for her. "Paula," Rose began, "whether you scare people off or not, I've always known you to be a very kind and caring person and I'm sure those who matter can see it too. Maybe because of your career, a very successful one at that, you've never been in the right place at the right time to find that someone who could be there for you. Perhaps now that your life has changed there is space for that someone. It could happen when you least expect it, you just never know."

Their eyes met and for a moment Rose could see how vulnerable her friend was now she'd let her guard down. She put her hand over Paula's forearm and held it there. "Thank you for thinking that," said Paula after a moment's silence. She stubbed out her cigarette and pushed her chair back, making to leave. "Let's get your records home and into their slots."

"Yes, whatever you say," said Rose. She drained her cup of tea and followed Paula out of the coffee shop like a dutiful pet, but she didn't mind.

Her own life, although it had had its ups and downs, had taught her what love meant, and she was ever grateful for that.

"Here we are, *Jambalaya* is number nineteen, I knew it!" declared Paula triumphantly. "Now I'll just have a tot of your delicious whisky, and then I'll be off."

After Paula had left, Rose slumped down into her favourite chair with a cup of tea and a custard cream biscuit. She couldn't be bothered to make anything substantial for her evening meal, she was worn out. Drinking whisky in the middle of the afternoon wasn't the best of ideas, but one always did what Paula Pilkington suggested. Only Arthur would question what she had to say, and that was only occasionally. Life was easier when one went along with Paula's plans and ideas. Rose thought about what Paula had said about Arthur; that he always looked after her. She looked after him too, but just considered it as being neighbourly, having totally dismissed his earlier romantic declarations as someone who had his wires crossed; another peril to be put down to time travel. She wondered why Paula had read more into it but concluded that it was because she didn't have anyone she could rely on in that way. Rose resolved to keep her eye open for likely candidates. 'Rose Brown, retired nurse, now matchmaker.' She chuckled at the thought.

A couple of weeks later Rose was in town and happened to bump into Sister Dawkins who'd taken the hospital ward over from Rose upon her retirement. They were outside the market hall, coming through the doors at the same time. They crossed over to Woolworths and went upstairs into the café so they could have a chat in relative comfort. Rose was given all the hospital gossip; who'd got the sister's post on ward sixteen, male orthopaedics; a most unexpected choice. Dr Mildew had been having an affair with Sister Prendergast on ward nine for years and nobody knew till now; discipline amongst the student nurses was horrendous, they were continually flouting the rules re uniform, the junior doctors were absolutely useless, and so on. "Oh, and about Dr Alistair, did you know his wife, Dr Fox, had died last month?"

"No, I hadn't heard. Was she ill?"

"I heard it was a sudden heart attack. No great loss there, she was a dreadful woman, couldn't stand having any of her patients on the ward and having to put up with her ill temper. Could never understand why he'd married her in the first place."

"Well," considered Rose, "I might have the answer to that."

"Really, what?" Sister Dawkins put down her coffee cup and sat forward in anticipation.

"Jealousy, plain and simple. I recall Dr Alistair was sweet on Matron Pilkington; well, that's how it seemed to me anyway, but Dr Eileen Fox had her sights on him and set about trapping him in the web she wove around him. He didn't stand a chance, and they were married within six months. Of course, everyone knew it would never work, he was, or is, so full of kindness and humility and she, well you know what she's like, or what she *was* like. I suppose I shouldn't speak ill of the dead, but I'll just say I don't think there was any love lost between them, it's probably come as a blessed release."

"Why didn't they get divorced?"

"Both Catholics, wouldn't ever have happened," replied Rose.

Sister Dawkins reached for her cup of coffee, took a sip and then changed the subject, but still keeping to a work flavour. "Talking of Matron, you heard she retired?"

"Oh yes, she's a friend of mine."

"Did she know that Dr Alistair had liked her?"

"I have no idea," replied Rose and changed the subject again to how her old ward was doing and listened contentedly to the familiar stories of the continual belligerence of some of the consultants, and how busy and unmanageable the ward could be when the hospital was 'on take' for the area's emergency admissions. However, she kept Paula Pilkington in mind, and also Dr Alistair. She was thinking they would make a very handsome couple, a very handsome couple indeed. There was a chance that her friend might find love yet; this chance encounter with Sister Dawkins might prove rather fruitful, and that could only be good news.

Chapter Sixteen

1970

Rose was in the park. She'd been there all morning, not knowing what time to expect anything to occur. Arthur was also there, on the park bench next to her, giving much needed moral support, and to satisfy his own curiosity. He'd been up and about from the early hours checking the swing of his pendulum around the stone circles and across the street near to Flat one, Meadowsring Road. It was a big day today; a day Rose had been both dreading and looking forward to for many a year. Today was the day that her mother was arriving from the year eighteen seventy-eight, and would prove that what she knew in her heart to be true, was real.

Arthur and Rose sat in silence, marvelling at nature's beauty around them; the May sunshine warming their bones and simultaneously shining on the blossom-laden trees, setting the already luminous pink, ablaze. Yet the glory of spring would be over too soon, already a carpet of discarded petals was strewn on the ground. Upon the undulating pond, the ducks' first hatchlings were being paraded with pride and vigilance. From where they were sitting, however, the scene was lost to them. As was that of a youth finding exactly the right shape of pebble to skilfully skim across the water's surface with perfected precision, briefly moulding the water's surface into a line of circulating ripples with its every bounce. It may have been a magnificent example of transitory art in motion, but it caused a flurry of agitated quacking and a sharp reprimand from a lady wielding a bag of stale breadcrumbs which she was feeding to the little flock. The youngster, with shoulders hunched, slunk away from the criticism and over to the swings.

Shuffling their positions from time to time, Rose and Arthur waited and watched. But Arthur was becoming agitated. He didn't like to be still for very long and idling the time away doing nothing wasn't his idea of being relaxed. In fact, it made him anxious rather than peaceful. He pulled his pendulum out and held it aloft for the umpteenth time and then stuffed it back in his jacket pocket. He got up for a second and then sat back down again, but he couldn't settle.

"For goodness' sake, sit still Arthur." His heels were off the ground and his knees were bouncing up and down as his feet jiggled.

"I can't, you know how it gets to me, when I have nothing to do. I need to keep busy, keep my mind occupied." He stood up again and began treading a path back and forth, in an attempt to steady his breathing. Rose remembered how her mother had been sometimes; erratic behaviour coming from some unseen fear, and Arthur was no different. It was the time travel of course; she couldn't think of another explanation, especially as they both exhibited such similar behaviour.

"It will pass soon Arthur, it always does."

"That's easy for you to say, you don't know what it feels like. I can't get my breath, my heart's thumping and I'm scared to death of something, but I don't know what that something is."

"Slow your breathing, stop panting."

"I'm trying to, but..."

Then there she was, walking awkwardly towards the main gates. Rose had determined it was her many months ago by keeping an eye on Flat one, number twenty-three, Meadowsring Road. In fact, she'd observed the place for years, and had known it before it had ever been divided into flats. Rose soon noticed when a young couple had moved in. The woman was an ample and rather glamorous lady. And the man; smaller, bespectacled and bookish. They had to be Glenda and Tony who'd brought her mother up, she just knew it.

"Sit down Arthur, she's there. Look, it's Glenda." He sat back down; his panic easing now he had something to focus on. The two of them watched as one, following her every torturous move with captivated eyes. "She looks far from comfortable," Rose determined. "When I've seen her before she has her hair up and lipstick on, like Paula."

"Yes, you're right, I've seen her walking a black Labrador, and she always looks as though she's on her way to Hollywood."

"Well today she's on her way to the doctor for her check-up. She's right at the end of her pregnancy and it's obviously taking its toll, poor thing. If only there was something we could do."

"We can't stop what will be, everything would change. But it hasn't, so we know that we don't interfere."

Rose sighed heavily. "I know you're right; but the boy; it's so very sad."

"There are many things in life that are sad, as well you know," said Arthur doggedly.

"I suppose so," said Rose. "We must wait until she's on her way home, but I don't know how long it will be after that."

"Well then, there's nothing else for it, we'll just have to watch and see. Why don't we go into the café for a cup of tea meanwhile? We'll be able to see her when she comes back."

"Glad you're feeling better," declared Rose as she got up from the bench.

"So am I, believe me," replied Arthur.

Around forty-five minutes later they saw Glenda on her way back from seeing the doctor. "Oh dear, she looks worse than ever," sighed Rose. They left the café and onto the pathway to get a better view. "Hold on a minute, she's sitting down." They loitered under a cherry tree and pretended to be admiring the blossom, which they had been doing in earnest earlier, but now a drama was playing out, and nature was unashamedly usurped.

"Oh no, so that's how it happens," said Rose, weeping at what she was watching. She and Arthur had seen Glenda get up from the seat, presumably not looking where she was going, and walk smack bang into a lamp post, her pregnant tummy taking all of the impact. Arthur was at pains to stop Rose going to help. He pulled her back by the arm. "But she's bleeding, she's going to lose her baby."

"Yes," replied Arthur, "and she *will* lose the baby. It's what happens. You have to let it take place. You cannot interfere."

Rose looked at Arthur, looked over at Glenda, and then back to Arthur. Arthur felt in his pocket for his handkerchief to wipe the tears that had formed at her eyes and remained strong while his heart was breaking. He knew they had to stay where they were, even though a young woman might be going to lose her baby because of their inaction. But it was not out of insensitivity that they did this; they didn't feel it was right to impede what they knew must come to pass. Rose accepted the handkerchief and saw

Glenda reach her home safely. She took solace from knowing that although Glenda was about to lose a son, she was also about to gain a daughter, Rose's mother. Now they would have to continue their vigil and wait.

They were good walkers, Arthur was always out and about, and Rose had spent a lifetime treading up and down hospital wards. All the same, continually dragging themselves up and down the street and around the immediate vicinity and back again, listening as hard as they could as they passed Glenda's doorway, and the emotion of it all, had them both worn out. In the end, they went back in the park and sat on the closest park bench to Glenda's flat to wait it out. At length, an ambulance came past and pulled to a halt across the road. Rose clutched at Arthur. "It's happened, she must be here. Goodness me, this is it!" she exclaimed and started to get up.

"Wait," instructed Arthur, "let them get inside and then we'll go over." Rose did as she was told and sat back down, but right on the edge of the bench and poised for action, being more than ready to play her part in the story her mother had told her all those years ago. Rose hoped her mother's narrative of events had remained close to what actually happened, or rather was about to befall.

Shortly after the ambulance men had gone inside, Arthur said they should go over. Someone else was already there hovering, with a nose to what the ambulance was doing, and then a door opened along the road, and someone came out. "Goodness, there's going to be quite a crowd at this rate, at least we won't be conspicuous," said Rose. They stood at the back of the ambulance where they knew Glenda would be taken to get inside it. Sure enough, one of the ambulance men reappeared, bringing with him a bedraggled, pale, terrified-looking Glenda in a semi-recumbent position on a stretcher-cum-wheelchair, clutching a baby to her breast so tightly, Rose was worried she might suffocate.

"She looks terrible," whispered Rose, and moved towards her as the ambulance man pushed her up the ramps and into the ambulance. He left her momentarily; there seemed to be a problem with her dog inside the house; his colleague was shouting for his help. Rose had her chance and stepped forward. She very gently stroked Glenda's cheek with her hand. Glenda turned towards her slightly, and slowly focussed upon the older woman, who was all but a stranger to her. Rose knew she needed to be kept warm, she was looking shocked, and though already covered by a blanket,

Rose took off the cloak she was wearing. "Here, let me put this around you," and placed the cloak carefully around the young woman's shoulders. "This will keep you warm."

"Thank you," replied Glenda.

"Your baby is beautiful," she whispered, and kissed her own fingers and then touched the baby's cheek with them lovingly. Her own mother. It was certainly challenging to construe the juxtaposition of the situation. But it was how it was, and time was getting on, and she still had to tell this poor young woman, who to all intents and purposes, had just had a cuckoo planted in her nest, what to call her.

"Have you a name for her?"

"No, not yet."

"My Grandmother wanted my mother to be called Jasmine, but it wasn't to be."

"What a pretty name," replied Glenda. Rose beamed a smile.

"Yes, isn't it. I never had children of my own, you are very blessed. Take good care of her, none of this was her fault."

The ambulance men were returning and Rose, with yet more tears in her eyes, retreated into the crowd of people that had now gathered. "How did it go?" asked Arthur after the ambulance had driven off and the crowd had dissipated.

"Well, I think. It must be like seeing your grandchild for the first time, but it's not your grandchild, it's your mother, but this feeling I have in my heart, it has to be similar. Don't you think?"

"I'm sure you're right," replied Arthur. "What have you done with your cloak, have you left it somewhere?"

"I gave it to Glenda, that's what my mother said happened, so that's what I did."

Arthur took his own coat off and placed it carefully about Rose's shoulders. "Come on lass, let's get us both home, it's been a long day."

"A long one but a significant one. Oh Arthur, it's all coming to pass, isn't it?"

"And so it is," replied Arthur both simply and prophetically.

"And I *will* see her again, just like she, my mum said."

"And so you shall."

It was some time before Rose had a chance to speak with Glenda again. She had taken to the regular habit of sitting on the seat near to the standing stones where she not only had a good view in several directions, but also of Glenda's flat. However, it was only the occasional glimpse that she caught of her out pushing the pram, and once in Marks and Spencer, when it was clear she was again with child.

Not having attached any significance to the day, one particular sunny afternoon in May, Rose was sitting in her usual place, enjoying the late spring offerings in the park. Her own garden, although lush with tulips, iris and peonies, was nothing like these neatly laid borders. Her favourite though, was always the cherry blossom, and today was no exception. She was marvelling in its now fading beauty, and hadn't noticed who had sat beside her along with a pram.

"Jasmine, be careful, I don't want you to hurt your knee again."

"I won't Mummy," a little voice shouted back.

It took a moment for Rose to feel composed enough to make conversation, she was content enough to see Jasmine, her mother-to-be, at play. Rose had jumped on and off those very stones as a girl and her mother had called out to her to be careful in an almost identical manner.

"That takes me back," declared Rose. "I remember clambering over those standing stones at around the same age.

Glenda looked across at her and smiled, but then her face changed to that of curiosity. "You look familiar somehow, sorry, I'm afraid I don't recall from where," she said apologetically.

"I'm often sat here, maybe that's it."

"Maybe," answered Glenda unconvinced.

"How old is your baby?" asked Rose, keeping the conversation going.

"She'll be one year-old next week," replied Glenda and pulled back the covers in the pram inviting Rose to have a look at the sleeping bundle.

"Oh how lovely," exclaimed Rose. "A girl?"

"Yes, she's called Lucy," said Glenda, surprised the old lady seemed to know she was a girl, for she'd dressed her all in white.

"I thought so, she looks like a girl, boys have a different air about them even at this age I think." She sighed before carrying on. "Two girls hey, how lovely, congratulations."

"Thank you, yes, having Lucy has made me very happy."

"And Jasmine? I heard you call out her name, it is Jasmine isn't it"

"Oh, er yes of course," replied Glenda, but then had a fit of coughing and didn't say any more until Jasmine came running up wanting to check that her baby sister was still asleep.

"Yes, she is fast asleep," replied Glenda. "Don't poke your dirty fingers at her, you'll wake her up." Jasmine pulled her eager fingers away and looked towards Rose.

"Old, old lady," Jasmine whispered loudly in Glenda's ear.

"It's rude to whisper, why don't you say hello to her?" said Glenda. But Jasmine retreated behind the pram not wanting to engage with the stranger.

"Hello to you, your Mummy tells me your name is Jasmine, is that right?" asked Rose gently. Jasmine withdrew further by climbing up beside Glenda and nestling into her arm on the other side to where Rose was sitting but gave a concession by nodding her head.

"You have a very pretty name and I'm very pleased to meet you, Jasmine. My name is the name of a flower too, just like yours. It's Rose, my name is Rose." Rose emphasised the 'oh' sound as if it were of importance, and it seemed to have the desired effect, for Jasmine was imitating the shape of the 'oh' with her own mouth. "Yes, that's right, you've got it, 'R-oh-se'." She put out her hand to try and shake Jasmine's, but that was too much for the three-year-old and she hid both her hands behind her back and looked away. Crestfallen, Rose sighed silently, but she understood. No young child would openly warm to a wrinkly old stranger, even if they might happen to be their own daughter.

The best plan of action, she decided, was to keep quiet and savour being in her company and watching her at play for as long as possible. This proved to be correct; a further twenty minutes went by before Lucy began to stir and Glenda thought it best to get her home. Glenda explained that it was Jasmine's birthday today, and they had made her birthday cake, leaving it to cool down before going back to put on the icing. The only outward response Rose made at the realisation it was her mother's birthday was a tighter grip of her handbag. Inwardly she was annoyed she'd forgotten the significance of the day. Glenda called over to Jasmine, who came running back with a clutch of daisies.

"Flowers," declared Jasmine, showing them to Glenda.

"Daises," Glenda replied. "We'll put them in some water when we get home, it looks as though they'll need some."

"Happy birthday Jasmine," said Rose. Jasmine couldn't help herself and responded with the sweetest of smiles reaching into every corner of Rose's being. She smiled back and looked into her mother's eyes and felt her essence, just how she remembered it to be.

"I got a dolly," declared Jasmine and put her hands into the tray underneath the pram and picked out a blanket bundle which she began to rock and coo at.

"Does your dolly have a name" asked Rose.

"Tiny Tears," answered Jasmine distinctly.

"We must go. Jasmine, put Tiny Tears back in the pram and hold onto the handle with me." Jasmine did as she was told, and they went on their way at toddler speed until they reached the road where Glenda scooped Jasmine up under her arm. Rose watched them all the way home in the hope that Jasmine would glance back so she could wave to her. She didn't. Rose shed a silent tear.

A few weeks later, after coming back from Woods with a stack of records for the jukebox, Rose saw two women she didn't recognise coming out of Glenda's front door.

"I think they've moved on," said Rose to Arthur. They were sitting in the café in the park. Arthur knew exactly who Rose was talking about; the time was about right from what she'd remembered of her mother's story.

"At least you got to meet her."

"Yes, at least I had that." She drank her tea, swallowing her emotions along with it.

"How many records did you buy?" Arthur asked, gesturing towards Rose's shopping bag with his eyes, realising a change of subject was in order.

"Four more. Nice to fill a few more spaces, almost done!"

"Which ones?"

"Number eleven, *Nights in White Satin* by some group called The Moody Blues, number thirteen, *I Heard it Through the Grape Vine* by Marvin Gaye..."

"Ah Yes," Arthur interrupted, "I've heard that one on the radio, it's quite catchy I think."

"... and number twenty-three, *I Can Hear Music* by The Beach Boys. I like their songs; they make me want to dance. Not that I have ever done much dancing, but the rhythms are always so upbeat don't you think?"

"Can't beat a good rhythm, that's for sure."

"Then number eighteen, *1900 Yesterday,* by Liz Damon's Orient Express - don't know that one at all. Mmm, this flapjack is delicious, are you sure you don't want to have some?" Arthur shook his head and waved his arms by way of saying no thanks. That's the lot for the moment," continued Rose, finishing the remaining flapjack.

"You have a crumb on your top lip," said Arthur, wishing he could reach over and brush it off for her. Her mouth had wrinkled, and her eyes weren't as clear, but Arthur saw beyond her ageing skin and stooping frame, to her strength of heart, her resilience and her steadfast determination through thick and thin. It was that which he admired, no, loved about her; that knowing to keep going onwards. She was his inspiration to do the same despite his joking sometimes that she preferred to be looking back.

"Has it gone?" Rose asked, having scrubbed at her mouth with a tissue in earnest.

"Can't see it, you must have got it," Arthur verified. "Busy in here today don't you think?" Someone had bumped his chair as they'd squeezed between Arthur and Rose's table and the one next to them, without offering any form of apology. Arthur had only just managed to save his tea from being spilled by a deft shoulder manoeuvre. He looked daggers at the miscreant, approving of manners and decorum rather than impropriety. Everything in its place; he needed to be in control, or that old nervous condition of his could take over, God forbid!

I got number twenty-four, *Needles and Pins* by the Searchers and number fourteen, *Mr Tambourine Man* by The Byrds some time ago too. I forgot to tell you," continued Rose, the minor disturbance having passed.

"Can't be many more to get then."

"Four more, number three, *Every Breath You Take* by Sting and the Police, number twenty, *After the Goldrush* by Prelude, number twenty-two, *Maggie May* by Rod Stewart and number twenty-five, *El Condor Pasa* by Simon And Garfunkel."

"And you've still no idea why these particular songs? I must confess, most of the ones you have already aren't really to my taste," declared Arthur.

"Nor mine. However she must have chosen them for a reason, but I have no idea what that reason is, or was. Perhaps they mean something to my other father, but I haven't the foggiest notion."

"I see, some sort of message perhaps?" replied Arthur.

"We may never know; we may never know," said Rose sighing and thinking back to the day a few months before when she'd met her mother as a three-year-old. She had now to come to terms with the fact that the little family from flat one, twenty-three Meadowsring road, had moved out of town and she would never see or hear of them again. But how lovely the encounter had been. Such a gift, and perhaps why her mother had never mentioned it, and so keep it as a wonderful surprise.

Chapter Seventeen

1990

Arthur had got himself a puppy. "Keeps me on my toes," was his explanation to Rose. He'd bumped into her in the park having wanted to be out before the rain set in. It had already started to spit, but the puppy needed walking.

"At your age," she scoffed. "You'll have to take it for walks twice a day, including in the rain, wind and fog. Do you realise what you've committed yourself to?"

"Well I'm out and doing that anyway, so that doesn't faze me. And now I'll have good company. Besides, I thought having a dog would help keep me calm. They say stroking a dog is good for you; helps with stress and blood pressure and all that." He bent down to pat his dog affectionately, who reciprocated by jumping up at him.

"And you'll need to teach him some manners, he can't be jumping up like that all the time. People don't like it." Rose bent down and stroked the dog who immediately started pawing at her skirt. "See what I mean?" said Rose. "Is he house trained? I don't want him in my house if he isn't."

"Rose, when am I ever in your house? It must be years. You come to mine or we meet in the park. I can't remember what yours even looks like inside."

"Well not much has changed apart from some damp getting into the library; no damp-proof course you see. It's just as well I moved all my old photographs out of there and up into the attic when I did. I quite like it in the old servant's rooms, nice and dry up there. The larger one of the two would be very cosy if I could manage to get a fire lit in the grate. Not much draw you understand, up there. Don't know how the servants ever managed it."

"You shouldn't be dragging coal all the way up to the attic Rose, at your age, now you're the one who's being idiotic."

"Well it was just the once and it did do me in rather, but nice all the same looking at all the old photographs one more time. I haven't done that for years; quite took me back."

"You are always looking backwards Rose. I like to look forward, it keeps me going. That's why I got this little rascal."

"What have I got to look forward to I ask you Arthur Pickford, but more old age?"

"It doesn't matter what your age is, it's how you embrace life. Seize the day, that's what I say. And you appear to be doing the same actually, otherwise I wouldn't have bumped into you."

"You know how much I like to wander around the park, it's what keeps me going. But I have my father's old walking stick with me these days; frightened of falling you know. However, I neither need nor desire a dog, it would surely pull me over."

"Well, yes, maybe you're right. Anyway," said Arthur looking up at the sky, "must get this little one home and dry before the weather gets any worse. Oh, and by the way, he's a she."

"Oh sorry; my mistake."

"No problem; nice to see you Rose."

"Yes, and you," came the reply.

That was several hours ago, and now the disappearing daylight prompted Rose to turn on her reading lamp. Rose had been sitting stoically, like she always did. Waiting, just waiting, until the day her mother promised would happen. The day she would meet her real father. But that still seemed to be so far away; she could barely imagine it, feeling as she did now. What would it be like to be one hundred years old? A bag of old bones was all she could imagine.

Heaving up her old and stiffening bones from out of her favourite armchair, she reached for the switch and then walked carefully to the window. It took her a bit of time to get going, especially as she'd been sitting in the same position most of the afternoon with her head in a book. She wiped her fingers over the build-up of condensation on the windowpane and peered into the dreary gloaming over the top of her reading glasses tutting at the continuous mizzling rain. Dusk had arrived an hour early thanks to the hour change the previous night. She wasn't looking forward to winter; the house wasn't the warmest, unless she lit all the fires, and there was never a need for that; she never had guests. She gazed absentmindedly through the window immersed in contemplation

Jasmine House. How its tender heart had throbbed in days gone by when thronged with her parents and brother, cousins and uncles and aunts, and the servants of course. All long gone or moved to the far reaches of the globe, leaving Rose with mere memories of those faraway days. Christmas cards were Rose's main communication of family news now, bringing updates of who was born, who had died, and all the things that distant relatives thought she ought to know. She hardly knew who the younger members were, having never ventured out of her native Yorkshire to meet them, nor had they come to see her. For them, she was but a distant once or twice-removed cousin from some historic generation, someone who they possibly knew existed, but not necessarily. Her first cousins, the two she had left, for many had gone with the war and then steadily since, were as old and decrepit as she was, and neither one was local.

A car came down the street, its headlights blinded Rose as they shone directly into the window. The spell was broken. She averted her eyes until it had passed the bend in the road out of her line of vision and she drew the curtains, shutting out the external world in retort. The fire needed her attention; there were only embers left. Rose lifted the coal scuttle carefully and threw a little of its contents in amongst the glowing cinders. She poked at it a bit, and moved the damper for a better draw. She then repaired to the kitchen to put the kettle on for a cup of tea before making something to eat for her evening meal, leaving the fire to pick up by itself.

By the time she went back into the sitting room the fire was roaring. She turned the damper back down, it wouldn't do to have it blazing so furiously, it would burn itself out in no time and she didn't feel like having to heave more coal from the coal cellar. What she had left in the scuttle would have to last the evening. She double checked, the damper was definitely closed off, but she could still hear the sound of a fire roaring and crackling loudly, and there was a popping noise. She knew, almost before the dense thick smoke started coming down from above and into the fireplace what it was. For a moment she was rooted to the spot, not knowing what to do first, then the doorbell rang and someone was banging on the front door urgently, so she went to see who it was.

"Your chimney's on fire," yelled a concerned looking Arthur as she opened the door to him. She stepped aside to let him in, along with his dog.

"Where's your phone?" His manner was crisp, but she understood the urgency and gestured towards the small table in the hall. Arthur went straight to it and dialled the number nine three times at the same time as gesticulating to Rose to get outside. Emotionally confused, Rose did as she was bidden but without thinking to take her walking stick or put on her coat. Her ears caught Arthur's voice relaying her address down the phone as she stepped into the cold dank drizzle outside.

There were mini explosions bursting out from the top of the chimney and Rose felt something she had never in her life allowed herself to feel. Standing as still as a statue, panic and terror flooded her body. "Don't worry love," said a voice from somebody who had come outside to watch the spectacle, "it's just the chimney, a bird's nest probably, they'll soon put it out."

"Do you have plenty of salt?" asked Arthur. He had come out to find her and see if she was all right.

"Plenty, yes thank you," replied Rose in a daze.

"Would you show me where it is, and quickly?"

"It'll be in the kitchen cupboard next to the cooker where it always is I expect," said Rose, completely disconnected.

"And the kitchen is where? I can't remember."

"First door on the left as you go in."

"Thank you, I'll try to put out the fire in the grate with it." Arthur dashed back inside leaving Rose with those who had gathered to gawp.

It wasn't long before the fire brigade arrived, but long enough for the fire to have spread into the space above the attic through loose mortar in the chimney breast. There was quite a blaze for them to deal with as now some of the roof timbers had caught light and part of the roof was falling in. All the while in silent vigil and getting colder and wetter, Rose stood watching her beloved house burn and the firemen with their hoses. her frailty suddenly apparent, so much so the firemen had asked for an ambulance to attend.

Somebody put a blanket around her shivering frame, Arthur asked her if he could take her door key, thankful to have been passing by with his dog at the right moment. Another helped her into the ambulance which took her to the hospital, where a kind individual helped her onto a hospital trolley and gave her a cup of tea. Rose lay there, seemingly hemmed in by a wall of curtains, her tea untouched; she couldn't reach it while laying down. A face then appeared through a chink in the curtain screen, just in time before her tea grew cold. It grinned at her and introduced itself as Dr Fleming, the junior house officer, and asked how she was. "I can't reach my tea," she answered feebly.

"I'll help you," Dr Fleming replied with benevolence, and he lifted the back of the trolley so she could sit up.

"That's better, thank you," said Rose.

"Could you tell me your name?" asked the good doctor.

"Yes," replied Rose.

"Well, what is it?"

"Miss Brown, Miss Rose Brown."

"And do you know what has happened to you?"

"Yes."

"Please would you tell me," he asked patiently.

"I thought they would have told you," replied Rose, and took another sip of tea. She looked around inquisitively. "I don't suppose they have any custard creams, do they? I'm quite partial to them."

"I'm sorry, I don't think they do. Who do you think would have told me?"

"The very nice ambulance men who brought me here. Didn't they give you their report?"

"Er yes, I have it here on the sheet, but I wanted to hear it from you too."

"Yes I understand. You want to see if I have all my faculties. I am perfectly well doctor, the only thing that is wrong is that my house has been on fire and that, and that..." Rose could say no more and broke down in tears and Dr Fleming could do no other than put a consoling arm around her and say that a nurse would come shortly to attend to her. He then disappeared through the curtain barrier as abruptly as he had appeared.

It had happened so unexpectedly, she'd had little time to take it in, Rose could only imagine the devastation. She appreciated it was only bricks and mortar, but it was all she knew, she'd never lived anywhere else. Apart that is, from the student nurses' accommodation during her nurse training. And of course at her grandparents, helping to bring the injured officers back to health. Jasmine House was her home and it meant more to her than anyone could ever know. It needed to be intact, *they* would never buy it if it were in such a state. Rose looked at the familiar patterns of the curtain material that surrounded her and the trolley she lay upon and began to warm up; her thoughts becoming more rational in response. Of course she knew *they* bought it because her mother had said, so somehow she would have it restored. "Oh my!" she exclaimed out loud, "I have an enormous task ahead of me."

Another face appeared through the curtains. "So it *is* you. When I heard the name I had to come and see for myself."

"Nurse Simpson?" enquired Rose tentatively.

"The very same, I'm surprised you recognised me; I have surely changed in the last thirty-five years. And it's not Nurse Simpson, it's Senior Nurse Blenkinsop."

"You got to be Matron then, I always knew you'd go far. Congratulations to you." Rose bowed her head slightly in respect.

"Ha, that post doesn't exist, Matron Smith was the last one, she came after Matron Pilkington who I'm sure you will remember."

"They might alter the name, but the office is the same, and no doubt they'll change it back; it all goes round in circles, nothing really changes; people will still get ill and need nursing back to health."

"Well you certainly haven't changed, that's for sure," replied Senior Nurse Blenkinsop.

"Hmm, I'm not so certain about that," said Rose softly, remembering the circumstances that had brought her to the hospital. "I'm not fit to be on my own, I've set my house on fire, and now I've nowhere to live."

"Dear me, I understand it was a chimney fire, and that can happen to anyone, so don't think it was anything that you did. And as for having nowhere to live, we have a bed for you on your old ward; it's women's medical now, we'll keep an eye on you for any sign of delayed shock, and then tomorrow we'll set about finding you a place to stay while your house is repaired. I expect the insurance will cover it. You do have insurance?"

"Yes, of course."

"Why did I ever think I needed to ask," giggled Senior Nurse Blenkinsop. "You were always super-efficient in all things; of course you have! Now, is there anyone that we need to contact for you?"

Senior Nurse Blenkinsop took complete charge of Rose while she was in the accident and emergency department, and as Rose had been an important and influential part of The Royal's nursing team for such a long time, the on-call consultant was called to come and give her a thorough examination. She then escorted Rose onto the ward and into a bed. "I've asked the nurses to take good care of you, and I'll be back to see you in the morning," she told Rose fondly.

"Thank you, you have been very kind," answered Rose, settling to sleep, cocooned for the moment from reality by the pampering of the nurses and another cup of tea along with, delightfully, a custard cream biscuit! All indeed would be well, the fire had been extinguished and Arthur would no doubt sort out 'the necessaries,' which is how he had described them to her. Good old Arthur, he always came to her rescue when she needed him, and she was so grateful, and thank goodness he happened to be walking past with his new dog and noticed the fire.

Alas for Rose, the emotional strain of the evening's misfortune managed to sneak its way in just when most good people felt safe and secure and sound asleep. As a result, things didn't go quite to plan. Rather than staying overnight, Rose was to remain in hospital for several weeks, due to a small matter of her falling out of an unfamiliar bed in the middle of the night and fracturing her hip. By the time Rose was ready to be discharged from the hospital ward, she was still unsteady on her broken hip, and very much daunted by the prospect of having to look after herself in her very large and empty house. It wasn't ready for her to move back into anyway, according to Arthur, despite his best efforts.

The insurance company had asked two local builders to come up with quotes for the building works. Following Arthur's advice, Rose opted for the more expensive one anticipating they would do a better job. It meant she had to dig deep into her savings having been advised to have a completely new roof rather than patching up the old one. The insurance did not cover her for all that. On top of the gaping hole from the fire, slates were either broken, loose or missing in various places and there was no form of insulation whatsoever. Rose knew her home would fare better with a sound roof; it would never do to have the risk of leakage and for it all to crumble away. She might feel rather dilapidated herself, but her house didn't need to fall away along with her, at least she had the power to rejuvenate a building.

Always living frugally, her nursing and state pension more than adequate, Rose had never needed to dip into her inherited family money. But she could think of no better way to spend it now than on herself and her own family, the ones she believed would be buying her home a few years hence. Thus while it was being sorted and she felt ready to return, Rose made a decision. She would be looked after by caring persons who would cook, clean and look after all her needs. It would be like the old days, when Mrs Cook, Polly, Charles, and the rest of the lovely staff had been in her father's employment, cooking, cleaning and taking her out for rides in the motorcar. She'd rather enjoyed the same during her stay in hospital, and was keen for it to continue, at least for the moment. She would look for a care home; somewhere local so she could be near to what she knew and loved. The one in Greenhead Road would do, she thought, until she was able to return home when all the work was completed. Friends from over the years had all moved away or were deceased, so any ideas of moving in with them were a no go. Even Paula had deserted her when she'd married Dr Alistair and moved to Cornwall of all places. There was only Arthur left, and she couldn't possibly stay with him; it wouldn't do, not at all. Consequently, there was a plan in place for her move into Greenhead Care Home to convalesce.

Meanwhile, Rose was keen to see how the workmen had put her beloved house back together. Arthur had been keeping her well-informed, but she'd wanted to see it for herself. So, when the day came to move to the care home for her rehabilitation, he made it all possible. He picked her up in a taxi from the hospital and took her back to Jasmine House first. It had been Rose who'd chosen the name 'Jasmine House.' It was after her mother had died. She knew her mother as Estelle, but it had never been her intended name. The lovely old rose that had given her her name wasn't the only creeper. There was also, giving out its sweet fragrance when in bloom, a white jasmine vine climbing up the south wall. Rose couldn't think of a more apt name to remember her mother by.

Rose hobbled inside onto the familiar chequerboard floor of the hall and gave a sigh. She was home! Slowly, gingerly, she raised her head above her stooped body and looked up. Relief washed over her. No smoke, no fire, no difference. The high ceiling of the galleried landing was clean and bright and only the airy aroma of fresh new paint filled her nostrils. Her visions of fire-damage everywhere, even though Arthur had reassured her it had all been contained in the roof, had been unfounded. Even the water damage from the fire-fighter's hose pipes had been mainly confined to the attic. Nevertheless, Rose insisted on inspecting everywhere. They started in the cellar and worked their way up. Rose had always remained active despite approaching ninety, but now her progress through the house was painfully slow. All appeared well, until, that is, they went up to the attic. Rose was looking for something, Arthur could tell by the way her anxious eyes were darting frantically around the room.

"They're just waiting for the plaster to dry out before they can redecorate in here," encouraged Arthur.

"My photographs, what did they do with my photographs?" Arthur's stomach lurched in dread for the next part of the conversation.

"Rose," were they up here before the fire?"

"Yes, I brought them all up along with some letters from my nursing days and my silver belt buckle and badge. It was drier here I thought, than in the library; it gets damp in there you know. I'm sure I told you that I'd put them up here."

"Oh dear me, dear me Rose. Perhaps if you'd lit the fire in the library occasionally it wouldn't have felt as damp. I'm afraid they will have burned along with everything else in this room. The fire began in the roof space above and caught the rafters, but the flames also spread into here as the fire burned its way through the lath and plaster ceiling. I'm so very sorry, there was nothing left in here, nothing at all apart from your belt buckle. If your badge was with it, it's been lost in all the debris. It was only by chance I saw your buckle. It was in a sorry state, black from the fire. I hadn't thought to mention it till you'd just remarked on it. I took it home thinking to try and clean it but haven't got round to it as yet. Oh dear, oh deary me."

Rose's hand had been resting lightly on her walking stick, but all of a sudden, she crumpled like a balloon having had all its air sucked out. The break in the neck of her femur had been a huge shock, but she'd pulled through with valour, and still had much of her old spirit. But not at this moment.

"Hold on old lass, I've got you," said a breathless Arthur. Age was gaining the upper hand on him also, and it took all his strength in keeping her upright. He managed to set her down onto an old milk crate that the workmen had been using to stand on. It was some time before he was able to help her get downstairs and call for another taxi and escort the distraught old lady the few hundred yards to Greenhead.

PART THREE

Chapter Eighteen

Wednesday, January 5th, 2000

The aroma that assailed his nostrils was sickly-sweet, with an underlying odour of stale urine, and what he could only imagine as, that of impending death. It was as it was the first time Steve had come to Greenhead Care Home to see the old lady. And what was so haunting amongst the wrinkles and sagging skin of the residents, was that he knew he was looking directly into his future. Deeply lined faces, each set to expressions of worry and fear and woe.

On his previous visit though, all had been regular and ordinary, when he knew exactly where Jasmine was, and he'd been comparatively content. However, all that he knew to be true had disappeared along with her. Everything, including these old folk, seemed to be reminding him that the only thing he knew for certain was that if nothing got us beforehand, old age would. We were all doomed. It was as if time were suspended in this place; where one came when life ceased to move forward, where everything stopped, and one simply waited for the inevitable destination.

Both he and Trevor were led over to where Miss Brown was seated. It was the same spot where Steve had seen her on New Year's Eve and for a moment he allowed himself to imagine that like in this room, time had stood still, and he'd left Jasmine at home and all was well. Alas, even though only a few days had elapsed since he had done just that, it seemed a lifetime ago now. Steve glanced at Trevor who appeared to have an inane kind of half grin fixed on his face.

"My goodness Rose no sooner than one set of visitors leaves, another lot arrives. It's two young gentlemen this time, they say they've both been here before. Are you happy to see them?"

Rose came out of some sort of reverie and looked up. It was clear she was going to say something but it was some time before any words were formed. "My glasses please," she mouthed eventually.

The nurse-assistant found her glasses on the side table next to Rose and helped her to put them on. When they both appeared satisfied they were properly placed, Rose focussed on her visitors and her face lit up. Her smile was lovely; curiously, almost familiar.

"Hello again," began Steve. "I was here the other day. I, er, live in your house."

"And I'm Trevor his friend, you know, the dentist," added Trevor. Steve gave his friend a sidelong look while Rose regarded him and nodded, and then looked back towards Steve. After a very long moment, she spoke. "I wondered when you would be back. Has your father told you already? I'm sure it was only a few minutes since he was here."

"My father, here?"

Rose studied him for a while, as if looking for something in his face. "Ah, so he hasn't." Steve thought she looked a little disappointed, but about what, he hadn't a clue; it made no sense. Why would his father have been here anyway? He thought it best to stick to the matter in hand. "Er, you were asking about the letters. We have brought them for you." He held them out to her. She looked at them in recognition, but gently raised her hand as if in defence.

"Oh no, they aren't mine. They're for you. Have you read them?" she asked hesitantly.

"Er, yes, some of them. I found them very interesting, but why are you giving them to me?" The old lady, hands clasped together at her chest, looked at Steve with such tenderness it made him feel awkward.

"Oh dear, I think you are going to need to sit down," came the reply. Steve sat down on an adjoining chair. Trevor pulled one over from a few feet away and sat down too, eager to hear what she was about to say. "So here it is," Rose began with wavering voice. "Many years ago, when I was about fourteen, I came across these letters in the same place where you will have found them, behind the drawer of my mother's dressing table. They weren't mine to read, but I was a curious girl and I couldn't help myself. At the time, I wished I hadn't, for they rocked my foundations as to who I thought I was. But if I hadn't, then so much might have been different." Rose paused a while before continuing, her breathing had become quite rapid and shallow and it was clearly difficult for her to talk for so long. "In them, as you can see, it was evident that the father I thought was my flesh and blood, was not at all. Another man was my father; a secret man that my mother loved till her dying day but could never tell a soul."

Rose stopped talking in order to rest, she'd already told her story once today. Steve remembered the content of the letters - life in the nineteen hundreds, but written as if the writer was telling someone about her life. Someone who she would never see again, and there had been a poignancy about them. The writer had found herself to be pregnant, but she could not be with her lover so she married someone else and pretended the baby was his. She named the baby Rose, he recalled. He waited until Rose was ready to continue, still not sure where it was all leading.

"Don't you recognise her handwriting?" Rose asked presently.

"Her handwriting? Should I? Whose is it? It's certainly from someone who finds writing with a nib difficult, it's full of blots of ink."

"Yes, she never got used to having to dip her pen into the inkwell. Anyway, when my mother realised I had read the letters, rather than scold me, she tried to explain what had happened. Oh dear, this is difficult." She stopped again. After a few minutes she began again. "I'll say it exactly how my mother said it to me, it's the only way I can do it. It was New Year's Eve, and she was walking home from a party."

'Sounds familiar,' thought Steve.

"And she found it harder and harder to see because of the fog, and she had such a pain in her head and ringing in her ears."

Steve glanced at Trevor; this story was a little too close to home. He remembered what the police officer had said about Jasmine being seen on camera rubbing her head because a ladder had fallen on her head after, after... their lovemaking in the broom cupboard.

"She thinks she was around the East Gate of the park. Well that's where she was in our time when it happened."

"What happened?" said Trevor. He was on the edge of his seat.

"She went through some sort of time warp. Well, that's how she explained it to me anyway." She stopped there, for two pennies to drop.

Steve was first to break the silence. "So you mean that Jasmine went through time, and, and that's where she is now?" Rose nodded affirmatively and studied his response thoroughly, she understood how hard it would be for him to comprehend. This may be all an upset for him, but at the same time, it was full of joy for her. She had waited a lifetime to meet him and all her love for him was now pouring out. Her heart may have been tired and old, but it was still able to feel and to love. He was her real father... and a close and proper relative at that. Since meeting Steve when he came to see her for the first time on New Year's Eve, she knew her dreary existence would be changing. Even a much relieved Arthur had noticed a glow about her when he'd visited that afternoon. She had no idea how much more life she had to live with her old bones, but she intended to live it with zest.

Steve tried his hardest, but it was a struggle. Computing this crazily irrational information was agonisingly challenging. He got up from his seat and circled around Trevor, whose eyes followed him in their own orbital whirl. Trevor was glad he was sat down - he was becoming rather dizzy watching Steve so avidly. They were both thinking the same. How could this ridiculous impossibility actually be real!? In the end, Steve conceded and came and sat back down. "And she was pregnant?"

"Yes, she was. I was conceived on New Year's Eve. You could never have known," Rose replied.

'She got pregnant in the broom cupboard. I made her pregnant! I'm going to be a father,' thought an overjoyed Steve, until he realised the connotations of what he was hearing and quickly bumped back down to earth. "So what you are saying is that you, you are my daughter."

"Yes, I am."

Silence. That's all Trevor noted until Rose broke it. He sat agog, feeling deeply for his mate. He couldn't imagine what he was thinking, what he was imagining or going through. Hell maybe. Was this good news or bad that they now knew what had happened? At least Jasmine was safe, or had been safe, once upon a time; for she was surely dead now; her daughter was nigh on one hundred.

"I know this is shocking for you," Rose continued, "but she told me you would come to see me on the eve before the century turned. Such a long time to wait, but wait I did for that moment; the moment when I would finally see you, my real father. Time and again I was ready to give up, but then I held onto what she said to me, that you would come on that day, and that I would know who you were. She was my mother, and I trusted her through and through, and I held on so I could meet you. I couldn't tell you then, on that day, because she hadn't yet gone back, and anyway, you wouldn't have been able to understand."

"I'm not sure I understand now," replied Steve, overwhelmed by this old woman's extraordinary words. "How can this be true? Why didn't you warn me so I could stop her, stop it happening?"

"Because it had already happened; it would have been impossible to change it. A lot of history has happened because of it."

He looked into Rose's eyes, and he knew, even though they were aged and faded, that they were like her mother's. He took her shaking wrinkled hands into his and wept. It was all too impossible to imagine, let alone realising it to be true. Rose squeezed his hands as best as she was able. "Do you have any photographs of her?" he asked at length. If he were to see her picture, it would prove everything, but he already knew it to be so, he could feel it in his bones and Rose's face spoke volumes.

"Unfortunately not, they got burned in a fire. I thought I was keeping them safe for you, but it was the opposite. I was devastated about that." Rose sighed, remembering the sad events; her deeply lined face drooping, corroborating her desolation.

Steve sank into the chair, head in hands, he wasn't even to see a picture of his beloved Jasmine from this other place, this other time. "Oh, I never thought," Rose piped up suddenly, "your father might have some."

"My father?" He lifted his head in surprise. Yet again his father was popping up in unexpected spots.

"Yes, his grandfather, I think, would have had some of my mother, of all of us in fact. He had many interests, one of which was photography."

"You mean Jason Bartram?"

"I do! He was married to my father's, my stepfather's sister. You are his descendent."

"Yes I know, we had many pictures, but Mum wanted to declutter and threw them out. I kept one of Jason Bartram though as I could see how I looked like him."

"Yes you do, I could see the likeness immediately, but in all my years I didn't know my mother had married his relation. No wonder she always had a good rapport with him, *he* reminded her of *you*. It must have been such a comfort to her." Rose thought she was going to cry, her emotions were getting the better of her, and she preferred to keep them in check. She cleared her throat, her quivering hands finding their way up to her nose to wipe it with a tissue she had crumpled on her lap. She was tired now, the last few days had brought renewed vigour and so much joy, but her aged body was not used to it, and she needed rest.

Trevor had managed to sit in quiet observance throughout, for he had no part to play in the surrealistic drama that was unfolding before him, other than thinking that Steve's father had been right all the time to think it had something to do with the energies of the stone circle. He thought to listen more carefully to what Penny said about invisible forces and ley lines for there was no way he wanted to get sucked back to some awful time in history. He was quite happy where he was, thank you very much. How Steve was going to live with this he had no idea, but he would be there for him as far as he was able, he knew that at least. "I'll take him home so he can think about all this. I'll make sure he comes back before long."

"Yes, this is a lot for us both to take in," replied Rose, "I will look forward to it."

"One more thing," began Steve. "What year was it she went to please?"

"It was the very early hours of the new century. The first of January nineteen hundred," declared Rose.

Trevor glanced at Steve whose eyes were in a blank stare. "The - millennium - bug - was - real - then," declared Trevor giving voice slowly and deliberately to what Steve was thinking.

The two men got up and moved outside, normal conversation eluding them, but once in the car and seatbelts on, Trevor felt moved to say something. "What do you think to it all?"

Steve looked across at him, almost raging. Trevor had never seen him like this and shifted slightly in his seat in attempt to keep his distance.

"What do I think? How would you feel if you found out that Penny had slipped back a century and had your baby that you had no idea about? It's not like she's gone on holiday is it? Not only will I never see her again, but our daughter is older than me and about to die because she's almost a hundred years old! How do you think I think? What I don't think is, I don't think I can take this, it's too weird. Trevor, am I sane, is all this real?" Steve then took hold of Trevor's arms in a grip so firm, and with eyes so menacing that Trevor wondered if his pal was going to get violent. But he was good in unpredictable situations, he was a dentist after all and ever prepared for a patient who might take umbrage and lash out at a critical moment during a root canal, or while injecting a bit of local anaesthetic.

"Oh mate, I don't know what to say, but your dad might. Rose said he'd been to visit before we came. Let's see what he has to tell."

Steve loosened his grip on Trevor's arms. "Yes, he's been keeping something very quiet, that's for sure. I'd like to see what he has to say for himself."

"Good, sounds like a plan then," replied Trevor. He gave his arms a quick rub to make sure they were still intact, breathed a quiet sigh of relief, and turned the ignition. The Golf burst into life and they headed back to Jasmine House.

Chapter Nineteen

January 5th, pm

Tom Downey was the first to arrive at the blue-painted front door of number three Luck Lane and he rang the doorbell casually. Meanwhile, Jim Manning lagged behind on the pavement, keeping his distance and feeling uneasy about the whole expedition. With his coat collar upturned, he shifted from one foot to the other. In fact his manner was so furtive as he looked up and down the street, he could have been mistaken for someone operating on the wrong side of the law. He willed the door would open, and soon, so he could get inside and out of the way of the viewing public. He absolutely did not want to be recognised, not here. The normally cool-headed well-worn policeman was definitely out of his comfort zone.

Fortuitously for Jim Manning, the blue door opened promptly, and to his surprise, revealed a rather attractive middle-aged lady who lay rather too easily on the inspector's eyes. Not at all what he had imagined; very well turned out if he was pushed to give an opinion. Tom Downey didn't think anything much; he'd done as instructed and secured an appointment with 'Maureen the Medium' and was now accompanying his DI because it was expected of him.

"Good evening gentlemen, thank you for being so very prompt. Please come in." The two policemen followed Maureen indoors, Tom Downey giving way to his superior, who shot inside like a bullet heading down a gun barrel having reached muzzle velocity. They were led down a bright and airy corridor, through a very well-appointed modern kitchen and into a rather plush glass extension, in which it appeared as though one was outside and in the middle of a beautiful garden. Jim Manning's well-practiced eye took it all in. His uncharacteristic cloak-and-dagger behaviour melted away, uncovering yet another side to his character that even he didn't know he possessed; that given the right circumstances, even the great Jim Manning could be wooed. He was quite mesmerised. It was totally different from the picture he'd created mentally; a dark, crystal-heavy candle-lit milieu. They were invited to take a seat and he made himself comfortable in an Arne Jacobsen Egg chair and nodded to his hostess. "Very nice, very nice all this."

"Thank you, I'm pleased you like it, I like my guests to feel at ease. Shall we make a start? There's no time like the present is there?"

'That's debatable,' thought Jim Manning under his breath. "Absolutely," he declared out loud.

"So, began Maureen, "as you already know, my name is Maureen, and since childhood, I've had the ability to talk to the spirit world. My clients are usually those who are seeking contact with a loved-one who has departed the physical world. But I understand from our telephone conversation Tom, may I call you Tom?"

"Yes, please do," answered Tom Downey. He sat up a little straighter having quickly sunk into a rather plush red velvet sofa which appeared to be swallowing him into its softness.

"And please call me Jim Manning," declared Jim Manning, a broad smile appearing across his face.

"Will do. I understand that you are asking for my help in locating a woman who has gone missing over New Year. Is that right?"

Yes, in the early hours of the first of January," answered Tom Downey.

"The one that I have seen in leaflets in all the shops; the midwife?"

"Yes, that's correct," Jim Manning answered.

"You are familiar with my work; I don't need to elaborate further?" Maureen asked.

"I believe you have worked with the police before," replied Jim Manning, dismissing any more explanations from Maureen with a wave of his hand.

"Yes I have, but what I find is what I find. Sometimes it's only snippets of information that are difficult to interpret. Do you understand?"

"I understand."

"You've brought something that belongs to her?"

"Er, no, sorry."

"No matter, it's only an aid, I can work without. Give me a few minutes."

The two men sat comfortably albeit with some apprehension while Maureen closed her eyes and did some deep breathing. She then reopened her eyes and looked rather puzzled. "I have a lady here who says she's a lady. 'Yes, thank you.'" Maureen looked over her shoulder and nodded as if someone was there. The two policemen looked but saw no one. They fixed their gaze back to Maureen. "I'm getting mother energy. Pea, Pete, Peter? 'Ah, you are a *Lady*! I understand, thank you.'" Maureen was looking over her shoulder again. She then looked back towards her very captive audience. "When you see me looking over my shoulder like that, I'm speaking to my guide who is assisting me, so don't be alarmed, I'm not really talking to the air!"

Jim Manning thought she could talk to anything; so long as he could stay spellbound.

"The lady that comes to me," Maureen continued, "wishes to be known as Lady Peters. The name is very distinct. She's speaking on behalf of her daughter because her daughter, who is here, is letting her mother speak for the both of them. J; J, A, S something; Jasmine. I'm getting the word Jasmine."

'That can't be right, her mother is called Glenda,' thought Jim Manning. But then recalled what both Arthur Pickford and Rose Brown had stated that Jasmine had been born in the eighteen hundreds, been transported to nineteen seventy a few hours after birth; that was where he himself had been involved with the stillbirth investigation; before going back to nineteen hundred, which was when she disappeared from the present.

"'Yes, Lady Peters thank you, I'll tell them.' She says Jasmine, but the name is wrong; only it's the same woman; she passed at the end of the Great War quite quickly and unexpectedly. Oh, I think it was something respiratory, I can't breathe. 'Can you take it off me please,'" she said, looking over her shoulder once again and seemingly gasping for breath. "'Flu, thank you.' She had the flu. She wants you to know Jasmine, no, Esther? No, not Esther, Estelle, is fine and to tell Steve and Rose how much she loves them. What? Now I'm hearing *I Want to Hold Your Hand* by the Beatles, and an image of an old jukebox. 'Yes, thank you, I will.' Now she's showing me an old vinyl record and saying it's all in the letters, for him to look at the letters. 'Who has to look at the letters?' Oh, she's gone, I'm afraid. It's hard to hold the vibration for long sometimes. Did any of that make sense to you? I have to say I was more confused than anything else. I got the impression that Lady Peters, lived in an earlier age. She came across as a Victorian lady but the vibration I got was that of her mother, and she definitely conveyed the impression that Jasmine's passing was many years ago. It's as if she has lived twice, but that doesn't feel right either."

Maureen sighed, she had received the messages easily and plainly, but it hadn't made any sense. However, she explained, it wasn't her job to analyse the communications she received, only to convey them. "I got the sense that Jasmine, the woman you are looking for, was concerned about something, as if there was a message from her to be discovered. She kept showing me music. What I mean is, I kept hearing snippets of nineteen fifties dance music and sixties rock and roll, that type of thing. I suppose that is why I got a picture of a jukebox. I'm sorry, it was a very mixed reading."

"Actually," began Jim Manning, "what you've said makes things very clear for me. Thank you very much."

"Oh good, I'm glad you are able to fathom it," replied Maureen. "For me, it was as though I was looking at two different periods of time and that's the bit that wasn't making sense."

"But it did to me." Jim Manning stood up and looked round; he seemed loathed to go. "Nice, very nice," he declared, and reluctantly made a move. "I'll leave the monies to my colleague here."

"Lovely, thank you. Oh!" Maureen stopped short. Jim Manning had all but left the room when she called out. "It's in the details James, it's always in the details." The words stopped Jim Manning dead in his tracks. He breathed in sharply till his lungs were full. He hardly dared to turn around.

"What did you just say?" he asked warily when he felt ready.

"A message, it was a message. They come through like that indiscriminately sometimes, when they're eager to pass information across, or whenever they get the opportunity, like through a medium. It was for you wasn't it?"

"Hmm, maybe," he answered grudgingly, and walked away towards the front door and outside, needing some fresh air. The other stuff was all well and good, but *that!?* Of all the things to hear, it had been most unexpected.

It was at times like this he wished he still smoked. A minute or two went by and Tom Downey joined him outside and ventured to quiz his boss as to what had just happened.

"I thought you knew which way I was conducting this investigation, otherwise I would never have asked you to make the appointment with Mystic Maureen in the first place," his senior snapped, not looking at Tom, but at the ground instead.

"I meant the last bit, the 'it's in the details' bit. The rest made some sense, but not that."

Jim Manning managed to prise his gaze away from the floor and looked up. "No, it wouldn't have, for you, but it did for me. It was what my father always used to say. He was a copper too, and when he saw I was stuck on a case, he would always advise, 'it's in the details,' just like she said. Took me by surprise; didn't expect anything like that, no, definitely nothing like that. Fancy a drink, I could do with one after that. Come on, let's grab a pint down the Crown."

Chapter Twenty

January 5th, pm

"Where on earth have you been?" Steve had barely passed through the front door when Glenda bawled out the question, and before he was able to form any sort of reply, his mother-in-law continued with more. "Your father went off with that Inspector whatchamacallit and was cagey about why when he returned, and then you vanished, and I don't know what's going on or what's happening because nobody is telling me a thing!" Anne tried to console her long-time neighbour but Glenda moved out of reach.

"That's because there isn't anything to tell," answered Lucy, throwing her arms around her mother and hugging her tight. "No news is good news," she added when her mother appeared calmer.

She's not coming back," stated Steve.

"You don't know that," said Lucy, retaliating.

"Yes I do, and I'll prove it." Steve put his hand into his coat pocket and pulled out a roll of papers, tied with ribbon. "These are some letters from Jasmine telling me all about where she is."

"Telling you where she is?" repeated Glenda, unravelling herself from her daughter's arms. "Why didn't you say so before?"

"Because I didn't know until today that they were from her. Rose told me Jas had written them. Do you remember Rose, the lady in the park you spoke to when Jasmine was small?"

"Yes, I, I remember. But what's *she* got to do with all this?"

"Quite a lot actually," said Paul, realising instinctively that Steve also knew the truth. He and Tony had come out of the kitchen to see what was going on. "Come on son, I think we have got a lot to tell them between us. Shall we go somewhere more comfortable?"

They all repaired into the sitting room and sat down. "I'll start," said Paul obligingly. Steve felt relieved, he didn't know if he had the strength to speak; the truth was overwhelming. How could he ever make sense of this topsy-turvy universe he now found himself in? And what about Jas? How terrifying for her; how scared she must have been all on her own. At least he had his family. His family - his daughter was an old woman! No one could take that in their stride, no one. It wasn't right, the world wasn't playing fair; it was all too much. He felt; well, he didn't really know how he felt. Numb, wholly numb.

"As you all know," Paul began, "I've been busy with some calculations. I fully understand that maybe some of you haven't been able to appreciate why I felt they were of so much import, and why I've been spending more than a little time on them while Jasmine has been missing. What I think wasn't appreciated by some of you, was that I, just like all of you, have been trying to understand what's happened to her; to find where she is. The police haven't found any conclusive signs of attack, we know she wasn't planning to leave, yet still she disappeared. There had to be an explanation, an answer. And when Penny showed me the standing stones in the park, I had an improbable thought. I wrestled with it, but it wouldn't go away and I had to look further before dismissing my line of thinking. My theory was outlandish, but unlikely events happen all the time. In mathematics it is known as the improbability principle. Having explored along this rule before, I couldn't let it rest, and so my investigations began."

"Investigations?" quizzed Glenda.

"Penny explained to me how her interest in dowsing had proved that there was an energetic resonance in between and all around the stone circles," continued Paul and ignoring Glenda. "We also discovered that the doorstep of flat one, number twenty-three, Meadowsring Road was also a standing stone."

"The doorstep where we used to live was a standing stone?" asked Glenda, determined to be heard.

"Yes, and it still is," answered Paul, at last giving Glenda the satisfaction of having some attention.

"Well I still can't see what this has to do with anything," she huffed.

"I'm coming to that," continued Paul. "After mapping the stones, their relationship to each other et cetera, I found a remarkable similarity to the mathematical analysis of black holes in the theory of general relativity, to that which I found in the standing stones."

"I have no idea what you are talking about," sneered Glenda. All that mathematical mumbo jumbo of yours has nothing to do with my Jasmine."

"I'm afraid the science of quantum physics has everything to do with, as you say, your Jasmine. You see, if you take the doorstep into the calculations, depending on the constellations in the heavens being in the correct alignment, it could be feasible for a black hole to exist somewhere along the imaginary line from the doorstep of flat one, up to the outer ring of the circle."

Glenda was incredulous. "Imaginary line, black holes?"

"Correct, yes," Paul agreed, straining to address Glenda's confrontational manner as calmly as he could. "...And within a black hole it is theorised that the spacetime continuum can bend, which means time is able to bend back on itself."

"So where is my daughter in all this? I don't understand a thing you're telling me." Glenda was almost standing beside herself. Tony put his arm around her plentiful waist to steady her; he thought she might lose control, which under the circumstances, would be accepted as a normal and reasonable response; he was finding it rather difficult himself.

"It means," Steve continued, interrupting his father, "that Jasmine didn't go anywhere. She stayed exactly where she was, but our time bent towards the time of nineteen hundred, and she somehow slipped through, back into that time."

"A black hole," murmured Lucy.

"WHAT?" shrieked Glenda, Anne and Tony in unison.

"Jasmine went back in time. I know this because her daughter, *our* daughter, has told me this," said Steve.

"Daughter? Are you mad? Jasmine doesn't have a daughter," declared Glenda, still unbeaten.

"Oh but she has, or she did have. She was pregnant before she went back."

"Pregnant?" Glenda interrupted. "She never said she was pregnant."

"No, she didn't even know herself, until she went back to the year nineteen hundred. Her daughter..." Steve stopped; he was choking up.

"Rose," Paul interjected. "Their daughter's name is Rose. The same Rose you met in the park. The same Rose you spoke to the day you gave birth at home. She was there, waiting, waiting to see her mother, waiting to tell you that her name was meant to be Jasmine."

Glenda had begun to shake uncontrollably; Tony clung to her bravely, wondering if it was now *she* who was holding *him* up rather than the other way round. But the words filling up Glenda's ears seemed somehow to feel right, and she stopped interjecting. The voice of truth needed to be heeded, even she understood that. "You see," continued Paul as gently as he could, "Jasmine was born in eighteen seventy-eight and not nineteen seventy as we all very naturally, took for granted. The day she was born, the maid who was attending her, put her down on the doorstep while she chased after a delivery boy." Steve listened attentively; this was news to him. "And then she disappeared, reappearing just as you had given birth to your son."

"On the doorstep," said Tony; realisation coming.

"Yes," said Paul. And somehow, on New Year's Eve, she was taken back to, or replaced where she had originally come from." No one spoke. Everyone was processing what both Paul and Steve had said. At length Glenda was the one to break the silence.

"You know, it all makes so much sense, I have never had any recollection of giving birth to her. Only Andrew, our beautiful boy. I always thought I couldn't remember because it was all so traumatic. Now I realise I never gave birth to her. She wasn't my baby, not my little girl at all. Oh Tony, what have we done?"

With great reverence, her husband answered. "We have loved and cherished a beautiful child as our own, that is what we have done." But his heart was breaking into tiny little pieces and like an imploding bomb, hitting him with immeasurable hurt.

Glenda wept openly, her pain clear to see, but there was nothing anyone could do, and it touched the same wound inside them all. Jasmine was lost to them; fact.

At length, Steve remembered about the letters; he had been clutching them all the while. He looked down at them and fumbled with the ribbon that held them together. Other eyes, hungry for that elusive something looked on.

"We found these a few days before Christmas. I read some of them then, but of course never in a million years thought it was Jasmine who'd written them. Why would I? They weren't addressed to anyone, nor did she sign her name. I suppose if she had when we saw them it would have been too freaky. Maybe that's why she didn't, thinking I would work it out after she'd... after she'd..." He couldn't finish the sentence, he was distraught.

"May I"? Glenda asked, putting her hand out towards the little bundle. She undid the ribbon that Steve hadn't quite managed, and taking one of the letters, started to read out loud.

August 1918

My Dearest Love,

It seems so long since I last wrote, I swore to my mother I wouldn't write to you anymore. She felt it best that I try and forget. How could I ever do that when I love you still? I felt I had to write now. It's the war, oh my love, the war has started and I've dreaded this moment for years because I know how horrible it all is and yet I have to stay silent. They all think it won't last long. How can I say what I know? They would think me insane. But I'm so scared for my stepson George, if he doesn't enlist voluntarily, he'll have no choice eventually. They're just boys, I've watched so many of them grow, and I can't bear it. Four years, I'll have to wait it out for four years, and what then? I have no idea how everyone I know is going to fare. This is awful, I wouldn't wish it on anybody.

All my love, always yours x

Glenda put the letter into her lap and continued to sob. As ever, with eyes red raw to match his heart, Tony was there to put a tender arm around her. Anne too, was crying quietly as she listened to Glenda read, and Lucy's cheeks were wet with tears cascading down and dripping unheeded onto her cardigan.

"Rose's boyfriend died in the war," declared Steve. He felt he needed to talk, for there was little else to do. "His name was Francis. He was nineteen years old. She never married after that."

"That sounds so very sad don't you think?" said Lucy.

"It was on the Somme. There was a photograph of him along with these letters. Jas and I assumed that the letters were for him, but Jas, after she went back to there... to the past, must have put it with the letters so that I would give it to Rose all these years later. It would be nice to see some photographs of Jas, you know - there. Rose said they were all destroyed in a fire. Dad, we may have had some; you are related by marriage to Jasmine. I mean when she went back in time, she got married to the person who was living in this house, John Brown. His sister Vicky was our ancestor, Great Grandfather Jason's wife. But you threw all those old photos out didn't you?"

"She got married, again?" chipped in Glenda.

"Yes, when she realised she was pregnant, she married. It's in one of the letters, I remember reading about it."

"Oh my poor girl," wept Glenda.

Paul looked thoughtful; his brow furrowed while he rubbed at his chin. "Those photos, we didn't exactly put them in the bin when we were having a clear out you know. I gave them to a cousin of mine who has an interest in family trees. He keeps all of the family records; thought he could make use of them. I'll try and get hold of him."

"So he might have some pictures of Jasmine back then? That would really prove it all," said Anne.

"I'm not looking for proof Mum," declared Steve. "I know what has happened. I'd just like to see her as she - as she grows older; because she's dead now isn't she, and I'll never see her again. It would be nice though, to see what sort of life she had after - after she left here."

Life in the nineteen hundreds appeared so long ago, yet only a few days had passed since Jasmine had been in the here and now and in his arms. He would never see her again because she was living somewhere else in time. For her, it would be the present, but for him and everyone else, years and years had passed since then. This riddle got him thinking. If what happened to Jasmine was because time had bent back on itself, then it could be said that all of time was happening at the same time. He'd heard his father speak of this theory over the years, but it had been such an enormous computation for Steve's brain, he hadn't given it any credence. Even so, without understanding it, because of what had taken place, he saw there was truth to it. He could now see that Jasmine still existed, she was merely on a different sort of wavelength, another dimension, another timeline. Like he'd felt in the park the other day, when he'd imagined she was there all around him. It was consoling in a way, if only he could reach out and touch her... He wondered though, coming back to linear time, surely she would have left more than letters for him. Information, evidence; she would do everything she could to communicate, to get a message to him.

Steve gave himself a sudden start. He'd remembered something. They'd been sitting in a pub together soon after Steve had returned from the States reacquainting themselves. He could hear Jasmine's voice in his head echoing through the years...

"I would always write to you if we were ever separated," Jasmine had told him. The letters of course; that was proof. What else was there? The name of their home of course! When they'd first come to view it. *"This is my house,"* Jasmine had exclaimed after she'd seen the words 'Jasmine House' written on the side gate. *"Wow, that's unbelievable!"* Perfectly believable if it had been another message, Steve thought. (He wasn't to know that it had been Rose who had chosen the name after her mother's death.) And what else? The dress they'd found under the floorboards that she wore for Trevor's New Year party. She will have put it there because that was what she was wearing when she went back in time. She must have put it there for precisely that reason. Then there was the jukebox. It was such an odd thing to have been in the house. Oh how they'd danced to the music! Dancing. He remembered he'd taught her his family's 'happy dance' when they first set eyes on the house. They'd danced and pranced a polka-like step, going from room to room in glee.

The doorbell sounded, snapping Steve back to the present. Lucy went to answer it and came back with Trevor and Penny, who added to the little group of mourners. Lucy brought in some tea and biscuits which brought some sort of normality, helping to bring everyone back down to earth.

"There must be a grave," said Penny abruptly. Her proclamation came as a surprise; none of them had thought about it. "I mean, it might be helpful to see where she's buried."

"Yes," said Glenda, "I think I'd like to find out where that is and see it."

"Er, do we know when she erm, died?" asked Lucy tentatively.

"No and I don't want to talk about it," retorted Steve. He'd wondered that himself but wasn't ready to know the answer, not yet anyway; he was getting too choked up just thinking about it.

"I believe her name was Estelle Brown," said Paul, steering the conversation away from the very emotive subject. "Apparently, she pretended she'd lost her memory, and so they chose a name for her. And of course, her surname became Brown upon her marriage."

"And you know all this how?" asked Lucy, pointedly. Paul explained that he and the police inspector had been to see Rose, and it was she who had told them.

"Estelle?" said Steve, finding his voice. "Star?" He looked at his father questioningly.

"Her birthmark; precisely," said Paul in answer.

"How very appropriate," agreed Lucy. "It must have been so hard for Jas. She couldn't have told anyone what had happened to her, they would have thought her deranged. Pretending to lose her memory was smart, she wouldn't then have to explain anything about where she had come from."

"And realising she was pregnant. No wonder she got married. She'd have had no choice of course, it was difficult enough to be pregnant and not be married in my day let alone a hundred years ago," added Glenda. "Oh Tony, our poor girl, our poor poor girl, she must have felt so trapped. I cannot imagine what it must have been like."

Steve looked over at Trevor and caught his eye. They rose as one and made their escape away from Glenda's tears. "Couldn't take much more of that," said Steve once they were in the relative safety of the entrance hall.

"I could tell," replied Trevor.

In comparative peace, they savoured the moment drinking their tea and munching ginger biscuits; their crunchiness sounding all the louder in the quiet of the hall. Steve's attention was drawn to the towering Norway Spruce. Steadfast in its silent presence and evocative festive fragrance, yet able to offer nothing more than faded memories of lost joy, and a rapidly thickening carpet of discarded needles around its base. His idle gaze then moved on to the jukebox. For a moment, he wondered again if it was another clue that Jasmine may have left.

"You know," he began, his mouth not fully empty of ginger crumbs, "Jas left messages for me like the letters, but what about the jukebox, do you think it might hold something too, for why else would Rose have it? I've had it apart before now to look inside and check it's workings, but there were no notes or anything. I'm convinced it's communicating something, because it's so incongruous, so random."

When Steve and Jasmine had purchased the large old house, they also purchased its contents. It had never been emptied from when Rose left to live in the care home. Little by little, they had sifted through all sorts of belongings, keeping some, selling some and taking some to the tip. It was all the normal type of furniture and stuffs that one would expect in a house belonging to someone who had spent a lifetime in the same place. But the jukebox was an unexplained anomaly. At the same time as enjoying playing the music, and dancing with Jasmine around the hall with the thing at full volume, Steve had always wondered about it, as Trevor knew well.

"Ah yes, I may be able to help with that," said Trevor, realising this was the moment to come clean. "When I spoke to Rose,"

"You spoke to Rose?" Steve interrupted. "When did you speak to Rose? I didn't notice that you did."

"Yes, I keep telling you, on Sunday, when I was the 'on call' dentist and was at the care home to treat a patient. Remember?"

"Oh yes, so you did, sorry, my mind is all over the place," replied Steve.

"I, er," Trevor continued falteringly, "thought to go and have a chat with her, seeing as I was there. It was precisely the jukebox that I wanted to chat about as I knew you were curious about it. It was then when she asked me about the letters."

The fact that it was more like 'I fully intended to,' rather than 'seeing I was there,' was still giving Trevor a guilty conscience. He took a drink of tea before saying any more, attempting to swallow the little white lie. "Now, according to Rose, her mother; er Jasmine, told her about the jukebox - to get it. And not only that, told her which songs she had to put in."

"Jasmine told her which songs? I wonder why, some of them are quite obscure, and it can't have been because we like them, as they aren't all to our taste." Steve put the last of his biscuit into his mouth and still clutching his mug of tea, approached the jukebox in order to examine it more closely. Looking back later, he didn't know how nor why the juke box had selected that moment over any other to reveal its secrets, or what had prompted them to think there really had to be a clue somewhere within it. What was he; stressed out, confused, not in his right mind, feeling weak and ineffectual and clutching at straws? Maybe all of those things, or maybe the colourful retro shapes lured him over. He looked at the play list. Indeed, some songs he loved, but some he couldn't understand why they were there, especially when there were far more popular tracks available.

"She also told her which ones must go where," added Trevor.

"Just a minute," began Steve, "there must have been a motive for choosing these ones in particular. Jasmine must have selected them for a reason." They stared at each other, both their brains working hard. Steve spoke first.

"Do you think there's a clue in the order they're in rather than what the songs are?" Steve began reading down the list of songs: *I Want to Hold Your Hand, White Christmas, Every Breath You Take, Night Train, That'll be the Day,* were the first five. Then he noticed that the first letter of each song title happened to spell out 'I went.' He looked curiously at the list and wondered if the rest of the twenty-five discs would continue to make words. He scrambled a pen and paper and wrote out the first letter of each song as Trevor called them out. They stared at each other as they read the sentence that had formed on Steve's bit of scrap paper. "Oh my God," said Steve.

"Jesus," replied Trevor as the revelation hit them both at the same time. Steve had written on his piece of paper the words,

'*I went back in time to 1900 Jasmine.*'

The only non-word was the number 1900, from the song *1900 Yesterday,* by Liz Damon's Orient Express; the lyrics almost an exact fit to how Jasmine must have felt after what happened to her. Each time they had played that particular disc, they danced slowly to it and in a loving embrace and sang along with it. Steve knew that this song from now on, would be his all-time favourite. He shrugged and went to put on his coat. "Well that's that then."

"Where are you going," asked Trevor.

"The police station of course, to tell them there's no point in looking for her."

"You can't tell them anything, they'll think you're mad," said Trevor.

"I wouldn't be too sure of that," said Paul. He had come into the hall unnoticed. "Detective Inspector Manning, he's the man to talk to, but hadn't you better ring first, he may not be on duty."

"I could do with the walk," replied Steve. "See you later."

Trevor and Paul looked at each other, both knowing there was little they could do to help. Steve needed space. Somewhere where he could make sense of this awful situation.

Outside and alone, with head hung low, Steve had nothing to look at but the flagged pavement beneath his feet. His unchecked imagination began wreaking havoc. One careless step could send him into the realms of time. *'Don't tread on the lines,'* he recalled from his youth that kids would shout out to each other. He deliberately stepped on as many as he could to prove that nothing would happen. Or maybe he just got lucky? Wrong answer, as according to his dad, the danger point was a line between the stone circle and a doorstep. His father only knew so much though. Anything could happen at any moment, and if you didn't have your wits about you, then who knows what?

His ears pricked. Something had alerted his senses; he needed to stay vigilant. Someone was there, he could feel them. He deepened his stride hoping to dodge into an alley and wait for whoever it might be. He'd had enough mystery. Why were they following his every move? If it was the police because they thought he'd done something to Jas, well God help them when he caught them. But if it wasn't them, then who was his stalker?

Steve reached the end of the road and turned into Meadowsring Road and saw his chance to conceal himself. Dodging through an open gateway into a garden, he hid behind the tall privet hedge, and panting slightly from a huge adrenalin rush, he waited in suspense and uncertainty. Footsteps approached; slightly uneven, a little doddery if he had to make any judgement about them, and they were about to walk past. Should he jump out and apprehend them? No, he thought, he must see who it is, and maybe follow them.

It was an oldish-looking man. Steve was about to start tailing him but the man had stopped and was looking in every direction as if he was looking for something. Steve could see him through a gap in the hedge, and as he looked more closely, he recognised who it was and broke his cover.

"Mr Pickford, have you lost your dog?"

"Goodness me, you gave me such a start there lad," replied Arthur Pickford. "Almost jumped out of my skin. You shouldn't go around startling people like that, thought I was under attack for a moment." Steve was taken aback, he hadn't expected such a retort, but then he supposed he *had* startled him. Then he put two and two together. He was an old man, he'd been around a bit, he knew Rose, he *knew* what was going on, he *knew* what had happened to Jasmine.

"Mr Pickford, have you been following me?"

"Er, just checking you are all right."

"You *have* been following me haven't you. It was *you!* Why have you been following me?

Arthur gave a big sigh. "As I said, just keeping my eye on you, checking you are keeping safe."

"You think I'm in danger?"

"No, I, er didn't mean that. Just wanting to keep an eye on you because I was worried about you. You know, with your wife missing and everything.

But I can see you are rattled, please, don't be alarmed, I never wanted for you to know..."

"Know what?" Steve interrupted.

"That I have been keeping an eye on you."

"And why would you want to do that Mr Pickford?" Steve was annoyed that he had been so spooked by what turned out to be just an old man watching his moves. He'd imagined all sorts on unimaginable encounters with unknown assailants. It had added to his stress and he could do with a lot less of that.

"I'm so very sorry to have alarmed you, I've been attempting to monitor your progress in your search for your wife, nothing more, and please call me Arthur. You've needed to know what happened to her of course, but how to go about helping you in understanding the truth of it; that has been the most difficult. But then, when your father was measuring the stones, I, we, well, we thought he might listen."

My father, again. He manages to crop up everywhere thought Steve. "You know my father?"

"We have met, yes. He was with the inspector."

"Yes, they went to see Rose together, the lady who used to live in our house."

"Yes," replied Arthur, "I took them. I wanted them to hear what she had to say.

"Oh, I see." After a short pause, an infuriated Steve continued. "So, as well as knowing Rose, are you now saying that you know what happened to Jasmine as well?"

"Yes, I suppose I am. So now you might begin to understand that that is why I've been watching over you, and then reporting back to Rose. We didn't know the right way or the right moment to tell you."

"Well the right moment came. I know what happened now. I've been to see Rose this afternoon. I know Rose is my daughter."

"I do hope, once the shock that has hit you has lessened you are able to find some sort of peace. Knowing what I know, I've been so concerned for you. You must be feeling terrible."

With that, Steve began to understand that Arthur Pickford, rather than spying on him, had, in his own way been caring for him. Everything else was the conjecture of his mind in overload. In that same moment, he knew all the anger and exasperation he was holding onto over losing Jasmine, had no place here. He managed to calm down, for he could tell that the old man wanted to say more.

"You see," Arthur continued, "I've known Rose for many many years. We've looked after each other in a way, and I know much about your wife, Rose's mother. If there is anything I can help you with. Because, in fact," Arthur hesitated for a moment, "I knew your wife back, you know, then."

"You did? Then we have a lot to talk about. But why didn't you say so before?"

"And you would have believed me? I didn't know where to begin. I tried going to the police but they supposed I was telling them rubbish. I thought that if I followed you I could maybe help you to understand what happened gradually, but meanwhile, your father seems to have worked it out for himself. I just helped to fill in a few blanks. And then you spoke to Rose. I know about your visit, I've just come from her, the second time today, she told me you'd been and you knew. It can't be easy for you, just as it can't have been easy for Mrs Brown, Estelle."

"Who?"

"Estelle, your wife was called Estelle back then."

"Oh yes, I forgot. Look Mr Pickford,"

"Arthur."

"Arthur, I'm on my way to the police station to tell them not to bother looking for her anymore."

"I don't think there's much need for that, now that the inspector has heard what Rose had to say."

"You sure? I know my Dad understands, but the police?"

"I don't know about the rest of the police force, but certainly Inspector Manning looked convinced. I doubt he'll still be there now though, and it might be better you speak to him as opposed to someone else. What about waiting till tomorrow when you'll be sure of seeing him?"

Steve knew he was right, but he wasn't ready to go home. He looked at Arthur, then up the street, then back at Arthur. "Look, if you've got time, I'd love to hear what you've got to say about Jas, do you fancy a drink?"

Slightly bewildered, Arthur peered at him. "Jazz? I'm afraid I don't know much at all, it's not my kind of music."

Steve realised his mistake. "No, I mean Jas short for Jasmine, my wife."

"Ah, I see what you mean. My apologies. Yes, I will join you for a drink and tell you what I know, but I can't stay too long as I've left my dog home alone.

Once installed in the Regent; Steve with a pint of Landlord and Arthur with a half of shandy, the two men spent an hour in deep conversation before Arthur reluctantly said he really had to leave and get back home to his dog. Steve stayed on for another pint, he needed to mull over not only what Arthur had told him about what he knew of Jasmine's life a hundred years ago, but also the astounding fact that he had come forward in time himself. Clearly, there was so much to life that Steve had no idea about.

The pub was filling up swiftly with a noisy mix of revellers still in the party mood of the new millennium. Steve, oblivious, had only his thoughts for company and was straying steadily into a mix of time travel, loss and confusion - and nearing the end of his pint. He looked at his glass and swished its liquid remains around it deducing he needed something normal in his life, and thought of Trevor. He messaged him to apologise for his hasty exit and to say where he was and if he fancied joining him. There'd been a text from Lucy, asking where and how he was. He messaged back and said to come and join him as it might be an escape from the elders. Twenty minutes later and Trevor was with him trying out the guest beer and listening to what Steve had to tell him. He and Penny had just been leaving for home as Penny had a lot of schoolwork to catch up on. Trevor however, never needing to bring his work home apart from the odd dental research paper, welcomed the invitation of a pint and was straight round after dropping Penny off. He was in the middle of hearing from Steve about why he hadn't gone to the police station and how Arthur had not only seen Jasmine disappear as a baby and reappear as an adult but had also been there the other day when she'd disappeared allowing her to reappear to where Arthur had seen her before, when Trevor noticed a familiar-looking face waiting to be served.

"Isn't he a copper?" he interrupted and nodding towards the bar, glad that he could stop Steve for a bit as he was getting rather confused with all the Jasmine appearances and disappearances. Steve turned round to look.

"Yes, it's that police constable who gave me a lift home so he could pick up Jas's phone. Downey, Tom Downey, that's his name."

"Never seen him in here before," declared Trevor. He sipped his beer with eyes glued to the policeman, speculating as to what Tom Downey might be doing in their local. Trevor could see that he'd been pulled a pint of Boddy's by the barman together with a glass of white wine. Trevor's eyes followed the policeman across the pub lounge and saw him settle over at the other side in one of the booths.

"Good grief, he's with your Lucy!"

"What?" Steve exclaimed. I've just sent her a text to come and join us. I'd better go and see what she's doing."

"No, don't do that, it's obvious what she's doing, she's on a date! She left your house just before I did; she never said she was seeing someone."

"But she can't be, I've just messaged her to come here because she texted me asking where I was, and I said 'here,' so that's why *she's* here!"

"Well mate, I think her plans have changed! Message her now. Say you can see her and ask her what she's doing. Wait a minute, she's coming over."

"Hello Trevor, again," began Lucy before addressing her brother-in-law. "Thanks for inviting me over to the pub. I needed to get out for a bit, only I've bumped into someone I used to know. Got a lot to catch up on, so if you don't mind, I'll see you later."

"Yes, of course," replied Steve.

"Go for it," said Trevor, winking at her. She gave him a half smile and turned round and went and sat back with Tom Downey. "She's a quick worker," mumbled Trevor under his breath while taking another slug of beer.

"Well I never saw that coming, you're quite right." agreed Steve. They sat quietly for a while, pretending they weren't watching the proceedings, but then Trevor spoke up.

"Hey, just a minute, how could the old man have seen Jasmine as a baby all those years ago and still be alive? It's not possible."

"Ah my friend, but you are forgetting something," replied Steve.

"I am?"

"Yes, you are. Time travel."

"Am I?"

"Yes. Arthur has travelled through time too! He travelled from nineteen-eighteen to nineteen fifty-five!"

"No way!"

"Yes, it's true. He met Rose in nineteen fifty-five and she recognised him from when she was a girl in nineteen-eighteen and he looked exactly the same to her; no ageing, and it gave her proof that Jasmine, her mother, had come from here; that is, our time."

"Never!"

"And even more than that, he's the one who's been following me. He's been reporting back to Rose and they've been trying to find a way to tell me about where Jasmine is, but meanwhile we've already found it out."

"I'm speechless!" declared Trevor.

Chapter Twenty-one

January 6th, am

DI Manning made himself a coffee and then sprawled into his office chair. For the moment he just sat contemplating nothing in particular; it felt good to drink hot coffee. However, he also understood that idling his time away wouldn't help to wrap up a case that couldn't be solved, or rather, couldn't be solved with any rational explanation. All the normal lines of enquiry had exhausted any possible leads, and the trail was well and truly cold. This of course, was inevitable given what he now understood to be, however extraordinary, the genuine explanation. Without bringing any supernatural goings on into the equation though, there wasn't much more they could do.

He opened the file on his desk computer and leafed through the material. The lack of any substantial evidence other than the footage of her clutching her head that a possible crime had been committed, made the case difficult; for even that could be explained away by a head injury she had sustained during the party. Everything that old Arthur Pickford had given them when interviewed, had been construed as the unhelpful ramblings of an old man and he certainly wasn't going to contest that. There was no real point in going through the motions looking for her when he knew she would never be found. The best way forward for all parties, he supposed, was for the case file to remain open, but inactive.

There was a knock on the door and Tom Downey's head poked round. Jim Manning noticed he was looking slightly the worse for wear. "All right Tom?" he remarked by way of a greeting. "Getting enough sleep, or is the Bird-wing case getting to you? I can understand, it's taken an unusual direction and I've just been contemplating where to go from here. Got any ideas?"

Tom cleared his throat before speaking and straightened his tie. "Well sir, a report has just come in that Steve Bartram was seen at the New Year party to have been in some sort of embrace with the girlfriend of whose party it was. And the witness states that he wasn't sure, but Jasmine may have seen this before she left, and been a bit put out."

"Hmmm," began Jim Manning, "that all sounds a bit like someone who likes stirring the dirt up and pointing the finger. So he gave someone a hug at New Year? Don't think we need to read too much into it, and I don't think it's relevant to what we both understand to have happened. However it may throw a bit of weight to the idea that she's gone to ground for a while." He drank down the last of his coffee. "Right then, I suppose we'll need to follow it up. Let's pay another visit to the husband and see what he has to say about this. Another partygoer was it?"

"Yes sir, so I believe."

Jim Manning, perked up by the coffee, heaved himself out of his chair, grabbed his jacket and strode out of the office with DC Downey dutifully on his tail. Hopefully this bit of intel would lean more towards downgrading the case into 'cold,' as it would look, to all intents and purposes, as though Mrs Jasmine Bartram had simply walked out. He would give his final report to the National Missing Persons Bureau after he'd spoken to Steve Bartram, and then file it. Not the usual Jim Manning approach, but the only one he could think of to stop actively working on something that was patently a waste of precious police resources.

Glenda opened the door to the two officers, eyeing them up and down with demonstrable suspicion. "What can we do for you?" she asked. She couldn't help but keep her eyes fixed on the older one, there was just something about him. She just couldn't think what.

"Good morning Mrs Simmons, we would like to speak to Stephen Bartram if he's here."

"Of course he's here, where else might he be?" she scoffed. She escorted them into the sitting room and pulled her son-in-law out of the kitchen saying, "to go and see to them," as if they were a bothersome encumbrance.

"Hello," Steve offered by way of greeting. He didn't know what more he could say, seeing as the detective inspector knew what had happened to Jasmine. Another night had passed without her, and it wasn't getting any easier.

"Good morning," began Jim Manning a little awkwardly. "An eyewitness has come forward and said that Jasmine may have been distressed prior to leaving the party on New Year's Eve. Have you anything to say about that?"

Jas hadn't been distressed Steve thought. They'd just watched the firework display with their arms around each other minutes before she'd left. He stared at the Detective Inspector in confusion. But then he remembered that kiss. Someone had pulled at his arm and the next thing he knew he was snogging Penny. A very brief, but significant event and in more ways than one, for now he knew with more certainty that Jas must have seen them. He sat down, his legs more or less buckling beneath him. The betrayal. He'd destroyed the trust between them and she'd left feeling deeply hurt. More than that, she would have had to live with it for the rest of her life as she'd never had a way of confronting him.

"Oh Jas, I'm so sorry," he cried out loud, and wept openly.

"Mr Bartram, Steve?" said Jim Manning gently after a suitable interlude. Men crying. He always gave them a little space. It didn't help matters to jump in straight away with more questions.

In his own time, Steve wiped his face and blew his nose and when ready, looked back up at DI Manning. "It was a kiss, just a New Year kiss under the mistletoe with Penny. Jas must have seen us as she was leaving. She would have been fuming. She should have come over. Why didn't she come over, what on earth must she have thought?"

"Whatever she thought or didn't think, did not contribute in any way to what happened next. I know that, and in time, *you* will know it too. Meanwhile, this information helps to make it look as though she might have decided to disappear for a while. This is advantageous for us in that it helps us with the decision-making process of how we go forward with the investigation. Officially the case will remain open, but inactive. That is, unless any new evidence comes to light." Jim Manning paused briefly before continuing. "How do you feel about us handling it in this way?"

Steve stayed quiet for a while. What could he say? It wasn't anything to do with him how the police handled their investigations. But then he understood the futility of searching for someone they would never find, especially when they knew where she'd gone. "How many of you know what happened to Jas?" he asked.

Jim Manning looked towards Tom Downey who was standing very quietly over by the window. "Only the two of us. And I think you can understand why it won't be any more than that. It's hard enough for you and me, for Tom here, for the rest of your family, to reason what has happened, except maybe for your father; but anyone else? No way!"

Steve shrugged. "I know you're right. If I go around saying Jas got pulled back through time people will regard me as nuts, but to have to say that she left me because of a stupid misunderstanding; that will be hard."

"Well in a sense you *did* mess up," declared Tom Downey rather abruptly and quite loudly. Both Jim Manning and Steve stared at him in blank astonishment. "What I mean is," he continued, "you kissed another woman in full view of your wife. That alone constitutes a break-up in many relationships wouldn't you think?"

"But it was just a kiss, and Penny only did it because Trevor was trying to kiss Jas."

"I think a kiss is between two people, meaning she was kissing you, you were kissing her," Tom Downey retorted back. Jim Manning thought his DC clearly had a bee in his bonnet about something. He chose to stay out of it, for now anyway, and would reprimand him later.

"Yes but," began Steve, and then stopped. DC Downey was right, he was guilty. And he also knew that Jasmine would have been extremely upset if she had witnessed it. Now she was lost, and he could never offer her an explanation, or rather, an excuse. He looked straight at Jim Manning. "Do whatever you think is right with your investigations. Jas is gone, and that's that."

There was a knock at the door and Lucy walked in tentatively and looked at the three men, but especially looked at Tom Downey.

"Hello, is everything all right?" she asked, "only I thought I heard raised voices."

"Everything is fine," Steve answered.

Lucy put her arm through Steve's. "Oh Steve, it isn't though is it, and it never will be after this, but at least we know what's happened, I mean where she went. And your dad has got hold of his cousin who says he has some old photos, so we may be able to piece together bits of her life. You also have all the letters that Jasmine wrote to you." Steve took Lucy in his arms; he could see she was weeping silently. Little Luce had lost her big sister. He needed to remember that others loved Jasmine too, and he wasn't the only one suffering.

"Letters?" asked Jim Manning, keen to avert any female lamentations. Men crying was one thing, but women? They seemed able to turn the taps on and off to suit themselves. Besides, his curiosity and the detective in him had got the better of him. Lucy obliged his conviction by shrugging off her tears and elaborated. She told him of the letters Steve had found and that Jasmine had penned them over the years when she was in the nineteen-hundreds.

"They're about what was happening in her life and how she felt about it all," Lucy concluded. Steve went to get them so the Detective Inspector could have a look.

"Well," said Jim Manning, after he had read a few pages, "these don't sound like they are from a woman who is at odds with her husband because of a quick kiss under the mistletoe with someone else. They sound like someone who stayed very much in love with you. It's like," he thought, "it's like she's overseas and cannot get back. Like someone in the forces writing to their loved ones back home."

"Maybe that's how I should look at it then," pondered Steve.

"In time," answered Jim Manning. "Maybe in time."

"In time being the operative words," Steve quipped back.

"Indeed," replied Jim Manning. "We shall leave you with that then."

Tom Downey hung back awkwardly, like he wasn't quite ready to leave. Lucy walked over to him and put her arm on his. "I'll see you later," she whispered quietly.

"Okay," he replied, and caught up with his boss, who eyed him quizzically.

"Don't ask," said Tom Downey in response.

"None of my business," replied Jim Manning. "My next job back at the nick is to cold case all this. I take it you're on board with this?"

"Absolutely Sir."

"Interesting that Maureen the Medium mentioned that," Jim Manning added while giving a nod towards the jukebox.

"Definitely Sir."

Chapter Twenty-two

One month later

It was another mild day, unusual for the month of February. Whether the steady drizzle might clear up any time soon though, was debatable. Steve arrived first, with Arthur and Rose. A special taxi that took wheelchairs to accommodate Rose's needs had been booked, for she had insisted on coming. The taxi dropped them off on Cemetery Road by the tennis club. Once they were organised, and with Rose suitably wrapped up in a blanket, they crossed the road and passed through the aged Gothic gates of the cemetery. Rose pointed the way and they progressed slowly along the downward sloping path, Steve honing his wheelchair skills. She then gesticulated vaguely in another direction and they altered course. The terrain changed from tarmac to tufted grass with yet more opportunities to challenge wheelchair manoeuvrability for Steve.

"There," declared Rose with quivering index finger pointing at an unassuming headstone metres away, and looking totally inaccessible for a wheelchair. Their progress was halted momentarily until they found a better route. Steve reversed and jostled his charge over the bumpy terrain determined to reach their destination. Meanwhile, some of the others were arriving.

"Over here," Arthur hailed, gesticulating with his cap that he'd removed from his head out of respect. Tony, Glenda, Anne and Paul had all come together in Paul's car.

"Good morning," said Jim Manning. Steve swung round to see the inspector standing behind him. "Weather could have been a bit kinder to us," he added, looking up at the skies.

"Thank you for coming," replied Steve.

Jim Manning nodded back. "I'm expecting Tom Downey to be here. He said he would be, but he's on annual leave and coming under his own steam."

"He's coming with Lucy," replied Steve. He then thought he'd better elaborate. "They go way back; used to be an item years ago apparently, but then Lucy caught him in an embrace with another girl so walked off and wouldn't speak to him, until that is, they bumped into each other last month outside the Regent pub."

A wry smile spread across Jim Manning's face. "That explains a lot. No wonder he was so scathing to you over your mistletoe kiss, don't you think?"

Steve shrugged his shoulders in response and replied that most people mess up some time or another, but it's the consequences that cause the problems, be they great or small. Jim Manning agreed, and the two of them watched Lucy and Tom walking along the path hand in hand. However, as soon as Tom became aware of his DI's eyes upon him, he hastily extricated himself, continuing by making sure there was an arm's length between them. "Don't know what he's trying to hide, she looks like a lovely girl," said Jim Manning.

"Yes she is, just like her sister," agreed Steve.

Steve managed to get Rose's wheelchair into position and the rest of the group gathered round. The grave was in a family plot and part of a row of four, the other three being John Brown, whom Jasmine had married after she'd gone back in time, John Brown's first wife Eleanor, who had died following childbirth Rose informed them, and Rose's brother George. "Or rather my stepbrother, but he felt like a real brother. Got blown up in the Blitz; it was a dreadful time," said Rose.

"How terribly sad," said Anne. But all eyes were fixed on the other headstone.

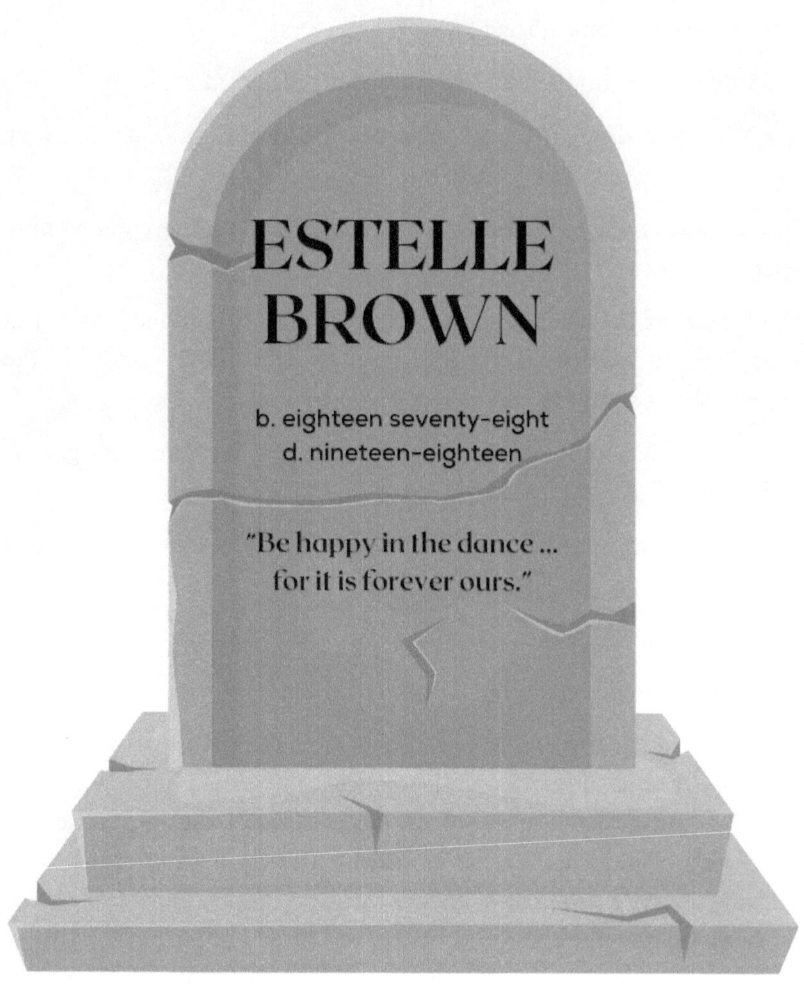

"She asked me to make sure she had that inscription put on her tombstone during her last hours of life," said Rose. Rose's voice, hard to hear at the best of times, was carried away by the wind licking amongst the graves.

"The happy dance," said Steve.

"The happy dance," declared Paul.

Rose sighed, "Yes, the happy dance. I understand you danced it together when you first looked around Jasmine House before you bought it, and then my mother danced it with your great-grandfather Jason after she'd helped his wife Aunty Vicky give birth to their first child."

"Yes, so we did," remembered Steve.

"And I danced it throughout my childhood," declared Paul.

"I still see you doing the steps on occasion," remarked Anne, smirking slightly.

"Yes, I dance it when I'm happy." He started dancing. Steve joined him. Rose clapped in time to their dancing feet.

"And that's why it's called the happy dance I presume," said Jim Manning. "You all look so happy. But who invented it first? Sounds like the chicken and the egg story to me."

"You do realise you are dancing almost on top of my daughter's grave," declared Glenda. "Maybe you should move slightly away?"

"Our daughter, but then she never was our *real* daughter," said Tony under his breath.

"What did you say?" asked Glenda.

"I said, we have flowers to lay for our daughter."

"Yes, they are in my carrier bag. Get it will you? It's just over there, where I put it down." Tony did as he was told, as was his duty. When the dancing was over, the little group of mourners amassed together in hushed sorrow. Glenda placed a spray of white jasmine flowers in front of the tomb stone; it might have a different name inscribed on it, but it was her Jasmine that lay beneath, nonetheless.

They didn't stay long after that, the weather was deteriorating. The wind had got stronger and the skies were darkening. Paul coaxed them away by inviting them to look at the old photographs he had received from his cousin.

Later, and unbeknown to them, a myriad particles of quartz crystal sand, carried hundreds of miles on the wind from the Sahara Desert, came to lay as dust upon the graves. When the sun came out again, shining its blessings, they twinkled in its reflected light,

Rose appeared to be having a new lease of life as she was wheeled into her former home. Arthur had been noticing a steady improvement in her vitality from the beginning of the year, but this was unprecedented. Her eyes sparkled and she gasped in amazement as she was pushed from room to room by Steve.

"It's just how she described. It's lovely," said Rose.

"I'm glad you approve," answered Steve. "It's taken some doing though, but she, Jasmine, did most of the redecorations. Everyone's congregating in the sitting room, shall we go in?"

"Would you like a sherry, Rose?" asked Paul after Steve had pushed the wheelchair in through the door and into a position that she was happy with, by the window.

"Dad, there's no sherry," Steve whispered.

"Yes there is, I brought some. There you go Rose."

"Thank you, how very kind," she replied and took the glass Paul was offering into both of her hands.

"Inspector?"

"Er, unfortunately I'm on duty."

"Ah yes, of course. I'll get you a cup of tea," replied Paul.

"Er, any coffee?"

"Certainly, coming up right away."

"Ah, lovely, thank you," said Jim Manning gratefully a few minutes later when Paul produced a mug of coffee for him. "So, tell me about this so-called happy dance. Who do you think made it up?"

"Who knows," replied Paul. "My grandfather taught my father and I taught Steve. But it appears that my grandfather danced it first with, well, with Jasmine and she learned it from Steve. So you are right, who danced it initially? A conundrum if ever there was one and a scientific one at that. Time could be spiral rather than linear, or at least fractal."

"Okay, I'll leave that one with you," said Jim Manning, and after taking a sip of the freshly-ground Jamaica Blue Mountain coffee, which was emanating its enticing aromas, he quickly changed the subject. "That's certainly a good cup of coffee. Thank you for inviting me today, I appreciate it."

"Thank you for coming. And thank you for seeing beyond the surface in our loss of Jasmine."

"Well, officially she is still a missing person. I don't think the good old British police force is ready to accept what has really happened. They'd have no idea how to categorise and file it."

"Quite," agreed Paul.

"It's no easy task for me either," declared the inspector. "I'd always taken anything supernatural with a pinch of salt but the evidence here – well, I'm a changed man because of it."

"Where are these pictures then," asked Lucy loudly, above the hubbub of conversation.

"Ah yes, coming up. My cousin has sent me quite a few I think." Paul left the room and came back a few minutes later carrying a large unopened envelope. He placed it down on the coffee table. "Stephen, would you open it please and show them to Rose so she can tell us who is who?"

"You think I won't be able to recognise her?" Steve retaliated.

"No it's not that, I thought Rose would be able to place them in some sort of chronological order so we can have a story of the events of Jasmine's life there."

"Oh sorry, I wasn't thinking," said Steve.

"No worries," replied his father. Steve picked up the envelope but held onto it, hesitating.

"Well get on with it then!" said an impatient Paul, "we're all waiting."

Steve looked round at all the expectant faces staring at him, then down at the envelope. Tentatively, he began to open it, trying not to tear it to pieces, then stopped. "I can't do it. I can't see her. There, I mean. It'll make it all real won't it?"

Slowly, Rose stretched out her arm and placed her aged hand on his in reassurance. "Please," she asked, "may I see them?" Steve could see tears forming in her eyes, Rose had lost Jasmine too, and of course wanted to see what was inside. He finished opening the envelope, pulled the photographs out and put them in her lap without looking at them. She picked up the one on the top. "Could I have my glasses please? They are in my bag." Lucy pounced upon the retro-looking leather patchwork nineteen-seventies handbag with great curiosity. It was the genuine article. 'Amazing!' she thought, while pulling out a pair of spectacles. She helped put them onto Rose's wizened face, her hands over Rose's, guiding them home. "Ah, that's better. Rose peered at the picture before passing it onto Steve. "This one is my mother, my brother George and me. We were at a birthday party for one of my cousins."

Steve stared desirously at it while Rose continued to talk. She hadn't been so animated for years. "Uncle Jason insisted on taking our picture when we had just arrived and before we had time to get ourselves into a mess. I would have been about eight years old I think."

"So," began Steve, his voice croaking with emotion, "this would be more than eight years later than now."

"You mean she would have already been there for eight years," said Glenda. She was looking over his shoulder and trying to get a closer look. Steve passed the grainy photograph towards her. She looked intently for a moment. "You can't see all that much can you. They are too far away from the camera."

"I can see what I need to see," replied Steve. Rose passed him another.

"That one is right before the First World War broke out. We were all about to go into the park for a picnic. That's Father, that's Aunty Vicky, that's Algie..." Steve had stopped listening; his eyes fixated on the figure who Rose had described as her father. Tall, dark, handsome; for a second he was filled with rage. Then he remembered what Jasmine had written in one of the letters.

John is a good man but he can never replace you. Please do not ever be jealous of him. I had to stage-manage things so he would believe Rose belongs to him. I shall never tell him that you are her <u>real</u> father as he looks after me well and I could never hurt him. You are my true love and you always will be for the rest of my life, I miss you so."

"Your father was a good man," he said to Rose when she had finished explaining who everyone was in the photograph.

"I'll second that," declared Arthur.

"Yes, he was," Rose answered. She rummaged through the pile on her lap. "Here's one of their wedding day." She passed the picture to Steve, but then retracted her arm. "Oh, I'm not thinking. This isn't easy for you is it."

"I'm okay thank you. I'd like to see."

Steve studied the photograph. It was Jasmine. She looked sensational, although her face was slightly rounder, but then she was pregnant of course. With his child. He looked at Rose. His child. Certainly, there were familiar characteristics in her. But how could he truly get his head around it all? They had become close in the last weeks, but she felt more like an elderly grandmother rather than his daughter. He looked back at the picture and tried to imagine how Jasmine had been feeling. He couldn't; it was too much. There she was, standing next to *him,* marrying ***him***! It was like a final insult. He knew he was being irrational, and tried to think of something else.

"What on earth has she got on her head?" he said thrusting the photo at Lucy who regarded it with fascination.

"How stunning she looks," said Lucy. "It's a hat, a very large hat. Height of fashion for the Edwardians. She must have been trail-blazing. They're ostrich feathers by the look. How amazing is that, wish it was around now."

"But she kept it," declared Rose quietly.

"Sorry, what did you say?" asked Steve.

"She kept it, and I never threw it out."

"I don't think we came across it, and we've pretty much had this place turned inside out," said Steve.

Rose was thoughtful. "What about the blue room, the one with the connecting door to the master bedroom?"

"The one where the letters were, behind the door in the dressing table?" asked Steve.

"Yes, that's the one. It's in there."

Steve looked doubtful. The only item of clothing they'd found in there was a dressing gown hanging on the door of an otherwise empty wardrobe, and said so.

"The silk dressing gown?" asked Rose. Steve nodded. "That's hers too, she loved that dressing gown. She said she would always keep hold of it, because she knew it would last and last. Now I understand why she said that. The wardrobe may look empty, but it has a false bottom. Did you know?"

Steve shook his head and raced upstairs with Lucy close behind, leaving the others to carry on looking at the photographs. "Bit like detective work," muttered Tom Downey to Jim Manning, who chuckled quietly, but then said he was doing a little private detective work himself and asked his junior if he might be a-courting. The junior looked at his senior. He hadn't understood the question. "Er, not sure what you mean Sir."

"Ha, sorry, it's an old expression but a good one. It's a bit brutal when turned into modern speak, but here goes." Jim Manning nodded towards the door that Lucy had just gone through. "Are you two an item?"

Tom Downey looked down at the floor and a broad grin spread across his face. "I do hope so," he said in answer.

Jim Manning's phone chimed in his pocket. He pulled it out as he walked out of the room so he could speak into it freely. "DI Manning," he bellowed as he closed the door.

Steve and Lucy looked inside the mahogany wardrobe immediately after entering the blue bedroom. Presumably it was known by Rose as the blue room because of the original William Morris blue patterned wallpaper. It had become unstuck in various places. Steve and Jasmine had planned to redecorate in the coming New Year, preserving what they could of the old vintage wallpaper. But that plan had gone out of the window along with the rest of his life, Steve had decided, when in moments of despair.

Lucy soon found the false bottom in the wardrobe. Steve, meanwhile, reached for the dressing gown and held it tenderly against his skin, feeling its shiny smoothness through his fingers and recalling how Jasmine had thought it would come up beautifully with a careful wash. He thought that he could never wash it now that he knew it had belonged to her... back then.

"Hey, look at this," exclaimed Lucy. "There's a dress too, I think it's the one in the photograph, the wedding-dress. Just look at these puffed sleeves tapering down tight at the forearm." Lucy stroked them fondly. "And the amount of frills on the bodice. Wow, the collar is higher than I would have imagined too."

She looked across at her brother-in-law. He looked lost, helpless even. "Oh I'm so sorry, how thoughtless of me. It's my job. Costumes. I get so excited when I see the authentic ones."

"It's okay, I understand. It's just me. It's hard to know she got married to someone else, even though it was the best thing she could have done in the circumstances." He looked over at the wedding dress and hat. The dress looked lovely, he supposed for a bride of that era, but he still wasn't sure about the hat.

"Have them if you want, I'm sure that's why they're there. She'd have stowed them away especially for you."

"D'you think?"

"Why else? She would know I wouldn't want them. Come on, let's go back down and have a look at the rest of the photos."

Neither of them made any move though, both feeling the need to sit a while in contemplation. At length, Steve cut into the silence, expressing his thoughts. "I need to make sure Jas had a good life after leaving here and becoming Estelle. There, I've said it. I didn't think I would be able to admit that she sort of turned into another person. Estelle. Jasmine. The same, but not entirely. She would have had to change so much to fit in with those times. How courageous of her don't you think? Did you know she built the very maternity hospital she trained in?"

"Yes, Mum told me all about it. You must be so proud of her."

"I am. Did she tell you her real parents were titled? They were a Lord and Lady!"

"Ha! I should have sussed that one. She had that sort of air about her. Lady Jasmine, the very thought! How hilarious. Seriously though Steve, that's what you have to remember, her brilliance, which, manifestly, didn't stop just because she was taken from us. It was meant to be, you know, her going through time, don't you agree?"

"Yes, you may be right."

Oh, there's one thing I don't know; I daren't ask."

"How did she die you mean?" Steve anticipated.

"Yes, I couldn't help but see the date on the grave. She was still so very young."

"Forty-eight. The Spanish flu. Straight after the First World War ended. According to Rose, she died the same day that she caught it."

"Oh, right," said Lucy. And then tears formed in her eyes. It had been but a month since she'd first heard the terrible news that her sister had gone missing. A deep wound had formed throughout her whole being, and it still lay open and raw, and the slightest thing set her off. She pulled out a tissue from her pocket and dried her face. "The reality of it all comes at you suddenly doesn't it? And I've just felt it again. Oh dear what a shock. She was taken abruptly away from them as well as us."

"Yes, I suppose she was." said Steve. He suddenly felt empathy for John, Jasmine's second husband, the man in the picture. The man who had taken her in, nurtured her, loved her. "He must have been devastated."

"Yes, I suppose he must have been," agreed Lucy. They both reverted back to their own thoughts again. Both remained sat on the old fourposter bed, still not making a move to reappear downstairs despite the lure of the old photographs.

"We need cheering up don't we. Shall we play the jukebox and show Rose what was hidden in plain sight. She'll be amazed at her mum's ingenuity!" said Steve finally.

"The steps she took to let us know she's close to us were surely great!" said Lucy. "That's not even mentioning she birthed a hospital. I bet she never imagined that one! What an amazing achievement. Shame it closed don't you think?"

"Yes, she loved working there, and hated when it shut down and all was moved to the Clarendon Wing. But then she would have known that of course, you know, back then, that it would close. Yet she still went ahead because she loved it so much. Oh come on Luce, they'll wonder where we've got to."

Steve and Lucy prised themselves out of the blue bedroom and joined the others, now minus Jim Manning who had been obliged to leave. Apparently a small boy had gone missing from near the stone circle in the park and he was needed for the immediate investigation. Steve put on a selection of music from the jukebox and pointed out Jasmine's message to Rose.

"Well I never did," Rose laughed. And she listened to the familiar *I want to Hold Your Hand* by the Beatles and her feet stepped in time to its beat, and bade Arthur over to jiggle her wheelchair back and forth. But she could see he was agitated. "What's wrong with you, what's set you off?" she asked.

For some reason, Arthur had turned a little light-headed. Assuming it was an attack of anxiety, he'd begun pacing about the room trying to ward it off. It hadn't worked, it was just making him more and more hot and bothered. He started to take off his jumper, pulling his shirt up with it. Tom Downey reached over to help, pulling his shirt back down while Arthur tugged at his jumper. It was then that Tom saw it, but didn't think anything of it till later, when he was back at the nick after his leave, and was catching up with the missing child case. The small child was described as having a small birthmark on his back, in the shape of a star, just like Tom had seen on Arthur's back.

After a few moments of reflection, Arthur answered Rose. "It's something my dear brother once said about my mother finding me in the meadow, where the park is now, and bringing me home. I am that missing boy. Now I understand what I've been searching for all my life. And even more curious, how can I have been living as a little boy and as I am now at the same time?"

But Rose had drifted off while the harmonies of *I Can Hear Music* were reverberating around the hallway, not heeding his reply. And in her mind's eye, she watched her beloved mother and her beloved Francis, waiting for her to come and join them when she felt ready. When the time was right.